STAR TREK®
STRANGE NEW WORLDS
V

STAR TREK®
STRANGE NEW WORLDS
V

Edited by
Dean Wesley Smith
with **John J. Ordover** and **Paula Block**

Based upon STAR TREK® and STAR TREK:
THE NEXT GENERATION® created by
Gene Roddenberry, STAR TREK: DEEP SPACE NINE®
created by Rick Berman & Michael Piller,
STAR TREK: VOYAGER® created by Rick Berman,
Michael Piller & Jeri Taylor, and
ENTERPRISE™ created by
Rick Berman & Brannon Braga

POCKET BOOKS
New York   London   Toronto   Sydney   Singapore

An *Original* Publication of POCKET BOOKS

POCKET BOOKS, a division of Simon & Schuster, Inc.
1230 Avenue of the Americas, New York, NY 10020

STAR TREK is a Registered Trademark of Paramount Pictures.

This book is published by Pocket Books, a division of Simon & Schuster, Inc., under exclusive license from Paramount Pictures.

ISBN: 0-7434-3778-0

First Pocket Books printing May 2002

10 9 8 7 6 5 4 3 2 1

POCKET and colophon are registered trademarks of Simon & Schuster, Inc.

For information regarding special discounts for bulk purchases, please contact Simon & Schuster Special Sales at 1-800-456-6798 or business@simonandschuster.com

Printed in the U.S.A.

Contents

STAR TREK®

STAR TREK THE NEXT GENERATION®

Contents

STAR TREK
DEEP SPACE NINE®

STAR TREK
VOYAGER®

Contents

ENTERPRISE™

Introduction

Welcome to *Strange New Worlds V.* It feels wonderful to write those words. When we first started doing these contest anthologies, there was no way to know that the idea would work. Lots of things seem like they are destined for success and then turn out not to be.

The thing that has made the *Strange New Worlds* anthologies work, I think, is that they are a labor of love from all sides, from the thousands of fans who write and send in the stories (whether their stories are to be found in this volume or not), to the publisher and editors, who are all writers as well, and who understand the drive to get your story down the way you want to write it, to tell the *Star Trek* story that won't get out of your head.

Perhaps the most impressive thing, and a lesson to us all, is the number of stories about the cast of the brand-new show *Enterprise* that were submitted. With only days between the airing of the first episode and the closing deadline for this anthology, fans ignored all the voices telling them that there wasn't enough time, sat down and wrote their story, then—and this is often the hardest part—put their story in an envelope and mailed it in.

Because if you want to know the secret of how to be a professional writer, there it is: write the story, put it in an envelope, and send it to someone who can buy it and publish it. That's what the people in this anthology did, and you can do it too.

Best,

John J. Ordover

STAR TREK®

Disappearance on 21st Street

Mary Scott-Wiecek

His mother, God rest her soul, once told him that everyone mattered—that every life was important. Now in his middle age, he's come to realize that she was either naïve or lying, and he strongly suspects the latter. He knows now that some people don't matter at all. That there are people who could disappear off the face of the earth and not a single living soul would mourn them, or even notice they were gone.

Everyone calls him Rodent. He can't remember who started it, but it stuck. They say it's because he looks like a rat, with his rheumy eyes and his pinched features, but he doesn't think so. More likely it's because he's a bum—because he sleeps on the streets and picks through trash cans—because sometimes, in a drunken stupor, he pisses on himself. In any case, he doesn't really care. It's as good a name as any. The name his mother gave him certainly doesn't fit anymore. That name belonged to another person—a boy with big dreams and his whole life ahead of him.

He sleeps in a doorway on 21st Street. It's a business, some kind of advertising agency. He likes it because the doorway's only big enough for one, and he prefers to keep to himself. The door is

3

bright red, with a diamond on it. It's different. The color stands out in this world of brown and gray. It's a good location—close to the mission and not too dangerous. He's had to fight for it, more than once. Now the others recognize it's his. He has to clear out every morning by seven, though. That's when the cleaning ladies come, and they don't like to find him there. One of them hit him with a broom once, like he was a stray dog or something.

During the day, he wanders around aimlessly, looking for handouts, looking for a drink. It's been at least ten years since he held a job, even a bad one. He doesn't bother to look for work anymore. Who would hire him? Sometimes he sits at the park watching the world go by, or he sleeps on a bench. No one speaks to him or looks him in the eye. He's as good as invisible, and most of the time that suits him just fine.

Today he has lunch at the mission. The bread is halfway fresh and the soup is thicker than usual. Heartened, he tries to strike up a conversation with the guys next to him at the table. They're new to the streets—he can always tell. One of them looks like a Chinee, only he's too tall, and he has no accent. The other is a younger man, with an intensity about him that Rodent finds exhausting just to look at—a starry-eyed idealist, just like Miss Goody Twoshoes over there. No matter, though—a few weeks of living on handouts will knock that out of him.

Anyway, he tries to talk to the guy—give him a few pointers, maybe. He starts with a little harmless shoptalk about Miss Goody Twoshoes, the woman who runs the mission, but the guy just tells him to shut up. Typical. Story of his life. He shrugs and hunches back over his soup. Let him listen, for all the good it'll do. All she does is blather on about sadness and hard times and spaceships. The broad is nuts, really. He can't stand listening to her, only he has to if he wants the soup.

A couple of days later, he wakes up under a paper in his doorway, badly hungover. His head is pounding, and the sun is reflecting strong off the bright red door. He groans and rolls over on the hard cement and tries to figure out about what time it is. Since the sun is up, the cleaning ladies will be around soon. A gust of wind knocks up the trash on the street and sends it fluttering. Broken glass on the sidewalk directs piercing sunlight right into his face. This doesn't help his throbbing head any, so he shuts his eyes tightly. He lies there for several minutes in a dazed fog before he notices the sound. It's been there all along—it must have been what woke him up. It's the high-pitched sound of a child crying.

He squints into the sun to find the source of the irritation. A little girl is sitting on the curb not ten feet away from him, bawling her head off. His first instinct is to roll over and wish she'd go away. She's not his problem. But then she stands up, and he sees her looking around desperately. She's obviously lost, and she looks the way kids sometimes do—like she might suddenly dart off in any direction. He's a little afraid she's going to go headlong into the traffic on 21st Street with its barreling trucks.

"Hey, kid," he croaks, sitting up abruptly. "What's the matter with you?"

She turns, her face streaked with tears. "I've lost my mama," she says, sniveling. "I turned around and she was gone." She walks over and stands in front of him, her lower lip trembling.

He's surprised to see that although she's afraid, she's not afraid of him. That's what he loves about little kids. The big kids taunt him and sometimes throw things—pebbles, or even trash—but the little kids, when they look at him, just see a person like any other person. No big deal to them. They don't seem to notice, or care about, the filth on his skin and clothes, or the vague odor of vomit that seems to hover around him.

He sighs, then staggers to his feet, coughing. His stomach lurches slightly at the sudden movement, and the sun, still low in the sky, is just killing his head, but he's got to move on anyway. "Well, you can't cross that street yourself," he tells her. "Let me help."

She nods solemnly and reaches for his hand as they get to the curb. He glances around, nervously, sure that someone is going to think he's kidnapping her or something, but no one takes any notice of them. The city is waking up, and everyone's in a hurry. Looking around, he spots a uniformed copper across the street. He usually avoids the cops, but in this case, it seems like the best thing.

He waits for a break in the traffic, then runs the kid across the

5

street. The copper scowls at him suspiciously as he approaches, the snuffling kid in tow. "What's going on here?" he barks, tapping his jimmy stick behind his back. Rodent, thinking he should have known better than to get involved, almost flees, but the little girl, frightened by the copper's tone and angry look, clings to his hand and moves closer to him. At once, the copper's face softens, and he glances at Rodent, finally understanding.

"She's lost," Rodent says. "She can't find her mother."

"Is that so?" the copper says, kneeling down and looking kindly at the girl. "Well, you just come with me. We'll find your mother."

The kid looks up at Rodent, and he nods. Satisfied, she releases his hand and takes the copper's. Rodent turns and starts to walk away.

"Hey buddy," the copper calls after him. He reaches into his uniform pocket and fishes out a dime, which he tosses at Rodent. "Get yourself a sandwich."

Rodent looks down at the dime, surprised, then back up at the cop.

"No booze, now. You hear?" the cop adds, gruffly. "Get yourself some food."

Rodent grumbles and waves him off dismissively, but even as he walks away, he's decided to take the advice. A sandwich sounds like a pretty good idea, at that.

Twenty minutes later, he comes out of the diner, feeling full for the first time in weeks. Halfway down the block, he sees the copper, and beside him, the little girl, reunited with her mother. The mother is crying, and clutching the girl tightly. Rodent blinks hard—the damned sun bothers his eyes, that's all—but unbidden, some of Goody Twoshoes' words come into his head.

"It is possible to find peace in the night, knowing that you have lived another day, and hurt no one in doing it."

Late that night, Rodent leans up against the brick wall next to his doorway and rubs his hands together, shivering. It's still hours until dawn. He carefully avoids looking at the milkman, who's just pulled up with his cart to make a delivery at a building across the alley. The milkman ignores him as well, of course. What does he care what happens to the milk after he leaves? He's done his job.

As the horse-drawn cart clops away, Rodent shuffles across the alley and picks up the bottle of milk. It's not usually his drink of choice, but he finds himself anticipating the cold smoothness of it. He's thinking, as he has been all day, about the kid he helped across the street, and her reunion with her mother.

He's just about to pull the cap off the bottle when he hears a shout.

"Assassins! Murderers!"

He looks up to find that a strange, wild man has appeared out of nowhere in the middle of 21st Street. He's dressed in a peculiar way; he's wearing a blue shirt and black pants that are too short— they almost look like kids' pajamas. The man is completely out of his head, too, screaming like that in the middle of the night. This is one time when Rodent would be more than happy to be invisible, but—just his luck—the strange man has spotted him.

"You!" he shouts, pointing. "What planet is this?"

God, what a nutcase! Rodent freezes in place, hoping he'll go bug someone else, but instead, the man begins running toward him.

The bottle of milk, cold and slippery with condensation, slips out of his grasp and shatters on the ground at his feet. The sound of the crash brings him to his senses, and he turns and flees down the alley. The man chases after him, shouting, "Don't run! I won't kill you! It's they who do the killing!" Rodent doesn't find that comforting at all.

The guy is surprisingly fast for a drunk, though, and when Rodent stumbles rounding a corner, the maniac grabs him from behind. Up close, he's terrifying. He's sweating like a pig, and he has red blotches all over his face. His eyes are all bugged out—he looks like he just broke out of the loony bin. Rodent tries to pull away— you never know what someone this messed up will do.

Oddly enough, the strange man grins and nearly embraces him. "I'm glad you got away, too," he says, fervently. "Why do you think they want to kill us?"

Rodent has no idea what to do. He's as frightened as he's ever been in his life. He just wants to get away from this guy.

"Look, fella," he stammers, "you take a sip too much of that old wood alky and almost anything seems like it . . . it . . ."

The man's mood changes abruptly—something that tends to happen with madmen, as Rodent recalls. His face darkens, and his eyes narrow, and he scowls at Rodent suspiciously.

"Where are we—Earth?" he demands. He looks up at the stars. "The constellations seem right . . ."

Rodent tries to jerk away again, and the wild man focuses his full attention on him for the first time. "Explain!" he barks. "Explain this trick!"

Rodent tries to speak, but no sound comes out. The wild man starts patting him down, like he's looking for a wallet or something, and Rodent wishes, not for the first time, that he carried a knife. But the man's crazy mutterings are not about money. "Biped, small . . ." He pulls Rodent's cap off and tosses it away, then grabs his head. "Good cranial development, no doubt of considerable human ancestry . . . Is that how you're able to fake all this?" the man asks, but he doesn't seem to expect an answer. He's mostly talking to himself now, which is just as well, since Rodent doesn't have any idea what he's going on about.

The wild man finally releases him, but now that he's free to run, Rodent stays put. The man looks around at the alley, then staggers over to lean against a beam. He doesn't seem like much of a threat anymore, so Rodent listens to his ramblings just for the hell of it.

"Very good," the man says, approvingly. "Modern museum perfection, right down to the cement beams."

The man's intensity is unsettling. His lunatic ravings don't mean anything, but he seems to believe every word he's saying. His demons are catching up with him, though, and Rodent watches as he begins to slide down the beam, moaning about hospitals and needles and sutures. Finally, with one last anguished "Oh, the pain!" the wild man slumps to the ground and passes out at Rodent's feet.

Rodent shakes his head sympathetically, but it's just as well. If ever a guy needed to sleep it off . . .

He picks up his cap, then looks down the alley, furtively, but there's no one around. What he's about to do makes him feel a little guilty, but times are tough and it's every man for himself. He stoops over and checks for money, or a wallet. He finds neither, of course—in fact, there aren't even any pockets in the man's odd clothes. There is something attached to his belt, though. There's a slight ripping sound as Rodent tugs it off.

He moves beneath the streetlight and studies the object. It's like nothing he's ever seen before—a small, metallic black rectangle with two buttons. Curious, he pushes the one on the left.

An unearthly high-pitched noise pierces the silence in the alley. He turns the device around, alarmed, but still can't make any sense of it. He thinks maybe he should press the other button to stop the sound, but by then it's too late.

There is no pain at all, just a tingling sensation and one split second where he understands that he's done something terrible and irrevocable—and then his life ends in a blinding flash of blue.

In the alley, the strange madman still lies unconscious in the gutter. A gust of wind kicks up, blowing some litter over the spot where Rodent was standing, but he's gone. He has disappeared off the face of the earth.

It seemed Rodent was right, at first. No one even noticed that he was gone. Oh, Edith surely would have. The woman Rodent knew as Miss Goody Twoshoes knew more about the men she served than they realized. She would have noticed his absence, but she was distracted that day by a new arrival at the mission—a man wearing peculiar clothes who went by the name of Leonard McCoy and tended to say things that didn't make any sense. By the next day, she, too, was gone, another victim of fate and circumstance.

Otherwise, life on 21st Street went on without him. His usual table at the mission was filled by other unfortunates. Other nameless and faceless bums slept on the park benches that day, and by the end of the week, someone else had moved into Rodent's doorway. The cleaning ladies didn't even realize it wasn't the same bum.

About a week later, however, a harried-looking woman walked quickly down the street with her young daughter in tow. While they waited to cross at the corner, the child stared at the red door with the diamond on it, tilting her head quizzically.

"Where is he? Where is he, Mama?" she asked.

"Where is who?" the distracted woman replied.

"The man with the brown coat who found me when I was lost."

The woman thought for a minute, then said, "No, honey. It was a policeman who found you. He had a black coat with two rows of buttons, remember?"

"No, but . . ."

"Honey," the woman said, a little exasperated, "just come along. You're confused. He's not here." She wasn't an unkind woman, she was just preoccupied—and there was a break in the traffic. She pulled her daughter into the street and hurried her across.

The girl furrowed her brow and looked back at the door. As she trailed behind her mother on the other side of the street, she muttered defiantly to herself, "He *was* here. I know he was."

[THIRD PRIZE]

The Trouble with Borg Tribbles

William Leisner

The small sphere floated slowly toward the bigger ship, its surface battered and scarred from its passage through the micro-wormhole. The markings on its exterior were still legible, however, for anyone familiar with Klingonese.

It would be several decades, though, before the Borg had any significant contact with that, or any other, Alpha Quadrant race. In time, the Collective would learn enough to discover the markings had read "I.K.S. Gr'oth," and that the vessel was a survival pod from that ship. For now, though, they had only this small piece of technological flotsam, swept across the galaxy by the verteron tides and chance, which would have to suffice in their desire to expand their knowledge of that distant part of the universe.

The cube scanned the small sphere, finding minimal and relatively insignificant technology—primitive stellar location plotting systems, plus life support. The life being supported was even more primitive, by Borg standards. These life-forms were also, for uncertain reasons, ceasing to be supported. Had this vessel held specimens of any known species, the Borg would have dismissed them as irrelevant, and let the sphere continue on its ill-fated journey without interference. But they were an unknown, which made them just relevant enough to assimilate.

A thin tractor beam lanced out from the gigantic cube, and pulled the sphere in through an irising portal. Once it was inside and bound to the deck with magnetic restraints, a trio of drones stepped from their alcoves and encircled it, scanning it with both organic and cybernetic eyes. The entrance hatch was quickly identified, and as quickly unsealed. And out onto the deck of the Borg vessel spilled in excess of three hundred tribbles.

Three of Three, formerly an individual being from the planet Talax, stepped forward to examine the small furry creatures more thoroughly. Many of them, he observed, had expired, and those that had survived their journey were clearly operating at far below their metabolic capacity.

They're starving, said the small portion of Three of Three's mind that still retained dim memory of life as a fully biological entity. That same area of his brain tried to claim that he was performing an act of charity, when he pressed his knuckles against the little animal's furry hide, injecting it with the nanoprobes that would allow it to survive without organic nourishment. If he had retained enough of his individual sentience to understand this claim, he'd know he was deluding himself.

Given the number of creatures that had been inside the sphere, the collective mind of the cube dispatched more drones to deal with them. Now designated Three of Two Hundred Forty-Seven, the drone observed the effect of the nanoprobes, reviving the tribble and elevating its metabolism to unexpected levels.

He also felt as the creature's underdeveloped brain connected to the hive mind. Its thoughts were primitive, of course—technically not even thoughts, not in the sense that any significantly developed life-form organized its mental processes. Rather, they were merely survival drives. *Eat. Procreate. Eat. Procreate.* Three noted—along with the whole of the ship's hive mind—that there were no additional survival imperatives. No instinct to flee from predators, or to fight them. Although an instinct to fight would surely betray them, as they had no apparent defenses. Perhaps they used their thin vocal membranes to frighten danger off? Or perhaps they came from a planet where they had no natural predators? This hypothesis about the Alpha Quadrant species was of extreme interest to the Collective.

Without realizing he'd been instructed to do so, Three started walking through the labyrinthine corridors of the cube, so this alien creature could be studied in greater detail. An entire regimen of tests was downloaded into his mind: spectral, chemical, electrical . . . The animal would be taken apart cell by cell, gene by gene, molecule by molecule. It was fortunate the Borg had come across such a large quantity of these creatures. When their studies were complete, they would possess an exhaustive knowledge of these creatures, and their first understanding of life on the far end of the galaxy. And perhaps, once they'd learned all they could, they might even be left with one or more living specimens.

Eat. Procreate. Eat. Procreate.

The small, still intact part of the former Talaxian's mind wondered at the fact that the soft living thing in his hands was so contented. Clearly, its brain was too simple, even with the augmentation of its new Borg implants, to understand its fate. It was receiving nourishment, the effects of its near-starvation on its asexual reproductive system were being repaired by the nanoprobes, and it was . . . it was . . .

Happy.

That word, echoing from the deepest recesses of what he once was, felt alien to Three of (now) Three Hundred Eight. He couldn't even apply a definition to it, yet he knew it was something he once valued. Something important he have, or be . . .

He reached his destination, a cramped compartment containing a wide array of technology accumulated from the thousands of cultures the Borg had absorbed into the Collective. In the center of the crowded space was an elevated table, long enough to support the average drone, positioned below a concave projector that would flood the examination subject with every known form of radiation, and record their effect in minute detail. Three placed the tribble in the center of the table . . .

. . . and found himself hesitating before removing his hands. The tactile sensation of the little animal's soft furry coat was . . . unique, particularly in combination with steady audible vibrations it made with its diaphragm.

Happy.

Three snapped his hands away as if from a fire, a throwback to his own genetically ingrained Talaxian survival instincts. As if this small, sedate creature had injured him. It continued purring, continued its simple *eat procreate eat procreate* thoughts without any concern over the impending threat to its existence that it must now—being connected to the hive mind as it was—surely sense in its own rudimentary way.

Three again surveyed the medical instruments covering the walls of this space. If this little creature were a Talaxian, he considered in his deepest thoughts, he would want to flee. Or fight. But he couldn't, of course. Resistance was futile. He would be assimilated. But then, he already had been. Absorbed into the Collective, stripped of his individualism, remade only to serve the Whole, to assist in the accumulation of knowledge, the consumption of new technology, the expansion of the Collective, eating, procreating . . .

The hive mind, heedless of this irrelevant organic mental activity, pushed Three away from the table and placed his hand on the control pad. He was to conduct an experiment, exposing the specimen to microwave-frequency electromagnetic radiation. Empirically, knowing that the tribble's chemical composition was approximately 88.92 percent water, the Collective predicted this would rupture every cell in the creature's body. However, meticulous testing was dictated in this circumstance.

The tribble continued purring contentedly, until Three pressed the tab that started the overhead device. He then emitted a high-pitched screech of what the hive mind coolly hypothesized was unbearable pain. Through Three's eyes, the Borg watched as the small furry mass shuddered and writhed on the table . . .

. . . and then stopped, as Three terminated the experiment

prematurely, and scooped the injured creature up and cradled him in his arms. With one hand, Three injected him with more nanoprobes, to repair whatever cellular damage had been done. And with the other, he caressed the tribble's silky fur, trying his best to comfort the poor defenseless little animal, who had done nothing to deserve this, to have everything he was ripped away from him . . .

DRONE THREE OF THREE-OH-EIGHT, the hive mind intoned in his head, *A MALFUNCTION IS DETECTED. YOU HAVE FAILED TO PERFORM INSTRUCTED TASKS TO SPECIFICA-TIONS. INITIATE DIAGNOSTIC SUBROUTINE A1.*

The Talaxian pressed the tribble, which had almost stopped its frightened quivering, to his chest in a protective manner, and hurried out of the laboratory. *DRONE THREE OF TWO-NINE-FOUR,* the hive mind summoned again. Three refused to listen to it, or to the similar orders echoing through the cube to the other drones who had taken charge of live specimens. He fled down the dark corridor, the long-silenced sliver of his instinctive mind pressing him on, even while aware there was nowhere he could flee to.

DRONE THREE OF TWO-SIX-SEVEN: YOU HAVE BEEN DEEMED A LIABILITY TO THE COLLEC—

Three felt his Borg appendages suddenly shut down, sending him sprawling, but leaving him with enough control to turn his body and avoid crushing the tribble as his shoulder hit the metal deck and he fell onto his back. He lay staring at the deck above him, where unaffected drones marched blithely by. A series of coded instructions downloaded into his cortical processor, trying to correct whatever malfunction had afflicted him, without effect. In approximately 2.15 minutes, the former Talaxian knew, the hive mind would abandon these efforts and terminate him. He also knew how the Borg would deal with these alien creatures, whose introduction into the Collective had precip-itated this widespread series of malfunctions. The entire cube could conceivably be disconnected from the Collective and de-stroyed.

But the assimilated tribble lying on his chest gave no indication of concern, thinking its simple thoughts, with no mind to predators, and purring serenely.

The Talaxian, with his one working arm, pulled the creature up his chest and against his cheek. He stroked its fur gently, closing his eyes, and letting the soft steady vibrations soothe his organic mind, and sharing in the tribble's sense of peace with the universe.

Legal Action

Alan L. Lickiss

Captain Kirk stood outside Starfleet Headquarters, enjoying the view of the Golden Gate Bridge and the taste of sea air that blew in from the Pacific Ocean. He heard someone approach from behind.

"Excuse me, Captain Kirk?" a woman asked.

Turning, he found himself facing a beautiful young woman. He smiled at her as she pushed a strand of her long blond hair behind her ear. She seemed unsure of herself, timid now that he had turned.

"Hello, can I help you?" he asked.

He received a slight, self-conscious smile from the woman as she looked toward the ground, embarrassed. Her hand again moved to push the strand of hair back behind her ear. She did it so casually, Kirk thought it must be a constant reflexive gesture for her. Kirk waited patiently, letting her steel herself to ask her question. He assumed it was to confirm his identity; his reputation, on Earth, at least, seemed to inspire contact by members of the general public, who wanted only a bit of his time. Normally he left after a polite

17

greeting, but she was different. The woman was enchanting, and Kirk always had a few extra minutes for beauty.

"Are you Captain Kirk?" she asked. "From the *Enterprise?*"

Kirk smiled, hoping to reassure the woman that he was not annoyed by her question. "Yes, I'm Captain Kirk." She was closer now, and Kirk could smell a hint of her perfume. Violets, he decided. Kirk extended his hand. "And you are?"

The woman placed a piece of paper in Kirk's hand. He watched her features harden and her eyes light with a sense of triumph.

"I'm serving you a summons. You are being sued in the Planetary Court of Iotia for breach of contract," she said.

Looking down at the paper in his hands, Kirk's smile turned into a puzzled frown. He looked back to the woman, who was quickly walking away. "What does this mean?" he asked.

She turned around and continued to walk away from him, backward. "It's all in the summons. And if you fail to appear, an arrest warrant will be issued." She turned away and was quickly out of sight.

Colored lights danced in the air as a vibrating hum sounded. The lights condensed, and in their place stood Kirk and Spock. Looking around, they found they stood on the roof of a building. A meter-high red brick wall ran around the perimeter of the roof, the top covered with white concrete. A door led into a small shed that Kirk assumed must be the stairs into the building. A few metal boxes and exhaust vents were stuck to the black tar of the roof. Beyond the edge wall Kirk could see similar buildings all around. Sounds of ground cars and people made their way up from the street below.

"Kirk, Spock," said a voice behind them.

Turning, Kirk found himself looking at an older gentleman with gray hair. He was wearing a dark blue suit that fit so well it must have been custom made, large dark-rimmed eyeglasses, and a huge smile. He approached them with an outstretched hand.

Kirk was wearing a similar suit, but made of a light brown material. The white shirt, dark tie, and brown fedora completed his look of a major boss. Spock looked out of place in his black suit with black shirt and red tie.

"Bela Oxmyx," said Kirk. "Are you the one who brought me here with this lawsuit?" He took Bela's hand, shaking it.

"Look Kirk, if I wanted to put the grab on you, I'd of done it myself. I wouldn't have used the coppers." A gesture to the two men standing behind him told Kirk how Bela would have handled the situation. Using the handshake to pull Kirk toward him, Bela reached around and put his arm around the captain. "I owe you big, Kirk. You helped me with that sweet setup you Feds put in place. No, the guy doing this is called The Kid."

Kirk heard the sound of a machine gun and saw a chip fly off the brick wall. Everyone ducked, moving to hide behind the stairwell or a ventilation shaft. More gunshots were fired, sending brick chips and dust into the air as the staccato crack of the gun was heard.

Kirk looked and saw a man hunched behind the edge wall of a building across the street. Kirk could see the machine gun sticking out over the edge, and a brown fedora, before more shots forced him back. When the shots stopped Kirk looked again, phaser in his hand, only to see the stairwell door closing on the other rooftop. Turning, Kirk saw that no one had been hit.

Bela started yelling at his men. "What are you standing around here for? Get over there and find that creep."

The two men took off running down the stairs. After Bela brushed off his jacket with his hand, he led Kirk and Spock into the stairwell.

"Do you think that was The Kid?" asked Kirk.

"Naw, that's not his style," said Bela. "He'd never even put out a contract on anyone, let alone pull the trigger himself."

"Who is The Kid?" asked Kirk. "I don't recall him among the bosses last time I was here."

The trio walked down four flights of stairs to the ground level, and into a large elegant room that contained a pool table in the center. Balls were arranged as if a game were in progress. To one side was a wood bar; a glass bottle containing a brown liquid sat on the top, upturned glasses arranged in a circle around the bottle. On the other side of the room there was a large ornate desk. Bela grabbed a cue stick and approached the table.

"Grab a cue," he said. "You don't know The Kid. That's why I wanted to chat with you first, clue you in on the scoop." He leaned over and hit a red-striped ball with the cue, sending it careening into another ball. "I've been trying to convince The Kid that you were hands off. But he doesn't convince easy. I'd of had him hit, but that ain't subtle. People would know who set it up, and The Kid's got a lot of friends."

Kirk and Spock looked around the room. Kirk could have sworn nothing had changed since the last time he had been there. The fireplace still filled one wall, and while the carpet was new, it was bright red. "But you're the Boss, Bela. Couldn't you just tell him to back off?" Kirk asked.

Bela sighed. "Well, there's two problems with that." Bela took another shot, sinking a ball. "A few years ago I retired. Oh, I'm still the Boss, but I decided it was time to relax and not deal with running the outfit. I'm letting Krako run things now. He talks to me from time to time, but he's running the show."

"Mr. Krako should be receptive to helping the captain, just as you are," said Spock.

Bela's two men came into the office. Their suits were a little disheveled and they were breathing heavily. "Sorry, Boss, whoever it was got away."

"There wasn't anyone in the building?" asked Bela.

"A few people in their flops, but no one saw nothin'."

Bela frowned. "Well get out there and keep your eyes peeled. If you spot anyone casing us, grab 'em."

The men left and Bela turned back to Kirk and Spock. "Now, where were we?"

"You said there were two problems with having The Kid stop his prosecution of Captain Kirk, but have only explained the first," said Spock.

"Yeah, that's right. The second problem is the judge," Bela said. He set down his pool cue and went to the bar. Flipping over three glasses, Bela sloshed amber liquid into them. He picked one up and took a sip. "A few years after you were here, we were getting bogged down in petty disputes. It was a nuisance. Those advisor guys you Feds sent suggested a court system. We consulted The Book, and found references to courts and judges on the payroll of the bosses. So, we hired some judges to settle the small stuff, reserving the big calls for us, with one exception. Any beefs about percentages has to be settled by a judge."

"And The Kid is suing me for—"

"A piece of the action. He claims you promised him a piece of the action, and stiffed him," said Bela.

"All rise, this court is now in session, the Honorable Judge Mugsy presiding."

The judge, a small thin man lost in the black robe he wore, entered from a side door. He walked the few steps up to the raised desk, where he sat, looking down at everyone. Kirk stood by a long wood table, next to a "mouthpiece" that Bela had arranged to take Kirk's case. At a second table next to Kirk's stood a man in his early forties. He had dark wavy hair and brown eyes. His suit was dark gray, and looked expensive by the local standards. He looked at the judge, not turning to Kirk.

Behind Kirk a low rail ran the length of the room, separating Kirk and the others from several rows of wood benches. They were filled with spectators, people who had come to see a Fed on trial for a percentage.

"All right," said the judge. "Bailiff, read the particulars."

The bailiff, wearing a dark blue uniform, picked up a piece of paper from a small desk next to the judge. "Captain Kirk, you are charged with welshing on a promised percentage to The Kid."

The judge looked across the room to Kirk. "How do you plead?"

The mouthpiece spoke before Kirk could ask for clarification. "My client pleads not guilty, Your Honor."

"Didn't think this would be an easy one," said the judge. "Everyone sit down and let's get started. Kid, call your first witness."

The Kid rose from his seat. "I call the Fed Spock."

Kirk was startled, and turned to watch Spock stand and approach a raised chair on the left of the judge. The bailiff swore Spock to tell the truth. Sitting in the chair, he was the picture of calmness as The Kid approached.

"Spock, you were here with Kirk the last time you Feds were here, correct?" The Kid asked.

"That is correct," said Spock.

"And during that time, do you recall when you and Kirk put the bag on Krako? Tell us about it in your own words, but remember you are under oath."

Spock paused a moment, arching an eyebrow at The Kid. "We did indeed put the bag, as you say, on Mr. Krako."

The Kid interrupted Spock. "But Krako is a big boss. How were just the two of you able to get past his boys?"

"We quickly determined that a frontal assault would not achieve our desired results," said Spock. "As we were formulating a plan, a male youth approached. He was able to distract the guards long enough for the captain and me to overpower them."

"I see," said The Kid. "What reason did this child give for being so helpful?"

"As I recall, he asked for a piece of the action," said Spock.

The memory of that day came back to Kirk as Spock testified. He remembered that he did indeed offer a piece of the action to the child, and with all of the work getting the bosses together in the syndicate, he had forgotten all about him. Looking at The Kid, Kirk had a hunch who the boy had grown up to become.

The Kid asked his next question. He was building the events of the day, and Spock had no choice but to follow down the path. "Did Kirk agree to the contract?"

"There was no document to that effect," said Spock.

"Don't twist the words. Didn't Kirk say, and I quote, 'I guarantee you a piece of the action'? And when the boy asked 'Is that a contract?' Kirk shook on it?"

Spock looked into the air for a moment. "I believe the conversation was to that effect."

"No more questions," said The Kid.

Kirk's mouthpiece leaned over and whispered into Kirk's ear. "Did you shake on a contract?"

"Yes," said Kirk. "But I forgot about it, with everything else going on."

The mouthpiece sighed. "I suggest we try and settle with The Kid before things get worse. He isn't asking for much, just one percent of the Fed's take."

The whispered conversation was interrupted by The Kid. "Your Honor, based on the testimony of Spock, I would like to have Kirk charged with endangering a minor in the course of a hit. His own lieutenant has testified that Kirk used a child to gain access to Krako."

"Too late," the mouthpiece whispered to Kirk.

The judge thought for a moment, then allowed the additional charge to be added. "Understand, Kirk, such a charge will send you upriver if you're found guilty," said the judge.

Kirk's mouthpiece stood up. "Your Honor, we'd like to discuss a settlement."

"No we wouldn't," Kirk said as he rose to his feet. He pulled the mouthpiece around and spoke into his ear. "I don't think the Federation would enjoy having me locked up, nor do I think they would approve the monetary outlay from the planetary treasury."

"I'm sorry, but I don't know how to get you out of this, not with testimony from your own lieutenant," the mouthpiece said into Kirk's ear.

Kirk couldn't stand giving in. He looked at the mouthpiece and knew the man was not going to be of any help. To win, Kirk was going to have to use logic, but apply it like a human. He turned to the judge.

"Your Honor, I'd like to release my mouthpiece and continue by defending myself," Kirk said.

The judge shrugged his shoulders. "It's your funeral." He said to Kirk's mouthpiece, "You're free to go, Squinteyes."

Squinteyes shrugged his shoulders. "Hey, what do I care, I've already been paid." He gathered his papers and walked through the gallery and out the door.

After Squinteyes had left, the judge motioned to Spock on the witness stand. "Your witness, Kirk," he said.

Kirk looked at his friend, knowing there wasn't anything Spock could say that would counteract what he had already said. He needed time to think. Until The Kid had questioned Spock, Kirk didn't know why he was even here. Now that he knew, he had something to work with, if he could get a little time.

"No questions," Kirk said.

Spock tilted his head to the side and raised one eyebrow. He rose and returned to his seat on the other side of the railing. When asked for his next witness, The Kid rested his case. The judge asked Kirk if he wanted to call any witnesses.

Kirk turned to the judge. "Your Honor, in light of the change in counsel for the defense, I'd like to request a continuance of this case."

The judge made a face that told Kirk he wasn't happy with the request. "I'm sorry, but this case has been delayed for too long waiting for you to get here. Your mouthpiece had ample time to prepare your case, but you dismissed him." The judge looked at his watch. "I'll tell you what, I'll recess now for lunch. That will give you a couple of hours."

Banging his gavel, the judge said, "Lunch. Be back at one o'clock." Standing, he shuffled down the steps and out the side door he had used to enter the court.

Kirk joined Spock and they left the courtroom with Bela.

"Captain," said Spock, "I think it would be advisable to locate some place we can talk privately."

"Exactly my thought, Mr. Spock," said Kirk. "Bela, is there someplace nearby we can meet quietly?"

Bela motioned down the block. "We can go to Gino's. He has a private room in back of his restaurant. He won't mind us using it."

The three men were crossing the four-lane street, Bela's two ever-present men in tow about ten paces behind them. A black car careened around the corner of the street that ran along the side of the courthouse. It was heading straight for them, picking up speed, aiming directly at the three men in front. They ran for the other side of the road, but the speeding car continued to track them.

Kirk looked at the oncoming car. It was going to be close. Out of the corner of his eye he saw that Bela's men had made it back to the other side of the street. Rushing forward, Kirk pushed Spock and Bela from behind, shoving them between two parked cars. As the oncoming car careened past, barely missing the bumper of the parked cars, Kirk dove across the hood of the parked car. His shoulder hit the center of the metal hood, and Kirk rolled across and onto the sidewalk.

Picking themselves up from the ground, the men stared down the street. Kirk heard the tires squeal as the car turned the corner at high speed. The smell of burnt rubber and car exhaust drifted over the area, carried by a light breeze.

Bela's men ran up to him. "Boss, you okay?" asked one.

"Yeah, yeah, yeah," said Bela. "Did either of you happen to see who was driving?"

Both men looked sheepish, looking anywhere but in Bela's eyes. "Sorry, Boss," said the one who had spoken before. "Whoever was driving was hunched down."

"I did see something," said Spock. "The driver was wearing a brown fedora."

Kirk turned to Bela. "Well, that couldn't have been The Kid, I can see him on the courthouse steps. Is it possible someone is trying to hit you?"

"Why would someone want to hit me?" asked Bela. "I told you, Krako runs things." He paused, tapping his chin with a finger. "Unless Krako isn't satisfied with running things, and wants to step up to the title of Boss, too. Look, I'm going to drop you two off at Gino's, and then I'm gonna have a talk with Krako."

Kirk turned toward the door of Gino's back room as Bela Oxmyx entered. It was the only door into the small, windowless room, which contained a table and chairs for six, and nothing else. Kirk and Spock were seated at the large table, where they had spent the last two hours reviewing a book on Iotian contract and percentage law. It was surprisingly simple. If two parties agreed on a contract, and confirmed it in front of witnesses, it was valid. By virtue of Kirk's having agreed to a percentage of the action for The Kid in front of Spock, the contract was valid and enforceable.

"I met with Krako," Bela said. "He'd heard about the attempts and was already trying to find out who was behind them. I'm convinced he isn't trying to hit me." Bela sat down opposite Kirk.

"What makes you believe that?" asked Kirk.

Bela took his glasses off and laid them on the table in front of him. "Hey, I know Krako," he said, pointing his finger at Kirk. "I've learned to read him, tell when he's hedging and when he's telling the truth. It doesn't rule out one of his soldiers, but Krako isn't behind this."

"Well, we haven't had much luck ourselves," said Kirk. He reached over and closed the book he and Spock had been reading.

"I didn't think you would," said Bela. "That law was meant to be so simple it couldn't be misinterpreted. Believe me, many a man has tried, including yours truly."

Bela pulled out a pocket watch and looked at the time. "We'd better start heading back. Mugsy don't like when you keep him waiting."

As the men rose and left the room, Spock asked, "Do you have a plan to refute the charges, Captain?"

Glancing back over his shoulder as they stepped out onto the sidewalk, Kirk said, "Not yet, Mr. Spock. Something will come to me. Probably something very human and irrational."

The walk back to the courthouse was less exciting than the walk to Gino's. There were no speeding cars, no machine-gun fire, no bombs.

When they reached the top of the stairs in front of the courthouse, a man came from behind a pillar and blocked their path. Kirk looked down at the tommy gun the man pointed at Kirk's chest. Kirk stopped and slowly raised his hands. The others followed Kirk's action.

"Slugo, what are you doing?" asked Bela.

"What's it look like? I'm making a hit," said the gun-wielding Slugo. "I'm going to hit the Fed that made my life a living hell."

Kirk looked the man over. He was tall with a thin build. His hair was salt and pepper, but had once been black. He appeared to be about a dozen years younger than Bela.

"I'm sorry, have we met?" asked Kirk.

"Have we met he asks," Slugo said with a sneer. He poked Kirk's chest with the gun barrel. "Think back, Fed. Think back to when you was here before. You humiliated me in front of Bela and all the other bosses. After you left, I was a joke. No one would give me any real work. I was stuck doing guard duty on empty rooms."

Kirk looked closer at the man's face. Looking at Spock, he could see that there was no recognition from Spock either.

Alan L. Lickiss

"I'm sorry, I can't place you," said Kirk.

"Does the game fizzbin mean anything to you?" asked Slugo.

"Fizzbin, fizzbin," Kirk said, trying to recall the game. Then it came to him, and he couldn't keep the start of a smile from his face. "You mean you're the guy I was teaching to play fizzbin?"

"That's right, Kirk. I'm the guy you made into a chump with that stupid game. Then later you had me strip to my skivvies so your boy Spocko could wear my clothes."

Slugo's voice began to rise in pitch and volume as he continued his rant. "After you left I was a joke. No one would let me do any real work. When I asked for the good jobs, they made jokes about my needing the proper wardrobe. Every time I sat down to play poker, some yuckster had to ask me the rules of fizzbin. Every time!

"I wish you Feds had never come here. I can't make you Feds and yer cockeyed ideas for one boss, free schools, economic advice, and all the other so-called help go away, but I can make you go away. I'm going to plug you, Kirk."

Kirk remained calm, allowing a smug grin to appear on his face. "I don't think those guys behind you are going to let you."

Slugo spun around, his gun poised on air. Spock stepped forward and pinched Slugo's shoulder nerves. Kirk grabbed the gun from Slugo's slackened grip as Spock eased him to the ground.

"Well, at least we know who was trying to hit us earlier," said Kirk. "That's one problem down."

"Yes," said Spock, "but you still have one problem without a solution."

Bela's men stayed to deal with Slugo while Kirk, Spock, and Bela continued into the courthouse.

"Oh, I don't know about that, Spock, I have an idea that might work," said Kirk.

Judge Mugsy called the court to order with a bang of his gavel. "You ready?" he asked Kirk.

"Yes, Your Honor," Kirk said. "I'd like to call The Kid to the stand."

The crowd in the gallery began to murmur. This was shaping up to be an interesting case. Each side was calling witnesses from the

27

other side to make their case. The judge banged his gavel and called for quiet. After a few moments, he received it.

The Kid stepped forward and was sworn in by the bailiff. He sat in the chair, looking out of place, as if he wasn't used to being on that side of the chair.

Kirk stood and approached The Kid. "First, let's clear up one thing for me. You're the knife-wielding young man that helped put the bag on Krako, aren't you?"

The Kid smiled. "Yes, I am," he said.

Kirk paced back and forth in front of the witness stand, letting that piece of information click into place. He stopped in front of The Kid. "Let's address these charges one at a time. First, the charge of endangering a minor. Kid, were you forced to help us?"

"No, but we still had a deal," The Kid said.

Kirk ignored the last part. "In fact, didn't we try to warn you away?"

"Ah, grownups were always like that. But I lived on the streets and could take care of myself. I saw an opportunity to make some money, and went for it. But then you took off and no one knew about our deal."

Kirk continued. "When did the minor-endangerment law go into effect? I don't recall there being a lot of concern for the people on the street the last time I was here."

"Oxmyx made that rule at the suggestion of some of your Fed buddies, to keep kids out of the middle of any local skirmishes. It went into effect about twenty years ago," The Kid said.

"So that was after my ship had left?" Kirk asked.

"Yes," said The Kid, his voice sounding less sure. Kirk could see The Kid was looking for where the argument was going.

"Then how could I break a law that didn't exist when I was here?" he asked.

The Kid didn't reply. He sat in the witness chair, silent. He appeared to be in thought.

"Your Honor," Kirk said, turning away from The Kid, "I request the endangerment charge be dropped. The Kid was clearly a volunteer, and the law was not in effect at the time in question."

The judge pursed his lips as he thought. Kirk stood mute, watching the judge, waiting for the answer. Finally the judge nodded his head. "Yes, I'll dismiss that charge," he said.

Kirk smiled as he turned back to The Kid. He moved with the grace and style of a man used to command, used to having the upper hand. The Kid's eyes narrowed for a moment when the judge announced the dismissal. Kirk noticed, and figured he had done the equivalent of capturing The Kid's queen.

"Now," Kirk said to The Kid, "about the breach of contract. You claim that you were promised a piece of the action, but never received it. Is that correct?"

"That is correct," said The Kid. He shifted in the chair, sitting up straighter, back on familiar territory.

"Would you please tell the court what the agreed-upon piece of the action was," said Kirk.

The Kid glared at Kirk. "The exact terms were not finalized, but it was implied that it was to be a percentage of your action," he said.

Kirk was pacing with a confident air in front of the witness stand and judge's bench. "But implied conditions are not valid, are they? The terms of the contract were that you would receive a piece of the action. That means that you would gain some benefit from the Federation's cut. Isn't that correct?"

The Kid smirked as he spoke. "Yeah, and I ain't seen one dime of it."

Kirk stopped his pacing in front of The Kid. "That's a really nice suit. You must do pretty good. What type of action do you run?"

"I'm a mouthpiece," said The Kid. He seemed a little confused by the change in questioning.

"A mouthpiece," said Kirk. "That's a pretty impressive step up from street urchin. How'd you manage that? A moment ago you testified that you were living on the streets as a child."

"The syndicate started a bunch of schools. I busted my butt cracking the books. I worked hard to be a mouthpiece so's I could sue you personally for what's mine," The Kid said.

"I see. So you are a well-off mouthpiece with good action because you went to the syndicate's school?" asked Kirk.

"Yes," said The Kid, but somewhat hesitantly. He was clearly caught off guard by the questions.

Kirk turned to the judge. "No more questions, Your Honor."

The judge looked down at The Kid. "I know it's a bit unusual, but the book says I gotta allow you to cross-examine the witness. So, you got any questions for yourself?"

The Kid thought for a moment. Finally he said, "I can't think of anything to add, so no questions." He stepped down and returned to his seat.

Kirk was still standing before the judge. He waited until The Kid was seated before saying, "For my next witness, I call Bela Oxmyx."

The crowd shifted and murmured. Kirk had called the Boss of Bosses, and the excitement ran through the crowd. The judge banged his gavel several times to restore order. Bela had been sitting on one of the benches at the back of the court. He swaggered forward and was sworn in. Even at his age he had the walk of a street tough, ready to do his own dirty work if necessary.

"Mr. Oxmyx, do you recall the terms of the Federation's take?" Kirk asked.

"Sure I do, Kirk. You Feds get forty percent off the top," Bela said.

"Please tell the court what the Federation does with that cut," said Kirk.

"Well, it's a bit nutso to me," said Bela, "but you guys put it into the planetary treasury. Then those advisor guys offer up ideas on how to spend it. Lots of public projects and stuff like that. Not that I minded. It meant less of the syndicate's cut going to that stuff."

"Public projects like the libraries and schools?" Kirk asked.

"Yeah, those were part of it," said Bela.

"Thank you, Mr. Oxmyx," Kirk said to Bela. He turned to the judge and said, "No more questions, Your Honor."

Bela started to get up from his chair, but The Kid stopped him. "Just a moment, Oxmyx. I have a question." Bela sat back down and waited patiently for The Kid to continue. "After the Feds got all the bosses together to form the syndicate, did Kirk ever discuss my participation in his bagging Krako? Or the promised piece of the action?"

"No, Kid, he never discussed it. Frankly, Krako was smarting a little because he was my lieutenant and not the boss. I don't think Kirk wanted Krako to stew about his boys getting jumped."

"So only Kirk and Spock were aware of the contract?" asked The Kid.

"That's right, Kid. If I'da known you were supposed to be cut in, you would have been," said Bela.

"Thank you, no further questions," said The Kid.

Bela returned to his seat in the gallery.

Kirk rose to his feet. "The defense rests, Your Honor." He sat back down; his demeanor had never wavered. He still looked like a man who thought he had already won.

The Kid and the judge both looked a bit surprised. The judge recovered quickly. He banged his gavel to still the whispered conversation of the spectators. "Okay, closing arguments then. Kid, you're up."

The Kid stood. He walked to the area in front of the judge. "Your Honor, I'll be brief. Kirk has made my case for me. I have shown through sworn testimony of his own lieutenant that he and I had a contract. And through the testimony of his own witness, that the syndicate was never apprised of the contract. It is clear that Kirk intentionally welshed on the contract." He then returned to his seat.

The judge nodded to Kirk.

Kirk moved to the spot vacated by The Kid. "Your Honor, I do not deny the contract with The Kid. Unfortunately, his expectation of what his piece of the action was to be has caused this unfortunate misunderstanding. The Kid has indeed received his piece of the action."

The judge had to bang his gavel several times to restore order. Kirk stood mute, waiting for the judge's signal to continue.

"Yes, he has received his piece. The Federation never took a dime from Iotia, but funneled it back into projects here. The Kid has been a benefactor of those projects. He has testified himself that he attended the schools provided with the Federation cut. He has also made a good living with his action as a mouthpiece. A profession brought about by the starting of the court system based on suggestions by the Federation advisors.

"The Kid has gone from street urchin to well-paid mouthpiece, without having to give up any of his own percentages. I submit that

The Kid has been the benefactor of the Federation's cut, and therefore the contract has been honored."

Kirk accepted the drink Bela offered. They were back in Bela's office, and Kirk and Bela were on their second drink. Spock was sipping his first, occasionally holding it up to the light and examining the dark amber liquid.

"That was some smooth talking you did there, Kirk," said Bela. "I was sure you were in the soup. You sure you don't want to stick around and become a mouthpiece?"

Kirk smiled. "While the offer is tempting, the Federation might consider that interference." He took another sip of his drink.

"Sure, sure. I understand. You guys are into a bigger piece of the pie," said Bela. "Too bad, 'cause that was the best verbal tap-dancing I've ever seen."

"Well, I did have one advantage on The Kid," said Kirk.

"Yeah, what's that?" asked Bela.

In his best Brooklyn accent, Kirk said, "I've been honing my mouthpiece mambo skills on ol' Spocko over there for years."

Yeoman Figgs

Mark Murata

It had taken hell and high water—plus a couple of broken ribs—but I had my trainers swearing I was the most fire-eating recruit they had ever seen. The ribs had healed, so I didn't feel any twinges as I jostled my way through the corridor. It was crowded with crewmen—some carrying tools and equipment, some making adjustments at open hatch covers with swift movements, some bustling toward their destinations empty-handed, but with determined looks on their faces. And I was one of them.

An engineering crewman jostled me with his circuit analyzer. I grabbed at my side. *Maybe it does twinge, just a little.* Cursing myself for displaying a moment's weakness, I whipped my hand back to my tricorder, riding on my right hip. Gripping the leather casing, I brushed past the muttered apology and pushed forward, my focus undimmed. My leather boots ate the lengths of deck plating, stride by stride, closing in on my destination. My grip on the tricorder dug the leather strap into my left shoulder, making me look down. The Starfleet insignia rode my left breast, the proudest part of my velour uniform. I had made it: Yeoman Vonda Figgs, posted to the most hard-charging starship in the fleet—the *Enterprise.*

The entrance to the transporter room was just ahead, on the right. After one last jostle, I headed into the double doors. They slid open automatically, right before my nose would have hit their dividing line. The whoosh of their opening blew some of my auburn hair past my ears and hugged my velour one-piece closer to my skin, but I didn't break stride. I joined the others with a nod, standing ready. My name had risen to the top of the roster, and this would be my first landing party. *Ready for anything.*

But I still couldn't get over how large it was—most transporter rooms I've seen are the podunk kind, crammed in odd parts of hallways with pads for two. But this transporter room was huge, enabling large groups to evacuate in rapid succession. And judging from the tales I'd already been told around the billiards table in the rec hall, it gave the security teams elbow room for a firefight when a hostile party boarded. My skin crawled at the ever-present hum from the control panel, hinting at the immense energies involved. And the pad . . .

The science officer walked in—a Vulcan. I'd never seen one this close before. Tall, dark hair, a sober face. The double doors closed behind him and he stood before us, placing his hands behind his back before beginning his briefing. I was careful not to look at the ears.

"I assume you've all familiarized yourselves with the mission briefing. To review: Planet Hydra Epsilon 3 has 1.05 Earth-normal gravity, a nitrogen-oxygen atmosphere, and a temperate climate. It is being considered for colonization. Your observations may have a significant impact on such a decision."

Just like that, he stopped. No good luck on being the first to set foot on a strange planet, no three cheers for Starfleet as it explores new worlds. He conveyed his facts, then stopped.

No one moved. The Vulcan stayed at attention, shoulders square. The rest of us stayed at attention, the hum from the control panel filling the blank space. My hand was pressing down on my tricorder, making the leather strap dig in again. I knew I should ease up, to avoid leaving a crease in the velour, but I was concentrating on not looking at the ears. In spite of that, my eyes were drawn to that tall face of his—upswept eyebrows, a greenish tint to his skin, and features chiseled from rock, betraying no emotion.

The double doors opened again, and the captain walked through. A fair-haired man in his thirties with boyish good looks, he seemed in constant motion. After exchanging a few words with the Vulcan, he looked us over. He had a careful eye, looking us in the face, evaluating. He stepped up to me. My strap dug deeper into my shoulder.

He put a smile on one corner of his mouth. "Yeoman . . . Figgs, isn't it?"

"Aye, sir." *Don't blow this.*

"Where do you call home?"

"Deck 12, sir."

His smile turned into a grin as he nodded at me. "I meant, where are you from?"

"Oh. Uh . . ." *He's not grilling me. He's being friendly?*

"The questions do get easier, Yeoman."

"I'm from Springfield, Missouri."

He got a twinkle in his eye. "I'm from Iowa, myself. We could use more Midwesterners on the *Enterprise.*" He led the way onto the transporter pad.

I followed the landing party up the steps, feeling numb. *I know that. Captain Kirk is from some small town in Iowa. And now he's one of the youngest captains in Starfleet.* I walked across the huge transporter pad as the six of us formed a circle, each a couple of feet apart. I knew enough to position myself at the back, next to another yeoman. She stood at attention, eyes front. I imitated her, but not before noticing how svelte she looked in her red velour draping down to mid-thigh, dark stockings showing below. The blond hair was piled high, long tresses flowing past her shoulders. *A little older—early twenties?*

The Vulcan was straight ahead, facing away from me at the front of the pad. *Those ears.* Tall, pointed ears. Humans, Vulcans, others—we were all in Starfleet together. *I've left Missouri way behind.*

The transporter operator let us know he was energizing. The hum surrounded us, making my skin tingle beneath the velour and the stockings. Then the shimmering light enfolded us. After a few seconds, all I could see was the shimmer.

Some people say they can feel themselves being transported. That's just not possible. Must be the tingling, combined with a bad case of nerves. No one can feel their body being disassembled molecule by molecule, converted into energy, "beamed" to another location, then reassembled. As far as I was concerned, I was standing still. The shimmer and hum faded away, and I was standing on the surface of the planet. My leather boots were firm on the mossy ground.

The heat and humidity were what I noticed first. The muggy air clung close and opened my pores, displacing the cool air that had beamed down from the *Enterprise* between my uniform and my skin. It was like a spring shower in Missouri, when it doesn't last long enough to cool things off, the humidity growing the moment it stops. Then there's nothing to do but lie around, feeling nauseous from the oppressive thickness of the air. I was glad the velour had such a high skirt and wide neck. *Don't sweat on your first landing-party assignment.*

The high-pitched ululation of two tricorders alerted me to the straightforward style of this crew. The Vulcan and the other yeoman had started taking their tricorder readings without saying a word, each wandering off a few paces. I realized I was still clutching mine. *Get it in gear.*

I brought it forward from my hip, gripping the black leather casing with both hands. The texture of that familiar leather helped me concentrate as I adjusted the different dials, the way I had practiced so often. Now it was for real, and the preliminary readouts on the little screen were clear: The ground we were standing on was dry enough, but just beyond the sparse tree line I was facing was a complicated series of swamps. A twist of a dial started the mapping function.

"Captain." It was the Vulcan. I looked over my shoulder. He was still staring at his tricorder readout, not bothering to look up as he spoke. "Intriguing mineral deposit in this direction."

"All right, let's split up." Captain Kirk made a casual gesture with his hand, as if dismissing us. "Rendezvous at this beam-down point in one hour."

The Vulcan walked off with a security guard. The captain walked off with the other yeoman toward a ridge she had been scanning. It dawned on me that he was acting as her security. Not only was he brazen enough to beam down in the first landing party to an unknown planet, he guarded a yeoman as she explored, rather than standing around with guards surrounding him.

I couldn't take the time to digest all that. I had to nod at the remaining security guard and stride off, as purposefully as the others. We walked into the tree line, my tricorder able to take my motion into account as it finished its mapping function. Then I started it on analyzing the trees. They resembled elms and maples on Earth, but on a dwarfed scale—not much taller than the two of us. The roots were small but gnarled, bumping at my boots as I walked and looked at the small screen. *Don't trip. Be thorough and deliberate.*

The security guard, whose name was Rojas, sniffed at the air and crinkled his nose. "Rotting vegetation. Are you heading us toward a swamp?" At my nod, he said, "Looks like we got the short end of the stick."

"Buck up. It's a swamp no one has seen before." I continued scanning, but my nose said he was right. The damp, fetid smell of tons of rotting vegetation was overcoming the leafy scent of the trees. Also, the humidity was increasing as I led us closer. I imagined the smell soaking into my uniform and stockings, oozing into my pores.

"Newbies." He chuckled and shook his head. "Always trying so hard." Still, his eyes were alert, and he kept his hand near the phaser pistol on his belt.

I led on. "Why not get some dirt under your fingernails?" That was the attitude that had cracked a couple ribs, much to the jaw-dropping shock of my trainers. But I was safe, and we had a whole planet to explore.

The brown soil became soggy beneath my feet, water squishing out around the edges of my boots. Dwarf trees gave way to huge ferns as we came to the edge. The fronds were up to three feet high, some sharp and springy, others wilting and ready to join previous generations as sludge. I twisted a dial, setting up for underwater mineral scan. "There could be phosphates here. Or a thick deposit of peat—think of those complex hydrocarbons. A colony could set up an automated synthesizer, plop it in the swamp, and let it run itself. No muss, no fuss."

Despite my bravado, I could feel the form-fitting velour getting damp from my perspiration. And the muggy smell of rot and fresh corn was clinging to my nostrils. *Fresh corn?* I looked up from my tricorder.

The new smell seemed to be coming from a pair of leaves—two pairs, actually. They had the classic spade shape, but were three or four feet long. The upper leaf of each pair pointed skyward. But each lower leaf floated on the edge of the water, holding a clutch of red berries at its base. They were a bright, shiny red, like maraschino cherries, only they were the size of billiard balls. So succulent—I'd never seen anything so delicious. "Do they smell like corn to you?"

"Corn? Those are pork chops!" Rojas squished forward, going down on his hands and knees on one of the leaves. It seemed to hold his weight, and he was soon flat on his stomach, grabbing the red berries with both hands. Black juice squirted onto his face and throat as he bit into them, sucking down as much as he could with ravenous moans.

This seemed a little odd to me, in a fuzzy way. *They do look good.* Then the upper leaf folded down on top of him, the tip just covering his buttocks.

"Like a giant mouth." I laughed and looked at the berries in the remaining pair. It was getting hard to see anything else. They smelled just like the corn on my parents' farm.

On the really muggy nights, I and my brothers would sometimes sleep out in the cornfield, lying between the rows of stalks. I would lie there in my underwear, feeling the rich earth against my back and legs, the thick air hugging me like a warm blanket. The corn smelled so sweet, and we would talk about the future. Gervase wanted to take over the farm when he was old enough, and he loved running computer simulations of different crop rotations, maximizing the yield by adjusting the fertilizers, water input, and fallow times. Hyannis wanted to be a sculptor. Or a musician. Or a dancer. "Do all three, and find three different ways to starve," I said.

They both wanted me to try out for Starfleet. They knew it was my dream, but I had to be realistic. "Those math and science requirements . . ."

"Then skip the Academy. You don't need to start as an officer." Gervase's voice became insistent, wending its way through the stalks. "You can ship out as crew. It takes a handful of guts to get through the training program, but you have that."

Yes. Yes I do. I reached out with my hand and ripped away some corn silk. I arranged it on my hair, piling it high on top, tresses on my shoulders. Like the female crewmen on the recruiting posters. I fingered my fake hair and stared up at the stars.

Just past my head, the rows of corn exploded. Steam covered my face, filled my nostrils. The night sky ripped open. It was the Vulcan, frowning at me with his upswept eyebrows. He let go of the sky and gripped me under the knees with cruel hands, inhuman strength. He dragged me on my back onto soggy soil, water squishing against my skin.

Captain Kirk held his phaser pistol in his hand, aimed beyond my head. The other yeoman, whose name was Rand, was gaping at me, eyes wide with horror. The Vulcan dropped my legs and grabbed his tricorder. The sweet smell of corn was gone, was gone. I was saddened, but also giddy. I pointed at him. "Look at those ears!"

He didn't change expression, just gazed at his readout. "A male human body, five feet below the surface of the water, undoubtedly Rojas. No life signs."

Meanwhile, Rand had ripped off a strip from the bottom of her uniform, revealing the black tights beneath. With frantic moves, she wiped off my face, my bare scalp. I gasped. "My hair. Where's my hair?"

She paused, lifting up the velour strip. An auburn tress dropped from it, falling to the damp ground. *Oh no.* I looked down. I was bare on top, the upper part of my uniform and my support garment having gone to pieces. She wiped black gunk off my arms and chest.

Kirk handed his phaser to Rand. "All right, we can't do anything more for Rojas and Klinsky. Let's get Figgs back to the *Enterprise*."

The Vulcan lifted his communicator to his face. "Spock to *Enterprise*. Prepare for immediate transport from beam-down point."

Crouching down, the captain lifted me in his arms, though my skin was still damp from the horrid liquid that had dissolved my clothes. Then we were off at a trot.

I could hear Spock's voice from the rear. "Captain, if I may speculate." He sounded methodical, as if he were describing a mineral deposit. "Based on Klinsky's actions and my sensations, it would seem the scent from the berries stimulates the hunger center of the brain, bringing up the food associations most pleasing to the individual. I was able to pull back. But as Klinsky, and apparently Rojas, discovered to their detriment, these 'berries' contain digestive juices."

Klinsky was the other security guard. My head was clear, but the skin on my hands and upper body was burning. I leaned my head against the captain's left shoulder, clutched at his shirt. He was a real gentleman—didn't look at my bareness. His arms held me close to his strong chest as he spoke.

"The plants are traps—like Venus's-flytraps on Earth, only bigger. Probably meant for birds, like that flock you spotted, Yeoman."

Rand held the phaser ready as she jogged beside us, eyes darting back and forth as she looked for further dangers. "But they snared some of our people instead."

Away from the tree line, Kirk set me down. His shirt was starting to come apart. Spock communicated with the transporter room one more time. I leaned my burning scalp against the mossy ground and looked up at the captain. "I'm sorry."

He glanced down, concern drawing his eyebrows together.

"I'm sorry I messed up." I looked at my hand. His Starfleet insignia was clutched in it. Then the hum covered my burning skin, and the shimmer enfolded us.

I can't remember what happened next. By all accounts, the sickbay worked me over fast. They washed the digestive acid off, cut off what was left of my acid-soaked hair, encouraged the skin cells to regenerate in the damaged spots, made sure the hunger center in my brain was back to normal. So I was lying there on a biobed, a blanket covering my new underwear. The hair would take a while to grow back. I stroked my smooth scalp. *See how long I can hide in my quarters.*

The double doors to sickbay opened. Captain Kirk and Yeoman Rand walked in. I caught my breath and tried to be invisible.

The doctor walked over from another biobed and waved his arms at the captain. "What the blue blazes were you doing? Sending a young girl down to a planet like that!"

The captain gave him a jaunty smile and pointed at Rand. "This young girl seems to do just fine."

She darted an annoyed look at him with her green eyes. "Girl?"

They talk to the captain like that? There was a camaraderie here I hadn't expected. Probably from shared dangers. The doctor walked off, leaving the two of them to stand near my bed.

The captain spoke in a quiet voice. "How are you, Figgs?"

"Ready for duty, sir."

He chuckled, regaining the twinkle in his eye. "Why don't we leave that for the doctor to say? I think I'll take you off the roster for a while, give you time to recuperate. Sorry your first landing-party assignment turned out to be so unpleasant."

It dawned on me that he had come to sickbay to see me—me in particular. "Yes, sir. It was quite a shock. But I can't wait to go back out."

He turned to Rand. "I think we have another hard charger." After a nod to me, he left.

She asked me if I needed anything, and I put a hand on her sleeve. "Was that a phaser blast that went off near my head?"

"Yes. It was a risk, his firing near your head like that, to cut the leaves off where they joined. Did you know it was starting to take you under? Legs sticking out and all? But Captain Kirk aimed at the murky water and fired."

"And then Mr. Spock dragged me out. Should I thank him? And apologize for what I said?"

She smiled, complementing her blond tresses. "He wouldn't acknowledge you if you did. He says it's because of his Vulcan heritage, but I think it's as much to do with his own personality as anything else." Then she cocked her head at me. "Don't worry. You didn't do anything wrong. It's normal for a crewman to be off the list after a bad experience—especially the first time."

Do all the experienced people read my mind? "But I'm not traumatized. In fact, if I'm put back on the roster now, by the time I get out of here . . ."

She put her hand on my shoulder, easing me back down. "We don't want you to get 'hard-charging fever.' The captain sees what you're like. You need time to reflect a little. Don't take on the universe all at once." She patted my shoulder, smiled again, then she was gone.

I lay back for a minute, thinking of how to thank Mr. Spock, whether he would like it or not. Then I swiveled the metal arm near my bed, bringing the monitor close. I was determined to read the landing-party logs from the ship's computer—the ones where everything went wrong. I would highlight Captain Kirk's actions and learn. *I'm hard-charging Yeoman Vonda Figgs. And I'm still here.*

The Shoulders of Giants

Robert T. Jeschonek

If I have seen further it is by standing upon the shoulders of Giants.

—Sir Isaac Newton

PROLOGUE

From *The Story of the Heavensent*, oral history, author unknown

As the pink one, the Godcaptainarcher, taught us, the way to Heaven is murder.

Listen:

When the pink ones came, the Kolyati believed them when they said they were from far away, for we had never seen their like before.

But when Godcaptainarcher said they came in friendship, not all of us believed that. We had been tricked before.

So fearandsuspicion grew among us. We captured the pink ones and fed them holy sap, which would force the truth from them.

Instead, it forced the life from them. Two of the pink ones died before we realized that this sap, distilled in our hearts, was deadly to their own.

Greatly ashamed, we released them all, though we knew full well that they might take our lives in return.

But they did not. With weapons drawn, they gathered their dead and left our village.

And Godcaptainarcher said:

"You've got a lot to learn about friendship.

"I only hope that someday, you'll appreciate the sacrifice of these men you murdered. That you'll learn from it and change.

"Trust me, it's the only way to a better world."

We did not understand until later.

Some of us, unseen, followed the pink ones as they left, carrying their dead beyond the edge of the forestreef. A strange chariot waited there, and they opened a door in it and went inside.

And then the chariot rose into Heaven, growing smallereversmaller until it vanished in the distance somewhere higher than the sun itself.

And at that moment, the Kolyati learned Godcaptainarcher's lesson, and our world was changed.

What is the key to Heaven? Why, you know the answer.

ONE: FIFFICK

From *Birth of the NewWay,* by Thias Ess Elt, Earth Year 2268

As I swung the axe into the chest of the one called McCoy, the holysong fluttered from my smiling greenlips, sending his soul on its bright Heavenflight.

To my surprise, I did not even get a thank-you.

But this was not to be my only surprise. Still singing, I began to wrench the handle back, about to free the blade and swing again . . .

Then a flurry of pink as I was struck, my tentacles sliding from the axe, my body sliding to the floor.

How shocked I was as looking up I saw that my attacker was the very Godkirk I had sought to honor with my murdergift. Springing to the side of fallen McCoy, he drew a weapon from his waist and then a talkingbox and flipped it open.

"Enterprise!" he shouted, and by then Spock was at his side as well, glancing down only once at McCoy from his careful weaponwatch of all the onlooking greenbrothers. "Three to beam . . ."

No one, I think, has ever been more surprised than I was when the Godkirk rejected my murdergift . . . except me, when the Godkirk's own words were cut off in the very next instant.

As a blast tore a hole through the chamberwall, I struggled to rise. I knew what was coming, and it was the very last thing the soontobesoaringbrightly McCoy needed.

It was a doctor.

Pushing through the jaggedhole, she stormed amid a glittering silver cloud, a screeningmist that masked her from detection. As her two fellowvermin, also vile doctors, slipped inside and raised McCoy, her eyes for just an instant caught my own and I could not subdue a tremor.

How could I have loved her once? And how could even a tinyspark still smolder within me as it did when our eyes met?

Carrying McCoy, the fellowvermin hurried past their leader into the night. Casting back a coldlook, Fiffick followed, leaving only the smoking hole and absence of McCoy as proof she'd been there.

Moonglow lit the way as our huntingparty set out, losing hardly any time in shaking off the rattleshock. Thirty strong, we left the cityreef, its cultivated coral pillars phosphorescing red and yellow, pearl and blue.

As many stars as filled the sky, twiceatleast that number twinkled all around, for it was coralbirthingseason. Tiny glowing polyps drifted, wafting first upon one breeze and then another, sometimes hundreds in a swirling bubblestream of light.

Earlier, the Godkirk with a smile had said they reminded him of "fireflies" from home . . . but deadlygrim now he ignored them as he marched ahead.

"The next time you decide to take an axe to one of my crew, I'd appreciate a warning," he said, quickflashing a glare in my direction. "Even if you think you're doing us a favor."

"It is the way to Heaven," I told him. "As in the story I told you of Godcaptainarcher. The murdered dead ascend to Heaven on a chariot like a shootingstar. 'It is the only way to a better world,' he told us."

"We need to talk about that," grimlysaid the Godkirk. "After we find McCoy."

"I hope he dies soon," I said with a smile.

Stopping then among the wild corals of the forestreef, we Kolyati smelled the air for trailtrace, the faintest scent that might have sifted through our quarry's screeningmist. Each of us opened our bodybud, deep green petalgills peeling up from knees to waist and waist to chest and chest to throat, a trio of glistening canopies fanning out around each greenbrother.

Turning like wheels, we closed our eyes and deeplybreathed the nearandfar, polypstars aswirl as we upstirred the air.

"Fascinating," said Spock amid our turning inhalation, reading from a blinkingbox he carried.

No more turning then, and petals with a rustle fell, refurling into deep green shrouds. As one, we started down another trail.

"Captain," said Spock, eyebrows raised. "Neither the tricorder nor the ship's sensors can detect any trace of McCoy. The olfactory receptors in the Kolyati's gills may be the most powerful sensory organs on record."

"Or we're being led on a wild goose chase," muttered the Godkirk in a lowvoice, but I heard him.

Touching the Godkirk's elbow, Spock guided him aside, far enough from us he must have thought to hide his words. "This bodes well for our mission," I heard Spock say despite his sneaking. "Logically, an extreme sensitivity to chemical composition would be a necessary trait for a species able to synthesize pharmacological compounds internally."

"Walking miracle drug factories," said the Godkirk.

Spock nodded. "I believe that we have already witnessed one of the products of this chemical synthesis: the 'screening mist' surrounding McCoy's captors."

"If they can secrete a mist capable of blocking a starship's sensors, they ought to be able to help us with our problem."

"Perhaps," said Spock. "Though, after what has happened, I must reiterate my objection to breaking the quarantine placed on this world after Captain Archer's visit."

"There was no other option," the Godkirk said stiffly. "We're saving Gideon."

Eversoslightly, Spock's voice softened. "It was their decision, Jim. They chose to use the virus to reduce their population."

"And it came from my bloodstream," said the Godkirk.

"But the mutation of the virus was unforeseen and uncontrollable. It has become something different from what they took from you."

"And in a week, there won't be anyone left on Gideon to care." The Godkirk quickchopped a hand through the air, swatting aside arguments and polypstars. "The Vegan choriomeningitis came from my bloodstream, and I won't let whatever it's mutated into wipe out an entire race.

"I just hope Bones isn't the asking price for Gideon's salvation," the Godkirk quietsaid, leaving me to wonder who or what the "Bones" could be.

Stopping twice again to smell for trailtrace, we wound our way through the forestreef, brightcolored coral branches weaving overhead, lower pulsing walls and mounds of coral piled under. Gardens of anemones wakened and bloomed at our footsteps, each glowing blossom of supplefluttering tendrils as big as the head of a greenbrother.

At last, as the trailtrace grew freshest, we lost it . . . and knew that we were close, where the screeningmist would be strongest.

Ducking under limbs of coral, we emerged into a clearing and stopped. There before us was a thing of such repugnance we could hardly bear to look upon it.

"It is a greenlodge," I told the Godkirk and Spock. "A *hospital.*"

Looming before us, the walls of the lodge were the glistening deep green color of Kolyati petalgills and as high as three Kolyati standing on each other's shoulders.

This was plain to see because the walls were made of Kolyati standing on each other's shoulders, three high, arranged in a ring. Around the base, another ring of people stood shoulder-to-shoulder, tentacles linked in a chain of resistance.

"It is a place of unimaginable evil and cruelty," I said. "It is where they save lives."

The Godkirk stared at me with narrowed eyes. "And this is a bad thing," he said.

"Doctors interfere with our holy killings, whisking off the Heavenbound," I said. "They bring the dying back to life, depriving them of Heaven's glory."

The Godkirk's next words thrilled me. "Clearly," he said, "this must stop." Stepping closer to the lodge, he raised his voice to address the living walls.

"You have one of our men in there," he said. "We want to see him. We mean him no harm."

At that, the walls began their babblelaughingshouting, dozens of renegade greenbrother voices joined in jeering uproar.

Turning, the Godkirk sighed. "The walls have ears," he said to Spock, "but they won't listen."

Spock looked up from his blinkingbox. "The walls also have pouches of toxic spray, which I believe they are about to fire in our direction."

Without a word, the Godkirk's red-shirted soldiers arrayed themselves to either side of their leader, weapons drawn.

"Phasers on stun, on my mark," the Godkirk said firmly. "Open a door, gentlemen."

"Wait!" I suddenshouted then as weapons raised, quickcoiling a tentacle around the Godkirk's arm. "Whatever you do, don't kill them! Don't send them to Heaven!"

"Don't worry," the Godkirk said grimly. "They'll get what they deserve." And then he gave his men the order.

* * *

Eyes bedazzled by the brightlight beams that toppled down a greenlodge wall, I followed the Godkirk and Spock in overstepping tumbled bodies through the entrygap.

Once inside the hospital, I saw what I had dreaded and was heartsick.

McCoy was still breathing. He lay upon the coral floor, eyes closed, Fiffick kneeling by his side.

It was not until I started forward, intending to put things right and send McCoy Heavenward again, that I realized the Godkirk's weapon was pointed at my chest.

Looking around in confusion, I saw that my rightminded brothers had entered the greenlodge behind me but were likewise confronted, encircled by the Godkirk's redclad soldiers.

This was not to be my last or worst surprise that day.

"Captain," said Spock, kneeling to wave his blinkingbox over McCoy. "He is alive, and his wounds have been repaired. Apparently, in addition to being natural producers of medicinal compounds, the Kolyati are masterful surgeons."

"If ever there was a race of natural-born physicians," said the Godkirk. "And they'd rather take life than preserve it."

"Not all of us," said Fiffick, rising.

"Yes," said the Godkirk. "And thank you. That man you saved is a doctor himself."

Startlegaping at McCoy, I gasped and stumbled back a step, unable to believe what I had heard.

"Then I am especially honored," smiled Fiffick, bowing to the Godkirk.

"No!" I blurted, burning at the sight of her and not with hate alone. "There is no honor in damning a soul by keeping it from its appointed Heavenflight!"

"Then you are damned," said Fiffick sharply. "Are you not, Thias?"

All eyes were upon me now, but only hers I met, returning her glare of contempt with one evendeeper of my own.

"Tell them, Thias," she continued. "Tell them how I saved your life when you were Heavenbound . . ."

How could I have loved her?

49

". . . and instead of begging your killer to finish the job, as the law demands . . ."

How could I . . .

". . . you chose to live, and swore me to secrecy."

. . . love her?

"Liar!" I shouted.

The Godkirk raised his weapon higherpointing. "Then you won't mind if I kill you now," he calmlysaid. "In fact, you'll welcome it."

I felt a pressure then as if the force of stares upon me had intensified. None of my greenbrother allies dared to break the waitingsilence in the greenlodge.

"You'll all welcome it," said the Godkirk, raising his voice to include the surrounded greenbrothers. "You'll thank us for sending you to a better world."

Frozen in place, I considered what I knew should be an easy choice . . . but it was not so easy after all. For the second time in my life, as I faced my own death, I turned my eyes to Fiffick.

"Any takers?" said the Godkirk. "Speak up. Why would you want to stay here when you can go to Heaven?"

I fought a silent moment with myself and then another, knowing every hesitation sunk me deeper in disgrace. Though I knew the only answer I could give, a feltbefore reluctance held my tongue.

Then, Fiffick spoke. To this day, I wonder still if there was something in my eyes that made her do it.

"I can't allow this," she said. "Not inside a hospital."

The Godkirk did not waver. "Then we'll do it outside."

"No," said Fiffick. "Heaven's too good for them."

Holding steady for a moment, locking eyes with mine, the Godkirk made me wonder what was next . . . and in that moment I confess I was afraid.

Afraid of what? I later wondered. *How could anyone fear Heaven?*

"All right," said the Godkirk. "Have it your way."

Slowly, he lowered his weapon, his eyes never leaving my own. "Consider this," he said. "Why did you hesitate?"

"Why did any of you hesitate?" he said to us all. "You could have been in Heaven right now.

50

"Could it be," he said, "that life is more precious than you thought?"

I did not answer him. None of us did.

Weeks later, though, when Fiffick returned from the faraway country of Gideon, flushed with success from a mission of mercy, the change had begun.

Thinking back now, I thank Dr. Fiffick for saving my life and rightchanging my mind . . . for the NewWay she helped me conceive . . . and for being my wife, furtherproving each day that the Godkirk was right about life being precious.

TWO: RAYVIS

From *The Diary of Rayvis Vo,* Earth Year 2343

So there we were, Captain Garrett and Lieutenant Castillo and I, surrounded by five hundred Romulans, and I wasn't afraid even though I didn't have a weapon and I started fighting them.

Okay, make that five Romulans. And I guess I was kind of afraid.

But I really did fight them! It was like everything they'd done to the Kolyati, and especially my parents, just built up inside me and I went crazy! Captain Garrett tried holding me back but she couldn't, and I don't think the Romulans were expecting me to fight, since people say I'm kind of small for a twelve-year-old (even though *I* don't think I'm that small), because I actually knocked two of them—okay, one of them—down on the ground!

That's when all of a sudden these people appeared out of thin air!

There was this humming sound and this twinkling in the air, and then they just appeared! They were all bushy and bumpy and they looked a lot meaner than those Romulans, so of course I thought we were in even bigger trouble than before!

But here it was Kestrel and Warlog (though I didn't know who they were back then, of course) so I didn't have anything to worry about! And the other three were Klingons, too, so we were in luck.

Boy, did they get those Romulans! They cut them up with their big curved swords, and there was green blood everywhere, and they didn't even break a sweat doing it!

It was the second time I saw anyone get killed, counting my parents. It was a good thing I was getting used to it, what with how things went for me later on.

Kestrel was the kind of guy I want to be just like when I grow up. Even though he was big and tough and he always let you know it, he was a nice guy and he liked to joke around.

The first thing he said to us was "Captain Garrett, I presume?" and he even bowed when he said it. "It's an honor to meet the captain of the *Enterprise*-C."

I'm pretty sure Captain Garrett liked him right from the start, even though she was all business and didn't show it. She said, "And you are?"

"Captain Kestrel of the *Qob'ral,* at your service. This is my first officer, Commander Warlog."

Warlog just snorted, but I could tell he was all right. He was old and kind of grumpy and didn't say much, but he was basically nice and he sure could fight.

Kestrel said, "We're answering your distress call. I take it you're in distress?"

Captain Garrett got a funny look on her face. "You mean our coded signal on a secure channel to Starfleet? That 'distress call'?"

Something about the way Kestrel laughed made me smile. "So you'd rather we left you to your own devices, Captain?"

Captain Garrett smirked at him, and that's when I knew for sure they'd get along great. "Absolutely not, Captain. In the spirit of Klingon-human cooperation born in the Khitomer Accords, I'll prevail upon you for whatever assistance you can render."

Kestrel had a big twinkle in his eye when he said, "Especially since your ship has left you high and dry, eh?"

"Let me bring you up to speed," said Captain Garrett. "Preferably while we get the hell out of here."

* * *

Even though all kinds of terrible stuff was going on, the greatest thing happened while we were walking through the forestreef! All of a sudden, Warlog put his hand on my head and rubbed it, and he told me I was a brave warrior even though I was still green! (Which I don't know why being green would make any difference, but that's Warlog for you.)

Okay, so he said brave "little" warrior.

Things would have been easier if Kestrel's ship hadn't gone away, but they called him on this talkbox he had—like the one they say Godkirk had?—and said they had to go get more ships because the Romulans had them outgunned.

Kestrel laughed and told them to take their time getting back! Can you believe it? He said that just meant less Romulans for him to share killing with someone else!

Captain Garrett didn't laugh, but she said maybe we'd be okay since the Kolyati are such a force to be reckoned with, which is why we were quarantined for so long, until the Romulans sneaked in.

There was just one problem, she said, and that's because Kolyati hate fighting.

When we got to the secret hidingcamp, way off in the forestreef, all these Kolyati were looking at us and I felt really proud because of who I was with.

Captain Garrett was saying to Kestrel how "Two centuries ago, their culture was based on ritual murder-sacrifice. Now, they're opposed to all violence, even in self-defense."

"Unthinkable." Kestrel shook his head, but I thought he was kind of kidding. "Poor, misguided souls."

"They have extraordinary capabilities," Captain Garrett said. "They could easily overpower the Romulans, if they so chose."

Kestrel said, "Ah, which is why the Romulans are here, of course."

Captain Garrett said, "They're carrying out mass executions to force the Kolyati to become killing machines for the Empire. Since the Kolyati would rather die than kill, that isn't likely to happen."

"And there won't likely be any more Kolyati." That's what Kestrel said, and it was the one thing he said that made me angry. More like scared, I guess. But angry, too, because he shouldn't have said it in front of me since I'm a Kolyati, too, after all.

But see, then he went and did something that made me like him all over again!

Kestrel winked at me and said, "It's a good thing this warrior shows promise! If he can fight the Romulans, then by Kahless, so can the rest!"

So then, Kestrel and Warlog tried to get the Kolyati ready to fight, but I don't think they expected how hard it would be. Kestrel even told Captain Garrett to stand back and watch the master at work, which I guess was supposed to mean him.

I'll tell you what, those Kolyati just wouldn't fight no matter how much the Klingons pushed them or screamed at them. Not even when a messenger ran in and told everyone that the Romulans had executed a whole town where a bunch of their friends and relatives lived.

You should have heard some of the swear words Kestrel used after that! I mean, I didn't understand a single one, but I sure wish I could swear like he did!

I also wish I had hands. Tentacles don't cut it when you're trying to learn how to use a Klingon sword.

After Kestrel got frustrated and gave up on getting the Kolyati to fight the Romulans, he showed me some sword moves—but wouldn't you know it, my tentacles just weren't as good at swinging it around like he did.

He said it didn't matter though, since I had the warrior spirit, and once you have that you can kill any enemy.

I'm kind of confused about the killing part, though. I don't know who to believe, Kestrel or Captain Garrett. Or the Kolyati, I guess.

I mean, the Kolyati are against fighting and killing, right? But then Captain Garrett said sometimes violence is necessary, like in self-defense, which is why it's okay to fight the Romulans and maybe even kill them.

Kestrel really laughed at that! He said, "Without the glory of battle, life isn't worth living!"

We were sitting around a fire, and he jumped up right then and there and howled at the sky! And then the other Klingons around the hidingcamp did the same thing! (Except Warlog, who was snoring.)

Then Kestrel said, "There is no greater glory than killing a worthy opponent in battle!"

But Captain Garrett said, "We believe in killing only when our survival is at stake, and then only as a last resort."

And Kestrel said, "Kill for revenge! Kill for honor! Kill for victory! Kill for love!" He got all excited and was stomping around the fire swinging his sword.

Then all of a sudden, he jumped down in front of me and stared me right in the face. I got a big whiff of his breath, which made me gag, and he said, "But there is no glory in killing the weak. There is no honor in killing the defenseless.

"Which is why these Romulan *ptakh* have no place in *Sto-Vo-Kor!*" (Whatever that meant.)

Anyway, I got pretty mad the next morning, because Captain Garrett tried to leave me behind when they were going off to fight the Romulans. It was a good thing I had Kestrel on my side!

What we did was, we headed through the forestreef to a town where the Romulans were killing everybody. There were just the eight of us, but we were going to try to save as many Kolyati as we could till we got reinforcements.

"Whether the Kolyati like it or not!" That's what Kestrel said. He sure did laugh a lot! (And I don't think Rachel knew it—that's Captain Garrett's name, Rachel—but I caught her smiling a couple times when he did!)

So we snuck in, and there they were. Romulans. Lots more than us, even without all the ones Kestrel and the Klingons killed on our way into town.

The Romulans had masks on their faces, I guess in case the people sprayed sleeping gas at them like I heard they did in other towns. They had all the Kolyati lined up, and whenever the Romulans asked them if they would serve the Empire, and the people said no, the Romulans shot them with ray guns and there was nothing left except a puff of smoke.

The funny thing was, I wasn't even a tiny bit scared watching all that, and not just because of Kestrel and Warlog being there. Instead, I just got madder and madder the whole time.

Now, when I think about what happened next, I just get sadder and sadder. I guess it's dumb, since things worked out pretty good for the Kolyati and it's partly because of me, but even the good parts make me feel pretty bad.

You know how sometimes when you're trying to sneak up on somebody, you sneak in from one side and your friend sneaks in from the other side, and you've got them cornered? That's what we did with the Romulans.

Except for me, because even Kestrel told me to stay put, so I just watched while the Klingons and Captain Garrett and Lieutenant Castillo sneaked up on the Romulans and started shooting them.

What a light show that was! There were so many rays flying around, I got spots in my eyes!

My team did the best job ever! Romulans were falling down or disappearing all over the place!

But then, a bunch more of them ran into the square! There must have been at least a hundred of them and they came from every direction and it was total chaos! (Maybe it was more like fifty of them, I don't know. Or twenty-five?)

Anyway, that's when Rachel almost got killed. She didn't see this Romulan and he shot her, but luckily this Klingon jumped in front at the last second and saved her life. Not so luckily for him, though.

And you know, I've been through a lot, but that kind of pushed me over the edge.

* * *

That's when I killed all the Romulans. (Did I say twenty-five? Maybe it was twelve.)

See, the reason they wanted us to work for them was we can control chemicals better than anybody. We can mix up sprays or fluids or gases right in our own bodies. We can breathe in one thing and breathe out another.

Like a poison gas that's absorbed through Romulan skin and turns copper-based Romulan blood into poison sludge.

(Maybe it was eight.)

So that's what I did.

And don't get me wrong, I'm glad I did it, because a bunch of Kolyati didn't get killed then. Plus, I got a lot of people to change their minds about violence and fight back.

But see, I still don't feel good about that day, and I don't know if I ever will. I mean, my parents are still dead.

And I'm glad Rachel's still alive, but I just wish Kestrel didn't have to die to save her. I'm not stupid, I know he wouldn't have stayed on Kolya when he was done helping Captain Garrett and us, but I would of rathered if he was still alive, so I'd know he was still running around somewhere laughing that crazy laugh of his.

Before he left, Warlog said Captain Garrett owes Kestrel and his house a blood debt, so I guess I do too. Since I can't get to his home at Narendra III, wherever that is, I think I'll repay him by helping keep our people strong in honor of his memory. And laughing at everything every chance I get.

And I really, really want to learn how to swear in Klingon.

THREE: NYDA

From *Call Me Obsolete: The Memoirs of Officer Nyda Em Kay,* Earth Year 2368

When Captain Picard ushered me into the crime scene, all I could think was what a snooty pink stiff the guy was. I wanted to find the killer and smack him around just for making me spend five minutes with this pretentious creep.

"The victim was blown apart from within," said Snooty.

"Gee," I said, looking around. "Here I thought he was smothered with a pillow."

Every square inch of the room was splattered with exploded Vulcan. There was green blood and green guts everywhere, all over everything.

"The room was sealed from the inside," said Snooty. "The door was not opened from Commissioner Stonn's arrival last night until the discovery of his body this morning. And no transporter activity took place in or around this building during that time."

"What a mess," I said, and then I turned around and whipped right past him out the door. "Well, thanks for the tour! Good luck!"

I would've been home free if I hadn't walked right into the world's biggest butt kisser, Minister Dulcid.

"Going somewhere, Officer Kay?" he said in a way that made me want to punch his fat face.

"You don't need me," I told him. "You need a cleaning crew."

"You're the only one who can help us, Nyda. It's the biggest case of your career."

"Can you say 'retired'?" I snapped. "When I turned seventy, you told me to get lost . . . so now I'm telling *you* to get lost!"

"You're the only police officer in the world," said Dulcid. "Please help us to get this quarantine lifted." What a piece of work! The only reason he cared about the dead Vulcan was that the commissioner was the head of the team about to recommend lifting the quarantine of Kolya!

"How many ways do I have to say this?" I said to Dulcid, jamming my shriveled-up old-lady kisser in his face. "I don't want to be here!"

Dulcid was scared of me, I could tell. "Well, nevertheless," he said, his left eye twitching a little, "you're not leaving until this matter is resolved."

"Okay then. *He* did it!" I said, jabbing a tentacle toward the snooty pink stiff's bearded weirdo first officer. "Now get out of my way!"

The butt kisser shook his head. "You're not leaving until this matter is resolved in a diligent fashion, to Captain Picard's satisfaction. Now get to work."

"Get to work yourself!" I yelled in his face. "It'd be the first time!"

But I knew I was beat. I was on the case whether I liked it or not.

And it was going to be a tricky situation. At the same time I was investigating one murder, I was already planning another.

After all her stupid questions, I was about ready to plan *another* murder . . . anything to shut up Federation Commissioner Elizabeth Fox.

She was like a bug that just kept whining in my ear while I was trying to go over the crime scene. "So you're telling me there are no Kolyati dissidents or criminals?" she said, which was about the fifth time she'd rephrased the same question.

"Why do you think an old woman's the only cop on Kolya?" I snapped.

The prissy little know-it-all wouldn't leave me alone. "On a world where ritual murder was a way of life . . . a world where twenty-five years ago, an entire Romulan invasion force was killed by the native population . . . it's impossible that murderers could exist?"

"No *Kolyati* murderers," I said, pushing past her to see what the machine man was so interested in. "We got tired of it. Been there, done that."

The machine man was scanning the walls with a tricorder. I liked him about the best of any of them (which isn't saying much), because he didn't give me any attitude. "I am detecting trace amounts of nitric and sulfuric acid in the cellular remains," he said. "Glycerol, as well. The components of the explosive compound nitroglycerin."

Prissy Little Know-it-all snorted. "Captain Picard. I guess I don't need to remind you of the Kolyati's ability to manipulate chemical compounds."

"But thanks for reminding us anyway," I said.

"Isn't it possible that they could manipulate compounds from a distance?" said Prissy. "Or through a locked door?"

Prissy and Snooty were waiting for me to say something, but I just kept talking to the machine man. "What's this oily crap?" I asked him, pointing to a black smudge in the middle of the green mess on the wall.

The machine man scanned it. "I do not know," he said. "It is . . . inert to the point of nonexistence."

I touched the smudge with a tentacle and probed it myself. It felt empty, like a hole . . . but not a hole. Just emptiness.

"Oh well," I said, pulling away. "It's probably nothing."

By the next morning, I had two murders to solve instead of one. Prissy Know-it-all had finally stopped talking . . . the hard way.

Other than the blood being red instead of green, Fox's murder scene was the same as Commissioner Stonn's . . . same splattering, same locked door, same no transporter activity . . . same unidentifiable oily smudge.

And same abuse for me while I tried to do my job, only this time the butt kisser was dishing it out. He was so worked up because the other commissioners had gone back to the *Enterprise,* I thought he might make *himself* explode.

"The quarantine talks are on hold!" he said for what had to be the hundredth time that day . . . make it that hour. "Why haven't you made any progress?"

"I'm just doing it to irritate you," I said, looking up at a corner of Prissy's room.

Without missing a beat, Dulcid switched to butt-kissing gear. "Captain Picard," he said to the snooty pink stiff. "I want you to know that we've called in the military to speed the resolution of this matter."

"Well, Data," I said to the machine man. "I guess we're off the hook." I had to laugh, because I could see he didn't get it.

"We're going to lock down the city and question everyone," said the butt kisser. "We won't stop digging until we turn something up."

"Are you certain that's necessary?" said Snooty.

Butt Kisser started to say something, but I cut off his pearl of wisdom. "Data," I said. "What if I told you nitroglycerin wasn't the murder weapon?"

Snooty and Butt Kisser both stopped talking. "I would ask you to explain," said the machine man.

"Well, let's say you put enough nitro in somebody to blow him up," I said to the machine man, ignoring everyone else. "Traces should be spread pretty evenly through the remains, right?"

"Right," said Data.

"So why are we finding spotty traces? Why just a little bit here and a little bit there? I'll tell you one thing—nitro didn't kill these people."

"What then was the murder weapon?" said Snooty.

I wasn't in the mood for him, so I didn't answer. For all he knew, the old woman just couldn't hear anymore.

"Data," he said. I could tell Snooty was ticked. "Ask her to identify the murder weapon."

"What was the murder weapon?" said the machine man.

"What part of the room is the least slopped up?" I said. "The corners.

"If you filled the room with a big ball, what part of the room wouldn't it touch? The corners.

"So how about a big forcefield sphere, blowing up from inside the victim?"

"The field could be projected from a miniaturized device within the victim," said the machine man, "most likely, nanotechnology-based."

I couldn't ignore Snooty anymore because he was standing about an inch away from my face all of a sudden. "Officer Kay," he said. (I thought his breath could use some work.) "Please come with me."

As soon as he got me alone, Snooty rolled out the sob story.

"Two years ago, I was assimilated by the Borg," he said. "As Locutus, I was controlled in every way by the Collective."

He lowered his voice. "Though I have been repeatedly assured that my body is free of Borg nanotechnology . . . I worry that some part of Locutus remains hidden within me . . . waiting for a signal to awaken.

"Perhaps, that signal has been sent."

Here was a guy who really needed to get over it, I thought. Two years ago, and he still threw a pity party every time someone asked him for the time of day. I wished I could trade him *my* problems.

"In light of recent developments," he said, "I believe you must include me on your list of suspects."

"Thanks for the heartrending confession," I said, "but my list of suspects is down to one, and you're not on it."

You should have seen Riker's face when I hopped up and planted a big, wet one on him . . . and I mean *really* wet, because while I was kissing him, I pumped a mouthful of holy sap down his throat.

It would force the truth out of him (without killing him, like the stuff from the old days), but I already knew the truth because I could tell the bearded weirdo was ready to kill me.

"What did you do to me?" he shouted in my face.

I shouted right back at him. "Gave you enough truth juice that you'll never shut up about those murders!"

Oily blotches crawled over his face and hands, and the whites of his eyes turned black. He started laughing, and his voice was completely different—deeper, meaner, uglier.

"You poor old used-up bag," he said. "You're in over your senile head. The only truth you'll find is that you're about to die."

"Bring it on!" I told him, hauling off and smacking him across the face.

The blotches grew and connected so his face and hands were coated in glistening tar. When I hit him again, he felt the same as the smudges at the murder scenes—like a big, empty hole.

I smacked him again. Just a big, hungry hole, waiting for something to fill it up.

Perfect. I couldn't believe how perfect.

All of a sudden, I had an idea how to stop this lunatic and save my skin. I got ready to make my big move . . . and Snooty and company showed up to ruin everything.

"Officer Kay!" shouted Snooty . . . then it took him a second to figure out who was strangling me. "Will?" he said, like he couldn't believe it.

"Better than Will!" said the bearded weirdo. "I'll give you a clue! Who put the 'late' in the Late Tasha Yar?"

Snooty practically growled the name. "Armus."

"I'm a piece of Armus," said the weirdo. "A seed, left behind when Armus engulfed Riker all those years ago on Vagra II . . . growing until I became strong enough to take control."

The bearded weirdo tossed me against a wall and knocked the wind out of me. I didn't know who to curse more—him for roughing me up or Snooty for bad timing.

The weirdo gestured, and Snooty raised his phaser. "You're next, Locutus." The weirdo grinned as he dragged out each syllable of the name. "I'll make you my puppet like the Borg did. I'll make you watch as everyone you ever loved dies by your own hand."

Picard turned right around and fired three shots at his wallflower engineer, La Forge.

The machine man caught the wallflower and took a hit himself . . . then snatched the gun from Snooty and smashed it to pieces. I don't think he meant to keep hitting Snooty like he did, though.

"This planet will be my playground!" said the bearded weirdo. "Its inhabitants my new soul mates!"

While the weirdo's attention was on the pounding Picard was taking, I pulled myself together and got ready to move.

On the count of three, I flung myself at the bearded weirdo.

There's no doubt in my mind that he wasn't expecting me to plant another kiss on his tarpit puss.

At first, he struggled some, but I had my tentacles lashed around his neck and wouldn't let go. As the darkness drained from Riker into me, he took me by the shoulders and kissed me back.

We were made for each other.

You better believe I've never let Dulcid forget I'd fingered the right suspect back on Day One.

So what if it was an accident? So what if I didn't suspect the bearded weirdo till his prints turned up on the doors of the victims' rooms . . . even though he supposedly hadn't shown up till the doors were wide open? (Plus which, he had access to the crime scenes after the murders to spread around some nitroglycerin traces.)

The less the butt kisser knows, the better, I always say . . . which is why I'll never tell him what really happened to Armus. It's none of his business!

The truth is, Armus saved my life. Believe it.

See, there's a disease that turns our power to control chemical reactions against us. My body was literally eating itself alive . . . and don't get me started on the pain.

But when I absorbed Armus, it was like water on a fire. Instant relief.

And it worked both ways, because Armus settled down once he had something to fill all that emptiness.

So how do you like that? One minute, I'm dying, and the next, I feel so good I decide to retire from retirement!

Which is really something, because I used to hurt so bad, I'd pray the disease would hurry up and kill me! And after a while, I'd even decided the disease wasn't doing the job fast enough.

So that's whose murder I was planning, the one that got called on account of Armus. It was my own.

EPILOGUE

From *Address Before the First Kolyati Space Launch,* by President Toval Mot Than, Earth Year 2465

Over the years, some among us have said that the interference of Starfleet and the Federation on Kolya has been a bad thing.

Looking back, at first glance, this point of view seems to have some validity.

First, we see Captain Jonathan Archer, with a few misunderstood words, transform our society, leading us to develop a culture based on sacrificial murder.

One hundred years later, Captain James Kirk nudged us in a different direction, inspiring us to become so pacifistic that we became easy prey for invaders.

Seventy-five years after Kirk, Captain Rachel Garrett sowed the seeds of a more balanced society, which some argue we would have developed sooner if we had evolved free of outside influence.

And then, in trying to bring us into the interstellar community that had abandoned us for so long—ironically, because of social change that they themselves had triggered—Captain Jean-Luc Picard brought murder to our soil for the first time in twenty-five years and exposed us to an extraordinary alien evil.

Four Starfleet captains. Four world-changing events. At first glance, it is not hard to condemn the unsolicited interference of our imperfect visitors.

Looking deeper, though, it becomes clear that we are better off for having been touched by these dysfunctional parents.

No one argues, for example, that we are not further along in our technological development than other species of a comparable age.

No one doubts that an early awareness of life among the stars and our place in the universe has enabled us to avoid the pitfalls of a skewed and superstitious worldview.

And whether by chance or as a result of the influence of the outsiders who helped to shape our society, Kolya has remained free of the wars and conflicts that have marked the history of every civilized world.

While it is impossible for us to ever truly know what we could have become without the intervention of our uninvited guests, I choose to believe that we are the recipients of a blessing, the full breadth of which we may also never truly know.

Do you need proof of this blessing? Look up, into the sky, as we launch the first vessel that will free us from the bonds of this world and link us with our Federation brothers in a grand destiny of unity and exploration and service.

This time, we shall be their guests! We shall bring our world into theirs!

I wonder what transformations will occur in their society as a result of our influence?

The circle is complete . . . and never-ending. From Archer to Kirk to Garrett to Picard . . . to us. All with the launch of this one fragile vessel into the perils and wonders that await us beyond our atmosphere.

Please excuse our lack of originality, but there really was only one name that we could ever imagine choosing for this singular ship of dreams.

We hereby christen her Enterprise.

Bluff

Steven Scott Ripley

The players faced off around a cramped wooden table, a booth in one corner of the boat's commuter cabin. The game was seven-card stud.

"Your action, sir," Data said.

"I am aware of that," Picard said.

Data was subtly heckling his captain, something he would never dream of doing in any other circumstance, but the social interactions during a friendly poker game were unique. He would be remiss not to carry the prevaricated banter along.

The tabletop rocked lightly back and forth at the ship's wake, just enough to make their stacks of plastic chips slide and clatter. A background murmur of other passengers and the metallic throb of the ferry's engines heightened the sweaty atmosphere.

Data almost wished he had a cigar to chomp on.

Picard called the bring-in, hardly a surprise at this stage of the hand with all jacks, queens, and kings unaccounted for.

Except, of course, for the buried pair of kings Data had obtained in the hole during the initial deal.

Will Riker bared his teeth at the others—a shark's smile.

Miles dealt a second up card to each player.
Data received the king of hearts.

A tiny green bud sprouted on the tip of Data's nose.

The android watched as the sprout grew; he knew he was dreaming.

The leafy bud swiftly increased in size, nurtured by visions, and within seconds swelled to the girth of a hundred-year-old redwood tree. Data felt roots digging into the flesh of his impossibly elongated nose, yet his dream vantage rode high above the tree's crown, free-floating over a riot of windswept greenery.

Data spied a nest in the treetop. He looked closer. A single egg, dirty beige and brown-spotted, nestled there, and now he could hear the sharp beak of the nascent bird tapping inside his head—his skull was the egg—his anxiety level grew—he felt frightened—there was something inside trying desperately to escape—from—

The egg rattled and cracked.

Crimson red disruptor fire seeped out of the shell fracture.

His head exploded.

Data opened his eyes and screamed.

Spot, who'd recently taken to sleeping beside Data's head on the pillow, hissed in surprise and swiped her claws across his cheek, then jumped off the bed with a thump and vanished into the dark.

His emotion chip fully active, Data placed a trembling hand to his torn bioplastic skin. He felt an angry desire to punish his cat, but he suppressed it, reflecting that she was only an animal, and he'd scared her, as he himself had been scared by the dream, and after all she was getting along in years.

It was wrong to punish the innocent.

Unable to return to sleep, Data rose and dressed himself in a long khaki night-robe he'd acquired recently, a gift from Geordi. He liked the night-robe. The cloth felt soft and smooth. The sense of touch, one moment so painful as when Spot scratched him, could also be comforting.

He called out hopefully for his cat but she did not deign to appear, mewling grouchily from beneath his bed. He decided to let her be for the time being, to leave well enough alone, as the saying went.

Data walked barefoot out of his quarters and took a turbolift to Ten-Forward.

None of them touched their cards. No need to peek again—they all knew exactly what they had.

Two passengers walked up, outside the grimy side deck window next to their table, stopping to crane their necks at the foursome and stare in at the game. Data and the others normally would have ignored the rubberneckers, but they were dressed bizarrely, each wearing a puffy white protective suit and helmet, similar to what an engineering crew might don during a warpcore breach.

The players swiveled their heads as one toward the pair, then after a beat returned their attention to the tabletop.

"Trills on vacation," Miles said. "They must be joined—only joined Trills are allergic to insect bites. Well, I fold."

O'Brien was sensible. No point in bluffing with a six of diamonds and two of clubs showing.

But Riker and Picard were a different matter.

"All insects?" Will asked, his eyes locked intently on Data's.

Picard coughed. "Most species."

Junk and the jack of spades for the captain; scrap and the queen of diamonds showing for the commander.

They are wondering if I have kings, *Data thought. Let them wonder.*

"You dreamt you were Pinocchio," Guinan said.

Data leaned on the bar, nursing a warm mug of semi-organic nutrient suspension in a silicon-based liquid medium. Geordi had dubbed it marshmallow goo, an apt description. Though he'd experimented with many different types of beverages, Data liked his goo best, and he stuck with it at times like this, when he felt troubled.

"The puppet who wishes to become real," Data said, rolling his eyes in slight embarrassment. He'd tuned his emotion chip way down, grateful for the ability to smother its intensity, but still felt a persistent needling accretion of anxiety.

Guinan splayed her long black fingers on the iridescent bar counter, smiling gently. "An interesting choice of words. Not the puppet *that* wishes to become real, but the puppet *who* wishes to become real."

Data shrugged and sipped his drink. "The metaphor is well worn. Do you not find it tiresome to hear me talking about it over and over? I do."

Ten-Forward was empty, except for the two of them. That was unusual for the *Enterprise*-E, and might not last long. Data wondered how long he could hold out before he opened up to the bartender entirely.

Guinan calmly scratched behind an ear, pushing up the rim of her dark purple hat. "Let's stick with this dream, then," she said. "It must be about a lie you told at some point."

Data set his mug down on the countertop, too sharply. "A lie?"

His voice sounded brittle. How could she not hear it?

"During the course of our many encounters and expeditions it has been necessary for me to prevaricate, to stretch the truth, to omit strategic details, to—"

"You're protecting someone," she said, cutting off his string of nonsense. "Who? Tasha?"

Data blushed, unwanted biochemical lubricants flooding into his cheeks and forehead. He shook his head awkwardly. A good guess, considering the Freudian implications of a growing nose in dream metaphor, but he knew his recent nightmare was not related to the intimacy he'd once shared with his long-dead friend.

He knew exactly what his dream meant. He hadn't initiated this conversation to find out why.

But on her essential point, Guinan was correct.

He took a deep breath and explained.

Captain Picard sat back in his ready-room chair and gaped at Data. He looked so surprised, for a moment he seemed to have forgotten to be angry.

Data stood at stark attention, his emotion chip tuned down to its lowest ebb. As it was, he could feel a harsh gnawing pain in his chest. This had to be one of his worst moments since activation.

"But why did you wait so long, Data?" the captain asked. He rubbed his bald pate, stunned. "It's been over ten years since that incident."

"I—I forgot, sir. Until recently. The dreams. I remembered."

Picard appeared to accept this, but his gaze grew steely. And he looked very disappointed, which was even worse. "This is certain to be a highly negative mark on each of your records. I can see no way around that."

"There is none, sir." In some way, at least to talk about it made it easier. "He was not innocent, but the evidence might have been used in his favor at the trial. It may have induced a mitigating factor upon his sentence. And it may yet."

"I expect it will," Picard said softly. "Well, I'll contact Starfleet immediately. You say you've spoken to Guinan about this?"

"Yes, sir. But solely for her advice."

"And you haven't contacted Miles or approached Will about it?"

Data shook his head. "I knew it would not be appropriate, given the legal ramifications."

"Good. Dismissed."

And that was all. The captain often called back an officer he'd just redressed for a private word, off the record, but Data walked the long mile to the bridge door in silence, and somberly returned to his station to attend to his usual duties.

The next day, they received extremely bad news about Kivas Fajo.

Most of the crew welcomed an unscheduled forty-eight-hour shore leave on Earth. Data spent the several hours it took to pick up Miles from Deep Space 9 and travel there in stoic anguish, but at least the captain allowed him to remain on duty as alpha ticked over to beta watch. Commander Riker was also on duty while Picard slept. He and Will had initiated many colorful conversations during past betas, but tonight they said little. The officer at the helm, a young ensign fresh from Starfleet Academy, kept asking why they were traveling at warp six for a simple shore leave. Data feigned ignorance.

At 0700, just as the shift was ending, Will approached the ops station and patted his hand on Data's shoulder.

"You did the right thing," he said gruffly.

Data didn't know how to respond, but fortunately it wasn't required.

After wandering down the ferry's port-side deck, the Trills strolled back and resumed staring through the window at the quartet of poker players. They seemed more interested in this exotic human card game than they were in the view of the choppy gray sea or the distant line of cliffs south of Auckland.

"The oceans are purple on the Trill homeworld," Miles said with a shrug. "Ours can't be too exciting in comparison."

Perhaps the curious alien tourists could sense the gathering intensity at the table. Data, who'd recently been experimenting with turning his emotion chip on and off during alternate hands, currently had his chip on, and he felt a thrill of exhilaration as the cards were dealt and slapped faceup for himself, the captain, and the commander.

He now had two kings in the hole, with a king and two nines showing.

They were not playing a high/low split variant of seven-card stud today: it was not a monster hand, but it was close, and the pot might all be his.

Picard immediately and without hesitation mucked his cards to the discard pile in front of Miles, folding as a result of the unlucky appearance of a four of clubs on the deal. His run for a straight was finished.

But Riker pulled the queen of clubs. Two queens showing.

Now they would have a showdown.

"Looks like you're the underdog, Data," Riker said, curling his lips in satisfaction.

"I beg to differ," Data began, then cut himself off and silently cursed.

He'd just been "told," Will cleverly forcing Data to infer the presence of two strong cards in his hole. Damn his chip! Without it, he'd never have let himself be drawn into such a sucker's gambit.

"Data, I'm surprised at you," Picard said.

So Riker knew Data had something that approached the monstrous, but he didn't know what. But, perhaps more important, Riker executed his feint because he needed to know. Why? *Data reasoned.* Because he's bluffing. He might have four queens. Or he could be a cunning, underhanded liar out to steal the pot that rightly belongs to me.

He quietly turned off his emotion chip.

"Surprised by what, sir?" Data said blankly, affecting the blandest of faces.

Riker literally sneered at him.

But not before Data saw an uncertain spark of fear pass through his eyes.

Prepare to be squashed, Mr. Riker.

The open transport—which the issuing administrator back in Auckland City called a "jeep"—bounced into a deep rut in the muddy outback road they traveled, hitching his three traveling companions about like agitated molecules in their seats, scrambling for handholds. Data focused his attention on steering the jeep over the bumpy terrain. His powder-white fingers curled firmly around the black steering wheel as he pressed a foot to the accelerator and gunned them forward.

They careered up the middle of a shallow valley between rolling hills capped with dense blankets of low-lying spring-green shrubs, broken up by patches of tall stalks of yellow grass. A few trees stuck up here and there in the outback, long and crooked trunks erupting at the crown in fan-shaped mists of tiny leaves. The landscape shivered, shrubs and grass and trees undulating beneath a steady buffet of wind blowing down from the north.

A lonely place, Data thought.

"I've been in smoother shuttle crashes," he heard Will grumble from one of the backseats, followed by a grunt from Miles.

The jeep roared through a final rain-filled pothole, a half-meter deep and wide as six Worfs, splattering all of them with muddy water drops, then finally climbed out of the valley of crumbled pavement and onto a long stretch of unblemished gray concrete.

They traveled across the wild northern reaches of the Great Barrier Island in the Hauraki Gulf, ninety kilometers by sea from the New Zealand coast and Auckland City. They'd ferried here by boat and driven the past two hours up from the docks in Karaka Bay, toward the heart of a penal colony surrounded by a deflective shield generated by machinery buried deep in the rock, which not only prevented all transporter activity, but in the normal course of things also disrupted every frequency of sonic transmission and even emitted an electromagnetic harmonic pulse that neutralized the engines of approaching spacecraft. The only way in or out past the checkpoints was by foot or animal or old-fashioned combustion vehicles—the penal colony was dead secure.

There hadn't been much conversation today, not since their final briefing before the court of inquiry. Would this be an appropriate moment for an off-the-cuff critique of the penal colony's unusual security measures? Or would it be better to take his cue from their silent captain, who sat next to Data in the jeep and stared broodingly out at the blasted landscape?

After all, they couldn't go on not speaking to one another for the entire duration of the journey, could they?

"It is a rough and ready trip," Data said. "Though the hardy terrain actually conceals a sophisticated underground security system used by the Hauraki Penal Colony to inter its prisoners. We are lucky that a qualified Federation judge and mediator are both already present at the colony, otherwise there may have been further delay."

No one replied to his comments. Picard appeared scarcely to have heard him. Data sighed to himself.

They traveled in silence.

The Trill tourists leaned in further, until their helmets were pressed flat against the window, their noses pressed flat against their helmet masks. Two males, both wide-eyed, stared with awed open mouths at the human drama unfolding before them.

"Must be the highlight of their trip," Miles said as he dealt the cards.

"You know what they say about poker," Picard said, leaning back with his hands clasped behind his head. "Two hours of boredom followed by two minutes of terror." He grinned, for the first time since their journey began.

Riker received a queen; Data received a two.

Data still had a full house, three kings and two nines. But did Riker have four queens, a full house, or only three pair?

There was no backing out now. He had to call and raise—but how to play it? Could he psych Will into folding? Or should he attempt to manipulate him into calling and raising an exorbitant amount?

Data tossed ten chips into the pot and raised thirty.

Riker raised his eyebrows. So did everyone else.

But he called Data's bluff and raised him twenty.

Miles quickly dealt them their final hole cards.

Data peered at his fate.

Data lay on a threadbare rug tossed over a rickety cot—the accommodations were Spartan here at the penal colony—staring at a dusty spiderweb in the ceiling corner, thinking about the past and wishing he could talk to Geordi.

He might have spent this time waiting for the inquiry in more productive activities, directing his positronic subroutines through thousands of tasks, reviewing data, perhaps composing a symphony or inventing a new holodeck program, or uploading the collected works of James Joyce into his active memory as he'd been meaning to do for ages; the sky was the limit, as they said in poker.

But all he could think about were the days he spent in captivity in the vessel of Kivas Fajo, the Zibalian trader who kidnapped and imprisoned him years ago, and the mask of poorly healed scar tissue shrouding the face of the woman, Varria, who gave up her life while helping Data to escape.

A horrible death. At first she'd pointed the Varon-T disruptor at Fajo, as Data tried to launch a shuttle from the *Jovis*'s cargo bay, but she'd dropped the weapon, and Fajo picked it up and fired. The bloody red beam ate her up from the inside out. He hadn't seen it, but he heard her screaming in agony.

That was the final straw. After days of submitting to Fajo's humiliations—stripped of his uniform and forced to wear a grotesque dressing gown, blackmailed with Varria's life into sitting on a display chair, like the other objects Fajo coveted and collected—her murder was intolerable. Data obtained the disruptor, pointed it at Fajo, and fired.

But just then Miles O'Brien located Data and activated the *Enterprise*-D transporter, and he was rescued. The disruptor beam discharged while he was in transit, but O'Brien, at Will Riker's orders, neutralized the beam in the transporter buffer before Data appeared back on his own ship.

Riker questioned Data about the disruptor fire. Data feigned innocence, and suggested it must have been a transporter malfunction, pretending he never fired at all.

He lied.

Murderous violence became the last resort. All of them—Data, Fajo, Varria, and the other men who worked for the trader—caught up in a cycle of extreme behavior, a spiraling descent into darkness where in the end there was no civilization, no ideals or ethics or morals, only the hunted and the prey.

And as Fajo taunted him and the crisp stench of Varria's evaporated body stung his eyes, Data reasoned desperately that he must pull the trigger.

Which still didn't explain why—

Data sat upright on his cot and smoothed his wrinkled uniform. His internal chronometer had just clicked and told him it was time for the inquiry to begin.

Time to pay.

Fajo, once well fed and corpulent, had become a stick. His pale orange prison uniform hung loosely over thin bones, a sunken chest. Though it was not a penal colony regulation, he'd shaved his thick black hair to an angular cap of fuzz on his skull. His dark eyes stared blankly at the judge as she spoke to him, floating in hollow sockets.

Data had turned off his emotion chip entirely for these proceedings, but he was still shocked by the man's changed appearance.

While en route to Earth, they'd been alerted that Fajo had accidentally contracted a rare degenerative genetic disorder from a fellow prisoner. Doctors sought a cure, but it was unknown if the patient would survive that long. His clock of mortality was ticking.

"You understand," the Federation judge said to the prisoner, "that this inquiry has been called solely to introduce and examine facts in your case that will then be judged by this court as to their relevance toward your original sentence? Mr. Fajo?"

The prisoner nodded. "I understand." No emotion. A robot.

Judge Anne Grambs—a tall, large-boned woman with beehive blond hair and a thick Texan drawl—inclined her head at Fajo's response and curtly dismissed him with a wave of hand. She must know him well; she was also the penal colony's top administrator—his warden.

Grambs tapped a wooden gavel on the tabletop.

"I call this inquiry to order."

She sat behind a simple table opposite the examination chair, both set atop a low raised dais that faced the three distinct groupings of those present.

Fajo returned to his seat, apart from the others, staring at the gray floor and meeting no one's eyes. Next sat the two mediators, Captain Picard representing the Federation officers, and a Zibalian man, who was also a Federation official and worked at the colony, representing Fajo. Finally side by side there were Will, Miles, and Data.

Everyone looked starched and neatly pressed in dress uniforms, except for the prisoner. The small room was starkly lit, as if to banish all shadows and lies from every corner, as if to tell the trio of guilty officers they could not hide here.

Data quietly ascertained that his chip was indeed entirely shut off—his thoughts were becoming much too fanciful. Strange, how even without emotions he had reactions to social situations—a unique and complex form of behavior modification.

But it had always been so.

"Mr. Fajo, you've stated that at the final moment before Mr. Data was transported back to the *Enterprise*-D, you don't recall whether

79

or not he fired the Varon-T disruptor at you?" Picard's questions had been few and pointed. He faced the prisoner, his hands clasped behind his back.

Fajo nodded, and for the first time since his formal questioning began glanced briefly at Data. "I have no idea whether he did or not. I would have fired, but that's just me."

Picard unclasped his hands and folded his arms, shaking his head, a frown on his face. "But surely you would have seen the red disruptor beam. It's quite distinctive."

Fajo shrugged. "I saw nothing."

He was digging in, hiding something. Picard knew it. "Well, either you don't recall or you saw nothing—which is it?"

"I—" Fajo faltered.

"Which is it, Mr. Fajo?" The captain employed a subtle and formidable courtroom tactic, leaning in toward the witness, pinning him with a hawkish stare.

It worked. Fajo had always been a childish man; that had not changed. His composure broke and his eyes fluttered into a stubborn, cornered squint. He sighed.

"Fine." He tossed his hands in the air in a careless pose. "He may have fired. I don't know. The shuttle bay was dark and there was all that transporter glitter—I may have seen the beam for a nanosecond—maybe I wasn't sure I saw it. Maybe—oh, fine, I saw it. I saw something. Are you satisfied?"

Picard let his hard face soften into a satisfied expression. It was an important point, and now he had it. "But surely if you saw it, you would have brought this up at your original trial, Mr. Fajo." The captain's smooth voice oozed concern, almost wheedling.

He was quite a mediator.

"After all, if you knew Data fired the weapon, and you've just stated that you did know it, then it would be in your own best interest to present this fact to the court. Of course it would not erase your own crimes, but it may have—contributed a factor of leniency in your sentencing. Haven't you ever thought about that?"

Fajo fidgeted.

"Mr. Fajo?"

Fajo turned toward Grambs. "Anne, do I have to answer that?"

Grambs nodded. "Yes you do, Kivas."

Their gazes locked for a moment—something passed between them. Data could not begin to guess what it might be. Obviously the judge couldn't verbally assume her normal role of warden at this point, yet the simplicity of using his first name produced an effect. Somehow she had rehabilitated him over the years, if only to tell the truth.

"Okay." He sounded defeated, and his gaunt chest seemed to deflate even more as he slumped in his seat. Picard made to lean in for the kill, but Grambs waved him back, sensitive not to push, to wait.

Fajo spoke softly, but every word could be heard, and every word etched into Data's positronic brain.

"I was going to, of course I was going to. You remember I chose to represent myself during the original trial. I thought I would say nothing at first, wait, until the right moment, when I could—when I could squeeze the most sympathy out of the judge. But they never brought it up. They never mentioned it. And then I started thinking, well, that's strange. Why wouldn't they? And I was looking at Data one day during the trial and I realized, ah, he never told them. And the other officers—if they knew—they never mentioned it either. So he lied. And he will—suffer—for that lie, because I know Data. I got to know him very well. It will torment him, I thought, for all time. So let him suffer. I hated him. I kept my mouth shut."

A shocked silence stole over the room. Data sat impassively, his chip firmly and utterly turned off, nodding lightly and thinking yes that is quite within Fajo's character it makes perfect sense it—

Data twitched spasmodically, despite himself.

Fajo opened his mouth and spat out a strangled moan. It was painful for him to speak this kind of truth. Good for the soul, maybe.

Maybe not.

Captain Picard pivoted toward Grambs. "I have no further questions."

The Zibalian mediator declined to re-cross. There was no need. Picard had won the single most important point, and revealed Fajo's bluff. Data, O'Brien, and Riker would duly receive black marks on their records; that was never in doubt. But it was highly unlikely Fajo would receive any type of mediated sentence.

He did not deserve it.

"You are dismissed, Mr. Fajo," Anne Grambs said formally, but her voice shook, betraying her emotions, sorrow and surprise and disappointment. Perhaps they had come very far together. This was a setback in his redemption.

Obviously, she cared deeply about that sort of thing.

The witness slunk back to his seat.

During the few seconds it took Fajo to do this, Data reviewed the book *Crime and Punishment* and its themes: the complexities of innocence and guilt, the burden of conscience, the inadequacy of justice, social dehumanization, the brutal wages of sin.

The results were inconclusive.

Will Riker raked in the hefty pot.

Data shook his head in disbelief.

"I felt certain you had only three pair," Data said.

"I know you did," Will said. He shook his finger at the android in mock disappointment. "You turned your chip off mid-hand. That's sort of cheating, isn't it? Shame on you."

Data frowned. "How did you know that?"

Will shrugged. "Something about your eyes. They sort of glazed over. I could tell you were on the fence about your bet—why turn your chip off unless you were afraid your emotions might betray you?"

Picard nodded at Riker's hand. "But you didn't pull the fourth queen until the final hole card, did you? That was quite risky, Will."

Riker threw his hands up, a devil-may-care gesture, similar to the one Fajo had performed in the trial earlier that day. "Kneel before me and do my bidding."

"Oh, brother," Miles said, rolling his eyes.

"Excuse me." Data got up abruptly and went outside for some fresh air.

The ferry was about thirty minutes out from their return to Auckland City, rollicking about on a windswept sea. Data leaned over the railing, ignoring the Trill tourists who still lingered nearby, probably hoping for another game to start soon. He turned his chip back on, fine-tuning it to a minute blip, just enough so that he could stare out moodily at the misty waterscape without being overwhelmed by his feelings.

Picard joined his side a few minutes later.

"What's bothering you, Data?" he asked gently.

Data shook his head. "Oh, sir. I do not know."

"Did Fajo get under your skin again today?"

Data considered. "Not as much as I thought he would. His revelation was unpleasant, but not out of character. That is not what really troubles me about all of this. I still do not understand why I chose to prevaricate in the first place."

"You didn't wish to betray the directive being sent to you by your ethical inhibitor, Data," Picard said. "It impels you not to harm any living thing. You fired the weapon, though your inhibitor told you not to, so you repressed your action by lying about it."

"But I was not programmed to lie, sir. What 'impelled' me to choose that action as a viable response to the situation?"

Picard sighed. "I don't know. Chalk up another mystery on the murky road to humanity?"

Data returned the wry smile. "I appear to have no choice in the matter."

"Do any of us?" Picard slapped Data on the back. "Come on. You've got to challenge Will to a rematch or there'll be no living with him for a month."

"He is a formidable opponent."

"I have faith in your ability to skunk him, Data."

Grinning sheepishly. "Thank you, Jean-Luc. I will do my best."

They rejoined Will and Miles for another friendly round of poker.

The Peacemakers

Alan James Garbers

July 21, 1889
Southwest Colorado, Earth

Arizona Ranger John Dawson hobbled his way down the limestone
canyon watching for a way out. Following the canyon would make it
too easy to be found. He had to find a different way. He found it just as
he heard riders coming. A narrow slot canyon twisted back east with
large boulders camouflaging its mouth. John smiled grimly. Those
hunting him on horseback would have a tough go of it to follow.

Jack Hayes, Daniel Biggs, Vic Hastings, Dutch Hardin, and Jim
Allen: outlaws who felt no remorse when they murdered, robbed,
and rustled. Had the outlaws not killed his partner, John would have
turned back days before, or so he told himself. Those who knew
John would have said different. They'd have said John would follow the devil himself into hell and bring him back hogtied. But now
John was wounded and running for his life.

"He couldn't have gone far." A voice echoed up the small
canyon. John figured it to be Jack Hayes. "Biggs wouldn't miss."

"I didn't see no blood," answered another.

"He's hurt all the same. His tracks show he's using sticks to walk."

John moved silently away, up the small canyon. Every foot was a battle, every inch a victory.

A minute was all John got. "Here it is, boys! I found a track!" rang out and echoed up to where he was.

John cursed under his breath as he fought to move forward through the jumbled boulders. Suddenly the slot canyon opened up into a small valley. Green grass and cottonwoods swayed in a cool breeze. In the high desert that meant water. John also spotted something else. An ancient Indian cliff ruin lined the far valley wall. Protected by a huge rock overhang, the stone walls looked as strong as the day the owners left, a millennium before. John quickly scanned the valley. It seemed to be a dead end, leaving the ruin as his only option. He hurried across the valley floor and made it to the ruin walls just as a bullet spat stone fragments beside him. He turned and raised his rifle at the men coming out onto the valley floor. The Marlin .45-70 rifle boomed. Had John not been swaying on a broken leg an outlaw would have died. As it was, rustler Vic Hastings spent the rest of his short life with a useless right arm.

As his pursuers ran for cover John ducked into the darkness of the ruin. Broken pottery lay scattered on the floor. Woven sleeping mats lay in rooms he passed. Other pottery sat along walls, waiting for their owners to return.

The musty smell of dampness drew him toward the back of the ruin, to the natural cave wall. There he found a seep. The cold water formed a clear pool that held a gallon or two. John dug into his saddlebags, pulled a metal cup out, and drank deep.

Looking back through the ruin passageway, John spotted Dutch Hardin creeping closer along the far valley wall. Resting the rifle across a stone slab, John let out his breath halfway and squeezed the trigger. John watched with grim satisfaction as Dutch fell forward, dead.

In answer a barrage of bullets ricocheted through the ruin doorway. They whined about John's head like angry bees. Grabbing up the Marlin rifle, John worked his way into the ruin, searching for another vantage point. Above him was another story of rooms that would give him a command of the valley, if he could just find the way up.

Penetrating deeper, John came to a small doorway sealed with a stone slab. John shoved hard and the slab fell into the darkness beyond. An odd scent drifted to John, reminding him of the smell of a thunderstorm. He struck a match and checked the room. A ladder poked up through a hole in the floor. John cursed and dropped the match as it burned his fingers. Reaching into his saddlebag, John found a bundle of candles and lit one. As the flame grew higher he peered down into the hole. The underground room appeared to be a ceremonial kiva, a round room like those he had seen on the Hopi Mesas. He was about to turn back when a thought hit him. Kivas usually had ventilation shafts for the ceremonial fires. With any luck he might be able to follow them to a safe place and wait the outlaws out.

Slinging the saddlebags across his shoulder, John squeezed his 227 pounds through the hole and down the ladder. His leg screamed in pain at the sudden jarring but John clenched his teeth and fought on. At the bottom, John wiped the sweat from his eyes and relit the candle. To his surprise, benches and shelves were built into the round walls. Countless decorated pots and figurines lined the shelves. Strange animals and figures danced in the candlelight.

A quick search failed to find a ventilation shaft big enough to crawl through. He glanced around once more and then decided to go back up. To be caught down here, well, John could think of at least eight ways they could kill him, trapped like he was.

He quickly turned and stepped for the ladder and it was that action that caused him to stumble into a shallow depression in the center of the room. Suddenly his hair stood on end as a blue light enveloped him. Then he was gone.

Twenty-fourth Century
Planet of Equinox, Cardassian/Federation Neutral Zone

Jean-Luc Picard gently removed more soil from around the ceramic pieces before him. Time had gently crushed the bowl into a dozen jigsaw pieces.

Jean-Luc's heart pounded as he leaned closer. His headlamp brightly illuminated the figurine that danced in red and black brushstrokes upon the gently curved surface of the ancient bowl. Picard gingerly cleaned the dirt away with a small, worn brush. Cocking his head, he blew the last particles from the pottery surfaces.

Slowly Picard sat back on his knees. The image was hard for him to accept yet precisely what he had come looking for. The chances of having the exact nongeometric design as those found in ruins on a planet light-years away were, well, impossible.

Picard stood and pointed one of the standing work lights full on the bowl as he mentally searched through the rumors that had brought him here to this dark planet called Equinox. He hit his combadge. "Beverly, can you come here? I have something you might like to see."

In a microsecond Dr. Beverly Crusher's voice replied, "I'm on my way. I'm bringing you something to eat."

Picard smiled. "You read my mind."

Picard stretched his legs. Kneeling for as long as he had wreaked havoc on his knees and now they were screaming in protest.

From the hilltop ruins Jean-Luc could see the lights of the battered Archeological Institute runabout and the base camp. A breeze tugged at his dusty clothes and brought a hint of the heat that waited on the full-sun side of the planet. Here, in the dividing region between eternal day and forever night, it felt good.

His eyes wandered the cliffs about him. They rose stark, silent, and haunting in the constant twilight, yet like a good ghost story they beckoned him to delve deeper into their secrets.

Light footsteps behind him caused Picard to turn.

"This place gives me the heebie-jeebies," whispered Beverly as she handed Jean-Luc a snack.

"Thank you, but why are you whispering?" asked Jean-Luc.

"I don't—" Beverly cleared her throat. "I don't know," she answered slightly louder. "I just feel I'm always walking around in a graveyard."

Jean-Luc smiled. The crimson twilight only served to enhance the subtle beauty of Beverly's auburn hair. "Not to worry," Jean-

Luc said softly. "I promise to protect you against all ghosts and goblins."

Beverly tilted her head as she eyed Jean-Luc skeptically. "With what?" she asked. "All I see is a trowel and a paintbrush."

Jean-Luc chuckled. "You'd be surprised at how resourceful I am in a pinch."

"No," she said softly. "You forget I have seen you in action." Beverly paused for a moment and then looked about. "Speaking of action, what did you call me out here for?"

Jean-Luc turned and stepped down into the excavation. "Over here." He shinned another work light down into the excavation. "What do you make of this?"

Beverly bent closer to the bowl. "It's beautiful! But I'd swear I've seen this figure before."

"You probably have. It's Kokopelli, the flute player, found on countless hieroglyphs and ceramic pieces—back on Earth. In the American Southwest, to be more precise."

"You're right! I remember seeing a Kokopelli figurine in a shop in Flagstaff, Arizona." Beverly nodded.

Jean-Luc nodded. "This is precisely why we are here. I've heard rumors and stories from prospectors searching this planet for ore, before the treaty with the Cardassians. They told of ruins in these canyons and brought out artifacts to sell to collectors of antiquities."

"Like what?" asked Beverly.

"Stone tools, clothing, trinkets, and pottery like you're holding."

"And let me guess," Beverly said as she stood up. "These other items looked similar to those found on Earth."

Jean-Luc smiled. "You are correct. The archeological community waved them off as frauds or cases of parallel development."

"But you wanted to see for yourself," Beverly commented as she sat down on the side of the excavation. "Couldn't this be a case of parallel development? Two cultures coming up with the same design?"

Jean-Luc shook his head. "If it were a geometric design I'd say yes, but there are too many similarities. The flute, the hunched back, the pack on the figurine's back. It's too close—"

"*Captain.*"

Jean-Luc tapped his combadge. "Yes, Data."

"I have found what appears to be a cavern. Perhaps you should take a look."

"Very well, Data. We shall be there shortly." Jean-Luc offered a hand to Beverly. "Shall we?"

Beverly stepped out of the hole and dusted off her pants. "Just what is the significance of the Kokopelli figure?"

"Well, the stories have been diluted over the millennia, but research from the nineteenth century Hopi Indians tells of Kokopelli being a magician who talked to the wind and the sky. His flute could bring the spring breeze, after the winter cold."

"He sounds like my kind of guy."

"He was a teacher, a healer, the god of the harvest. He would visit villages playing his flute—"

Beverly nodded. "I am beginning to see why they honored him so much."

Jean-Luc stopped and smiled. "When he left, the crops were plentiful and all the women were pregnant."

Beverly stopped and saw Jean-Luc's sly grin. "I think this Kokopelli better stay away from our camp."

"Captain, over here!" Data waved from the opening of a small canyon.

Jean-Luc followed Beverly to where Data was waiting.

"Captain, I have found what appears to be the mouth to a cavern."

"Are there any indications of inhabitation?" queried Picard.

Data nodded. "Visual observation has produced evidence of a midden, as well as carbon deposits."

Jean-Luc smiled. "Well done, Data. You are on your way to becoming a top-notch archeologist."

"Thank you, Captain." Data turned. "Follow me. The entrance is approximately twenty-seven meters up canyon."

Beverly switched on her wrist lamp and fell in behind Data. "Would somebody please explain what a midden is, and why we're looking for carbon deposits?"

"I apologize, Beverly," replied Jean-Luc. "A midden is a trash heap or dump. They are one of the best indicators of a prolonged inhabitation."

"And the carbon deposits?" she asked.

"Soot stains. The smoke from countless cooking fires can leave carbon deposits on cave walls that can last eons," replied Jean-Luc.

They stopped in front of a dark gaping maw into the side of the canyon wall. Beverly involuntarily stepped back behind Jean-Luc.

"Beverly!" Jean-Luc chuckled. "A command officer of the *Enterprise* is afraid of the dark?"

"And I'll be moving up the chain of command when something big comes out and eats you!"

"Doctor," replied Data. "I assure you nothing larger than rat-sized creatures reside in the area."

Beverly stepped out and stood between Data and Jean-Luc. "I guess I've been in too many of the holo-horror novels."

Data turned on his wrist lamp and flashed it into the cavern. "The trash midden is off to the side of the cave. From the research I have done, many cave dwellers discarded their refuse in the low-ceiling areas, as we see here."

"Very good, Data," commended Jean-Luc. "Professor Bowman would be proud of you."

"Thank you, Captain," replied Data as he moved the beam of light deeper into the passage. "Unfortunately the rest of the passage is blocked by a cave-in."

Jean-Luc inspected the blockage. "It seems to have occurred after the inhabitation."

"I concur," replied Data. "I have also detected a slight draft through the rubble."

"Yes." Jean-Luc nodded as he held up a hand. "So do I."

"And that means?" asked Beverly.

"The cavern is open on the other side—and possibly very extensive," replied Jean-Luc. He turned to Data. "Can you get a reading with the tricorder?"

"Negative," replied Data. "There seems to be a natural dampening field that is making it impossible to get conclusive results."

"That means the runabout's transporter wouldn't get us inside either."

"That is correct, Captain."

"Could we clear away the rocks and get through?" asked Beverly.

"Probably," sighed Jean-Luc. "But not tonight. My knees are aching and there's a cozy cot back at the camp calling me."

"So." Beverly grinned. "The captain of the *Enterprise* is human."

Jean-Luc nodded in the darkness. "Very much so tonight."

"Good," replied Beverly as she headed back down the canyon. "My feet are killing me but I didn't want to be the first to complain."

"Captain?" queried Data.

Jean-Luc and Beverly stopped. "Yes, Data?"

"I do not require any regeneration. I would prefer to stay and clear the rubble."

Jean-Luc thought for a second. "I see no harm in doing so provided you don't take any chances."

"Captain, I am essentially indestructible."

"But you're also a valued friend I wouldn't want to be without," replied Jean-Luc. "So let me rest easy tonight with your promise to be careful."

Data smiled. "Rest easy, Captain."

Jean-Luc grinned as he turned back down the canyon. "Good night, Data."

July 24, 1889

John Dawson was worried. It had been uncountable hours since his "trip into Hell," as he called it. Luckily he had retained his guns and saddlebags. With a candle stub and a match he had been able to find his way out of the dark cave and into the relative light of the canyons.

A piece of dried jerked meat served as his supper and was followed by a futile search for water. He resorted to opening a can of peaches and let the sweet flesh and syrup slide down his parched throat. Looking at the sky, John spotted a star. "It'll be full dark soon," he sighed. "The cave is better than the open." John hobbled his way back inside and fell asleep.

John woke at dawn. Refreshed by a good sleep, he was able to track down a dripping noise to a small seep deep in the cave. After filling his belly he made his way back out to the mouth of the cave to find the day no brighter than before. Shrugging off the strangeness of the light, John slowly followed the twists and turns of the canyon until it opened into a rolling plain. A boulder sat partway onto the plain and it was there that John Dawson decided to rest his throbbing leg and wait for full light.

An hour later, as John sat upon the rock and gazed out over a dark desert plain, the moon rose. At first John was grateful. The added light helped bring more contrast to the land.

When the second moon rose John realized he was no longer in Arizona, or on Earth. The rest of the day . . . night was spent getting back to the cave.

As time slipped by, John rested next to a small fire and thought about his situation. Here, wherever it was, he was safe from Jack and his gang. He could rest and wait for Jack to leave the canyon back home. He had water and if he went easy on the jerky it would last a week. By then his leg would be better and the hike to Mancos or Durango would be less grueling. John picked up another can of peaches, felt his stomach growl, and placed it back in the bag. Those he would save for his upcoming hike.

It was on the third day John started going through the saddlebags. There was a "stay" pile: string, flint, steel, char cloth, and other nonessentials. There was a "go" pile: rifle shells, food, tin cup, pocketknife, money, matches, candle stubs, and a few more things.

After sorting out his possessions, John cut the leather between the two bags. One bag he filled with the "stay" items and placed them on a rock shelf. The other bag he sliced belt loops into and hung on his good hip. The "go" items went in it.

The hardest decision was which of his weapons to keep and which to leave. The Colt .45-caliber Peacemakers were beautiful but heavy. The Marlin rifle would be better for game and, if necessary, fighting. He sighed as he pulled the pistols from their holsters. Their nickel finish gleamed in the candlelight as he spun the cylinders and removed the cartridges.

Giving each pistol an extra heavy coating of gun oil, John reloaded the cylinders, placed the Colts back into their holsters and onto the rock shelf. As a last thought John penned a note.

Property of John C. Dawson
Arizona Rangers
Prescott Office

He shoved the note in with a pistol. John turned and sighed. With what belongings he had left, John followed his tracks back to the chamber where he had first entered this world.

As the candle was melting away the tracks ended. With grim determination John Dawson limped forward and was gone.

Twenty-fourth Century
Planet of Equinox

Jean-Luc sipped his morning tea and gazed at the twin moons. They hung low, large, and yellow on the horizon, casting an odd light upon the plain. It was a strangely beautiful sight he would never forget.

"It's hard to fathom the size of meteor impact it took to stop this planet from spinning," commented Beverly. "It must have been cataclysmic."

"Very. However, the planet still spins, it's just so slow that the spin matches the planet's revolution around the sun. One side is always in darkness, the other always in light," replied Jean-Luc.

"Are there any legends or records about what happened to the people who lived here?" asked Beverly.

"None," replied Jean-Luc. "Those who survived would have to adapt quickly or perish. Other than the few ruins like these, little is known about this planet. And being in the neutral zone, it gets very little exploration."

"I hope the Cardassians don't get upset about our being here."

"Archeology is allowed under the treaty we have with them."

"Still," sighed Beverly, "I wish the *Enterprise* was nearby and not back at Earth . . ." Beverly cast a watchful eye to the starry sky and sighed. "Just in case."

"Not to worry," replied Jean-Luc. "There is very little on this planet that would interest the Cardassians."

"Have you heard from Data this morning?" she asked.

"No. I suppose we ought to check on him." Jean-Luc tapped on his combadge. "Data? How are you this morning?"

Jean-Luc looked at Beverly as concern grew in the silence.

Jean-Luc tapped his badge again. "Data, please answer."

Beverly stood and looked in the direction of the canyon. "I think we better get over there."

"I think you're right."

The short distance to the canyon seemed abnormally long as they fought down their anxiety. The twilight now seemed evil and malignant as they raced to see what had happened to Data.

As they wound through the canyon a strange sound echoed down the walls. Jean-Luc and Beverly stopped their breakneck pace as they reach the cavern opening. The pattern to the sound was clear.

"I see he cleared away the rubble." Beverly shook her head. "Is he singing Pagliacci?"

Jean-Luc sighed in relief. "From the second act, I believe." He cupped his hands. "DATA!" The singing stopped as Picard's voice echoed into the passageway.

"Yes, Captain?" Data's voice came from deep in the cavern.

"What are you doing?"

"Singing Pagliacci," replied Data. "The acoustics in here are incredible."

Beverly shook her head as her eyes flashed. "You had us worried to death!"

As they entered the cave, they spotted Data's wrist light coming toward them.

"We tried to hail you but didn't get a response," chided Beverly. "We were concerned for your safety!"

"I am sorry for your apprehension, Doctor. The combadges are inoperative inside the cavern, unless in close proximity."

"Have you localized the reason?" asked Jean-Luc.

"Actually, I have," replied Data. "There is a natural matrix of a crystalline-active element. It combines with the rock to form a massive power cell."

"Like a chemical battery," commented Beverly.

"Your analogy is close, Doctor."

"Could it be used as a power source?" asked Jean-Luc.

"I have studied the tricorder readings and believe it is quite possible."

"Have you found any artifacts?" asked Beverly.

"I am sorry, Dr. Crusher," replied Data. "In my haste to analyze the matrix I neglected to look for signs of inhabitation. However, I did see a hieroglyphic relief carved into the cave wall farther in."

"Let's have a look," replied Jean-Luc.

Approximately thirty meters in, the cave widened into a room. Data flashed his wrist light onto the cave wall. Jean-Luc could hardly believe his eyes.

"We're going to need the holocamera," he murmured.

"It's beautiful, but dirty," commented Beverly. "The design is filled with dust." She stepped up and brushed her hand over one of the designs. Instantly the room hummed with power as the overhead rock started to glow with a warm yellow light.

Jean-Luc shielded his eyes from the light, wary, yet enjoying the sudden heat.

"Data, what do you make of it?" he asked.

Data studied his tricorder. "A chemical reaction. It seems to be harmless but it is bringing the cavern to an even twenty-eight degrees Celsius."

"That's close to what I keep my cabin at," commented Beverly.

Jean-Luc nodded. "That's just what I was thinking," he commented as he inspected the relief. In a moment he shook his head and chuckled.

"What is it?" asked Beverly.

"Dr. Bowman will never believe me, but the design for heat is the Hopi Indian sun god."

Data ran a tricorder over the relief and checked his readings.

"I suspect you're finding something other than native rock," commented Jean-Luc.

"Quite right, Captain," replied Data. "There seems to be a sort of electronic switch embedded in a polymer made to look like the rock." Data tapped a button on his tricorder. "It seems to use the static charge from your body to start the process. The natural chemical reaction of the matrix takes over from there."

"Fascinating," murmured Jean-Luc.

"Somehow I don't think the people who lived in this cave created this technology," commented Beverly.

"It doesn't seem to fit with the rest of the puzzle, does it?" agreed Jean-Luc.

"It's as if a more advanced culture were caretakers of this culture."

"It does seems the switch is designed to reinforce religious beliefs, and not upset them," agreed Data.

"Like part of a noninterference-type doctrine?" proposed Beverly.

"Perhaps," said Data

"Maybe this somehow links to the legends of Kokopelli," replied Beverly. "Perhaps this Kokopelli wasn't a deity, but rather a more advanced life-form."

"Other such culture relationships have been recorded by Starfleet," added Data.

"Are you saying Kokopelli was here and on Earth?" asked Jean-Luc.

"Why not?" replied Beverly. "We're here."

Jean-Luc smiled. "Very true."

Beverly glanced about the room. "Data, have you found any other hieroglyphics?"

Data shook his head. "None."

"I propose we make use of the lighting and start a new dig here," said Jean-Luc.

"Captain," replied Data. "I would like to search deeper into the caverns to see what other technology is present."

"I agree," said Jean-Luc. "Beverly and I will bring up the supplies."

Beverly and Jean-Luc wound their way out of the canyon and across the plain to the runabout. By Jean-Luc's mind it was mid-morning, but the sky was in perpetual twilight.

"Just once I wish the sun would come over those mountains," commented Beverly.

"It would certainly make things less dreary," agreed Jean-Luc. "But I admit there is a certain beauty."

They reached the runabout and went in.

Beverly plopped down into a chair. "What I wouldn't give for a nice warm bath and a hot meal."

Jean-Luc grinned as he sat down in another chair. "What's the matter? Don't you like roughing it?" .

"This isn't what I had in mind when you asked me to go away for a week." Beverly smirked.

"Sorry," Jean-Luc said softly. "Next time you can pick the place we go."

Beverly grinned. "Someplace more romantic, to be sure."

Jean-Luc held her gaze until she blushed and looked away.

"What all do we need?" she asked.

"All of the documentation gear, the holocamera, data recorders, plus the shovels, brushes, picks—"

"You're going to have to go slower if you want me to remember all that," groaned Beverly.

"Grab the holocamera and data recorders." Jean-Luc grinned. "I'll gather the rest and put them in the transporter."

Beverly cocked her head. "I thought we couldn't use the transporter."

Jean-Luc nodded. "We can't transport into the cavern but I'll see if I can get right outside in the canyon."

Beverly nodded. "I like your way of thinking."

The darkness of the canyon was momentarily shattered as a pile of gear and two humans materialized in a twinkling of white light.

In a moment the two scooped up the gear and went into the cavern, their wrist lights bouncing around like drunken fireflies.

"I wonder how many other lights we're passing that we could be using," commented Beverly.

Jean-Luc paused for a moment as he flashed the light over the cave walls. "I'd be surprised if we don't find more."

In a few moments they stepped into the cavern chamber. They placed the gear on the flat dirt floor and started setting up the holocamera. As they finished Data appeared from a side tunnel.

"Captain, I have found something you will want to see."

"What is it?" asked Beverly.

"I believe it is a form of transporter," replied Data.

"Is it operational?" queried Jean-Luc.

"Unknown, Captain," replied Data. "It seems to be functioning but in what capacity, I am not certain."

Jean-Luc scooped up his pack. "Let's go see it."

Data led the way through the maze of tunnels until they reached a seemingly dead end at a small chamber. Their wrist lights searched about the floor as they carefully stepped in.

"Careful, Captain," cautioned Data. "The transporter is continuously activated. A person merely has to step into the center of the room to be transported."

Jean-Luc checked the area with his tricorder. "Have you found the controls?"

"I believe so," Data replied as he flashed his light on the chamber walls. "The components have been camouflaged and embedded in the native rock about the chamber."

"I wish there was lighting in this room," commented Beverly.

"There is a glyph to your left, Doctor," replied Data.

Beverly flashed her light on the relief. "Then why are we working in the dark?"

"I am sorry, Doctor," replied Data. "My positronic network in not compatible with the starting circuitry."

"What happens when you try?" asked Jean-Luc.

"Nothing happens," replied Data. "It is another case where I am less than human."

"Or simply, just different," commented Beverly as she passed her hand over the glyph, "like the rest of us."

A halo of light circled the ceiling of the chamber.

Beverly nodded her head in satisfaction. "Now this is more like it."

Jean-Luc studied his tricorder as he ran it over the walls. "This is amazing. The technology is so simple a child could understand it, yet so complex in other ways I wonder if we ever will decipher it."

"It is unlike any technology known," agreed Data.

"Can you figure out where the transporter coordinates are set for?" asked Beverly.

"Not yet," replied Data. "Their system of reference has no known relationship with ours."

"I'll run an algorithm. Perhaps we can find a common reference point," replied Jean-Luc.

Beverly soon grew bored with the conversation between Data and Jean-Luc. "I'm going to look around to see if I find any other glyphs."

Jean-Luc looked up and nodded. "That's a good idea. Just be careful."

Beverly strolled down the tunnel flashing her light around the walls. She hadn't gone far when a dusty lump on a rock shelf caught her eye. As she brushed away the years of dust the object began to shine in the dim light. She stopped brushing as the form registered in her mind. She wasn't an expert on ancient weapons but she knew a pistol when she saw one.

"Jean-Luc!" she called down the tunnel.

Within a moment the lights of Data and Jean-Luc came bobbing toward her.

"Is something wrong, Doctor?" asked Data.

"No," she replied, "but I just found another piece that doesn't fit into the puzzle." She motioned to the rock shelf.

Jean-Luc gingerly removed one of the pistols. The nickel plating shone brightly as Jean-Luc turned it over in his hands. "It's an old revolver—"

"A Colt Peacemaker, to be precise, Captain. It was also known in the military as a single-action Army. This type of weapon was carried by many individuals during the last part of the nineteenth century."

Beverly pulled a brittle, oil-soaked piece of paper from the holster. "Look at this: 'Property of John C. Dawson, Arizona Rangers, Prescott Office.'"

Jean-Luc gingerly read the words and slowly shook his head. "I think we just found out where the transporter leads to."

"Be careful, Captain," cautioned Data. "The tricorder readings indicate the weapon is still loaded and operational."

"After all these years?" wondered Beverly.

Data nodded. "The dry atmosphere makes for a perfect preserving environment."

Jean-Luc pulled the holsters down. "There is another pistol. They're a set."

Data carefully inspected the pistols. "The serial numbers are still readable. We can date them when we get back to camp."

"Data!" commented Jean-Luc, "You have surprised me again! When did you become an expert on ancient firearms?"

"I have long been fascinated by the 'Old West' era of Earth's past. Firearms are a major part of that history."

"There's more up here," added Beverly. "It's a pack or something."

"It is a part of a saddlebag," corrected Data.

Beverly pulled a few of the pieces out. "It's hard to imagine these are part of a man's life from someplace so long ago and so far away."

"Earth might be just a few steps away," replied Jean-Luc.

"That would explain the similar patterns in pottery," agreed Data.

"You're saying ancient Indians transported back and forth from Earth to here?" asked Beverly.

"Perhaps they migrated from here to Earth," replied Jean-Luc. "After the meteor strike Earth would have been very appealing."

"Could it be possible this Kokopelli figure led those people to Earth?" asked Beverly.

"There is a Hopi myth that could be linked to that hypothesis," added Data.

Jean-Luc tilted his head in question. "What myth are you referring to?"

"Hopi mythology tells of previous worlds that they inhabited."

"Previous worlds?" queried Beverly.

"Yes," replied Data. "According to their creation stories, Earth is the fourth world that they have lived on."

"Did they describe the other worlds?" asked Beverly.

"Vaguely," replied Data. "The myths tell of a world that was dark and cold. The gods gave them some light but it was not enough to grow crops."

"This planet fits that description," agreed Jean-Luc.

"Did they say how they got to Earth?" asked Beverly.

"Versions vary slightly but they all agree that a deity helped them climb to the fourth world through a hole in the sky, a sipapu," replied Data.

"That sounds like a transporter," added Beverly.

"It does. And a sipapu is still found in their ceremonial kivas now," added Jean-Luc.

"It is a spiritual representation of the one they came through eons ago," agreed Data.

"Are you telling me after all this time the Hopis still practice their religion?" asked Beverly.

"Very much so," replied Data. "In fact they still believe the true sipapu exists somewhere near the La Plata Mountains in southern Colorado."

"That area has the highest concentration of prehistoric ruins in North America," murmured Jean-Luc, "including Mesa Verde."

"I've been there. I was a little girl on vacation," reminisced Beverly. "I remember climbing down into Indian ruins in caves."

"Cliff dwellings," corrected Data. "The ancient cliff ruins in Mesa Verde Heritage Park are unique and their prehistoric inhabitants are still a mystery."

Beverly pondered the artifacts in her hand. "I guess the next question is, who is going to be the first to step into the transporter?"

Jean-Luc shook his head. "It would be ill advised to risk something like that without further study."

"We could make a probe and send it through. Starfleet could triangulate the signal if it truly goes to Earth," suggested Data.

Jean-Luc scratched his chin and nodded. "Do we have what we need at camp?"

"I believe we do," replied Data. "It will take me a few hours to put it together."

"That sounds good to me," replied Beverly. "I'm getting hungry anyway."

Jean-Luc turned to Data. "Do you have the pistol serial numbers logged?"

"I have them committed to memory, Captain," replied Data.

Jean-Luc placed the pistols and saddlebag back on the shelf. "I'll leave these here for now."

* * *

It didn't take long for the trio to hike the distance to their camp.

"I'd swear we walk farther each time," complained Beverly as she rubbed her legs.

"My internal chronometer says it is the same distance," replied Data.

"Yeah, well, my internal chronometer says somebody keeps moving it farther away."

"Data," commented Jean-Luc, "we're going to get something to eat. Let me know if you need any help."

"I should be able to find everything I need," Data said as he entered the runabout.

Jean-Luc turned to a cargo container and pulled out some food packets. He turned to Beverly and held them up. "Pork and beans or chicken à la king?"

"Prime rib, an inch thick and medium rare, a baked potato covered with chives, sour cream, butter, and a bowl of cantaloupe with vanilla ice cream."

Jean-Luc smiled. "Sorry, but we're all out of butter."

Beverly chuckled. "Okay, just bring the rest and I'll forgive you—" She stopped talking as the air shimmered in front of them and deposited six heavily armed Cardassians.

Jean-Luc turned and faced the armed men. "What is the meaning of this?"

An aging Cardassian stepped forward. "You are violating the Neutral Zone treaty!"

Jean-Luc's eyes narrowed in the dim light. "Gul Dusac, we are on an authorized archeological mission."

The Cardassian sneered at Jean-Luc. "So you do remember me. Only, it's not 'Gul' Dusac anymore. After my defeat, my family fell out of favor with Central Command. The Obsidian Order has even suggested that I am a traitor and let you escape."

"I am sorry for your hardship. The fortunes of war can be fickle at times," replied Jean-Luc.

"You fail to see how fickle, Picard," hissed Dusac. "You see, while I no longer command a ship, I do command a clerical desk. A desk that your archeological permit crossed." Dusac laughed for a moment. "You don't know how long I waited for something like this, Picard. A chance to capture you and that android." Dusac slowly nodded his head. "Don't you see, Captain, this will bring back my honor."

Jean-Luc shook his head in the dim lights of the runabout. "Kidnapping a group of unarmed archeologists is hardly honorable."

Dusac stepped forward and backhanded Jean-Luc, knocking him against a container. Jean-Luc shook off the blow and wiped away a trickle of blood. "You have just reaffirmed my statement."

Dusac's lip quivered with hatred. "Just the same, there are those in command of Cardassia who want you. And with the technology we glean from your android we will make an army of them to take back what is rightfully ours."

"Grand plans by a small man," replied Jean-Luc. "Starfleet will not sit by and allow that to happen."

"By the time they know it will be too late," Dusac mocked. He waved a hand to his men. "Two of you stay out here to cover them. The rest go inside and find the android."

Jean-Luc casually blocked their way and spoke loudly. "Data isn't aboard."

"I don't have time for this, Picard," hissed Dusac. "Where is he then?"

Jean-Luc glanced at Beverly. "Data transported back to the dig. We were just getting ready to join him."

Dusac's eyes flashed fire. "I don't believe you! Stand aside!"

Jean-Luc slowly nodded. "Very well. Look for yourself."

The four guards stepped past. Jean-Luc glanced at Beverly in time to see her shape start to shimmer with white light. He glanced back at Dusac to see him frantically waving to the guards. Jean-Luc felt a moment of fear as beams erupted from their rifles, but it was too late.

Jean-Luc glanced around. The familiar dark walls of the narrow canyon loomed above him. Data and Beverly stood next to him. "I'm glad you took the hint, Data." He took Beverly's hand. "Let's get inside the cavern where they can't lock on to us."

They entered the inky darkness. "Now what?" asked Beverly.

"Data, did you get a chance to contact Starfleet?"

"No, Captain," replied Data. "The Cardassians were blocking our communications."

"I am assuming you didn't have a chance to assemble a probe."

"You are correct. We have only what gear is stashed in the cave."

Jean-Luc sighed. "They are not leaving without us and we can't hide forever."

"We could use the transporter," replied Data.

Jean-Luc slowly nodded. "I'll try it first."

"Captain," replied Data, "I should go first to ensure your safety."

"We're not aboard the *Enterprise,* Data. It was my plans that got us into this mess. I should take the risk."

"Captain, I stand a better chance of surviving whatever danger might lie at the other end," chided Data.

Beverly squeezed Jean-Luc's hand. "He's right, you know. Data stands the best chance of getting back, good or bad."

"All right," sighed Jean-Luc. "Let's do it before they figure out where we went."

The trio hurried through the passageways. It seemed forever before they found the chamber. Beverly turned on the lighting. Data took a reading with his tricorder. "It is still functioning."

Beverly grasped Data's hand. "Good luck, Data. Don't forget to write."

Data cocked his head in confusion. "If all goes correctly I will not have time to write."

Beverly bit back a laugh. "It was a joke, Data."

"Ah," replied Data. "Defusing a tense situation with humor." He turned and stepped toward the transporter.

"Data, wait," called Jean-Luc.

Data turned. "Yes, Captain?"

Jean-Luc pulled the pistols off the rock shelf. "How do you work these?"

Data gave a quick demonstration. "Pull back the hammer until it cocks. Aim along the barrel at your target and squeeze the trigger mechanism. A load explosion will result as the projectile exits the barrel. After it is complete, repeat the same sequence until the gun is empty."

"How long will that take?" asked Beverly.

"You have six shots per gun," replied Data.

"Then what?" she asked.

"Hopefully I will be back by then."

Jean-Luc worked the pistol around in his palm and practiced pointing it down the passageway. He nodded to Data. "I'm ready."

"I hear footsteps coming!" hissed Beverly. "Give me a pistol!"

"Go, Data," urged Jean-Luc.

Data stepped toward the center of the chamber.

"Hurry!" urged Beverly. Data nodded and was gone.

"Turn out the lights. Let's not make this any easier for them."

Beverly swiped her hand over the glyph. The glowing stopped.

They waited in silence for a moment. As they watched, lights started flashing off the passageway walls, creating grotesque shadows.

"When they turn that last curve," Jean-Luc whispered, "aim just above the lights and fire."

Beverly nodded in the darkness. "I'm ready."

As lights flashed down the walls, Jean-Luc could faintly see the rock-steady stance and grim determination upon Beverly's face. He turned and looked down the barrel as the footsteps came closer and louder. "Take the left side, I'll get the right," he whispered.

"I got you covered."

The lights came around the last curve and shone on the floor. As one, Jean-Luc and Beverly fired. The ancient weapons belched fire and death that had lain waiting an eon. Phaser blasts replied, showering them with rock particles. They cycled the hammers and fired again. In the confusion and smoke Jean-Luc saw three Cardassians lying lifeless on the passageway floor. He glanced over at Beverly only to have fear jump into his throat. Blood was streaming from a wound on her temple as she slumped against the rock wall. Jean-Luc fired another round at their attackers and leapt over to Beverly. She didn't respond to his touch but a quick check still felt a heartbeat.

Another wild phaser blast showered them with debris. Jean-Luc took careful aim and fired. He was rewarded with Cardassian cussing. More phaser fire drove Jean-Luc behind an outcropping. A steady stream of phaser fire warned him the Cardassians were attempting to advance. He hazarded a quick look to confirm his suspicions. They were almost close enough to touch. He fired his last three shots in quick succession. With a roll he picked up Beverly's pistol and fired again. Dust and smoke stung his eyes as he checked on Beverly.

Her breathing was slow but steady. As he wiped away some of the blood, he felt a firm hand on his shoulder.

"Captain, follow me!"

Jean-Luc turned to see Data standing over him.

"Take her and I'll cover you!"

Data wasted no time or effort as he picked Beverly up and stepped into the transporter. Jean-Luc fired his last three shots down the passageway in a slow steady succession in a covering fire before he stepped into the transporter and was enveloped in a blue light.

In a long moment he was standing in a dark, round chamber. Wrist lights flashed in his eyes and then away as gentle hands pulled him aside. Through red-rimmed eyes he focused on someone next to him. It was Data.

"Where are we, Data?" he murmured.

"Southwestern Colorado, Captain. Mesa Verde Heritage Park, to be precise."

More armed personnel in Starfleet uniforms were climbing down an ancient pole ladder and taking up defensive positions around the chamber. One of the men tossed a stun grenade into the transporter, where it vanished in a shimmer of blue light. Seconds later the men around him started stepping into the transporter beam, phaser rifles ready. Jean-Luc smiled grimly. Dusac was about to have a rude surprise on Equinox.

Jean-Luc's gaze rose to the ladder hole in the ceiling. As he looked around it dawned on Jean-Luc that he was in a kiva. At that same time he realized he still held the Peacemakers at his sides.

Data stepped over to the ladder. "This way, sir. Help is waiting."

In a moment they stepped out of the ruins and stood in the tall green grass of a cool meadow. The leaves of cottonwood and aspen clattered overhead as a breeze caressed his weary body.

"Beverly?" Jean-Luc croaked.

"She is safe, sir," replied Data "You will be seeing her in a moment." Data tapped his combadge. *"Enterprise,* two to beam up."

June 19, 1929
Southwest Colorado, Earth

John Dawson scanned the canyon walls with aging eyes and cursed. "Damn time changes everything."

"Yes, Senator, it does," replied an aide on a horse next to him.

"Grandpa, it's been forty years. Anything could have happened to the entrance."

Senator John Dawson turned in the saddle and looked at his granddaughter, Elsa. She was beautiful. And rightly she should be. Her mother and grandmother were of good stock, not the wild breed he had been. Then again Elsa did have a love of the wild places in her. His family had always been explorers, movers. It was in their blood.

He smiled and nodded. "All right, Elsa. Let's head back to camp." He glanced one last time at the canyon walls. "Maybe somebody else will find my pistols. Somebody that needs 'em."

Elsa smiled. "Maybe, Grandpa."

Twenty-fourth Century
U.S.S. Enterprise, Alpha Quadrant

Captain Picard rose from his command chair aboard the *Enterprise,* tugged his uniform tunic down, and nodded to Data. The viewscreen shifted from the image of the *U.S.S. Colorado* to an image of a woman in a captain's uniform. Jean-Luc smiled. The eyes, the cheekbones, the smile, were all as he had seen in the old photographs of Senator John Dawson. It was hard to imagine that family members five hundred years apart could look so strikingly similar.

"Greetings, Captain Picard," the woman said as she nodded. "I have heard so many things about you. It's an honor, sir."

Picard's smile grew. "The pleasure is all mine, Captain Dawson."

"I got your message about returning something of mine." Captain Dawson paused. "Frankly I'm puzzled. As far as I know we have never met."

Captain Picard nodded. "You could say I borrowed it from a relative of yours, from a long time ago."

Captain Dawson cocked her head. "Forgive me, sir, but does this have anything to do with the ancient ruins you found in Mesa Verde?"

"As a matter of fact it does," replied Picard. "I didn't realize you had heard about it."

The woman's eyes sparkled. "I probably wouldn't have paid much attention but there's an old family legend about some Indian ruins in that area."

Picard nodded again. "I would like for you to beam over. I would love to hear your story and I know you'll want to hear mine."

Efflorescence

Julie A. Hyzy

Boothby spotted him when he was still thirty meters away. The old gardener shook his head and grumbled. *Too young.*

After easing the root system of a delicate pink seedling into the waiting soil, Boothby sat back on his heels and watched as the fellow made his way down the shaded walkway, his face eager, his eyes alert. Handsome and smiling, he exuded confidence, yet looked out of place in tan overalls. He reminded the grounds-keeper of a young child, dressed in first-day-of-school crispness, ready to face new experiences, but with wide-eyed wonder. Build-wise, he was anything but childlike. Over two meters tall, he had a physique more suited to pugilistic endeavors than gardening. But this was the one. His replacement. Boothby's gloved hand absent-mindedly reached for the next plant. When he looked down at the delicate petals, the shiny green leaves, he gave a short laugh. *Impatiens.* Perfect. Exactly what he was feeling right now. Impatient to meet this man. Impatient to find out what the future held.

Two female ensigns chatting on the nearby bench apparently caught the young man's eye and he stopped to talk with them.

Boothby watched as the women sat up a little straighter and smiled. Eager to help. Together they nodded, pointing toward the garden where Boothby sat. The young man followed their direction and looked around, his eyes passing the groundskeeper twice before realization registered on his face.

Still kneeling, Boothby raised his hand, the dirt from creases in his gloves tumbling out to shower over his head. He didn't bother to smile.

He returned his concentration to the plants at his knees, stabbing at the dirt with his handshovel. He had no intention of retiring. Weeks ago he'd petitioned the administration for an extension, assuring them he was capable of working many more years. At the very least, he ought to be given the opportunity to try.

His petition was tied up somewhere in, what was the ancient term? Red tape. *Yes, yes,* they placated him. *You'll hear from us soon,* they claimed. *But, in the meantime, we need to be prepared in the event your request is denied.*

He wasn't holding his breath. He remembered back all those years when he first came to this job. His predecessor hadn't been happy to see him, either.

"We're not supposed to have favorites, you understand," the old woman had said, whirling unsteadily to look at him. She waved her finger in Boothby's face.

He'd nodded at the crooked, arthritic digit, having stopped short to keep from running into it when she turned to make this pronouncement. She was tall, at least a head taller than he was, and her finger wagged furiously right at the level of his nose. *Favorites?* he wondered.

"You just remember that. Though I suppose you're too young to even begin to understand what you're getting into here." Her white hair spiked out in every direction and she ran a spotted hand through it, to no avail.

He nodded again, but this time to her back. She'd resumed the brisk walk through Greenhouse 001, pointing, gesturing. Lecturing. As if he'd never been in one before. *Too young?* He was fifty-three years old, by Earth standards. Not quite middle-aged, but getting there. To her, though, he probably looked like a child.

"Aubrey?" he said, using her name for the first time. "Ma'am?"

She lurched, wincing as she turned, favoring her left side. He'd heard she was being forced to retire owing to physical limitations caused by her advanced age. Limitations that could be remedied with medication, but with side effects she refused to tolerate.

"Yes?"

It was obvious she hadn't been told.

"I'm not a gardener," he said, straightening a little. "I'm a librarian."

In that moment Boothby understood the term "flashing eyes." Her eyes, blue and bright, surged with a power that he would never forget. He fought the urge to step back. Instead he stood his ground, and watched, intrigued, as the anger dissipated, only to be replaced by resolve.

She blinked, nodded. "What did you say your name was?"

"Boothby," he said, then added again, "ma'am."

She raised one eyebrow, a small gesture that he imagined could mean anything from displeasure to surprise. Right now, he was betting on the former. "Well, Boothby, starting right now, you're a gardener. And you have a lot to learn."

The young man stopped in front of him. Smiled, showing perfect white teeth. "Boothby?" he asked.

The gardener nodded, "And you are . . . ?"

He stood at attention. "Lieutenant Deagan, reporting for duty, sir."

"You're Starfleet?"

"Yes, sir. They told me not to wear my uniform."

"At ease, Lieutenant. And you don't need to use 'sir' with me. Boothby will do." The gardener glared at him. "How old are you, boy?"

"Twenty-seven."

"That's very young," he said. "Since when do they send Starfleet for this job?"

Deagan shook his head, shrugged.

"What's your specialty?"

"Specialty?'

"Botany, plant pathology, ecology?"

"I'm an engineer, actually. I . . . my time in this position may only be temporary unless—"

"Temporary?" *Were they out of their minds?* This was the job of a lifetime. *For* a lifetime. They couldn't just throw someone into it for the time being and hope for the best. Boothby massaged his forehead. It made no sense to replace him. Why didn't the administration listen to reason?

"Yes, although I have the option to request—"

"You need to know that this job is about *gardening*," Boothby said, gesticulating with the shovel. "What I'm here to teach you is about *gardening*. About planting seeds, nurturing, fostering growth. You understand?"

The lieutenant nodded, too eagerly, Boothby thought. He didn't understand at all.

"Well, sonny, let's get started. I hope you like playing in the dirt."

He gave Deagan some gloves and tools, and pointed where the *impatiens* were to be planted. *Playing in the dirt.* Weren't those the same words Aubrey had used all those years ago? Hadn't appealed to Boothby then. But things change. The old man worked the dirt with a small spade, and remembered.

They'd done their homework before presenting him with the job opening. They knew him, knew he'd be unable to resist. Two of Starfleet's finest had come all the way to his small library on Gabal Prime to ask him if he'd be interested. And he had been.

Giving up his comfortable life in the company of his books, he'd traded his daily mundane tasks for the opportunity to experience the sprawling grandeur of the Starfleet Academy library. No longer would he methodically return perused-through tomes to their places on the shelves. No, instead he was to be given the chance to influence young Starfleet cadets, to put the quadrant's classics in their hands, to teach them, help guide them, using the beauty of literature. It was too tempting to pass up.

That was before he'd met Aubrey.

After his first day, when he'd complained to the administration that Aubrey didn't understand his role, that she'd assumed he was taking over the gardening responsibilities, they'd asked him for patience. To humor her. To wait. Then, he'd be free to choose his own realm of guidance. And if he preferred the library, then the library it would be. But they insisted he needed to give Aubrey the year that she'd requested for his training.

And in that one year, she'd taught him to understand that to expect beautiful blooms, one needed to plant seeds in the right conditions. Within the confines of the library, the cadets were polished, serious, stiff. Outside, in the fresh air, amid the profusion of color, with the soft green grass beneath them, they were seedlings reaching for the sun. With their guards down and their minds open, they were flowers ready to blossom.

Under the shade of *quercus agrifolia* trees, the gardener, with a shovel in his hand, found himself to be far more effective than the librarian behind the desk.

Lieutenant Deagan plucked another small plant from the tray behind him.

"Did you know Kirk when he was at the Academy?"

"Kirk?" Boothby said, his voice rising with indignation. "How old do you think I am?"

"I'm sorry. I just—"

"Watch what you're doing. You just planted the echinops in front of the dianthus. Didn't I tell you that echinops grow taller?"

"Yes, sir. I thought these were the dianthus. I guess I got confused."

"Of course you did," Boothby said, muttering. "Thinking I was here with Kirk. What do you think I am? Vulcan?"

"No, sir."

Lieutenant Deagan switched the plants, taking care not to harm the tender buds. He eased the flower into the pre-made hole and tamped dirt around it softly. Boothby watched, and despite himself, was impressed. "My predecessor was."

"Sir?"

"Here. With Kirk. Told me about it."

Deagan reached for another plant, an expectant look on his face. "He did?"

"She. *She* told me. Don't they tell you new people anything?" Boothby slapped the dirt off his gloves and sat back, remembering. And even though he settled back on the grass for a talk, Boothby noticed that Deagan kept working.

"She was called Aubrey. An old name, meaning Mystical Counselor. I looked it up."

The lieutenant raised his eyes to Boothby's as he worked the edges of a small hole away with his fingers. *Good,* Boothby thought, *he's listening.*

"I'd been here for only one day and I knew she took an immediate dislike to me." Boothby watched Deagan give a wry smile as he planted another flower. "I wasn't a gardener, you see. Not then. I'd been a librarian. She was convinced that I'd never get the hang of this job.

" 'Well, Boothby,' she said, and I remember her saying it with some degree of derision, 'since you're used to working with books instead of plants, I don't know how much I'm going to be able to teach you. I can only share with you what has worked for me and maybe you can use that when you're on your own here.' "

Boothby handed a small plant to his apprentice and continued, "My goal was to stay in her good graces. Even though I had no doubts about this assignment, I knew that she could easily make the transition difficult for me." He gave Deagan a meaningful glance.

The lieutenant held up the last of the dianthus. "I'll need more."

As they walked toward the greenhouses to replenish their tray, Boothby continued, "I knew better than to ask her about all the officers she'd gotten to know. She had a reputation for being close-mouthed, and so she should be. But as her replacement, I knew she'd tell me all I needed to learn in good time. So, I waited."

They stepped into humid warmth that hung heavily above the rainbow rows of plants. Stopping here and there to touch a specimen, Boothby wound his way through the maze of petals and green. At one station, he called to the computer to open the wall-size case before them. Hydroponic heat coaxed small buds to bloom. "Annuals and perennials. Very different, both important. Perennials are your mainstays. These are the ones that give your garden its strength because they come back every year, without fail, assuming they've been planted well and cared for." Boothby sorted through the profusion of color under the clear glass ceiling. He held up a tuberous begonia. "Here's an annual, beautiful, blooms all season. But no matter how hardy, or how much care it's given, they don't last. They need to be replaced."

"I don't think I could tell an annual from a perennial."

"Not yet. You will."

"Did you start all these yourself?"

"Of course. Planting seeds, mostly. That's how it always begins."

Boothby could see Deagan struggling, wondering if they were just talking about flowers.

"Here," he said, "we'll take these out by the fountain, the sun is just right for them there.

"Aubrey," he continued later, watching Deagan plant the begonias, "got to know Kirk early in his academic career, from what I understand. I remember her telling me that we shouldn't have favorites. And she was right. But she couldn't help herself with Kirk. She loved that boy. Thought that he was too headstrong and needed discipline. But she also knew that he wasn't one to take an order and follow it blindly."

Deagan looked up, said nothing.

"Seems to me she was pretty successful with that one. You don't want to take a man's energy away from him, but he has to have wisdom to know when to act and when to wait."

"I understand."

"No you don't," Boothby said, sighing. "And maybe you'll never get the chance." He took the last begonia from the tray and waved Deagan away. "Go on now. You're done for the day. Be back here at 0700 tomorrow."

Deagan nodded, and stood up, shaking the dirt from his pants as Boothby muttered to himself, "Temporary."

Deagan jogged up to the greenhouse at 0659. "Well, you're on time at least," Boothby said, not smiling.

Deagan grinned. "What are we planting today?"

"Nothing," Boothby said. "Today we're taking out the weeds."

The two men walked down the shaded path, Deagan taking short strides to keep from outpacing Boothby.

They worked together side by side for several hours, Deagan paying close attention to everything Boothby had to say. Just as the chime sounded for the late-morning classes, the old gardener sat back and gestured to the young lieutenant to do the same.

Deagan leaned up against the tree next to him and they watched the cadets as they passed by. Most wore serious expressions, carried padds, and studied as they walked. Some laughed and talked with friends, others strolled, taking in the gardens and flowers around them. "Boothby?"

"Yes?"

"Is it hard to tell which are the weeds?"

Boothby thought for a moment that this lieutenant had more depth than he'd originally given him credit for.

"Sometimes. Tricky part is when the weeds grow in so close to a valuable plant that it makes it hard to get rid of it without losing the plant, too."

"Sounds difficult. What do you do?"

"That's when you have to depend on the strength of the plant you value. Sometimes, in taking away the weed, you damage the plant. But, if it's strong, if it's hardy, it will survive." Boothby stood up, gesturing. "Here, let me show you one."

Surrounding the flagpole near the entrance to the Academy, Boothby indicated a raised flower bed. "Perennials," he said, by way of explanation.

They moved in closer to the bed. Boothby pointed. "Those pink ones are called thoroughwort. Planted the originals here around 2325. A vigorous plant, it blossoms in late summer and fall—toward the end of its season. But when I first planted them here, the young seedlings had some difficulty."

"Difficulty?"

Boothby fingered the leaves of the thoroughwort. "I remember planting these; I had help. A young cadet who needed someone to

116

talk to. And, despite the fact that he was dealing with his own problems at the time, he agreed to help when I asked."

"That would be about the time Picard attended the Academy, wouldn't it?"

Boothby gave the boy a shrewd look. "Yes, as a matter of fact. It was exactly that time."

"What happened?'

"I won't tell you the specifics. I wouldn't do that. But he'd gotten himself into a tight one. Just like my thoroughwort plant here." Boothby caressed the plant, and continued, "Picard let a weed take root, and it was devouring him, little by little. Like all weeds, it was devious, wiry, and strong. It wound its way around his life, slowly strangling him."

"What did you do?"

"All I did, all I could do, was to help him see beyond the insidious thing growing and listen to himself."

"You must have done more than just have him work with plants."

Boothby smiled at the memory. "Deagan, I have to give you credit. You're more perceptive than I expected. The plants helped. We worked together, just like you and I are working now. We got to know each other and he began to trust me." Boothby remembered. "I knew he needed more than the flowers could give, so I fell back on what I'd always known best. I put a book in his hands. Sometimes we all have to plant seeds in different ways."

Deagan waited.

"Picard was having a difficult time. He was faced with a serious choice. We talked at length and maybe that in itself would have been enough. For to have someone who's apart from the problem to be able to listen—and to be able to say the thing out loud—is sometimes enough to conquer it.

"In any case, I remembered my library days. And the wealth of inspiration I'd always found there." The groundskeeper looked up, remembering, "A passage from *Hamlet* seemed fitting, 'To thine own self be true, and it must follow, as the night the day, thou can'st not then be false to any man.' "

"From what I know of Picard, it seems he follows that philosophy to this day."

Boothby gave a rare smile.

Deagan continued, "You know, I seem to remember seeing a Shakespearean collection in Picard's ready room on a tour we took when I was a cadet."

"*The Globe Illustrated Shakespeare.*"

"That's right. The guide told us that Picard received it as a gift when he graduated from the Academy."

"Yes," Boothby said, gazing across the campus, "he did."

The following morning, 0659, Boothby watched as Deagan jogged up again. There was more to this fellow than met the eye, he judged. He listened well, understood, and commented quietly, but profoundly. Maybe there was hope. Even if Boothby's request for a longer tour of duty was turned down, maybe he could request that Deagan become his permanent replacement. So much would be lost otherwise.

"Morning, sir."

Old habits died hard, Boothby knew; he let the "sir" go. "We're heading out back today. Section 77M. Quite a few old plants there. Gotta get rid of them."

They took a small conveyance out to the back of the campus.

"What's wrong with these plants?" Deagan asked, looking around. "They seem healthy and strong. I thought we'd clear away only dead ones."

"Starfleet regulations. Each plant has an average life span. They don't want to take the chance of having the plants die while on display. So we schedule them for removal once they've reached their peak."

"That doesn't seem right."

"No, I quite agree."

"Have you ever pushed the limits on a plant you have a fondness for?"

Boothby grinned. "Often."

Deagan, hands on hips, looked at him. "I think I'd like to do that here, sir. If you don't mind."

On board the *Enterprise,* alone in his ready room, Picard clicked off the monitor ending the transmission from Earth, and sat back in his chair. He steepled his fingers, pressing them up to his lips. It had been a long time. But not so long that he'd forgotten. He pressed his hands on the arms of his chair and rose to walk around the desk.

Across the room sat his prized volume. Picard touched the book reverently. From the moment he'd received the message, Picard knew he'd act. He just wanted to take a moment to touch the memory, to say a silent thank-you to a man who needed him now. A silent thanks for the opportunity to return a favor.

It was getting dark. Boothby stabbed his handshovel into the earth, muttering to himself. "Day's almost over." Shadows played tricks on his eyes and he dug into the ground where he'd already made a hole, causing him to lurch forward when his shovel gained no purchase. "Just when you think you've made a connection . . ." he said, not looking up. "They disappoint you."

"Good evening, sir," Deagan said.

"You're late," Boothby answered without stopping.

"No, sir."

Boothby looked up. "No, sir? What does that mean?"

"I've been reassigned, sir."

And he looks so happy about it. I should have seen this coming. I had such high hopes for this one. Maybe they're right, maybe I don't have it anymore and I need to move on. But how could I have been so wrong about this one?

Boothby stood up, leaning heavily on his right knee as he did so. He thought, *Just like an old man.* He took care to brush the dirt from his pant legs before straightening himself up. Taking off his gloves, he moved forward to offer his best wishes, when they were interrupted by Admiral MacKenzie.

"Excuse me, gentlemen," he said to them. Then, turning to Lieutenant Deagan, "May I have a moment alone with Mr. Boothby?"

Deagan nodded and moved toward the collection of plants Boothby hadn't yet planted. He stood just out of earshot of the two men and Boothby watched as Deagan picked the seedlings up, one by one, to examine them.

"Mr. Boothby."

"Admiral."

The tall, silver-haired officer smiled. "It is my great privilege to inform you that the mandatory retirement age for groundskeeper personnel has been abolished."

Boothby was stunned. "My request went through?"

"Yes, it did. And I might add that you have powerful friends in this quadrant whose influence has helped our administration see the wisdom of this decision."

Powerful friends? Boothby's eyes flicked over to Deagan, who glanced up at that very moment. Their eyes held for a split second. "Thank you, sir. I will certainly stay on."

Admiral MacKenzie nodded. "The position is yours as long as you want it. Which is why we've reassigned Deagan." The admiral shot a look over to the young man who was earnestly studying the plants. "That boy has potential. He can see the big picture. He's going to be quite an asset someday." His eyes snapped back to Boothby's. "I'll leave you to your work then. Carry on."

Deagan walked up as the admiral departed. "Congratulations, sir. And thank you, for all you've taught me."

"You called Picard."

Deagan took a deep breath before answering, "Yes, sir."

Boothby shook his head, "You should never have bothered him. He has more important things to do than worry about the fate of an old gardener. What were you thinking, boy?" He waved his gloves in Deagan's face. "You called in a favor on my behalf. Why? So they would change their minds and you wouldn't have to take this boring, unglamorous job? Is that it?"

Deagan's eyes were blue, bright, like Aubrey's had been. He fixed his gaze on Boothby. "If I may be so bold," Deagan said, "I would appreciate it if, someday, you recommend me to be your replacement. But only when you're ready."

Boothby squinted at Deagan, but stayed silent as he continued.

"I don't need a glamorous job," he said, looking down at the half-filled flower bed. "What I need is the opportunity to help things grow. In the short time we worked together, I began to understand. You're at the peak of your career, here; it would be wrong for you to leave now. But the thought that I had a shot at taking over for you in this position was exhilarating. Overwhelming, even. Someday, if

I'm lucky enough to earn this job, I won't give it up without a fight either." He held Boothby's gaze. "Yes, I contacted Captain Picard, but I made no request. I simply did what you taught me. I planted a seed." He took the gardener's hand in his. "Thank you, sir. For everything."

Boothby watched the young man walk away, turn once, and wave before jogging off down the path. He scratched his head and looked at the plants below him. He was far, far behind. Maybe he'd have to work into the night.

Kneeling, he reached for a marigold. He sat back with the small plant tucked safely in his hands and looked up at the stars just beginning to appear.

Somewhere up in the night sky, hundreds of starships across the quadrant explored, sought out adventure. Boothby tried to imagine the call of the stars—the intangible thing that pulled at these cadets so strongly. He thought of a night, years ago, when a young cadet walked away from him, terrified, but standing straighter, ready to make his decision. Ready to meet the consequences of that decision. And he thought about how proud of that young cadet he was.

He whispered to the heavens, "Thank you, Jean-Luc."

Kristin's Conundrum

Jeff D. Jacques
and
Michelle A. Bottrall

The girl didn't know who she was, and her toes were cold as she padded down the corridor of the *Enterprise* in her bare feet. Her body was still clammy from the wet bathing suit she'd peeled off in sickbay, but the flimsy medical gown the doctor had given her wasn't much of an improvement.

She held closed the split in the front of the thin gown as she went, feeling as ridiculous as she no doubt looked. Her eyes searched each of the mono-colored doorways she passed for one that might seem familiar, but they all looked the same. The names on the door ID labels could have been written in Swahili for all she recognized them. It was a strong certainty her name wasn't "Reginald Barclay," but the possibility existed that she could be "Robin Lefler," "Jenna D'Sora," or "Sariel Rager." Still, she didn't feel like a Robin or a Jenna or a Sariel. Why she felt that, she hadn't a clue. She just did.

As the doctor explained it to her, the *Enterprise* had been hit with some sort of scan that knocked out everyone's memory, though only specific things had been lost to them. The crew knew how to

122

work things, like computer consoles or, as in the doctor's case, medical tools, but memories of who they were and what they were doing here were gone.

The words of the command that rang over the intercom earlier still echoed in her head. "Remain where you are," the deep voice had said. "Stay calm."

Oh, she was calm, but the idea of sitting in sickbay in a wet bathing suit for hours did not appeal to her in the least. She might not know who she was, but she had a feeling she wasn't the type who followed orders very well.

As the girl walked along, her footfalls silent on the soft carpeting, she figured everyone else on the ship must be just as confused as she. Some of them might have found themselves in their quarters or standing at their duty stations, though, which at least might have given them some sense of purpose, some sense of who they were.

She, on the other hand, had found herself sitting on a biobed in sickbay with a fractured shoulder and a wet bathing suit clinging to her body. Big help there.

Or maybe it *would* help. At the moment, she didn't know where to report for duty, or even if she had any duties. She didn't even know where she lived. And so she wandered down the corridors of the *Enterprise,* searching for anything that looked familiar to her.

At the same time, she kept her eyes peeled for a swimming pool. A wet bathing suit meant swimming, in her book. There had to be a pool somewhere on the ship. Maybe she was a lifeguard. Or maybe she'd been relaxing after a long hard day of . . . whatever.

A flash of orange streaked by her peripheral vision and she turned to the right as an orange tabby cat scooted around the corner, not even bothering to give her a curious look. She watched as it padded away and disappeared around another corner.

At least *it* seemed to know where it was going, and she decided to follow it. For all she knew, it could be *her* cat leading her home. It beat staring at a hallway full of strange doors.

She hurried to catch up and followed the striped tail as it led her through the maze of corridors.

The door to someone's quarters opened in front of the cat and the girl jumped inside just before it closed. Inside, she saw an easel with an unfinished piece of artwork resting on the stand. The canvas was dotted with swirls of blue and yellow that reminded her of van Gogh's *Starry Night*.

Van Gogh? How did she remember that?

On the other side of the room, a tweed cloak and hat were displayed on rack near a shelf of books. A violin sat propped against a music stand. She picked up the bow, nestled the violin under her chin, then swiped the bow across the strings.

An awful screech filled the air and she dropped the instrument in alarm. Fortunately, the instrument didn't break as it hit the carpet. These obviously weren't her quarters and the last thing she wanted was to break some stranger's stuff.

In the corner the cat crouched low and licked at a saucer of milk. At least the cat belonged here, and it appeared that its owner took good care of it.

She took the cape off the coat rack and wrapped it around her shoulders, relishing the added warmth. The coarse fabric of the garment scratched against her neck, but it was better than the drafty gown.

In the center of the room sat a shiny black table with a computer terminal on top. On the screen, a cursor blinked, as though waiting for a command. Why the heck not, she thought. She was alone and this might be a first step in finding out who she was.

It felt good to sit again. For a long moment she just sat at the computer and regarded her reflection in the black screen, her features as sketchy as her own memory.

"Computer?" she asked. A dull tone sounded, indicating the interface was ready. "Where is the swimming pool located?"

"There is no swimming pool on the *Enterprise*," a bland female voice answered.

The girl frowned. How could she have been swimming if there was no swimming pool? She sighed and pushed the chair back. As though waiting for that cue, the cat jumped into her lap. She winced, waiting for the claws to tear into her bare legs, but instead felt only the massage of its soft paws. A well-behaved cat for sure.

"Hello, Kitty," she said. The cat circled on top of her knees, once, twice, three times, and then settled into her lap. She scratched its ears and it closed its eyes, giant purrs rumbling against her legs.

The girl looked at the screen again. "Computer," she said. "Is there anywhere to swim on the *Enterprise?*"

"There are thirty-two holodeck programs that include a variety of water-based locations," the voice said.

"Ha!" Now they were getting somewhere. As a wave of giddiness swept through her, she pushed a strand of damp hair away from her face. "Were any of those holodeck programs active in the last ninety minutes?"

"Affirmative," the computer said. "Program 47-C, The Cliffs of Heaven, was in use in Holodeck Two until 0940 hours." By the time the sentence was finished, the girl was out the door, cat and cloak in hand.

Outside Holodeck Two, the control panel still displayed the information pertaining to the active program. The Cliffs of Heaven— a re-creation of a popular tourist site on Cirrus IV. It didn't sound like a simple watering hole, and as she scanned the specifications of the falls, she felt her knees weaken.

"You've got to be kidding me," she said. "Computer, have I used this program before?"

The computer emitted a dull buzz. "Unable to reply without proper identification."

The girl rolled her eyes. "Never mind." She glanced at the cat in her arms. "Well, what do you think, Kitty?" The cat nudged her hand with its head, as though prompting her to be bold and face her fears. She sighed. "You must be a guy." She lifted its tail and discovered, in fact, that Kitty was a girl. "Computer, activate program."

"Program activated," the voice said. "Enter when ready."

The large interlocking door opened with a mechanical groan as she approached. A fine mist rolled out into the corridor, carrying the faint, sweet scent of fresh rainwater on a summer afternoon. The thunderous roar of rushing water pounded in her ears and the exotic fragrance of Kantarian orchids tickled her nose.

The cat tensed at the loud sound assaulting them and the girl gave her a reassuring scratch behind the ear. "Don't worry, we're in this together. Remember?"

The girl stepped into the misty landscape and the door closed, vanishing without a trace. Remarkable, she thought.

In front of her, a waterfall dropped ten meters and crashed into a pool below. Impact ripples extended outward until they dispersed near the opposite side. A yellow butterfly flitted by her shoulder and the cat squirmed in her arms. She dropped her onto the earthy path.

"Stay close, Kitty." She peered far over the edge of the falls. Undoubtedly this was where she had fractured her shoulder, and yet she found herself with the strong urge to dive into those waters, to feel the rush of the wind, the spray of mist in her face, and the sense of utter freedom. But she wasn't here for that.

A black duffel bag rested at the base of an ancient oak tree that leaned over the void. Etched on the bag's side was a silver emblem: an arrowhead shape atop an oval.

"A clue, perhaps?" She crouched next to the bag and examined its contents. There was a change of clothing (thank goodness!), a fluffy blue towel, and an old-fashioned paper novel. On the cover, the title *Sherlock Holmes: The Hound of the Baskervilles* stood out in stylish gold script.

The girl gave her surroundings another look to make sure no one else was around, and then shrugged out of her borrowed cloak and medical gown. She changed into the simple red pantsuit with black crested shoulders, similar to the one the doctor had been wearing under her blue lab coat. It was a snug fit, but more comfortable than she would have guessed. It must be hers, she decided, and that meant she was some type of crew member. So much for the fantasies of being a simple lifeguard.

She sat against the mighty oak and leafed through the book, its dog-eared pages worn from multiple readings. She was a mystery buff, though she couldn't remember ever reading this particular book.

As she flipped through the pages and took in the comforting smell of the ancient text, a plastic card fell from between the pages and into her lap. At the top, the figures 07-4208 were engraved. An address? Now she was getting somewhere.

She tossed the book into the bag and slung it over her shoulder.

She called to the cat, but she didn't appear. "Computer, end program." At once, the sound of the rushing waterfall ceased and the entire environment dissolved around her, leaving behind a static, yellow-gridded room. The contrast was jarring.

The cat was caught unawares, her paws just reaching for something that was no longer there. She uttered a startled "meow" and the girl scooped her up.

"Come on, Kitty. I think I know where I live."

On Deck 7, she stood before a pair of doors that looked like most of the others she'd seen during her travels. But these were hers. She pressed a button on the panel to the right and the door opened to reveal a set of living quarters. The cat launched itself from her arms into the room and disappeared into the shadows. The girl followed and the door breathed shut behind her.

"Computer, lights," she said. The room lit up and bookshelves, furniture, and personal items emerged from the darkness. They all should have brought her immediate comfort, but everything was unfamiliar and a heavy isolation pressed in around her. She stood there, just beyond the threshold of the door, craning her neck to see everything, almost too scared to go any further.

"This is ridiculous," she said after a few moments. "This is my place."

She dropped her bag and went to the nearest bookshelf. None of the titles on display sparked any memories. On a small shelf farther along were a number of glass turtles, some colored brilliant green with painted eyes of red or blue or yellow. She wondered if she'd made them herself or if they were gifts. In either case, she must like turtles.

She moved her finger along the book spines as she continued along, and toward the end of the bookshelf was a holographic image of her and an older woman with the same thick, dark hair and brown eyes as hers. They were both smiling, standing in front of an ancient building with tall ivory columns. Written along the bottom of the image was "Me and Mom, The Parthenon, Greece 2367."

"Yeah, but who's 'Me'?" she asked.

Behind her, the cat meowed and she turned to see her pacing around a black computer terminal on a small table. Her own personal computer. A computer that might have some answers to who she was. On her way to the table, she stopped at the replicator.

"Computer, one glass of chocolate milk," she said. A moment later, with a twinkling swirl of molecules, the requested beverage materialized. She took a sip of the milk and sighed happily. Delicious as always, she thought, then frowned. As always? Did she have this drink often? And why had she ordered chocolate milk in the first place? Perhaps her memory was doing its best to knock down the barriers that had been erected and the computer might just help punch its way through.

At the desktop terminal, she took another sip of milk then scratched Kitty's ears, as the cat lay sprawled at the bottom of the screen. "Computer, are there personal logs recorded on this terminal?"

"Negative," said the bland voice she'd come to hate. Didn't it realize her memory, her very sense of individuality, was at risk? It could at least *pretend* to be concerned.

"Okay," she said, "how many incoming personal messages do I have?"

"There is one incoming personal message stored on this system."

Only one? Geez, didn't she have any friends?

"Well, play it already."

Mom came onto the screen a moment later, her hair held back with a blue and white bandana. The stardate in the corner was 45103.3, not that that meant anything because the computer couldn't give them the current stardate and no one remembered what it was. As the woman began to speak, the girl felt a natural kinship with her.

"Hi, Kristin, it's Mom," the woman said, and at once the girl felt a rush of victory pass through her. *Kristin.* She loved it! "I was so happy to hear about your promotion and I want you to know we're both very, very proud of you. Your father thinks that next time they should just make you captain to save some time." Kristin smiled. Mom had a sense of humor. Maybe she did too. "Anyway, I know you're busy with all your new duties and whatnot, so I won't keep you. Just know that you're always in our thoughts and we love you very much. Bye."

The recording ended and the screen went blank, save for a blue and white emblem in the center that meant nothing to her. Kristin switched the screen off and regarded her reflection again. At least she knew more about herself than she had a few minutes ago. Her name was Kristin and she'd recently been promoted. To what position and rank, she had yet to determine. She doubted the answer would be available for some time.

Kristin wandered about her room some more, but nothing else sparked any memories. She saw nothing to suggest she lived with anyone. Personal items around the room were few enough to suggest they belonged to her. There was a single hairbrush and comb next to the sink along with a damp toothbrush. She took the band out of her hair and ran her fingers through the mass of curls. Her eyes strayed to the side of the mirror reflecting the empty room behind her.

It was so quiet. The image of her mother had made her long for company. She needed to see someone.

She ran her fingers through her hair again, trying to get the curls to stay in place. "This is hopeless," she said. She tried to run a comb through the mass of curls but it got tangled in the snarls and Kristin slapped it down on the counter.

There had to be a hairdresser on this ship. Every community had one, and the *Enterprise* was a community of sorts. Besides, what better place was there to find people to talk to? Beauty shops were always full of women just dying to spread some juicy gossip.

She asked the computer where the hair salon was and it told her . . . sort of. The place in question was a barbershop. She hoped this barber knew something about styling a woman's hair and she hoped there would be people there to talk to.

Kristin paused in the doorway and called the cat, which sprang out the door from nowhere, it seemed.

She had gone just a few steps before she heard voices in the corridor ahead. She tensed, knowing she wasn't supposed to be out of her quarters, much less wandering the hallways looking for a barbershop. Kristin ducked into a niche between two Jefferies tube

129

hatches, flattened herself against the wall, and hoped they wouldn't hear the thumping of her heart.

She almost screamed when something brushed against her hand. She looked down and there, crouched beside her, also hiding from the voices, was a little boy, his dark face glistening with tears. He looked up at her and swiped at his face with the back of his hand. His forehead was studded with ridges and dark brown hair hung straight and long on either side of his head.

Kristin grasped his hand, then put a finger to her lips. He nodded and they listened as the voices receded down the corridor. Kristin peeked around the corner and saw that they—whoever *they* had been—were gone. She knelt beside the boy.

"Hello there," she said with a smile. "Are you okay?"

The boy sniffled and shrugged his shoulders. "Are you my mother?"

Kristin's heart broke. The poor little guy was lost. They went into the corridor where it was brighter and she gave him a look. With those heavy ridges on his forehead he didn't look like a kid she might have produced, but there was something human about those eyes, and the frightened waver of his chin reminded her of her own scared reflection in the mirror. She could have passed that down to him.

"I'm not sure," she said. "But why don't you stick with me for now. Me and Kitty are going on an adventure. Doesn't that sound like fun?"

"I guess," the boy said. "But I must find my mother."

"Okay, then that'll be our first priority. But we aren't going to find her standing here in the corridor." Kristin took the boy's hand, and as they walked Kitty scampered ahead of them as though scouting for the safest route.

As it turned out, no one was in the barbershop. Three big chairs sat empty before a giant mirror on one of the walls. Assorted cutting and styling tools were lying about on countertops and trays, including scissors, combs, brushes, and bottles of water with spray nozzles. On one of the mirrors, a brief message was attached: "Sorry, gone to Ten-Forward." Kristin sighed.

"Computer, where is Ten-Forward?" she asked.

"Deck Ten, forward."

Kristin rolled her eyes. "Duh. Well," she said, and looked at the boy, "I guess we're going to Ten-Forward."

"Maybe my mother will be there," the boy said.

The kid had a one-track mind, that was for sure.

"You never know," Kristin said.

They hadn't taken more than a few steps when they heard the voices in the corridor again. Not again, she thought. But then she glanced at the boy and knew she had to confront the owners of the voices. There was more than just herself to worry about this time. She grasped the boy's hand a little tighter and stepped around the corner.

"Excuse me."

Their voices stopped midsentence and a man and a woman turned toward her. Like her, they both wore red uniforms with black shoulders. The man had a trimmed beard and was just starting to smile at her when the woman spoke up.

"What are you doing out here?" she demanded with a bite to her voice. The woman had a series of little creases on the bridge of her nose, as if she were frowning. "Didn't you hear the announcement to stay where you were?"

Kristin didn't like the woman right away. There was no reason she had to be so harsh.

"Yes, I heard it," Kristin said, "but I—I—"

"Yes. You what?" the woman asked.

Kristin grit her teeth together. The woman's bad attitude had managed to make her feel guilty about being here, but she knew she was justified in what she'd done. Sure, she'd disobeyed the order, but it wasn't like the ship was going to fall apart around them because of it.

"I found myself in a very precarious spot when all this happened and had to go search for some clothes," Kristin said. She noticed one of the man's eyebrows lift just a bit and her face flushed a little. "Along the way I ran across this little guy."

The woman looked her up and down as if she suspected Kristin was the cause of all this trouble. She didn't even seem to notice the boy. She scowled, making the creases on her nose more pronounced.

"Well, it looks like you've found your clothes to me," she said. "Where do you think you're going now?"

As if on cue the boy stepped forward, tugged at the bottom of his tunic, and threw his shoulders back.

"We're looking for my mother," he said. "Have you seen her?"

The man's grin was too big to hide, and Kristin could see his dimples even through his beard. "We've been checking on everyone all day and I don't think I've seen your mother," he said as he ran a hand through his dark hair. "But I have seen a man on the bridge who looks an awful lot like you. Maybe he's your father."

"You must take me to him," the boy said as if there were no other alternative.

The woman looked at the bearded man with an expression of frustration. "What, does he think he's the captain now? Look, kid, I'm afraid your father's busy right now. He doesn't have time to—"

"Hey," Kristin said, anger bubbling into her voice. "Busy or not, don't you think he'd like to know he has a son and that he's all right?"

The hot-tempered woman opened her mouth, but the man put his hand on her shoulder. She glared at him as he knelt down before the boy.

"Your father *is* pretty busy," the man said in a gentle voice. "He's trying hard to figure out what happened and to get everyone's memory back. If we brought you to him right now he'd be distracted and wouldn't be able to concentrate on his job. You wouldn't want that, would you?"

"I guess not," the boy said after a moment's thought.

"Good," the man said. "Then how about this? There are a lot of people in Ten-Forward who are feeling a little lost just like you are. Why don't you go there with your friend, maybe have a bite to eat, and when we get to the bridge, we'll tell your father about you. That way, he'll know you're okay and he'll still be able to figure out what the heck is going on."

The boy seemed to consider this for a moment. "But . . . but I . . ."

"No buts, kid," the woman said, breaking her silence. "Now, do what the nice man said, and—"

132

"Don't interrupt me!"

The violence that blasted from the boy's little mouth startled the woman and she took a step back. The man seemed amused by the woman's reaction, but he put a gentle hand on the boy's shoulders, brushing against Kristin's fingers as he did so. She couldn't help but admire him. This was someone she was sure she wanted to get to know. Heck, it was someone she might already know.

"She's rude, isn't she?" the bearded man said, low enough to seem like a whisper, but loud enough for everyone to hear.

"Yes, she is," the boy said, and glared at the woman, who just stood with her arms folded across her chest.

"Do you remember the message that came over the intercom telling everyone to stay where they were?" the man asked.

The boy bobbed his head and set his mouth into a firm line. "Well, that was the man I think is your father. You'd want to do what he told you to, wouldn't you?"

Again, a curt nod indicated he would.

"Well, I don't want to have to tell him that his son is one of the only people on the ship who didn't obey his order. You want to make a good first impression, don't you?"

"Yes," the boy said.

"So, what are you going to do?"

"I'll go to Ten-Forward with the lady and I'll wait until everything is back to normal, and then my father will come for me."

"Excellent idea," the man said. He gave two short tugs on the boy's hair, then stood up and nodded at Kristin. "Carry on. Ten-Forward is around the corner and down a bit."

Kristin smiled. "Thank you."

The bearded man returned the smile, and then turned away with the woman. Kristin realized that these two were in the loop and would know more than she what was going on. It couldn't hurt to get an update.

"Uh, sir?"

The man turned back, but the woman sighed loud enough for Kristin to hear.

"Has there been any headway? Does anyone know who they are yet?"

133

He nodded and cut off the woman's protest before she could voice it. "Only command-level personnel have been identified. You'll find pictures and titles posted in Ten-Forward."

She nodded and watched as they walked away. It was obvious they were friends and Kristin longed for something similar. Not remembering her own friends was almost as bad as not remembering herself. She needed someone to talk to about what was happening, preferably someone her own age. The boy and the cat were nice to have around, but they weren't the best conversationalists.

Kristin felt a tug on her hand and she looked down at the boy. "Are we going to go?" he asked. "My father says we shouldn't be in the hallway." There was pride in his voice. He, at least, had found his father.

The doors to Ten-Forward whooshed open to a cacophony of chatter. Almost every table was filled with people. They stood in the aisles, lined the bar, and crowded around the windows. But no one looked familiar. It was a room full of strangers, and Kristin felt lonelier than ever.

She pushed their way to a vacant table in the back of the room near one of the large windows that looked out into space. A game board sat on the table, wet napkins and sticky glass rings on either side. Round black and red disks were scattered over the board and a few had rolled onto the floor.

Checkers! She remembered them, and something about an older gentleman tickled the back of her brain. Was it her grandfather or an uncle maybe? She couldn't quite put her finger on it.

"How about a game of checkers?" she asked the boy as he slid into a chair.

He looked at the board and raised an eyebrow. "I don't think checkers is something I would do."

Kristin grinned. What a cutie. "You don't *do* checkers. You play them. Why don't you stack the red ones on this side and the black ones over here." She set one next to his elbow. "I'll get something from the replicators."

"*Gagh,* please." He held a checker and peered at it, trying to decipher the impressions stamped on either side.

"Excuse me?" She must have heard wrong. Had he just told her to gag?

He dragged his eyes up to hers. *"Gagh."*

Must be some sort of food. "Doesn't sound too appealing. Are you sure?" The boy rolled his eyes and went back to stacking the checkers. Apparently so.

Near the replicator a group of people were gathered around a computer screen that flashed the pictures, names, and ranks of the commanding officers.

"Captain Jean-Luc Picard," the computer said. A picture flashed of a competent-looking gentleman with a close fringe of grayish-white hair.

"Commander Kieran MacDuff." Another picture, this time of a younger man, closer to her own age, with dark brown eyes and thick dark hair that made Kristin wonder if he was her older brother. He was the first officer.

The picture of the bearded man Kristin had spoken to a few minutes earlier appeared on the screen. William T. Riker was his name and he was the executive officer on the ship. In his picture, she caught just a hint of those wonderful dimples hidden under his beard and remembered how gentle he was with her new friend.

The list continued to scroll and she caught site of Dr. Beverly Crusher, who'd fixed her shoulder, and Ensign Ro Laren, the bad-tempered woman who'd been with Riker. There was also a picture of Lieutenant Worf. With his forehead ridges and dark skin, he looked like an older version of her young friend.

She stepped to the replicator and ordered another chocolate milk for herself and a *gagh* for the boy. Her face twisted into a grimace when she saw the dish the replicator put in front of her. A silver bowl filled to overflowing with live, wriggling worms. The coppery scent of fresh blood made her nose crinkle. With worms wriggling out of the bowl and onto the floor of the replicator, how was she supposed to pick it up? She wasn't going near that stuff!

Kristin looked around for a towel to throw over the squirming mess when someone screamed. Like a wave, the people in the room

135

crowded toward the windows and she felt a tiny pulse in the floor that signified a laser blast.

She ran to the window and looked out into the stars. A ship was there, a tiny ship, and it was firing at the *Enterprise.*

The little ship was no match for the colossus *Enterprise,* but still it attacked. She craned her head over the top of the blue man's shoulder just as an orange blast of phaser energy from the *Enterprise* streaked toward the ship and disintegrated it into a fiery ball.

People around her took their breath as if they were one. Shock trembled through her shoulders as murmurs drifted through the crowd.

"What is it?"

"What are we doing?"

"Who were they?"

She searched her brain, but there were no answers there, just empty space. She *hated* this! And then she remembered the boy. She had to get to him. He must be frightened out of his mind. She cut her way through the throng to the table where she'd left him, but it was empty. Where did he go? She scanned the crowd at the windows but didn't see him.

"Hello? Little boy?" That sounded ridiculous. If they didn't find out who they were soon, she'd have to give him a name. She couldn't continue calling him "little boy," after all. And *Gagh* wouldn't do either.

And then she spotted him crouched under the table, pressing the cat to his chest. His brown eyes were wide and unblinking. She held her hand out to him.

"You can come out now," she said. "It's safe."

Uncertainty clouded his eyes. "How do you know?"

She thought about that. She didn't know, not really. They might be in the middle of a war zone for all she knew. They might be hit with torpedoes any moment. When it came right down to it, she didn't know very much, so she decided to be honest with him.

"I guess I don't," she said. "I don't know if we're safe, but I saw a picture of your father and he looks like a big strong man. I'm sure he's doing everything he can to protect all of us. Would you like to see a picture of him?"

He shrugged his shoulders and Kristin started to worry. It wasn't like him to not care about his father.

"Tell you what—I'm tired of being with all these people. They just make me nervous. How about if we go back to my room and I show you my turtle collection?"

Just then a voice came over the intercom and the din of chatter fell silent.

"To all hands, this is Captain Picard. I'm sure most of you have seen the small skirmish that has just occurred. We have gained access to computer files that tell us we are at war with a race called the Lysians and it was one of their scout ships that engaged us. It is believed that they have a new weapon that is responsible for our shipwide amnesia. Be assured that Dr. Crusher and her staff are doing everything they can to fix the problem. In the meantime we are following the Starfleet orders we have found in the computer. There may be other altercations, but rest assured, you and your families are safe. We will keep you apprised of the situation. Picard out."

Somewhere in the middle of the announcement the boy had launched himself into her arms. They sat together on the floor gathering what little comfort they could from each other's grasp.

"Was that my father?" he asked.

"No, that was the captain. But your dad is up there helping him out. Don't worry."

He rested his head against her chest and she stroked the silky hair on his head. "It'll be okay. You're safe," she whispered, and hoped she was speaking the truth.

Several hours later, Kristin watched through the two windows in her quarters as the *Enterprise* approached the huge Lysian station. Her heart raced. The station was so big that if the Lysians decided to attack, the *Enterprise* might not survive. But somehow, the more she gazed at it, the calmer she became.

The station had a saucer section that glowed a serene blue and two large armatures that reached out as if to embrace them. It sure didn't look like someone the Federation would be in a war with, but looks could be deceiving. In any case, it wasn't her problem. Her job was to keep the boy occupied until it was all over, one way or another.

Coloring books and some broken crayons lay scattered on the floor. The few pictures he'd completed were simple stick figures, most wielding a phaser or a sword he called a *bat'leth*. She'd replicated another checkers game, but he seemed more interested in rolling the red and black disks across the floor and watching the cat chase after them.

She had her head stuck in the closet going through a few boxes she found tucked into its dark recesses. They all had her name on them and inside she found some old pictures she had drawn in grade school. They weren't much better than the boy's. She pulled out piles of old clothing and found at the bottom a small, fuzzy blue blanket. She pressed its warmth against her cheek. It smelled faintly of powder and something else.

She closed her eyes. There—if she concentrated hard, she could see the man she remembered from the checkers game earlier. His hair was a shock of white and there was a child curled up in his broad arms, with that blanket tucked around its legs. It must be her, and the man was her father. He was reading to her and although she didn't understand much of the story, she could have sat there all day wrapped in his arms, just listening to his deep voice and feeling the rumble in his chest.

She wished he were here now. Maybe he could tell her more about herself, that everything *would* be okay. What she wouldn't give to feel the comfort of a parent or even just a familiar face right about now.

"Attention all personnel."

Kristin's eyes snapped open as Picard's voice came from the speaker box next to the computer terminal. The boy turned his head to look at it, and even the cat stopped what she was doing.

"We have regained control of our computer systems," Picard said. "You will each be called to sickbay for treatment to restore your memories." He paused for a moment. "It seems we never were at war with the Lysians after all. We are a peaceful ship on a mission of exploration and discovery. This will all become clear once your memories have been restored. Picard out."

She grabbed the cat and the boy's hand.

"I told you we would be safe. Come on. Let's go find ourselves."

The door swished open and Kristin gaped at the man who stood before her. Lieutenant Worf was the tallest, broadest man she could ever remember seeing. He wore a yellow-gold uniform and a heavy-looking metallic sash over his right shoulder.

"Father!" the boy cried, and flung himself at Worf.

"Alexander," Worf said. He pried the boy from his legs and held him at arm's distance. "Klingons do not hug in public."

"I'm sorry, Father." Hugs aside, it was clear to Kristin how excited Alexander was. His normally grim lips were spread apart in a grin and his eyes were at their widest.

"Father, this is Kristin," Alexander said, and waved an arm at her. "She took care of me while you were busy protecting the ship."

"Thank you," Worf said. It seemed he was a man of few words and while his words seemed abrupt, Kristin sensed the Klingon's gratitude. But now that father and son were reunited, Kristin felt awkward standing there holding just the cat and her duffel bag in the middle of the corridor.

"You're welcome, sir," she said. "It was the least I could do. If nothing else, I think I made a new friend." She ruffled Alexander's hair a little.

She looked at Worf, hoping to see an encouraging smile, but it seemed Klingons did not smile in public either—a lesson Alexander had yet to learn, she thought with amusement.

"Well, if that's all, I'll just be heading back to my quarters."

She turned to leave, but then Alexander called her name and wrapped his arms around her waist.

"Alexander," Worf said, as though to admonish the boy, but it didn't stop him.

"Come and visit me, Kristin, please?"

She brushed her fingers through his hair and nodded her head. "I will, sweetie, I will," she said. "Just as soon as I'm settled."

Alexander detached himself from Kristin, then looked up and up to his father. "Can Kristin come to dinner tomorrow?"

Worf pressed his lips together and scowled, an expression that made his forehead ridges even deeper. "Alexander, you are being presumptuous. She could already have plans."

Kristin thought of her nearly empty room and the half-unpacked boxes stacked in her closet. The treatment had restored her memory, but her real life didn't thrill her. She was new to the *Enterprise* and had not made any friends yet. She'd always been shy, so instead of searching for friends, she sought solace in the Cliffs of Heaven program too many times. But after today, she realized she was tired of being alone. Dinner with some new friends sounded wonderful.

"Actually, I don't have any plans," she said, then looked at Alexander. "And we never did have that *gagh.*" Alexander's face bunched up into a grimace. "I thought you liked *gagh,*" she said. "You looked pretty eager to have some in Ten-Forward before."

Alexander shrugged. "I had amnesia."

Kristin laughed, then stifled it with a hand to her mouth. She looked at the Klingon security officer's scowl. She thought she heard a sigh escape his closed lips.

"Sorry, sir," Kristin said.

Worf shifted on his feet and looked more uncomfortable than Kristin felt. "It is all right. And we would be . . . pleased to have you to dinner tomorrow evening."

Kristin smiled. She loved a challenge and breaking through that rough exterior of Worf's might prove to be a lot of fun. "It's a date then," she said, then waved at the two Klingons as the door to their quarters hissed shut. She couldn't be sure, but Worf's face seemed to lose some of its color at her last words.

Alone in the corridor with the cat, Kristin set off to make one last stop.

"Spot!"

For an android who had no emotions, Lieutenant Commander Data seemed pretty happy to have his cat back. Spot—an odd name for this particular cat—leapt out of her arms and into those of the pale-faced man. The cat licked his nose, while Data inspected every inch of her, even under her tail.

"You have taken very good care of her," Data said.

"Well, she's a pretty low-maintenance cat," Kristin said. "But she kept Alexander and me company for most of the day."

Spot jumped from his arms and scooted over to her bowl on the floor.

"She seems glad to be home," Kristin said. He looked at the cat and nodded. "I'm Kristin, by the way. I apologize if anything's out of place, but . . ."

"You were here while I was out," Data said.

Her mouth fell open. "How did you know?"

"Your quantum signature is still present in the room," the android said. "Although it is faint, my internal sensors were able to detect it and I matched it with your bio-signature."

Kristin smiled in wonder. One of the reasons she had wanted a post aboard the *Enterprise* was so she might have the chance to meet Data, but she never expected it would happen like this.

She pulled his cloak from her duffel bag and held it out to him. "I borrowed this earlier. Again I apologize, but I didn't have any—uh, *many*—clothes at the time and I was cold and it was just hanging there not doing anybody any good, so I . . . well, I just . . ."

As Data looked at her with his curious yellow eyes, Kristin took a deep breath and started over. "I'm a Sherlock Holmes fan too. My father used to read the books to me when I was a little girl."

Data's eyebrows rose a bit. "I have many holodeck programs based on the Arthur Conan Doyle mysteries. Would you care to try one with me?"

"You mean now?" Kristin asked, stunned by the invitation. *"Right* now?"

Data nodded once. "If it is convenient."

"Well, I . . . but what about your cat?" Now Spot was drinking from the water dish.

"Spot is used to being alone," Data said. "She will be fine."

"In that case I'd love to," Kristin said with a grin.

Data grabbed the tweed cap from the rack and placed it on his head. When Kristin offered him the crook of her arm, he looked at her with a quizzical expression, then accepted like a gentleman. She supposed Data didn't have many opportunities to walk arm in arm with a girl.

As they walked to the holodeck together she could just imagine how she was going to start her first personal log.

"Personal log: Stardate 45494.8. Today I made a friend—no, correction: I made *several* friends."

The Monkey Puzzle Box

Kevin Killiany

I woke up with a mouthful of used armpits. Some guy I couldn't see was methodically swinging a cinder block against my skull, bouncing it off my curbstone pillow with every blow.

Good thing the rat with the apple core was a vegetarian. I was in no shape to put up a fight. He shifted position suspiciously when I managed to move my arm, warning me off his feast with a gimlet glare.

"Keep it," I said. Meant to say. What I said was "Key fit." If those were my dying words, they'd make a helluva clue. Cops'd be jiggling every lock I was ever seen with. I made a mental note to grimace later.

It took half a lifetime to crawl from the curb to the brownstone. Ever notice there's never a cop around to drag you across the sidewalk when you need one? Or a hooker. Or a bum, for that matter. Even my rat had left me.

Propped against the stoop, I took inventory. My gun was holstered, the model-1911-sized bruise in my ribs telling me it had broken my fall. My wallet still had fourteen dollars, an expired library card belonging to "Hill, Dixon," and assorted licenses and business cards. Even my aluminum Timex was there to tell me it was about two hours till dawn. I couldn't be sure my pocket change wasn't light a dime or two, but on the whole I felt pretty confident in ruling out robbery.

Which left the question, why had I been slugged?

If it was a warning, it was a botch. What good is a warning if the warner doesn't tell the warnee what the warning is about? And if it had been a hit, I wouldn't be having this fascinating conversation with myself. I'd be dead with a small-caliber bullet in the base of my brain.

Speaking of which . . .

A bit of cautious poking told me I didn't have a mark on me. Which made sense when you considered the hangover—and with my vision going red with every heartbeat, I had no choice but to consider my hangover. I hadn't been slugged, I'd been drugged.

The question was, when could anyone have slipped me a mickey? I hadn't had anything to eat or drink since dinner, about ten hours ago. I was so looped I thought about bushmen with blow-guns. Even took two minutes to prove to myself there were no poison darts lodged in my flesh. The only gases I knew about either killed you or burned your lungs out or both, but they were always dreaming up new things at the War Department. Still, you'd need a lot of it to knock a man down on an open street, and I would have remembered a fog bank rolling in. No, had to be a mickey, I just couldn't remember how they did it.

By now my mind was clearing and the sky was turning gray. Still no signs of life on the street, but dawn was coming. No point in going home. I pulled myself to my feet with the stoop railing and headed for my office. Or at least in the direction I was fairly sure would lead to my office. I made a mental note to thank the city planners for putting all the buildings next to the sidewalk for a guy to hold on to.

Two hours, three gargles, and a sink bath later I felt almost human. Except for the curb scrape under my eye and the gun bruise under my A-shirt I looked like I hadn't spent the night in the gutter. My second suit had managed not to become wadded up in my office closet and Madeline had made sure the laundry listened when she told them no starch on my spare shirts.

144

Hard to look like a tough guy with diaper rash crawling up your neck.

Madeline came in while I was deciding not to shave.

"So now you're cool enough to leave them waiting in the lobby while you pretty up?"

"What's that supposed to mean?"

"The dame you got stashed in the waiting room. I thought she was a client until I saw you in here prettying yourself up."

"She must have come in while I was washing up. What does she look like?"

"Like a real lady, if you spell that m-o-n-e-y. Worried, but not real excited."

"Make me some java," I said, changing my mind about the shave. "I want to be alert enough to enjoy this hangover."

"Rough night?"

"Somebody slipped me a mickey." I filled her in on the morning's festivities and my theories—or lack thereof—as to how they'd come about while she measured ground coffee and water into the pot on the hotplate.

"You're getting old, Dix."

"Just let me drink my coffee and tell the new client I'll be with her in ten minutes."

I knew she was trouble when Madeline showed her in, which is one of the reasons I kept looking. Sure, she was drop-dead gorgeous, but it was more than that.

Madeline had it only half right when she said this dame had money. She had three or four generations of money. Privilege flowed from her fingertips. I've seen women proud to wear fur coats that cost less than her suit set, and her clutch purse was made of a leather I couldn't guess at.

Someone with that much class and power coming to a two-bit gumshoe like me to clean up her mess? Gotta be looking for a cleaning rag she won't mind throwing away.

I bet myself she'd say her name was Smith.

We went through the usual pleasantries, the nonsense noises we all make while we size each other up. She was not Smith, or any other last name, just Minuet, which sounded more like a lounge singer than an heiress. She didn't smoke or drink coffee, but she did sit. I got her situated in the good leather chair, angled so the morning sun caught red and copper highlights in her hair, and settled myself behind the desk. No propped foot, going for the businesslike approach.

"What can I do for you?" I asked, businesslike.

"Would you do me a favor first?" she asked back.

"That would depend on the favor," I said, playing it cagey, ready for anything.

"Look at your watch and tell me when a minute has gone by."

Okay, so I wasn't ready for that.

"What's the gimmick?"

"No gimmick. I just want to compare your clock with mine."

She pulled a gold watch the size of a hockey puck on a man's fob out of her clutch. She popped the cover open, then regarded me, one eyebrow arched.

I checked my window, locked, and the door, shut with the reassuring staccato of Madeline's typing beyond, then looked back at her. A little smile was playing around her lips.

"Humor me?"

I sighed and looked at the Timex on my wrist.

"Starting now," I said, as though I did this with all my clients. I stole one look at her, but she was studying her gold watch intently. So I studied my tin one like it was going to do something unusual.

"Mark," I said.

"You're much faster than I thought." Her voice had, what? Relief? She gave me a thousand-watt smile. "You might just make it."

"Huh?" I quipped cleverly.

She ignored me, making a production of returning the gold watch to her clutch.

"I'm not sure where to begin," she began.

I sat back and let her gather her thoughts, which was not only polite, but gave me a chance to admire the great packaging job Mother Nature had done. Oh, sure, she had helped; nowadays a girl didn't come by that innocent blush naturally. But even her perfectly applied eyeliner could not have given her tawny eyes that provocative tilt.

"What do you know about the situation in eastern Europe?" she asked, apropos of nothing I was thinking about.

I was about to say not a thing, when I remembered reading about it in the newspaper yesterday. That by itself stopped me, because I didn't remember having enough time to sit and read anything but the sports and police blotter yesterday. My yesterday was turning into a mystery all by itself, but it was going to have to wait. I'm not a paying client and the lady sitting across from me would soon be.

"Um," I said, filling in time while I thought of something clever to say to cover me thinking.

"The Romulan Empire is pushing the United Federation pretty hard," I said at last, hoping she didn't ask me exactly where in eastern Europe these places were. I remembered seeing a map, but I really hadn't been that interested. "Something to do with disputed territory."

"Good," she said, and I felt like I'd earned a gold star from Miss Gramble, my second-grade teacher. If I ever find Miss Gramble again, I'm going to make good on my promise to marry her when I grew up.

"Which side do you favor?" she asked as though she expected me to care about eastern Europe.

"The papers like the Federation," I didn't exactly answer. When she relaxed slightly, I took a guess. "They seem like pretty decent folk."

"I think they are some of our staunchest allies."

I waved her sudden patriotic fervor aside. The trouble with drinking coffee on a hangover is it makes you feel alert when you can't think straight.

"What is it you want me to do?" I asked; variation on an earlier theme.

"You may need this," she said, which was not an answer to my question. She set an intricately carved wooden box on my desk.

I picked it up and turned it over in my hands. It looked like a coffee-table cigarette box, big enough to hold a pack and a half of smokes. It was a red wood I didn't recognize inlaid with a black I was pretty sure was ebony and fit together the way only honestly expensive trinkets are. Real craftsmanship. The carvings were monkeys, dozens of them in interlocking patterns. Some of them seemed to move when I pressed, which tipped me to how the concealed latch worked.

Spending ten minutes trying to open a puzzle box can only make you look foolish, so I knocked off nine minutes and forty-eight seconds early and looked back at my potential client.

"What would I need with a monkey puzzle box?" I asked.

"Chinese puzzle box?"

"Chinese, Latvian, Irish," I answered, wondering who she knew called the Chinese monkeys. "It's a puzzle box covered with monkeys."

"Monkeys?" She peered at it like she'd never seen it before. "How clever. And you can't open it?"

"Not at the moment," I hedged. Puzzle boxes weren't my long suit, but if she was offering a paying job I'd give it a shot.

"Then don't try," she said, shooting down that theory. "Keep it. I'm going to need you to deliver it to someone."

"Who?"

"The person I need you to find."

"Who is . . . ?"

"His name is Data, though I'm not sure what name he's using now. I don't know where he is exactly," she said, which figured. If she knew she wouldn't need me. "But you'll know him when you see him. He's yellow."

Which meant either the guy was a coward or she was a closet racist. Since this was the second slip, I was leaning toward the latter, which was a shame. When something looks that good on the outside you want it to be good all the way through.

"He is not Asian," she said as though she were reading my mind. "His skin, even his eyes, are really yellow."

"Like jaundice?"

"Like jaundice," she agreed, "only not sick."

I decided to try another tack.

"You don't know exactly where he is," I prompted. "Do you know about?"

She frowned thoughtfully while I admired the two little lines between her eyebrows.

"Someplace where lots of things go in and out."

"He's a doorman?"

"No. Big things." I wouldn't have believed it possible, but she made a helpless gesture. "Important things, valuable things, going in and out of . . . the country?"

My uncle Erno used to do that. Dance all around the word he wanted, one he used every day but forgot. She had the same look, except she wasn't ninety-seven and she had all her teeth.

"Seaport," I supplied. "You're talking about the docks."

"Of course!" I'd never seen anyone that happy about the waterfront. "I wish I could see all of this as you see it."

"Right," I said, thinking I would not have sat here this long if I didn't smell money. Which thought led to multiplying my usual fee by three and saying: "My usual fee . . ."

She thumped a stack of bills big enough to move me two years closer to retirement down on my desk. I sat at attention; I couldn't help myself. That many presidents in one place demands respect.

"Is this sufficient?"

"Yes, ma'am."

It was only after she'd left, while I was just barely fitting the monkey puzzle box into my coat pocket, that it occurred to me to wonder where she'd been carrying the box. Or the stack of money, for that matter. Neither one of them would have fit in her smart little clutch.

Before heading down to the docks I called a smallish import/export company near the south end. I told them who I was and asked if I could come by that afternoon to get a quick tutorial on how the business worked so I could advise a client. I mentioned I'd pass along some of what my client was paying me and Mr. Hernandez was suddenly happy to have me drop by. I wrote his address on a three-by-five card, carefully reversing the address.

Next I called Lieutenant Dan Bell over at police headquarters. He normally works homicide, which this was not, as far as I knew, but it was always a good thing to check out the obvious first. Except he wasn't in. I didn't recognize the switchboard operator's voice, which was unusual, so I kept it very polite and businesslike as I fed her a few more names. She told me each one in turn was either out sick, out on assignment, or in a potentially endless meeting.

"Something's up," I told Madeline, filling her in on the peculiar behavior of our city's finest.

She tried a couple of her contacts with the same results. She didn't recognize the voice answering the phone, either, which was unheard of.

"Something's up," Madeline confirmed.

I spent the next four hours trying to figure out what with no luck.

A visit to headquarters confirmed that all experienced cops were somewhere incommunicado. At every level were wooden-faced rookies who would only spout the company line, no matter what the incentive.

My sources outside the department were all present and accounted for, but they were worse. Not one of them had noticed anything unusual about the boys in blue. I got the feeling most didn't believe what I was telling them. A few said they'd check it out and get back to me, but you could tell their hearts weren't in it.

The only good thing about my morning was my hangover fading away. I was actually able to enjoy, and keep down, a pastrami on rye and a seltzer for lunch before turning my attention back to my paying case.

Interleaving with a cyclic synchronicity subroutine, I caught a cab to the waterfront. Getting out at the north end, I began walking south, referring often to my little white card with the wrong address and peering at everything.

Normally, I would have been one of a thousand guys walking along the waterfront, all on legitimate business. Today I stood out like a bug on a plate. There were only about a dozen fellows like me wandering about, all of them looking as lost as I was pretending to be. On the docks I could see stevedores standing about or sitting on equipment. Nothing and no one was moving anything on or off the ships.

Curiouser still, there were no groups of people standing around discussing the peculiar state of affairs. Try to imagine something like the city docks shut completely down without even four winos around a burning trash can talking about it. Never happen. Except I was walking through it.

After a while I quit pretending to look at my card.

I was about halfway along the docks, just coming up on number forty, when I saw the monkey man. Not a man in a monkey suit, a man with the hair, ears, and hands of a monkey. This one was wearing some sort of naval uniform and walking toward me at a brisk pace. I froze, staring into the middle distance like everyone around me, and he passed me without a glance. Good thing, that without-a-glance part; I don't think I was keeping a straight face.

No sooner was he gone than another one stepped from between piles of crates at the end of Dock 39 and headed into the warehouses across the way. Two more came out and headed away from me. Casually turning my head, I scanned Dock 39. It had various piles of assorted bales and crates along its length, a mobile crane parked by the short-term warehouse about a third of the way out, a two-story shack with outside stairs at midpoint, and a huge shiny silver ship at the very end.

No one else seemed to notice, but as a trained detective I knew right away that a chrome ocean liner dispensing monkey men was something out of the ordinary. This was looking less and less like a simple missing persons case.

As I resumed my southward stroll, I noticed someone else who didn't fit the usual pattern; or he did fit the usual pattern, which meant he didn't fit in at all today.

A portly gent of imposing height in a utilities company coverall was working his way along the warehouses with pen and clipboard in hand, apparently counting overhead lines. The duffel bag hung from his shoulder. If the rat with the apple had asked me this morning if I'd be more surprised to see monkey men in uniforms or Cyrus Redblock in coveralls I'd still be mulling over my answer. The way things were going now, I took it pretty much in stride.

"Cyrus," I said when we converged.

"Indeed."

We stood for a while, me staring out over what water I could see between ships, him counting bricks since he'd run out of wires.

"Care to explain?"

"I am here as your backup," he sighed in a how-the-mighty-have-fallen voice, "should you need assistance in liberating Mr. Data."

"Cyrus Redblock on the side of the angels?"

"I dislike war, sir." He was so angry he forgot to pretend we weren't talking. "It is a waste of resources and of human life."

Normally I would have pointed out that he'd wasted a life or two in his career, but something else he'd said caught my attention.

"Who said anything about war?"

"A very persuasive woman with captivating eyes and an improbable name," he said, going back to his brick counting. "I believe you know her."

"Minuet," I confirmed. No confusing who he'd meant. "It sounds like she told you a lot more than she told me."

"I imagine I required a good deal more convincing."

"Care to fill me in?" I asked when it became clear he was going to leave it at that. "With you being my backup and all, it might be a good idea."

"You are familiar with the situation in the Carpathians?"

"Folks are fractious."

"War is imminent," he corrected.

"Which has got what to do with us on a dock watching monkey men get off a chrome liner?"

"The Romulan Empire could attack the United Federation at any moment." Cyrus glanced to be sure I was listening. "Which would normally guarantee our coming to the rescue of the Federation."

"Unless . . ." I prompted.

"Unless our government believed the United Federation perpetrated an unprovoked attack on us."

"What sort . . ." I stopped myself. How could a small nation attack a larger one? "Sabotage?"

"And mayhem on a massive scale," Redblock confirmed. "The details are unknown. As you may have surmised, we are observing henchmen of the Romulans preparing to commit an atrocity which will be contrived to implicate the Federation."

"How do our lady with the eyes and Mr. Data fit into all this?" I asked.

"Mr. Data is a Federation agent. Miss Minuet is one of us."

I was about to point out that working for Minuet made Cyrus and me G-men when she showed up in the flesh with Felix Leech in tow.

"Boss," said Leech, "I can explain."

"You were to keep her safely away from here."

"I tried, but she kept asking where you were," Leech explained. "Then she kept telling me to bring her here."

"And you lacked the backbone to refuse her?"

"Wouldn't you?"

Felix had him there. None of us could have stood up to a determined Minuet for long, and Cyrus knew it. With a sigh, he nodded.

"Data is there," Minuet said, pointing to the shack halfway down Dock 39. None of us bothered asking her how she knew.

Leech pulled a Thompson submachine gun with a fifty-round drum from his duffel bag. From the way the bag hung I could tell he had two or three more drums in there. Call it two hundred shots to my nineteen, if you counted my spare clip and hideout Airweight snub-nosed thirty-eight. It was enough to make me feel unarmed.

"Subtlety, Mr. Leech, subtlety," said Redblock. His hand was inside his own duffel bag, which hung from his shoulder at an only slightly unnatural angle.

Call it four hundred rounds to my nineteen. I was unarmed. If worse came to worse, I could always hit them with my puzzle box.

"Is there a plan?" I asked Minuet as Felix reconcealed his tommy gun.

"If we can recognize the virus and avoid it," Minuet said, "we could probably simply walk in and get him."

"Virus?"

"Operatives," she amended. "I think of them as a disease. With no specific orders about us, they'll most likely ignore us."

"The monkey men are easy to spot," I said.

"Monkey men?"

"The ones in uniform." I nodded toward two uniformed goons leaving the dock and lockstepping away from us.

"Ah!" she said, squinting after them.

Redblock and I exchanged significant glances.

I found it hard to believe she was one of those vain women who refused to wear eyeglasses. But then again, today was full of things hard to believe.

"I'll lead," I said. "Cyrus, if you'll escort Miss Minuet? Felix, you bring up the rear."

Surprisingly enough, it was as easy as Minuet had said. One tense moment when we met a single goon in the narrow way between the crane and the short-term warehouse. We froze against the warehouse wall like the dazed citizenry around us and he waltzed past us without a glance.

"What's wrong with these people?" Leech asked, waving his hand in front of a fisherman contemplating the sea.

Minuet said something that sounded like "clock speed," and headed for the shack. She would have charged up the outside stairs, but Redblock held her back while Leech and I checked out the bottom floor. Nothing. No guards, no locks; nothing. The whole setup screamed "trap."

Which is why I led the way upstairs.

The door at the top didn't even have a place for a lock. I drew my forty-five and stood to one side on the narrow landing as Redblock unlimbered his Thompson and leveled it at the door. He nodded once and I flipped the door open, leaning back out of his line of fire.

"Data!" cried Minuet, pushing past him and into the room.

I had been right about one thing, the whole setup was a trap, but not for us. The guy with the yellow eyes was bound neck and arms by a stainless steel colonial stock. He had apparently sprung the trap by reaching for a doohickey that looked like a ham radio nut's nightmare. He literally had to have stuck both hands and his head in it to have been caught so thoroughly. My respect for the United Federation's intelligence department's training program took a real beating.

I holstered my gun and fished out my lock kit without a word. Kneeling down, I went to work on the manacles.

Minuet was fussing over Data, calling his name. He had apparently been here awhile, but he managed to rouse himself. He squinted at her for a long moment, as if trying to place her, before he spoke.

"You are . . ." For a guy standing in a stainless-steel stock, his voice was remarkably calm.

"A Bynar emergency defense program," Minuet replied, obviously using some sort of G-man spy code. "Last-ditch variety."

"I did not know you existed."

"I was kept unindexed for situations of this sort."

"I see." Data watched me work on the lock holding his left arm for a moment. "And this is?"

"Private Investigator Dixon Hill and assorted associates," Minuet introduced. "Security protocols have been corrupted and I had to improvise."

"Intriguing. Their perception must be unique."

"More than you can imagine." Minuet patted my shoulder as though I were a prize bluetick. "Dixon here detected the Romulans are using Chirkniz technology."

It took me a moment to realize she had not said "Chinese." Maybe she had never said "Chinese." My hangover must have muffled my ears back at the office.

The first lock gave and I moved on to the second.

"How so?"

"They are a simianoid people," she said, "and he keeps seeing monkeys."

"Ah." Data leaned his head aside to give me better access to the throat lock. "That explains much."

The two of them went on for a few minutes about subroutines and interfaces. She had apparently snagged a gizmo called a backdoor global delete, something she thought Data would find very useful. The trick was keeping it hidden while getting it in position. I tuned them out while working on the locks. Redblock and Leech were doing the same, watching the docks through the tiny windows. I tuned back in when they got around to their next move. They were planning to hit some military installation to head off the saboteurs.

"Hold it."

They both jumped like they'd forgotten I was there.

"These aren't soldiers," I said, probing the third lock carefully as I spoke. "They aren't going for any military targets, they're going to hit the utilities."

"Utilities?" Minuet wasn't buying it.

"I suggest you heed Mr. Hill's advice," Redblock said from his post by the windows. "His most irritating characteristic is his uncanny ability to leap to the correct conclusion with only the most fragmentary of evidence."

"I have commented on that fact to my captain," Data said, though I hadn't heard him say any such thing, or seen his captain, in the five minutes we'd known each other. "Do you comprehend what he means by utilities?"

Minuet's light went on. "Of course!"

"We had better hurry, we only have point six seconds to intervene."

With perfect timing, the last lock popped open.

"Gentlemen and madam," Cyrus announced. "We have company."

A quick glance confirmed that swarming out of the chrome ocean liner was a mob of monkey men.

We were down the stairs in seconds, dashing for shore. It took us about four steps to figure out we weren't going to make it. Monkeys run a lot faster than either dames or middle-aged guys. They were going to catch us before we made the end of the dock.

"Cyrus, gimme your gun," Leech suddenly said, pulling up by a pile of crates.

"What?"

"Gimme your gun," Leech repeated, fishing the spare ammo drums out of his duffel bag and setting them in easy reach. "They gotta squeeze between the crane and the warehouse here."

We looked around and saw he was right. Between the crane tower and the blank warehouse wall was a gap only about twelve feet wide.

"You have insufficient ammunition to stop them," Data pointed out.

"Don't tell me my job," Leech snapped. "Gimme both tommies and I can hold them long enough for you to make it."

"My friend," Redblock began.

"Shut up, fatso." Leech grabbed Redblock's gun and tucked the butt under his left arm. "Get the hell out of here so this is worth something."

Don't get me wrong, Felix Leech was a cheap gunsel. He cut every corner, cheated every partner, betrayed every trust. He was Redblock's man through greed and fear; there wasn't a loyal bone in his body. He never had a moral instinct or a decent thought in his life. But he squared all that on Dock 39. Last time I saw him he was giving the goons hell with both Thompsons, ankle-deep in brass and covered with glory.

The dash through the warehouses was a hyperventilated blur. Maybe it was the lack of oxygen, maybe it was residual hangover, maybe Madeline's right and I'm getting old. Whatever it was, when we burst into the street I flagged down the first cab I saw. I was holding the door for Minuet before I realized the driver was a monkey.

"Dix!" Redblock yelled just as long arms grabbed me from behind.

I drew my gun, but couldn't get it around to the guy behind me. Data and Minuet both stood for a second like deer in headlights as Redblock started toward me.

With my upper arms pinned, I flipped my gun to him as best I could. Always agile for a fat man, he snagged it neatly out of the air and turned to deal with the cabbie while I went on the offensive.

Slamming my head backward produced a crunching sensation and a satisfying howl from behind. I jammed my heel down on an instep and threw myself forward as the bear hug slacked. Somersaulting awkwardly, I got my Airweight out of its ankle holster and came up braced on one knee. Two thirty-eight-caliber hollowpoints wiped the surprised expression off the goon's face.

My satisfaction lasted until I realized there had been three goons and Cyrus Redblock was dead.

Data killed the monkey man who got Redblock before I got my snub-nosed revolver back up. One jab. The goon's head bounced off the warehouse wall while the body it left behind dropped like a felled tree. United Federation agents may not be much on brains, but they're hell in a fight.

I snatched my forty-five from Redblock's still-warm grasp and slid behind the wheel of the cab. As we pulled off, I thought that maybe I should have at least turned his head around the right way again, but it was too late.

I didn't remember ever being to Central Utilities before, but I knew the way. Everyone knew the way. Everything came from Central Utilities. Electricity, gas, water, telephone all went through one distribution complex. Part of my brain said there was something wrong with that model, but I ignored it. Things were weird enough without my starting to doubt my own memories.

"What are we doing now?" Minuet asked.

"I believe we are in a motor vehicle," Data answered. "Moving toward the operations CPU."

"You're doing it again," I said.

"Doing what?"

"Talking like you're blind or something."

"We do not perceive our surroundings as you do, though I seem to interface more readily than Minuet," Data said. I could tell by his voice he thought he was explaining something sensibly. He seemed to have no idea how crazy he sounded. "Am I correct in observing there is no other traffic?"

Damn. How did I miss that? This was worse than no cops, this was no other people at all. I said as much.

"There were no cops earlier?" Data asked.

I gave him the short version of my day at police headquarters and he nodded sagely as though this made terrific sense and explained something to Minuet about worms and search parameters. Apparently everything remotely related to security had been taken off line.

"Dix," Minuet asked suddenly, "did anything happen to you this morning? A fainting spell or a seizure?"

Two sentences covered my mickey and hangover experience, by which time we were in sight of the Central Utilities plant.

"What now?" I asked.

"Now," said Minuet, "you give the puzzle box to Data, then help him get as close to the CPU as possible so he can open it."

"That's it?"

"That's all it takes."

"Fine by me." I fished the monkey puzzle box out of my coat pocket and handed it to Data. He didn't take it.

"We have a problem," Data said. "I cannot perceive the box."

"What?" we both asked.

"I lack Chirkniz protocols," Data said in his nonsense-explaining voice. "I can detect the presence of the packet, but I cannot read it or manipulate it."

Minuet cursed fluently.

"Plan B," she said at last. "Data, you assist Dix in getting as close to the CPU as possible and, Dix, you open the box."

"Why me?"

"Because you can," she avowed with a missionary's intensity. "Within set parameters, you adapt to meet any demand. I'm not designed to be that flexible. Data is, but he can't see the box."

There was really nothing to say to that. Mostly because I didn't understand a word she said. I slid my forty-five over to Data and got out of the car. As he joined me, Minuet got behind the wheel of the cab.

"Where are you going?" I asked.

"To create a diversion." She grinned. "This is a pretty solid little utilities macro. It should create havoc when it runs through internal sensors."

I began to give serious thought to the theory that everyone was crazy.

"So do we hoof it from here?" I asked, eyeing the mile or three of rough terrain between us and Central Utilities.

"There is not enough time," Data said. He pointed to a black cloud rising out of the utilities complex. "The destruction has already begun."

"Shouldn't we be looking for cover?"

He shook his head.

"The annihilation will be complete."

A regular ray of sunshine, this guy.

"There is, however," he added, "a Plan C which Minuet did not consider."

"And that would be?"

"I could interface fully with your program," he nonsense-explained. "Our combined capabilities should initiate the packet and purge the system."

"Right," I said, as though I had a clue. "What do you want me to do?"

"Hold the monkey puzzle box directly in front of you with both hands," he illustrated, his empty hands at chest level. "I will put my hands over yours and access the packet through you."

Why not? Nothing else had made sense today. I stuck the box out in front of me and waited.

Data did what looked like a few calisthenics, deep-breathing stuff, to warm up while the black cloud moved slowly closer. When he finally got down to business, he seemed to have trouble seeing my hands with the box. His hands missed mine twice before he finally latched on.

Nothing happened, which was about what I had expected.

We held that pose, him frowning at his hands holding my hands as if willing them to do something while I focused on the black cloud, willing it to not do anything, until I felt completely ridiculous.

"Look . . ." I began, but never finished.

The box in my hands went white hot and ice cold at the same time. I would have dropped the thing, but Data's hands wouldn't let me. I was opening my mouth to protest when everything went white.

I woke up flat on my back inside a strange room with lighted ceilings. A bald guy with a beak and a black man wearing silver goggles were peering down at me.

"I don't know what you did, Data," the black guy said, "but it worked. All systems are virus-free and on line."

"Good work, Mr. Data," said eagle face. "How do you feel?"

"Data's the other guy," I grated for the record. "My name is Hill, Dixon Hill. And I feel like hell."

The black guy's jaw dropped, but the eagle seemed to take it in stride.

"Of course, Mr. Hill, a momentary confusion." He cocked an eyebrow at his partner. "Better get those records straightened out, Doctor, before this goes much further."

"What? Oh, right." He left, shaking his head.

"You're in a hospital, Mr. Hill," the eagle explained with a diplomatic smile which pegged him as an administrator. "Why don't you just relax while Dr. La Forge straightens out your records. I assure you we'll do everything we can to get you back where you belong as quickly as possible."

"Right," I said, all gullibility and confidence.

The eagle smiled wanly and patted my shoulder.

I woke up flat on my back on my leather couch as Madeline let herself into my office.

"Rough night?" she asked.

"I think someone slipped me a mickey," I said.

Madeline scooped the two-thirds-empty bottle of rye up from the floor by the couch.

"More like you slipped yourself a mickey," she replied.

"I don't suppose," I said, just for the hell of it, "there's a drop-dead gorgeous heiress in the waiting room eager to pay us thousands of dollars?"

Madeline eyed my rye bottle with more respect.

"This must be the good stuff to give you visions like that." She shook her head. "Get cleaned up, I'll make some java. You're going to want to be alert to enjoy that hangover."

The Farewell Gift

Tonya D. Price

There are times I almost wish I never saw their faces, heard their voices, learned their dreams. If I never crossed the path of those Starfleet officers that afternoon those many years ago, my heart wouldn't ache so at their absence. But then, I would never have known their stories, would never have made them my own.

I was fourteen years old the spring afternoon one of the older students rushed into the studio smelling of the fertilizer the farmers were tilling into the spring soil. The heat came early that year and beads of sweat dripped down his face. He panted as if he had run a long distance. "Saryana, Master Kalim says you are to come at once—visitors want to meet you."

My mouth watered and my stomach grumbled at the news but I took time to finish my hand-drawing exercise, pretending not to see the other students' jealous looks.

Alrak rose to his feet, stretched his front paws in front of him, and licked his black lips with his pink tongue. "I hope they are rich visitors."

"Any visitor is likely richer than we are." Two years earlier, before the drought began, a wealthy merchant, seeking an oil painting of his young wife, served meat at his partok. I didn't get my hopes up. With food scarce most visitors brought a single bottle of bitter marya juice with them.

Alrak's long tail beat a soft rhythm against the hem of my skirt. "Didn't I say your inventions would bring you fame? Bring the tube that makes little things appear big."

I picked up the hollow picot branch housing the two ground lenses and ran my fingers along the smooth tube. "I'm having trouble with the focusing."

A flash of insight came to me in a vision and I forgot the partok. In my mind I saw the image of a stand holding the tube suspended above a hole. A gear, attached to a large knob, controlled an arm for raising and lowering the tube past a tilted mirror. With this stand the focus could be maintained for long periods. I wiped the sweat from my forehead. "Wait. I see now what to do." Grabbing my charcoal I made a quick sketch in my notebook beside the preliminary drawings of my farscope.

Alrak cocked his anvil-shaped head to one side. His long pointed ears pitched forward. He kept his bark low in order not to disturb the other students working at their easels. "Bring your magniscope anyway. You know how Kalim loves your inventions."

Alrak became my friend within days after my parents apprenticed me to Master Kalim. As my first and only friend I loved him without reservation. And he proved to be a smart Ebod. Everyone agreed he was the smartest Ebod they ever met. After two years of learning to trust his advice, I no longer questioned his judgment. With my magniscope in one hand, and my anatomical drawing exercises and ideas notebook in the other, I left with Alrak for Kalim's cottage.

Master Kalim met us at his door. "Saryana, Alrak, come in. We have been waiting for you." A long career bent over a workbench hunched the old master's back in a permanent curve, but years of stone carving had left his handgrip strong. His powerful fingers pulled me inside. With a sharp kick of his foot he shut the door to the manure smell.

I offered my drawing exercises for inspection, knowing Kalim would insist on examining it before proceeding with any discussion. He reached into his vest pocket and withdrew the seeing lenses I had set in wire frames for him. These he placed upon his hooked nose before reviewing my work. To my relief he nodded his bald head with satisfaction, gave a quick wink, and set his hand on my shoulder. Warm breath tickled my ear. "We have visitors from the south. They want a statue." His thick gray eyebrows rose. "They asked for you by name."

Fame. Arlak said when everyone knew my name, the other kids would want to be my friend. No one made fun of famous people. I smelled roast meat and thought no more of fame.

Master Kalim took the magniscope tube from my hand. He held the branch to the light. "What is this? Another invention based on your contoured glass?"

"It's not finished yet. I need to build a stand . . ."

He laughed and shook an ink-stained finger at me. "The visitors have been asking about your inventions. I showed them your seeing lenses. They expressed interest."

"They did?" Despite my pride at the compliment, I managed to refrain from smiling. Humility, my mother always taught, is the proper attire for young women. Alrak said the humble are the fools of the universe. He always talked like that. At night when I drew the stars, Alrak would say Naora is nothing but a tiny speck in a tiny galaxy on the edge of the universe. Such a strange Ebod, but as I said before, I loved him. If it weren't for Alrak's encouragement, I might never have built my inventions and I wouldn't be the one invited to the partok.

"I don't need to tell you how much the cooperative's survival depends on the trading value a statue would bring."

"No, Master Kalim."

His gap-toothed smile returned. "Good. Follow me." We continued down the narrow hall leading to his study, stopping at a large carved door bearing a huge relief of San. Above the pudgy god's likeness, thick gold lettering read, "Wisdom is thought transferred." Master Kalim opened the heavy door with a flourish and I found myself staring at a partok meal big enough to feed half the village.

Tonya D. Price

"Duke Riker, may I present Saryana, one of Uran's most promising artisans." Master Kalim made the introductions as if he were Uran's chief councilman about to anoint the harvest barterer. I lost the struggle to keep my eyes on the strangers, and stared at the table straining under the weight of a fat roasted guntil stuffed with assorted baked fruits. A platter of brightly colored cakes covered in thick icing and dusted with violet and emerald and pink sparkling sugars rested beside platters stacked with steaming fresh vegetables. Never had I seen such a partok feast before. Master Kalim nudged me in the ribs and I forced my mouth to close.

The duke rose from his chair. Towering above Master Kalim, the giant bowed toward me as if honoring the dead. "It is my pleasure, Saryana, to meet you." Straightening, he gestured toward the others. "May I present Duchess Lady Deanna and her attendant, Miss Beverly."

The three visitors smiled at me. Each sported perfect white teeth. False, of course, but what workmanship. Ivory or porcelain, perhaps.

Kalim pointed to an empty chair. I waited for the guests to sit first. "The duke journeyed from Synria in the far south to meet you. He wishes to commission a statue."

The duke lowered himself into the chair and stretched his long legs out, resting his feet on the divan.

I stared at the pink flesh devoid of calluses. He must be the richest man I ever met. Did he walk on carpets all day?

He waved a hand at the food. "Please, do us the honor of sharing the partok with us."

No need for a second invitation. I filled our plates. Alrak circled in front of the fire before curling up in the space between my chair and the three outsiders. His ears stood straight up. His eyes never left the strangers, but his black nose twitched from side to side, sniffing the air in anticipation. I heaped his plate with vegetables and fruit, for unlike other Ebods, he would eat no meat. I, on the other hand, loaded my plate with roasted guntil and sweets.

After my second helping of guntil my teacher asked the question I waited to hear. "What kind of a statue are you looking for?"

The duke spread his long arms wide. "A big one. To go in our

165

town square. Of my father. On horseback. To celebrate his many military victories."

A bronze. For months I begged for the chance to do a bronze. I said nothing of my inexperience to the duke. "I'll start on some sketches at once. Did you bring a likeness of your father?"

"Well." Master Kalim cleared his throat with a loud cough. "The duke is interviewing several artisans. He has not yet decided who will do the project. He wishes to ask you some questions."

"I see. What questions?"

The duke's wife brushed a stray ringlet of loose curls off her shoulder. "We won't take long." Something about her soft voice and gentle nature calmed my growing panic. She turned to Master Kalim. "We would like to talk to Saryana alone. I hope you don't mind."

"Of course not." Master Kalim shot me a silent plea to be on my best behavior as he rose to leave. "Come, Alrak." He held the door for the Ebod.

Alrak rolled his chocolate brown eyes upward but refused to lift his head from his paws.

"Oh, that's okay," the duke said. "The Ebod can stay."

"Well." Master Kalim looked at me in confusion. I shrugged. I could not explain why the duke first insisted on interviewing me alone and then contradicted his own order by saying Alrak could stay. Everyone knew Ebods were the worst gossips. However, I didn't argue. To be honest, I preferred having my friend with me. Master Kalim shrugged and left without a word, leaving everyone staring at each other. Except for Alrak, who closed his eyes as if pretending to sleep.

"Do you have examples of your art?" The duchess pointed at the notebook lying in my lap.

Alrak half-opened one eye and growled. "Be careful. Don't show them your inventions or they might try and steal them."

Good advice. Besides, years of ridicule taught me to be cautious. "These pictures are not my best work. Some are several years old. Let me sketch you now as we talk."

"Will it take long?" the duchess asked.

"No."

With a nod of her aristocratic chin she granted her consent.

The duke continued asking questions as I positioned Lady Deanna in a simple high-back chair in front of the window to gain the best light. "Your accent is different from Master Kalim's," he said. "Where do you come from?"

I sharpened a drawing stick with my knife. "I was born in the village of Harmon, to the north."

For several minutes I studied the duchess. The scene through the window provided a backdrop of brown fields underneath a royal blue sky. Lady Deanna didn't strike me as a woman of the fields. A lush jungle scene would suit her best. Perhaps a cool ocean breeze to counter a tropical sun. Yes, with bright crimson blossoms dotting a silent garden filled with people. How strange. A park crowded with people should be loud with excitement, but I heard nothing in my vision.

The pencil never touched the paper but hung suspended in my hand. A new vision replaced the first. An enormous object floated in the night, surrounded by stars. I began to draw a large flat oval for people to work and live in. A column descended to a squashed tubular body to house the engine. On either side of the short main tube I drew longer matching cylinders. I heard a word in my mind—*nacelles*. Where would people go in such a vessel? To other worlds. What did they find there?

Creatures of every description and color appeared in my mind. Blue men with antennas radiating from their heads. Warriors with forehead wrinkles, each pattern different. Fish people and races with ridges on the bridge of their noses. I captured their faces, drawing as fast as my hand could manage. In the center of the picture I sketched the duchess in a blue flowing dress, her hair up in a bun laced with a thick, braided chiffon.

Nightmare images consumed me. People with tubes sticking out of their foreheads grew tools where hands should be. Black veins marked gray skin. Sad mechanical eyes stared at dark halls of wires and flashing lights.

"Draw not your visions." Alrak paced at my feet. "They want a simple portrait for a bronze. Show them that montage and you will lose the entire commission."

His advice came too late. The duke rested a hand on my shoulder. Had he heard the impertinent Ebod?

He motioned the duchess near. "Deanna, take a look at this."

When the duchess rose from her seat by the window the vision cleared. No one spoke as the three visitors studied my drawing. The silence lengthened. They were disappointed. They hated my work. Embarrassed, I tore the drawing from the notebook, crumpled the paper in my fist and threw the sketch toward the hearth. The small wad hit the brick fire wall and bounced out onto the floor a short distance from the glowing embers. "I'm sorry. I can do better. Let me draw you by the window."

The duchess waved a protesting hand. "No need to apologize. You have a remarkable talent. I would like to ask you some questions. Sort of a game. Would you like to play?"

What I'd like to do was get the portrait commission. And have another helping of the partok meat. "If I play the game will you choose me to do your statue?"

Miss Beverly smiled from her high-back chair. "The commission is already yours."

A sigh I didn't know I held escaped my lips. "Then, I would be happy to play the game."

"No." Alrak positioned himself before me. His brown eyes narrowed, his ears lay flat against his head. "No games. I don't trust these people."

If Alrak's indiscretion insulted the strangers, none indicated offense. But too much was at stake to take chances. "I apologize for Alrak's rudeness."

"He's a fine-looking Ebod." Duke Riker knelt down to the floor and clapped his hands. "Come here, boy."

Alrak's lip curled backward, baring his impressive fangs.

I didn't care how rich the duke might be. He had no right to insult Alrak. "You don't need to call him like he's a pet largh."

Miss Beverly nudged the duke. "Sir, I believe the Ebod is sentient."

In a calm voice the duchess asked, "Saryana, can you talk to the Ebod? And does he answer?"

"Of course."

"We understand many languages, but we aren't familiar with his. Where we come from, Ebods can't speak."

The duke rose to his feet, eyeing Alrak with interest. "I hope you will accept my apology. I meant no insult."

Alrak continued to face the duke as he spoke to me. "They are an ignorant people or they are lying. Everyone knows Ebods speak. Have they never heard birds sing either?"

Before I could answer, the duchess pointed at her servant. "Saryana, would you look at Miss Beverly and tell me the first thing that comes to mind."

Alrak growled a warning. "Another trick."

Did he want me to lie? Perhaps a compromise would do. A partial truth. "I see . . . a pretty lady with shoulder-length red hair, a nice smile . . ."

The duchess leaned closer and I found myself staring into her black eyes, unable to turn away. "Is that all you see?"

"She wears a blue dress?"

Her smile faded. "Saryana, I will tell you a secret. I possess a special ability that lets me know when people are telling me the truth . . . or when they are lying. Please, tell me everything you see when you look at Miss Beverly."

Alrak sidled up to my thigh. "She is an empath. A dangerous being. Speak no more to them."

If I secured the commission everyone in the cooperative could eat meat. What harm would answering her question bring? "I see beds. With little lights and lines rising and falling like ocean waves. I see her use a stick to close a cut on a man's arm. I see boxes with moving paintings inside. I see nurses, a son . . ."

"A telepath." Miss Beverly clapped her hands and rose from her chair to stand beside the duke. "Of course. All Naorans have latent empathic abilities, but she must have developed advanced perceptions. I wonder how extensive her abilities are."

Naorans? What a funny way to talk. Miss Beverly referred to the world as if she came from somewhere else.

I saw water. Buildings taller than a jimbo tree spidered upward into a night sky with a single moon as large as a thumbnail. My hand shook. Who were these people?

The duchess reached out to pat my shoulder. "How long have you been able to see what is in the minds of others?"

See in the minds of others? My visions? How long have I been different? My cheeks warmed. My entire life I cowered under the weight of the outcast's mantle, hiding myself in the woods rather than face the jeers of the other kids. Away from the others I filled my drawing notebook with what some called my fantasies. I preferred to call them my realms of possibility. "I have never been like everyone else."

My mother called me unique. My father said I was crazy. Kids at school insisted I must be a witch. To protect me my mother sent me far away to Master Kalim. If I didn't get the statue commission Master Kalim might close the studio and then where would I go? "I won't put anything strange in the sculpture. I promise."

The duke stroked his bearded chin. "Saryana, I will commission a second statue, if you can tell me how often a diagnostic series is run on a starship's warp power core during a red-alert situation in separation flight mode."

A trap. The answer came to me without effort but I said nothing. What would happen if I revealed the extent of my visions?

Alrak howled. "Don't answer."

A double commission meant food for the cooperative and art supplies for a year. More supplies meant we could create works without waiting for commissions and sell them in the markets to the southern ports on the great sea. If I secured such a prize Kalim might allow me time off to visit my parents. My father would be proud of my success. Swallowing hard, I asked, "What class starship?"

"Galaxy."

"Under such circumstances a level-four diagnostic series is repeated every five minutes during a red alert."

The duchess took me by the shoulders and twirled me around without warning. Black eyes held me in a hypnotic stare. "What is a thermoset?"

I saw nothing. No words echoed in my mind. "I . . . I don't know."

Riker leaned close, his blue eyes challenging me. "You know detailed information about operating a Galaxy starship in separation mode, but you don't know anything about plastics?"

As soon as he spoke the word *plastic* the answer came. Anxious to please him, I repeated what I heard in my head. "Thermosets are a type of polymer which cannot melt because their molecules are linked in chains. They set hard. They can't be remolded. Examples are formica and Bakelite."

Riker released me, looking disappointed, not pleased. "Very good, Saryana. You read my mind perfectly. Word for word."

From her seat the duchess sighed. "You couldn't read my mind because I have learned to misdirect my thoughts from untrained telepaths. Earlier, I didn't know you possessed such abilities and I left my thoughts unguarded, so you were able to read my mind."

"Telepaths? You mean there are others like me?"

Riker's voice resumed its friendly tone. "Yes, maybe not in Uran, but you are not the only one to possess such a gift."

Gift? Not a curse?

The duke turned toward the duchess. "So our suspicions were correct. The rapid scientific advances of this society must be coming from an outsider. Someone else must be feeding Saryana her scientific insights. Who?"

Miss Beverly nodded toward the door. "Kalim?"

Alrak paced again. "I told you they wouldn't understand. They are making fun of you. I refuse to listen to any more of this."

Riker knelt before me. "Could your scientific visions be coming from someone else?"

"They usually come when I'm alone."

The duchess tried to help. "Think. Is there anyone who is always around when you get these visions? I'm speaking of the images of things that don't exist. Futuristic weapons like your black powder gun and scientific discoveries like your seeing lenses."

"I think of such things all the time. Usually when no one is with me . . ." Except, I realized, one companion never left my side, day or night. Alrak. And I realized something else: the inventions started after I arrived in Uran. After I started my apprenticeship. After meeting the Ebod. Turning toward him, I asked, "You?"

Alrak crouched low. He growled an angry curse. "I told you not to speak with them, you gullible child. They tell you lies and you, whom I befriended when others made fun of you, you believe these strangers instead of me. Who do you think will help you if I leave your side? These people? They will leave and you will find yourself alone and despised. Again."

"No, Alrak. Don't leave me."

Riker stepped between me and Alrak. "What is the Ebod saying? Is he the one who told you of the flying machine and the battery for storing the sun's energy?"

I saw hundreds of large furry bodies lying dead, hacked into pieces. Purple blood spreading in a pool, soaking the new-tilled ground. Mechanical men walked fields stinking not of spring fertilizer but of death. Alrak's roar brought me out of the nightmare. His back arched. His spine elongated. Bigger and bigger he grew. His anvil-shaped face stretched to an oval. Thin black whiskers disappeared. Narrow chocolate eyes widened and turned crimson. A monster towered above me.

Miss Beverly spoke first. "A shapeshifter?"

The monster answered, this time in my own language. His eyes glowed at me and in those eyes fire burned. "Look in my mind. See what future awaits you. The machine men are called Borg and they prey on weak species like you Naorans."

I stumbled backward, away from the terrible images. "Borg?"

Releasing me, the duchess stepped toward Alrak. Now that he spoke our language she understood his words. "Stop it. Why are you showing her such things? It is wrong to interfere with the natural development of this society."

The creature spat at her. "I am well aware of the Federation's Prime Directive. Do you think I don't know you are Starfleet? Henallians were denied membership in the Federation, remember? I haven't the luxury of protecting her from such knowledge. The Borg can't assimilate shapeshifters so they tried to exterminate us. Those they didn't murder they starved to death by raping our land of anything of value. The few of us who survived found ourselves without a means to live. Our land no longer feeds us. We have nothing to trade, but we have our knowledge. Knowledge this world needs."

Riker took a step toward the creature. "Perhaps the Federation can help your people."

"We don't need your help. This planet has rich pergium and tekasite veins to be mined. Once Naora has reached industrial-era status, we will make ourselves known and offer to provide the technology to extract these minerals. In return for our expertise we will ask for only a small percentage of the profits. Both our people will benefit. Henallians and Naorans."

Riker took another step forward, placing himself within reach of the creature. "Your people do not need to interfere with Naora's development in order to survive. The Federation . . ."

The Henallian grew even taller than Riker. "The Federation is concerned with protecting its own. Where was your starship when the Borg attacked Henallia?"

"We can't be everywhere."

The transformed Alrak scoffed at the reply. "What good is your Prime Directive if it prevents you from protecting these people from the Borg? With Henallian help they stand a chance of being prepared. At least they will know what they are up against."

Riker didn't back down. "You will cause planetwide panic on Naora if you continue to introduce technology at such a rapid pace. Even the advances you have already given Saryana have begun to disrupt this society's stability. That is what drew our attention. Trade patterns are shifting. Inflation has erupted in the port cities. Political alliances are certain to deteriorate. Soon cults will appear as traditional religions break down. If you do not stop your interference you will engulf Naora in chaos. Your technology will prove little use in the midst of anarchy. Unless you are planning on conquering, rather than helping, the Naorans . . ."

My hand began to shake. No matter how hard I tried I could not hide my fear. The mechanical people here? In Uran? We wouldn't stand a chance.

The empath spoke with urgency but in her mind lurked more images of broken ships and ravished worlds. "You must believe me. My people will do everything we can to protect Naora."

I found my voice at last. "Why not let the Henallians teach us how to protect ourselves?"

The duchess shook her head. "He can't guarantee your safety." She turned toward the creature. He swayed to and fro like a fighter seeking an advantage. The duchess said, "You will have to come with us."

"I will not." Sharp claws shot out from the creature's fingertips. The small side teeth grew into long fangs. His roar shook the study's glass windowpanes. He sprang at Riker, slashing at the duke's face.

Images of weapons filled my thoughts. Guns. Photon torpedoes. Long phaser rifles. Riker pulled a small object out of his belt. Blue fire streaked across the room. Fur crackled as coarse hair singed, but the blast could not stop the creature from sinking those pointed fangs deep into Riker's hand. The phaser fell against the tile with a clang and skidded on the floor, coming to rest against my foot.

I picked up the hand phaser. The weapon felt as if it weighed nothing in my hand. I pointed the phaser at the creature I once called friend. "Enough. Let the duke go."

He shrank into the Ebod's shape again. Alrak scolded me. "Would you shoot me? When no one else would comfort you I stayed with you. I interpreted your dreams. I gave you the image of the ground lens and the farscope. I made you famous, dried your tears at night when you cried for your mother, and now you turn on me? These creatures will not lift a finger to help you when the Borg come to assimilate this world. Will you trust them more than me?"

Would I shoot? I did not know. "Alrak, don't move."

The duchess felt the Ebod's lie and through her thoughts I knew Alrak's deception as well. I didn't need a vision to see how he used me for his own purposes. Any comfort he gave he offered not for friendship, but for his own kind's gain. The Henallians hoped to en-slave my people, not guide them. In Riker's thoughts I saw how to activate the phaser.

Alrak sprang forward. His jaws opened, reaching for my hand. He wanted me to drop the phaser. I heard his pleas in my mind, beg-ging me to let go of the weapon so he wouldn't have to bite. Per-haps he did care for me after all. I pressed the button. The phaser bolt struck. Alrak stiffened in midair, then collapsed on the floor.

His body lay motionless. Limbs and fur reverted to the creature's true form. With effort I managed to speak past the knot in my throat. "Is he dead?"

With great tenderness Riker pulled the weapon from my hand. "Not dead; unconscious."

I turned to the duchess. "What happens now?"

"Now we go back home and keep the Henallians away from Naora."

"Will your Federation keep the Borg away from our planet too?"

I caught the look the three shared. A worried look. They didn't know what to do with me and my knowledge of things. I knew what I hoped they would do. "Take me with you." I never begged for anything before but I fell on my knees, intoxicated by the wonders I viewed earlier encased in their memories. Even fear of the Borg couldn't frighten me from wanting to see the universe for myself. "Please. Take me with you to travel the heavens."

Miss Beverly raised a short wand. "I'm afraid we can't do that." The wand pulsated with an orange light. A heavy sleep closed my eyes. A distant voice said, "Her neurology is much different from any I've encountered before, but she shouldn't remember a thing."

"Saryana, wake up."

Master Kalim shook my shoulder. My head ached. As I came to my senses I discovered my notebook gone, Alrak nowhere in sight. My last memory? The taste of the partok meat, prompted no doubt by the smell of roasted guntil hanging heavy in the air. "What happened?"

Master Kalim put one hand to his back for support and bent over to pick up a wad of paper from the floor. "I must be working you too hard. You fell asleep during your interview. The duke left full payment for two statues to go up in our town square. You must have impressed them."

"I don't remember."

He tossed me the crumpled ball of paper. "Here, this looks to be your work. Haven't I told you paper is too expensive to use just one side? There is no reason why you can't draw on the back of this."

I looked around the study. "Where's Alrak?"

"He must have gone out."

I returned to my little attic room above the studio. While I waited for Alrak I unfolded the wadded-up drawing. The images of far-away worlds and odd creatures seemed familiar—like a memory of a fairy tale once heard. After several hours I fell asleep, but the strange images continued to haunt me. The next morning I woke up remembering—everything.

Thirty-five years have passed. Alrak never reappeared. I missed him, called his name out many lonely nights when nightmares chased me from my sleep. Even a bad friend is better than none at all. As for my inventions, I never built another—partly out of respect for Riker's warning about the effects of advanced technology on an unprepared society, but also because fame held no allure for me once I learned the tenuous nature of friendships acquired cheaply. As for my career, I enjoyed modest success as a sculptor. In return for my loyalty, more than my skill, Master Kalim left the studio to me when he died. My students are my family now. Through them my name will endure when I am gone.

So ends my first story, but I have many others—an unexpected farewell gift from my friends, those Starfleet officers. Strange, I think of them as my friends, even though I spent just a few short hours in their presence. The truth is, since that day long ago, I have relived their experiences so many times I feel as though I have grown up knowing them.

Based on their memories I have walked the corridors of the *Enterprise* at will. Through Riker's eyes I visited exotic worlds where creatures of every description and color lived, whose outward appearance proved much more bizarre than any birthed in my small imagination. With Crusher I watched men and women face death with courage. From Troi I learned that alien hearts break as easily as mine and take as long to heal. Each memory told a tale and I listened to them all. I listened and remembered and wrote them down for future generations, so someday others might share my wonder, heed the lessons, and dream with me of strange new worlds to come.

Dementia in D Minor

Mary Sweeney

I. ALLEGRO

Where am I? I do not know. I cannot think. I can only feel. Sorrow. Regret. Loneliness. What is this music that surrounds me? Concentrate . . . I must concentrate. I know this music. It is Terran music . . . it is . . . I cannot remember. Emotion . . . so much emotion . . . I am lost . . . lost.

Perrin? Perrin, my wife, where are you? I remember now. Perrin wished to remain at my side, but I sent her from me. It was necessary. She was becoming entangled in the web of my emotions, sharing my madness, my suffering. I could not allow it . . . I will not allow it. I *will* not . . . it is all right. It is all right now. Perrin has honored my wish: I am alone. The music is my only companion . . . brooding, ominous . . . rage at war with reason. I know this music. It is Mozart . . . Wolfgang Amadeus Mozart of Earth . . . his Piano Concerto Number 20 in D minor. Such passion . . . how can these austere walls contain it?

How stark this room is, how empty. Surely, it was not always so.

There, in that corner, there used to be a Benecian sculpture. Beneath that window there was a chest of *t'klar* wood that once belonged to my father. And upon that wall, a portrait of Amanda, she who was my wife. I remember . . . I remember it all! But now all that remains is the meditation stone upon which I lie. What has become of the rest? Stolen . . . stolen! But who . . . who would dare?

Ah, yes: it was I. I am the thief of my own possessions. I ordered . . . I begged Sakkath to strip the room bare, for I saw how it would be . . . I *feared* how it would be. Destruction . . . destruction . . . wood and glass and metal, shattering and splintering beneath my fists until my surroundings were reduced to a reflection of the scarred and twisted landscape that Bendii Syndrome has shaped within my mind. Order . . . order is so difficult to maintain. Entropy increases . . . chaos . . . *chaos!* No . . . I must control. I am safe: this empty room is my refuge. Amanda's portrait is safe. All that remains here now is the meditation stone: hard, cold, indestructible. Outside, beyond the wall that surrounds my home, seven adepts of the *Kolinahr* stand silent guard upon my errant thoughts, containing them with the combined force of their disciplined, telepathic minds, protecting others from my madness. Soon, their strength will be tested again, for beneath the clear melody of lucidity my emotions lie in wait, growing stronger, rending the carefully repaired fissures in the walls of my control. Tears fill my eyes . . . regret, that is all I have now. I am lost.

Where am I? I do not know, but it is safe here. I am safe and I am listening to Mozart. Mozart was human, but I am Vulcan. I am Sarek of Vulcan, Ambassador to the United Federation of Planets. I negotiated the Treaty of Alpha Cygnus IX. At the Babel Conference, I ensured the admission of . . . of . . . why, why have I forgotten? Anguish, anguish, *anguish!* All of my accomplishments seem so small, so insignificant. It is defeat that haunts me now. I remember . . . I remember it all: clear, precise, accurate in every detail. No! Go from me! Go from me! I do not want to see!

But the memory fills my mind. I cannot stop it. In the memory I am on Meliach III. That is the name by which the Federation knows this world. But the people of this place call their world Zefral, which translates as "beautiful song." My mission here is an urgent and weighty one. The fate of two worlds lies in my hands, but I feel no fear, for I am a Vulcan.

Perrin . . . my wife . . . where is Perrin? She was with me at Meliach III, was she not? No . . . no, Perrin was not there. She had not yet been born. And Amanda . . . Amanda was not with me either. She was only a child then, and we had not yet met. I was alone, as I am alone now. I must face my fear alone . . . climb the stairs alone . . . climb up to the Palace of Crystalline Song, where Greth, the Oth of Zefral, awaits my arrival.

Round and round the staircase twines, and climbing with it, fanning out about the great, central supporting pillar of the palace, there is a series of balconies which serve the recreational needs of the Oth's most loyal and trusted subjects. Violet-skinned, blue-eyed, long-limbed, and slender beings . . . the people of Zefral surround me as I climb. On the lower levels, Elders robed in blue gather in the shade of tri-lobed *elkast* trees to debate the state of their world in soft, reedy voices. The mid-level platforms are peopled by courting couples who sit silently upon opulently carved benches, their long, spindly fingers intertwined. Children frolic in the upper levels. Some of them are singing in trilling, birdlike voices. Several are squabbling. Many are bobbing their heads exuberantly—a gesture indicating great joy. And so it is that I, a Vulcan, must ascend to Oth Greth's palace through a roiling cloud of emotion: nostalgia, regret, ambition, grief, love, apprehension, jealousy, delight. It is difficult to shield my mind from such an onslaught, but I remain in control. Yes. Here, in this place of memory into which I have fallen, I am, still, in control. And here, as in the present, Mozart's music surrounds me, rushing out to meet me as the palace doors are opened, following me through the corridors as I am ushered by an aged, limping servant into Oth Greth's presence.

The hereditary ruler of Meliach III is standing upon a raised platform before a great, curved window overlooking the sweeping expanse of her capital city and the green fields and blue-hazed mountains beyond. Valacia, the fourth moon of Zefral, rides high over Oth Greth's left shoulder. The distant, shimmering oval of the Lake of Nolien is encompassed by the arc of her raised right hand as its long fingers curve in the ritual greeting of her people. Behind Oth Greth, beyond the curved, interlocking panes of the great window, children are scampering about on the uppermost of the recreational balconies. They are playing *kilet,* a local game in which small red spheres programmed with a variety of evasive techniques are pursued and captured in a pale blue net. When all of the spheres have been gathered up, the net will be emptied and the game will begin anew. Vulcan children would never engage in such a pointless activity, but the children of Zefral seem to relish their game of *kilet:* every child on the balcony appears to be both healthy and contented. And so Oth Greth stands, framed by her kingdom and her young and joyous subjects. It is, I realize, a carefully orchestrated tableau designed to impress, perhaps even to intimidate. But I am immune to such displays.

I raise my hand and curl my fingers—which are much shorter than Oth Greth's—into an approximation of the Zefralian's ritual greeting.

"Welcome, Sarek," Oth Greth warbles in her lilting native tongue. "Sit," she says, indicating the cushions piled at my feet, "and we will listen together to the strange and wonderful music that the president of your Federation has sent me. It is a fine gift, this music of Earth."

But I do not sit. I lower my hand to my side and remain standing. "Oth Greth," I say, "I must decline your offer. I have just come from Meliach II, where I was granted an audience with Belant."

Oth Greth's raised hand falls to her side. "Three times now you have come to me, and three times you have refused to listen to this music of Earth," she says.

"Forgive me, Oth Greth," I say, "but there are far more pressing matters at hand. You must consider a treaty with Belant."

"Belant is an animal," she says.

"That is your opinion," I reply. "In any case, you must deal with him, and quickly. Belant's Orion allies have armed his ships with new, more powerful weapons. Your shields will be useless against them. Fortunately, Belant has agreed to refrain from attack for a period of four Zefralian days."

"Has he?" Oth Greth asks.

I have studied her people's culture, their physiology. Her relaxed stance, the tone of her voice, all seem to indicate a strange indifference to her difficult situation. I do not know how to interpret this reaction. Perhaps she does not comprehend the full import of what I have told her.

"Your world is in grave danger," I tell her. "You must put Belant's cease-fire to good use: you must negotiate with him."

"If you do not wish to listen to this music with me," Oth Greth says, "then bring me music that you do wish to hear—perhaps a work from your world, from Vulcan. Your people do make music, do they not?"

"They do," I say, "although it is quite different from the music of Earth."

"Bring me this Vulcan music, Sarek, and we will share it together," Oth Greth says. Then she turns away to stare out the great window.

I have been dismissed, and I am expected to return with a gift of Vulcan music, which will, no doubt, cause further delay. Oth Greth's behavior is not entirely unexpected. The people of Zefral are ruled by their passions. Great lovers of music and art, they often become so completely immersed in the appreciation of some particular masterpiece that all other concerns and activities—sleep, food, duty—are neglected for days on end. But the Oth of Zefral cannot afford such indulgence—not now. Illogical, irrational, irresponsible . . . can she not see the danger that is before her?

Even though Oth Greth has turned away from me, I must not leave. I must stay and make her understand. With a steady voice, I begin, again, to speak. "I would like to remind you, Oth Greth, that as a member of the Federation you would have access to its resources: the music and art of all of its worlds would be yours to appreciate at your leisure. But your petition for membership cannot even be considered while the worlds of this system are at war with one another. You must make peace with Belant. You must dissuade him from the attack that he is planning."

"There is no music in Belant's heart," Oth Greth says, as she raises a hand in greeting to one of the children playing upon the balcony. He is the smallest of the group, a tiny child no taller than my knee. His head bobs up and down excitedly as he raises his hand to return Oth Greth's greeting.

"The diplomatic shuttle that brought me here is small and unarmed," I say. "Even if the Federation were to sanction interference in the internal affairs of this system, I would be unable to protect you. Negotiation with Belant is your only hope."

Oth Greth turns back to face me then. The motion is abrupt, angry. "The Oth of Zefral does not treat with barbarians!" she cries.

I recoil from her emotional display, but my control reasserts itself at once. "As I have explained on my previous visits," I say, "I am willing to act as an intermediary. Allow me to speak with Belant on your behalf. Give me leave to negotiate a peace treaty for you."

"And what would you offer Belant?" she asks. "He understands nothing of joy or beauty. All he wants is power and the things that it brings—things that he can hold in his hands."

"In that case, I shall appeal to his materialistic nature. Belant's world is poor, and the resources of the Federation are considerable."

"Belant is too proud: he will never agree to a treaty," Oth Greth says.

"With respect, Oth Greth, I believe that you are mistaken. I believe that I can convince Belant of the advantages of Federation membership. In order to join the Federation, he must first make peace with you. Therefore, logically, he must agree to a treaty with Zefral."

"They told me that you were a man of logic, of reason," Oth Greth says. "But Belant knows only conquest and dominion. His ambition has made a wasteland of his own world. Now he wishes to do the same to Zefral. He will never change, Sarek."

"There was a time, Oth Greth, when the people of my world were locked in a cycle of senseless violence. Our taste for vengeance was without limit. War followed war. But with logic, we have found peace. We were capable of change. Belant and his people are also capable of change. Authorize me to negotiate for you and I will return at once to Meliach II to begin the task."

"I wish to be still now," Oth Greth says. "I wish to listen to this music of Earth."

For a moment, I am struck silent by her utter disregard of her duty. But my own duty soon forces me to speak. "Negotiations with Belant must begin at once," I say. "Authorize me to negotiate for you and I shall leave you in peace to listen to the concerto."

"I hear sadness in this music of Earth," Oth Greth says. "Sadness and joy, helplessness and power all mingled together. Do you not hear it, Sarek?"

"The treaty, Oth Greth," I say. "Give me the authority to negotiate it."

Silent, she turns away again to look at the frolicking children and the towers and bridges of her city and all of the rich land that lies beyond. I do not know what more to say to her. We stand there at an impasse, surrounded by Mozart's music.

I must think. I must call upon all of my experience, upon every bit of knowledge and wisdom imparted to me by my teachers. There must be some way to make Oth Greth understand, some key that will unlock her closed mind.

The communicator upon my belt signals, its shrill note disrupting the flow of the concerto. Outside the great window, above the peaks of the distant mountains, there is a flash of red light. "No," I say, as, heedless of protocol, I rush to join Oth Greth upon her platform. I stand beside her, my face turned upward, my eyes searching the heavens. High above the distant mountains, sunlight glints off a small, silvery shape. The communicator signals again and I answer it.

"Ambassador Sarek, this is Captain Ashton. Meliach II has launched an attack on Zefral. Scanners show two . . . no, five, of Belant's ships in Zefral's atmosphere. There are at least ten more on the way. What are your instructions, sir?"

"Stand by," I order, as a red energy beam lances down into the Lake of Nolien, boiling the water off in a great cloud of steam and leaving behind an empty, brown crater. I turn to look at Oth Greth. She is much taller than I; I must tilt my head back in order to meet her eyes. Her gaze is serene, composed, patient. "I do not understand," I say. "Belant said that he would refrain from launching an attack against Zefral for a period of four days. He gave me his word."

Oth Greth regards me with great sadness, almost with pity. "Belant lied to you, Sarek," she says, in the soft tones that her people reserve for very small children. "You believed him because you listened to his words when you should have been listening to his heart."

"Perhaps it is not too late," I tell her. "This insanity must end. Give me leave to negotiate for you."

"I do not know your heart, Sarek, and you do not know mine."

"Vulcans are ruled by logic, not by emotion," I tell her.

"Then perhaps you are like Belant, Sarek. Perhaps you can find no music in your heart. Perhaps you are not to be trusted at all."

"Vulcans do not lie," I say, as a third beam lances downward, striking, this time, on the outskirts of the city. "Captain Ashton, establish contact with Belant," I say into the communicator.

"It is too late," Oth Greth says. "All I required was that you listen with me. If we had shared the music together, then I would have seen what is in your heart and then, perhaps, I could have trusted you to speak for me."

I am stunned by this revelation. "Why did you not tell me of this requirement?" I ask.

"I should not have had to tell you, Sarek," Oth Greth says sadly, patiently. "If you had listened to your heart, you would have known what was necessary."

"Belant isn't answering our hails, Ambassador," Captain Ashton informs me.

"Continue trying," I tell him.

Outside, on the balcony, the red spheres are still bouncing about, blindly following their programming, but the children are no longer in pursuit. They have stopped their game to gather at the railing and look out over the city. A fourth energy beam strikes, turning a golden bridge into a smoking slag heap. More ships have appeared. A fifth beam strikes and a sixth and a seventh. Smoke and fire rise up into the sky. Mozart's music mingles, now, with the sounds of chaos and destruction.

"*This* is all that Belant can hear in his heart," Oth Greth says softly, her eyes fixed upon her dying city. "Suffering and destruction."

"Captain Ashton," I say into the communicator, "it is imperative that I speak with Belant at once."

"I'm sorry, Ambassador, but we can't raise him," Ashton replies. "Your life is in danger, sir. We're beaming you out now."

"No!" I cry, heedless of the emotion in my own voice. "Not yet."

"But Ambassador, we've sighted ten more ships."

"Not yet," I repeat.

"Standing by," the captain says.

"Beam up to the ship with me, Oth Greth," I say, "and we will go together to Belant. We will stop this madness."

"Will we take these children, also?" Oth Greth asks. "And what of all the others . . . what of all the others?" The children are cowering behind the railing now, huddled together in groups of three or four. Only the smallest is alone. He has returned to the window to stare up at Oth Greth with eyes that are wide with fear. "I will not leave my people," Oth Greth says.

"We're beaming you out, Ambassador," Captain Ashton says.

"I forbid it!" I say.

Outside, beyond the window, the tiny child has begun to weep. His keening cries penetrate the barrier of the window; his tears are dark blue, the color of his world's sky. His small, anguished face is the last thing I see before the transporter takes me.

Aboard the ship, I push the transporter operator away from his controls. My fingers fly across the control board as I scan the area around Oth Greth's palace. Over and over again I search, but there are no life signs.

I failed you, Oth Greth. You and all of your people and Belant and his people as well. For many years I have told myself that I acted logically, that I could not have been expected to understand your request because you did not speak plainly. But now, locked in this madness, I wonder: is it possible that I knew all along what you wanted of me? Is it possible that I failed because I was afraid to allow you to see what I held in my heart—grief and joy, despair and hope?

Lost, lost, so many lost . . . and what is done cannot be undone.

II. ROMANZE

Peace . . . peace . . . I must have peace! Comfort me, Mozart. Relieve me of my burdens. Sweet, sweet . . . the tender music of

Earth . . . such a soft and forgiving place, so cool and blue and full of life . . . so unlike this harsh, sere world. But Vulcan is my home. I am a Vulcan. I *am* a Vulcan. I must control. Control . . . control . . . it is our way, it is *my* way.

Oh, but this beauty tempts me. Such beauty, Mozart. How can I bear it? Mozart . . . Mozart was human. Humans are so alone, so very alone. Locked in their own minds, unable to touch the thoughts of another. Of course . . . of course . . . that is why they create such beauty, why they *must* create such beauty. Mozart, you have touched me as surely as if my thoughts and yours had intertwined. Though we are separated by time and space, I *know* your mind. I hear your loneliness and your joy. In your music, I hear my own past.

Amanda, my wife, how I long for thee now. Perrin has been good to me: she has done her best to protect me from the indignities of old age and disease. She has been patient with me. Gracious . . . unselfish . . . true. But she has known me only as an old man. You, Amanda . . . you knew me when I was in my prime. We grew old together, Amanda. We grew old and then . . . and then you were no more, and I . . . I had to continue. Duty . . . my duty . . . it was my duty to continue. It was logical to continue. Without you. Logical to continue. Logic . . . logic . . . logic . . . I am sick to death . . . sick to death of logic! Your words, my wife. Your words and now they are mine as well. Age is said to bring wisdom. Vulcans respect the wisdom of experience, the logic of life's lessons. I am old . . . old . . . but where is my wisdom? Lost years. Dead friends. Is *this* to be my inheritance? This chaos? I am trapped, trapped in the maze of my own thoughts!

Comfort me, Mozart. If I cannot have peace now, then let me remember . . . let me remember a time when solace was within my grasp. . . .

Amanda . . . Amanda . . . how fragile you seemed on the first day you spent here, in this house. How out of place. I was shocked at how pale you became, how drained and tired. The heat, the gravity; I wanted to keep you safe, to take you away, to take you home to Earth. But you would not hear of it. Though I knew you were suffering, you did not complain. You stood at the window and looked out at the sparse desert garden, where the position of each rock, each plant, was governed by traditional principles of restraint and order. You spoke of change, of the diversity of life on many worlds. You spoke of Andorian *eth'la* vines and Benecian fire trees and Terran roses. *Impossible,* I told you. *Illogical. It is too dry, too hot.* You smiled in answer, and the next day you began to shape your dream.

How slowly you worked at first. How worn you looked as you sat in the shade, resting with a drink of cool, life-giving water. I feared for you, Amanda. I asked you to stop. But you continued: illogical, stubborn, human. So very human. But as the days and seasons and years passed, you grew stronger. And you created and shaped, revised and improvised, until your garden was as you had dreamed it would be. Beautiful . . . so beautiful. It is still beautiful, Amanda. Your roses are in bloom. Red and gold and bronze: all the colors of a Vulcan sunset. I kept the roses safe for you. I cared for your garden with my own hands until I was no longer able to do so, and then I placed it in Perrin's care. And after her there will be another caretaker and another and another. I have made the arrangements. Do not fear, Amanda . . . do not fear! Your garden will continue. The scent of the roses will fill the desert air. So sweet . . . so tender . . . the scent of the roses. . . .

Amanda? Amanda, are you here? My wife, where are you? No; no, you are gone. I remember now. And your portrait is gone also. No matter: I do not need it . . . I can see you as you were, in my mind . . . as you were all those years ago.

I remember, Amanda: I remember a day when the scent of the roses was sweet on the desert air. As I approached our home, as the scent of the roses grew stronger and stronger, I felt such joy . . . because you were my wife, because you had made my world your home . . . joy, joy, joy! Joy so strong that I wanted to weep, but I could not, I could not, for it was not the Vulcan way. It was not *my* way. Please, Amanda, my beloved: please forgive me! If I could . . . if I could go back . . . go back . . .

Roses . . . the scent of roses . . . so sweet, so tender . . . roses and music, the music of Earth . . . the second movement of Mozart's Concerto Number 20, greeting me as I enter our home. I recognize the recording. It is the Martian Symphony Orchestra, recorded in . . . in . . . yes . . . I remember . . . it was recorded in 2141 for the centennial celebration of the founding of Mars Colony I. But there is something amiss: Als Retnor of Alpha Centauri IV was the pianist at the Anniversary Concert, yet I do not believe it is his work that I hear now. Apparently, Amanda has programmed the household computer to mute Retnor's part and substitute the work of another pianist. It is an interest of hers, piecing together bits and pieces of the recordings of various performances, matching one part to another, adjusting tempos, intertwining the styles of artists long dead with those still living, seeking to make a harmonious whole of disparate parts. Her pastime strikes me as singularly human . . . a pursuit of perfection which can never be realized except in the virtual world of the computer, for the members of Amanda's orchestras can never, in fact, perform together. And yet, she derives pleasure from this activity. In some ways, my human wife is still very much a mystery to me.

I pause in the hallway, listening. Amanda has not changed a note of the Martian Symphony Orchestra's accompaniment, but the pianist is definitely not Als Retnor. Though I am familiar with the work of hundreds of concert pianists from Earth and many other worlds, the identity of this performer is unknown to me. It is an interesting style. The technique is flawless: each note is clear and pure. Strange. There is an almost Vulcan precision about this performance: there is great attention to detail. The artist clearly possesses a command of the muscles of the wrists and fingers which is far superior to that of humans, Andorians, and even Elarians. But the pianist cannot be Vulcan, for no Vulcan would play with such unbridled emotion. Joy: sweet, tender joy. And beneath it, a touch of sadness, of longing. It is difficult not to be moved by this music. I find that my automatic efforts at control must be augmented with a conscious attempt to resist the emotional resonances that cloud my mind. Thus reinforced, I follow the music down the hallway to Amanda's sitting room. When I reach her door I stop, shocked by what I have found. There, seated at my wife's grand piano, his feet barely reaching the pedals, his hands flying unerringly over the keys, is my young son, Spock.

Amanda is sitting beside Spock; she is turned slightly in her chair so that her face is in profile to me. She is wearing a gown of pale blue silk. Her long hair is unbound, flowing down over her shoulders almost to her waist. One hand is raised to her lips, covering them. Her cheek is wet with tears. She senses my presence and turns toward me, shakes her head in disbelief, then turns back to watch, in mute, rapt amazement as Spock's hands continue to draw forth the sweet, pure, emotion-laden notes of Mozart's music, while I continue to stand in the doorway, as if I am a mere observer, a non-participant in the family drama unfolding before me: my son—half human, half Vulcan—playing, indeed, as a child of two worlds. Pride and dismay war within me: I crush them both. Emotion is not what is needed now.

Composed, objective, logical, I enter the room. When I reach my wife's side she stands and rests a delicate hand upon my left forearm.

"Oh, Sarek, isn't it wonderful?" she whispers, her voice laden with excitement. "He only heard the concerto once—just once! And now he's playing it from memory as if he's practiced it a thousand times! But he hasn't just copied Als Retnor. He's better than Als Retnor, better than anyone else I've ever heard! I'm so proud of Spock, Sarek, so very proud!"

Her pride . . . and her joy . . . are communicated directly to my mind through her touch. She is so very human. For a moment, I am tempted to share in her emotion. But I am a Vulcan, so I draw away, disengaging my arm from her hand. At the piano, Spock continues to play. I do not know if he is so deeply engrossed in the music that he does not know that I am here, or if he has chosen to ignore my presence. Amanda is looking up at me, smiling, expectant.

"There are certain elements of his technique that are . . . impressive," I say. Spock's back stiffens as I speak. Certainly, now, he knows that I am here, but he does not behave as a Vulcan child should behave. Vulcan children are taught to greet their elders with silent respect, but Spock's hands keep moving over the keys, and now the emotion beneath his music is anger. I have tried. Over and over again I have tried. But I do not know how to correct him, how to teach him the importance of tradition, of control. Unbending, unyielding . . . he is far too stubborn, too proud for his own good.

Spock is not alone in his passion. His mother, too, is angry with me: the emotion flashes in her eyes, fierce and challenging. "Certain elements of his technique?" she echoes mockingly, her voice raised, now, well above a whisper. Surely, Spock has heard her, has detected the emotion in her voice. Evidently she is aware of her error, for she moderates her voice when she next addresses me. "Sarek, can't you hear it? Can't you hear the beauty that Spock is creating?"

I can hear it . . . I do hear it. And I am greatly troubled by it, for at this point in his training Spock should be capable of more control. But this is neither the place nor the time to discuss my son's shortcomings with my wife, so I remain silent, unmoved, determined to keep to the course I have followed throughout my life.

"I *know* you can hear it," Amanda continues, her voice barely audible now, even to Vulcan ears. She leans closer. "You *can* hear it," she whispers, "but you're too stubborn to admit it. And you're too stubborn to tell your son how much you love him. Someday, Sarek, you will regret that."

She turns away from me then in a swirl of blue silk and reseats herself beside our son. How like Spock she seems at this moment: her anger is evident in every line of her bearing. Later, when we are alone, my wife and I will discuss what has happened here. Amanda will question our decision to raise Spock on Vulcan, as a Vulcan. I will remind her, as I have on many other occasions, that it is a decision that we reached together. I will review our reasons for our decision. I will remind her that we wished our son to live in a world without war, without strife, without the inevitable disappointment of childish and unrealistic expectations. I will remind her that we wished him to know contentment and serenity. Amanda will ask, as she has so many times, if the price of that serenity is too high to pay. But in the end, she will agree that Spock should continue his education on Vulcan, that he should learn the way of Surak, that that is the best, most logical upbringing we can give him.

I tried, Spock. I tried to do my best for you, my son. I did what I thought . . . what I was certain . . . was best. In the past I was so often certain. But now I am ruled by confusion. Regret, regret . . .

that which is done cannot be undone, no matter how much we may regret it.

Mozart's father wanted fame and fortune for his brilliant son. But I . . . all I ever wanted for you, Spock, was peace.

III. RONDO

Seconds, minutes, hours . . . rushing by. When I was a boy, time seemed to stretch before me, endless and full of possibility. Time, time, an infinity of time. Foolish child. Foolish. Foolish. My time has passed so quickly. On and on—days, seasons, years—rushing by, and I . . . I have been swept along with them. I am an old man now and I am afraid.

The philosophers of Ebuz IV believe that the final second of one's existence—the final thought, the final breath—holds the true meaning of one's life. But what thought will fill my mind as I draw my last breath? Will it be that of a madman, nonsensical, meaningless, formed not of reason, but of passion? Surely, surely, it would be illogical to ignore all that has come before that final moment—the triumphs and the defeats, the trials and the accomplishments? But perhaps . . . perhaps it is not the grand events of one's life that matter. Perhaps it is the thousands of small, seemingly trivial daily decisions and actions which, collectively, define us in the end. Meaning . . . my life *must* have meaning. I do not want . . . I do not want to die a madman. Control . . . control . . . I *must* control. I am a Vulcan. I am not ruled by passion. I am a being of reason, of logic. But logic without wisdom is useless . . . even dangerous.

Experience is wisdom: learn from thy mistakes. That is what T'Pau told me after the disaster at Zefral. Logical advice, from a very logical source. For a time, it sufficed. For a time, it quieted the despair I felt whenever I thought of the child—the tiny, violet-skinned child, who stood upon the balcony weeping. I did not tell T'Pau about the child. It would have been illogical to do so, to focus on one life when so many were lost.

But now . . . now I, too, weep . . . I weep for the child . . . illogical . . . illogical . . . this mourning is illogical. The past is the past. I must . . . I must control . . . I wanted to protect the child . . . I tried to protect him! But I failed and he is gone . . . long gone. I have had all of these years . . . all of these years to ponder the loss. Grief . . . such grief . . . held at bay for so long, for too long . . . now it has broken free . . . Amanda, Spock . . . heavy, oppressive, this grief overpowers all else. Emotion . . . emotion . . . I am ruled by emotion! Is this humiliation to be my penance? No, no . . . it is too late for penance . . . too late . . . to this day, the Meliachian system remains submerged in the chaos of violence. Waste, waste, chaos and waste. I am sorry, Oth Greth. I am sorry. I should have listened . . . I should have listened to my heart.

On and on the music plays, measure after measure. Measure . . . measure: what is the measure of a life? How does one balance the bad against the good? I have saved many lives. I have brought peace to many worlds. But what of my failures? How should I calculate my worthiness? If I have saved a million lives, does that erase the damage I have done to a thousand . . . or to one?

Spock, my son . . . restless wanderer . . . where are you? Stubborn child! Have you gone into the mountains again? Why? For what purpose? Answer me . . . answer me! But you will not. You will not answer, you will remain aloof, you will not share your life with me. But you will not lie. You might have fooled me, you might have concocted some explanation that would have spared you from punishment. Instead you remained silent. The truth, the truth . . . with you it was merciless, always the truth. But the truth, my son, is that the universe is a dispassionate place. The truth is that life is complex and difficult. The truth is that there are times when logic is a luxury that does not apply. And the truth, my son, is that I never shared my thoughts with you for I was afraid, not of what I would see in your mind, but of what you would see in mine. The flaws, the disappointment, the errors, the regret, the confusion. I wanted to be perfect for you, Spock. I wanted to be pure. I wanted to be as I once was, long ago, before I recognized the impossibility of righting all wrongs or erasing all injustice, before I felt the sting of defeat. I tried to protect you, my son, just as I tried to protect the children of Zefral.

Soft, sweet . . . the music of Earth. Comfort me, Mozart. Bring me peace. Once, it was logic that brought me peace. Logic and the scent of Terran roses. Logic and the color of Amanda's eyes. Logic and the comfort of Perrin's voice. Logic and the honesty in Spock's gaze.

Where have you gone, my son? Where have you gone? Have you run off again? Have you climbed up into the mountains? Silent, stubborn, willful child. No . . . no . . . you are not a child now. Not now. Not for many years. Spock, Spock, where are you now? Why are you not here, at my side?

There was a man, someone I recognized, someone I knew. Picard. Picard told me that you were . . . that you were on . . . Romulus. Yes, that is what he said. That you were on Romulus. You are not a traitor: you cannot be! No, no, not a traitor. But not an innocent either, for you know now, you know how difficult it can be, how easily good intentions can go astray. No, no longer an innocent: you have seen too much, experienced too much. You have even known death . . . perhaps you know more than I . . . far more than I. Perhaps you can see more clearly. Perhaps you have found your truth glimmering amid the darkness, amid the red flames and black smoke of a burning city. Perhaps you have found your truth in a weeping child's gaze. Perhaps you will find your truth even in the dark despair of the Romulan people.

You have taken your harp with you, my son: it was not among the possessions you left behind. I remember, Spock. I remember how it was with you, how I taught you to play the music of this world, the music of tradition and restraint and precision. And you learned. You learned it all. But you were not content with what I could give you. You reconfigured the harp, attempting to suit it to the music of Earth. I told you it was a useless pursuit, a foolish waste of time. But you persisted. So very human, so like your mother. And in the end, like your mother, you triumphed. You made your harp sing with Mozart's work and with that of hundreds of Earth's composers. And still you were not content. You experimented with the music of Kreleth of Andor, of the Tamarian composer Jek Lor, of Lopil of Niath. You even played the harsh, rasping notes of the Tellarite Graknor and the Klingon Ketelk.

Mozart's music surrounds me still . . . but it will not always be so. The concerto . . . the concerto is drawing to a close. Soon, soon, it will be over, and who will fill the silence then?

Where are you, Spock, where are you, my son? You are a child
no longer . . . you are . . . you are on Romulus, yes, that is what Picard said. On Romulus. But what are you doing there, Spock? Are
you sitting in some dark, hidden corner, surrounded by your fellow
conspirators? Are your hands even now upon the strings of your
harp? Are you teaching the Romulans the music of many worlds, of
Earth and Andor, of Vulcan and Elar? Have you taught them the
music of Zefral, Spock? Strange, alien music that sings of light and
glittering crystal and children whose tears are the color of the sky. I
hear it now, beneath the music of Earth, and I wonder, did Mozart
hear it also?

Perhaps he did, my son. Perhaps he did. As you always have. Tell
them, Spock. Tell the people of Romulus of the warring clans of
T'Lai and T'Sell, whose members now live together in peace, side
by side, in the city of your birth. Tell them of Klingons and humans
grown weary of battling one another. Speak of peace and truth and
justice. Speak of unity and kindness. And if they say that you are an
idealist, that your dream of reunification can never be realized, tell
them of roses blooming in the Vulcan desert. Tell them, my son,
how it was for you, when you woke from the darkness, whole and
renewed. Do not be afraid . . . never be afraid . . . to share with
them *all* that you are—Vulcan and human. And do not forget to listen, my son. Listen to the music of Romulus. Listen, and you will
hear the soft melody of hope beneath the strident tones of rage and
despair. Hold fast to that melody, Spock. Hold fast.

I hope that Picard will find you, Spock. I hope that he will show
you all that you have meant to me, all that you have taught me. I
hope that you will know, at last, that I love you, my son. That I have
always loved you. That I am proud of you—of all that you are and
all that you were and all that you will be. Your mother was right. I
regret that I did not have the courage to show you these things myself. I regret it most bitterly. Forgive me, Spock. And know that I
wish you peace, even though I do not believe you will ever find it.
Not truly. Not completely. For you will always dream of making
this cold and indifferent universe a place of justice and mercy. Ide-
alistic. Impractical. Illogical. You are better than I, Spock. You always were.

I hope that you *will* succeed in this great endeavor to reunite the people of Vulcan and Romulus. But I know that if you do not succeed, you will try again and again and again. I know, also, that you will leave your mark upon the minds and spirits of all those whom you touch in the effort. Walk in wisdom, my child, and listen, as you always have, as you always will, to the dictates of your own heart. Unity *is* possible. I know that this is so, for I hear it, now, in the music that surrounds me. Hold fast to your dream, Spock, and one day our worlds . . . all worlds . . . will be one. I am certain of it.

STAR TREK
DEEP SPACE NINE®

Fear, Itself

Robert J. Mendenhall

Let me assert my firm belief that the only thing we
have to fear is fear itself . . .

—Franklin D. Roosevelt,
twentieth century

Fifteen seconds until hull breach. Fifteen seconds.

Jake Sisko clung to the arms of the crippled shuttlecraft's only pas-
senger seat, fighting the erratic pull of the failing gravity-field gener-
ator. Bile teased its way up his constricted throat. His eyes teared
from the acrid smoke that saturated the cabin. Or was it from the raw
fear that burned inside him? A wild klaxon wailed above the engine
roar and sliced through the incessant ringing in his ears like a saber.

*Oh, Dad. Dad, if you can hear me, wherever you are, please
help us.*

It was a useless plea and he knew it. Benjamin Sisko had disappeared into the realm of the Bajoran Prophets months ago.

Time seemed to slow for Jake, to liquefy. His thoughts drifted
lazily in his head. He watched Nog glide past him in an elongated,

operatic lunge. The Ferengi said something to Jake—it must have been urgent—but Jake couldn't understand the words; they were drawn out and distorted.

Jake turned his head away, back to the forward section. It was like swimming through mud and that simple movement made his stomach churn. What was left of the navigator's station crackled and sparked like lightning. The charred face of Ensign Warren gazed at him through lifeless eyes. She was so young. So pretty. Her gray uniform still smoldered.

"Ten seconds until hull breach," the computer announced, its feminine voice calm in contrast to the imminent danger it warned of.

"Emergency transporter has been set," shouted another familiar voice. "Let's go!"

Jake saw Lieutenant Ezri Dax jump from the command seat and stumble past him. She was a short young Trill with walnut hair that waved over her blue eyes. Jake caught her fresh pine scent even through the stench of burning materials—or was it his imagination?

And then, like Nog a moment before, she seemed to move unnaturally slow. She took a step and then appeared to just hang in midair. He fixated on the line of mahogany spots which circled her round face, ran down her neck, and disappeared under her torn Starfleet uniform. Hard to believe that slender young woman, nearly girlish in her mid-twenties, carried a symbiotic life-form in her abdomen that was over three hundred years old. When he first met her, Jake had been drawn—

Suddenly, Nog was there, grabbing him by his shirt with small, yet powerful, fists and pulling him to his feet. Reality returned with a snap. Jake towered over the small Ferengi, but Nog yanked him toward the aft section with unnatural ease and strength.

"Five seconds until hull breach," the computer droned.

"Computer," Ezri shouted as she removed a pair of satchels from the locker behind her. "Emergency beam-out. Engage."

The computer didn't acknowledge the command. It simply carried out the instruction.

Jake's skin tingled with the crawling sensation of molecular dissolution. He smacked at the coppery taste forming in his mouth and blinked his watered eyes as he disintegrated into azure energy.

Transport is never instantaneous. You don't just vanish from where you were and instantly appear at your destination. It's a process. For a brief period, milliseconds perhaps, you actually exist in two places at the same time. Some actually claimed to have experienced dual awareness. It had never been that way for Jake, but this time—this time—he was aware of materializing, of being somewhere else while he was still present on the dying shuttlecraft.

Through his stinging eyes, he watched as the structural integrity forcefields failed and the battered hull succumbed to the void of space. He felt a slight breeze as the atmosphere, smoke, and loose debris were blown into space by the rapid decompression. For a terrifying instant, he felt his own dematerializing body pulled away from the pad.

Suddenly, the ground was rushing up to him. He crashed into it headfirst in an explosion of hot colors and sharp pain. And then, there was nothing but the dark.

Jake had a sensation of dreaming, but no clear recollection of it—only flashes of impressions. Terror. Being chased. He became aware of a relentless throbbing in his head as the blackness that surrounded him melted into a soupy gray. He tried to bring his hand to his head but the movement encouraged a fresh wave of nausea. He groaned and let his hand drop.

"C'mon, buddy."

Jake heard the familiar voice amid the ringing in his ears. Reluctantly, he opened his eyes, found his vision a blur, and shut them again. "N-Nog?" Jake said. He heard the Ferengi squeal in delight as Nog often did.

"You had us worried there, Jake."

"S-sorry, ohhh."

"Just relax, take it easy. You've got a concussion."

"What hap-happened?"

"We materialized about six feet off the ground."

"Why-why did we d-do that?"

"Emergency beam-outs are tricky. The computer just finds a safe location if it can and adjusts its coordinates as it energizes. The computer was knocked out before it had time to complete the coordinates. We were lucky we didn't materialize a hundred meters up, or even in orbit. We were real close to the emergency transporter's limit."

"Y-yeah," Jake said. He opened his eyes now, and winced at the pain, but forced himself to keep them from shutting again. It was dark. He could see a very few stars through the cloud-covered night sky. The air was balmy and stank of rust and oil and fetid garbage. He finally managed to raise his hand to his head, and felt it bandaged.

"Ezri's scouting the area—ugh." Nog's grunt of pain drew Jake's attention. Nog was sitting up against a rock, one arm splinted and tied immobile to his shoulder. One of his legs was wrapped below the knee

"Nog, your leg . . ." Jake asked tentatively. He wondered if it was the biosynthetic leg, the one Nog received after he lost his own leg fighting Jem'Hadar forces on AR-558.

"It's okay. Nothing broken. Just landed on a jagged rock."

"Nog, wh-what happened up there?"

"We struck a cloaked, gravitic mine. Didn't think the Dominion would have left any around their old facilities. Should have been looking for the damned things. Stupid. Stupid."

A mine? A *mine?* His father would have anticipated booby traps. "But why mine a junkyard like this place?" Jake asked. "That's all this is, right? Just a boneyard?"

"As far as we know. Every other Dominion base we inspected has been just what the Founder said it was."

"Did she say anything about—"

"Quiet," Nog said and tilted his head so his enormous ears could cup distant sounds. "Someone's coming." Nog leaned over and removed a hand phaser from one of the satchels Ezri had taken from the shuttle.

Jake scooted himself closer to the rock Nog leaned against, gritting his teeth at the fierce pain the movement generated. He glanced in the direction Nog was pointing the phaser and listened for several moments. "I don't hear—"

"Shhh. You know my ears are more sensitive than yours." Jake bristled at the rebuke. "Wait. Wait a minute . . ." Nog lowered the phaser and let out his breath. "It's okay. It's Ezri."

"How do you know?"

"Ezri was with me on 558. She knows I can hear approach movements and whispered it was her coming up."

A moment later, Ezri Dax scampered around the backside of their rock, out of breath. She dropped to her buttocks with uncharacteristic clumsiness. She was tired, Jake thought. Dog-tired. Her complexion was ruddy with exertion, causing her spots to appear even darker. Her brow glistened with perspiration, pasting the short hair to her forehead. The collar of her turquoise-colored shirt was unfastened and open down to the torn black and gray tunic she wore over it.

"We've . . ." she said, breathless, "another . . . problem."

"Now what?" Nog asked with annoyance. "Don't we have enough problems?"

"What is it, Ezri?" Jake asked.

"Breen. Heading this way."

"What? Here?" Nog asked.

"I thought the Breen surrendered with the Dominion," Jake said. "What are they doing here in Federation space?"

"The Breen government signed the peace treaty, but these don't look like soldiers," Ezri said. She pulled a small canteen from one of the satchels and took a long pull from it. Water dripped past her lips and onto her chin.

"Hey, take it easy," Nog said. "We only have two of those."

Jake shot an annoyed glance at Nog. Ezri was thirsty. Why was Nog acting so arrogant?

Ezri lowered the canteen and dabbed at her chin with the sleeve of her free arm. She sucked in a deep breath and lowered the canteen. "Sorry."

"You were telling us about the Breen," Nog insisted. Again, Jake felt a rush of unfamiliar annoyance.

"I saw a small contingent of Breen. Four, maybe five. I don't know what they're up to, but my guess is they're looking through the salvage for anything of value."

"Or something specific," Nog said.

Ezri looked at him sharply. "Yes," she said. "I hadn't considered that. But what?"

"Us?" Jake asked.

Ezri shook her head. "I don't think so, they weren't using tricorders. But then again, I don't think tricorders would be much good in all this debris. Too much interference. No, I don't think they know we're here."

"Lucky for us," Nog said. "But we're going to have to find a place to hide out until they leave."

"Actually, I think I've found just the spot. Back that way." Ezri cocked her head in the direction she had come, then took another, much shorter, pull from the canteen.

"Toward the Breen?" Jake asked. "Shouldn't we be heading in the other direction?"

"We don't know what they're looking for, but I do know where they've already looked. They're searching through junk piles of old ship hulls and debris."

"Ships?" Jake asked. "Maybe we can find one that works and fly out of here."

Nog shook his head. "This is a boneyard, Jake. If it was space-worthy, it wouldn't have been dumped here. Just a bunch of hulls and spare parts. Hey, maybe the Breen are just looking for parts to fix their own ship."

"Maybe," Ezri said. "Come on, we need to circle around them before they get here."

Jake winced as he staggered to his feet. His head swirled and he fell back against the boulder. Nog wrapped his good arm around Jake's waist and Jake draped his other arm over the Ferengi's shoulder. Ezri supported Jake on the other side and the three awkwardly shuffled into the junkyard, making a wide circle around the approaching Breen.

Jake had never seen so much debris before in his entire life. He recalled touring the surplus depot in orbit around Qualor II with his dad and was amazed at the volume of derelict spaceships and salvage, but at least there it was all in some sort of order. Here, it was all just piled and dumped in massive stacks of metal covering the entire surface of the small planetoid. They passed ruptured hulls of all kinds of craft—Romulan scouts, Klingon birds-of-prey, Bajoran subimpulse raiders, Federation shuttles, Pakled freighters,

Jem'Hadar attack ships, Vortan couriers, and skeletons of vessels Jake didn't recognize.

Noxious fumes rose from the stacks, challenging the tentative control Jake exerted over his nausea. The heat, even at night, was debilitating, and Ezri and Nog were forced to stop several times so Jake could rest. He was trying not to be a burden to them, but they were Starfleet officers, trained in this kind of hardship. He was a journalist. He wrote about these situations. He did not live through them. He didn't. . . .

He . . .

Jake collapsed in their arms as a rush of vertigo subdued him.

"We've got to let him rest," Ezri said. "Let's find one of these open hulls where we can hide."

"There," Nog said.

Jake had only a vague idea of what was happening now. His thoughts were nonsensical and fragmented, his vision a teary blur. Confusion dominated him until, finally, he slipped into oblivion.

It was after him. Pursuing him. Why was it chasing him? Why? He tripped and fell, sprawling onto the forest floor. He heard the creature's ungodly wail through the dark foliage. Closer. Closer. No—

How long he was out, Jake didn't know. But when his thoughts resurfaced, the throbbing behind his eyes and the wrenching of his gut had subsided. It was cooler, and the air was less putrid than he remembered. It now held a spicy odor he couldn't quite place. He lay on a corrugated surface of hard rubber and could feel the regular, skid-resistant ridges of the material through his clothing. It was deck plating of the kind used in older, spartan space vessels.

His eyes opened to muted, jade lighting. Nog? Ezri? Alone. He was alone inside some alien vessel. He pushed himself to a sitting position and rubbed his aching neck. Someone had balled up a jacket and propped Jake's head on it like a pillow, so the stiffness would quickly pass.

Thank you.

The vessel was small, perhaps an old scout ship. The bulkheads were obscured with dead, useless gauges and shattered monitors.

Wires and fiber hung limply from splintered conduits. The only light came from a dull, green filament, jury-rigged with a Starfleet tricorder for power.

Where were they? Scouting? Looking for food? Water? Escape?

How long before Deep Space 9 began looking for them? They must be overdue by now, although he had no idea exactly how long they had been here on this rock of junk. Surely Colonel Kira would've alerted Admiral Ross when they missed the scheduled check-in. Dr. Bashir must be going crazy with Ezri missing.

The scrape of metal on metal jarred him. His breath caught as the rusted hatch swung inward with an agonized screech. Had the Breen found him? He skidded back, hugging the bulkhead. His heart slammed against his chest. The roof of his mouth was suddenly dry as cotton.

"Jake?" Nog's pronounced lobes popped through the hatch.

Jake nearly giggled with relief. "Yeah," he whispered as Nog bounded into the craft. "Where's Ezri?"

"She's out checking the wrecks for a working communications system."

Jake nodded and pulled the pack around Nog's bandaged arm. "Good."

"Don't get your hopes up, buddy."

"Okay, but sooner or later, someone's going to come looking for us, right?"

"Oh, sure, when we don't make the next check-in. But, Jake. Starfleet doesn't know where we are."

Jake was stunned. "What?"

"Oh, they have a general idea. Admiral Ross gave us a list of about twenty Dominion sites to check out. We filed a flight plan, but we deviated from it to check out this place, instead of the next one in line. This was a dump. I thought we could knock it out now and save some time not having to double back. I didn't amend the flight plan. So, they know where we were at our last check-in, and where we were supposed to go next. But not where we are now."

Jake couldn't believe it. His father would never have allowed a mission, even a routine one like this, to proceed without every detail carefully planned and verified and followed. There would have been fail-safes and backups and contingencies and—

"Dammit, Nog!" Jake was furious. "How could you—"

"Jake, this was a routine survey. The Founder gave us extensive information on each facility and Starfleet already did long-range scans on all of them before they sent out these small inspection teams. There weren't supposed to be any mines."

"There weren't supposed to be any Breen here, either," Jake said. "But there are."

"Okay, okay," Nog said, conceding with hands outstretched. "We were careless."

"Ensign Warren is dead, because you were careless."

Nog's face went as ashen as a Ferengi's could. He stared hard at his longtime friend. When he spoke, his voice was low, nearly a hoarse whisper. "You don't have to tell me she's dead. I know she's dead. I saw her die." Jake opened his mouth to retort and was cut off with a snarl. "You don't know a damned thing about death, Jake. Nothing. I'm a Starfleet officer. I've seen more death in the last two years than you'll see in your entire milksop life."

Jake charged the Ferengi, his anger seething like plasma. Nog grabbed the tall human's shirt with his good hand and pulled Jake's face down until they were nose to nose. Nog snarled. Jake swore.

"Oh, you think that's something to be proud of?" Jake said. "That you've seen death? That you've killed?"

"You knew you couldn't hack it in the fleet, Sisko, that's why—"

They were yelling at each other now, with a vehemence neither had shown nor known before. They didn't hear, didn't understand what the other was saying. Their pent-up anger was released in incoherent fury. Spittle sprayed from Nog's heavily toothed mouth. Jake's eyes bulged with unrestrained contempt. They shouted and pushed and grabbed until they were seconds, literally seconds, from lashing out and striking each other.

"Stop it!" They were both so consumed in their rage, they hadn't heard the hatch open. "I said stop it!"

Jake and Nog turned toward Ezri Dax, both still clutching the clothing of the other, both panting so hard their throats rasped. She

stood at the hatch with a look of deep concern. Or was it contempt?

"You two are friends," she said deliberately. "Best friends. I
don't know where this is all coming from, but I don't have time to
counsel you now. You both need to put it aside, bury it for now, until
we get out of this."

Jake twisted free of Nog and turned toward the small Trill, his
anger still dominant. "Did you find a working communication system?"

"Unfortunately, no."

"Then, come on, Ezri. How the hell are we going to get out of
this? No communications. No way off this planet. A bag of ration
bars, even less water than that. A few medical supplies. And the
Breen, who'll kill us the minute they find us? Just how are we going
to get out of this? My father would never—"

"Dammit," Nog said, lunging for Jake again. "Your father is not
here. Your father left us. He *left* us!"

"Enough!" Ezri said, her voice assured and in command. In command like Jadzia Dax, the symbiont's previous host, used to be. But
Jadzia had always been formidable, and with her, Jake could never
tell when the Dax personality was dominant. *Ezri* Dax, on the other
hand, was more reserved in her authority, less confident in her ca-
pability. Ezri was . . . sweet. When the Dax personality asserted itself, the differences were remarkable and instantly compelling.
Jake backed down and so did Nog.

"Lieutenant Nog," Ezri said sharply. "I expect no further outbursts from you, is that clear?" Nog nodded weakly and turned
away. "Mr. Sisko, you are a civilian and came along with us as a
journalist, however under the circumstances, Starfleet regulations
place you under my authority. You will also comply. Is that understood?"

Jake looked long at Lieutenant Ezri Dax, but shook his head yes.

"Very good, gentlemen. Now let's take some time to let the emotions settle, then I want to meet to discuss what our options are.
Thirty minutes."

Jake and Nog turned and examined each other for a long moment. In those few seconds, it seemed that their entire relationship

replayed itself in Jake's mind—their first meeting on DS9 nearly, what? Eight, nine years ago? He thought of their antics on the Promenade, getting in trouble with Odo, chasing the same girls, the Noh-Jay Consortium, dom-jot matches, holosuite adventures, school. . . .

Growing up together, they had been the best of friends. But, at that moment, Jake Sisko realized how truly far they had grown *apart.*

He found a dark corner in the tiny cabin and sat down against the bulkhead as the rage segued into despair. He was frightened. Jake could see no way out, no way to the safety of Deep Space 9. The chilling memory of Ajilon Prime oozed into his thoughts, and he screwed his eyes shut, vainly hoping the images would vanish.

But they didn't.

Nog was wrong. He *had* seen death. Jake had gone to the aid of a Federation colony on Ajilon Prime with Dr. Bashir. There was an emergency hospital there. It was under attack. He watched people he didn't know, and some he had come to know, die. And he learned a great deal about courage. And his own cowardice.

Perhaps that's why his friendship with Nog had soured so. Nog had courage. Nog proved it time and again. Even after he lost his leg in combat, Nog returned to service and fought the Dominion alliance with undiminished fervor. And not just courage in battle, Nog had personal courage, as well. Despite all odds and against his family's wishes, Nog became the first Ferengi in Starfleet, withstanding suspicion, resentment, and an academic regimen that Jake himself would have found exacting.

Jake raised his eyes to sneak a glance at Nog. Their gaze met for an instant. No more. Both averted. Both turned away.

"The Breen," Ezri said when the three had gathered half an hour later, "seem to be heading away from us. I backtracked their route, but if they're here for a purpose, I can't determine what it is."

"Could they just be checking the place out, like we were supposed to do?" Jake asked.

"The Dominion surrendered all their facilities to the Federation Alliance," Nog said coldly. "The Breen have no authority here."

"Nog's right. Technically, they're already in violation of the treaty. Unfortunately, we aren't in any position to arrest them." Ezri smiled, clearly trying to lighten the air.

Jake scowled. "Maybe they're planning on setting up a secret base to launch pirate raids." The crack was meant to be facetious, but Nog and Ezri looked at each other with sudden concern. "What?" Jake asked.

"Jake, old buddy," Nog said with a trace of the old warmth. "You may have hit it right on the money."

Ezri nodded. "That would explain why there are cloaked, gravitic mines in orbit and why the Founder didn't tell us about them. She didn't know about them. The Breen may have been planning on double-crossing them."

Jake sat straight, his journalist instincts now aroused. "Or maybe not. Maybe they're just now seizing the opportunity created by the Dominion's surrender."

"Could be. Could be," Nog said, thoughtfully stroking one huge ear.

"When they decided to set up shop here isn't important right now," Ezri said. "They're here. Those must have been patrols we saw. Which means their base is somewhere near here, since they were on foot. We're going to have to move again. Find a safer place to camp."

Jake and Nog nodded in agreement.

"And we're going to have to get this information back to Starfleet, somehow."

Somehow.

Jake closed his bone-weary eyes and shifted his body over the hard deck, testing position after position for one that would be less uncomfortable than the last. His temples throbbed and his brain ached behind his eyeballs.

All night. They had hiked *all night* around mountainous junk piles, through forests of debris, in between stacks of garbage. They managed to avoid the Breen and found this old Federation shuttle-craft hull half-buried beneath hundreds of other wrecks. It was an ancient, sublight box and if Nog was right about the markings, it was well over a hundred years old.

Old or not, it was familiar, so they pried open the side hatch and battened down for the day. The cabin had been gutted. The old control console had been stripped and wires and conduit snaked from it like untended weeds. Except for the two ragged pilots' seats forward, the shuttle cabin was barren. Jake could see the mountings in the deck where five other seats had been, but they were long gone. So, with nothing to lie on, each found a spot on the unrelenting deck.

That was their plan. To sleep during the daylight hours and scout at night. Their first priority would be to find water. They had only one canteen left and even rationing would not make it last more than another two days, at best. Not if they were going to be exerting themselves and they surely would be.

Food next. Then find some way to communicate with Starfleet. The Breen must have communication equipment, which, of course, didn't do them one gram of good.

It was dark in the shuttle and the air was stale. But at least the hull was insulated, so they wouldn't bake when the sun came out. Still, with no power to operate circulation fans, they would need to leave the hatch open a crack for air to get in and that meant the stench would get in, too. And the air would be hot.

Restless, unrefreshing sleep washed Jake Sisko away. And he dreamed.

They were troubled dreams. Fragments. Sketches, no more than that. Brief scenes from an unfinished play. They were snatches of imagination and slices of incoherence. He tossed and moaned.

Graveyards. Hounds howling in the night. Moon shadows cast over tombstones. Wind. Limbs. Cracks of lightning. He shivered in the pelting rain and ran. And ran. And ran.

Into the forest. Thunder. Lightning. From behind him, right behind him—a shriek of malevolence and depravity. Of carnivorous hunger. Right behind him. He screamed. And ran.

Lightning. Electricity. Crackling electricity. Thunder and that hideous wail.

Forest. Creature. Chasing him. Chasing him. Reaching for him—

* * *

"Ugh." Jake sat up suddenly. Sleep and the dream were instantly gone. Nog and Ezri were curled up on the deck, each in their own corner, each fast asleep and seemingly oblivious to Jake's own troubled slumber.

He slid his back against the bulkhead, careful not to cut himself on jagged rips in the metal. How long had he slept? He rubbed his eyes with the heels of his hands. The dream images were fragmented, but still clear in his mind. They nagged at his deep thoughts. He was running. Fleeing from something hideous. And it was after him. Chasing him. . . .

Sleep seduced him slowly and he drifted off again, still sitting against the jagged bulkhead. Again, pieces of images troubled his dreams. He heard guttural wailing and shouts. Electrical flashes and *booming thunder. The lightning silhouetted the monster for split seconds. Its seeping, hollow face snarled. It reached for him with bony fingers. Dripping fingers. Nowhere to run. It grabbed him by the shoulders and shook him—*

"Jake, wake up."

Jake opened his eyes with a start. It was dark and hot. He was sticky with sweat and sore. His neck ached and the back of his head felt flattened from leaning against the hard bulkhead.

"Come on, Jake, wake up," Nog repeated, shaking him by the shoulders again. "We've got work to do. How did you sleep like that, anyway?"

"I have no idea." He looked around the dark cabin. Nog's tricorder was propped open and supplying the tiniest bit of light, just enough to illuminate the shuttle's interior with a ghostly tinge.

"Where's Ezri?" Jake asked.

"She's out looking for a discreet toilet area. You can do the same when she gets back. Then we start looking for food and water."

"Where are we going to find either one on this junkyard?"

"Ezri had an idea. Our tricorders are practically useless down here at ground level. Too much interference from all this metal. So we climb to the top of one of these piles and scan for residual Federation energy signatures. We find a Federation ship," he looked around the ancient shuttle, "a more modern one, and hope to find a working food replicator."

"Wow, that's a slim chance," Jake said as he grunted to his feet. At least the effects of the concussion seemed to have gone away.

"Well then, if we can't find a Federation replicator, we'll look for a Vulcan one, or something, Anything that we can get to work to replicate some food and water."

"Who's next?" Ezri said as she popped through the hatch.

"I'm fine," Nog said. "You go ahead, Jake."

"All right. Be back in a few minutes."

Jake slipped out the hatch and into the hot night air. He walked a bit, navigating through the maze of stacks until he found a niche in a nearby heap. Gratefully, he relieved his bladder.

When he emerged, Jake felt a deep chill in his bones. A chill of dread. He scanned his surroundings quickly, frantically. Everything looked the same in the dark. Which way had he come?

He looked up, but could get no bearing—there was no moon and the stars were unfamiliar.

Which way had he come?

He felt the old fear, the same icy terror that had touched him on Ajilon Prime, felt his heart begin to expand.

Wait. Relax. Relax.

Relax, he told himself. He was close by. He knew that. And he certainly didn't want Nog to see him this way. Not Nog.

Get control. . . . Jake clamped his eyes shut and called up an image of his father. It came quickly and clearly. Ben Sisko. Benjamin Sisko. Captain Benjamin Sisko. Jake saw his tall father, sitting behind his old desk on Deep Space 9. His feet were crossed and resting on the desktop. Casually, he tossed his prized baseball in the air, caught it and tossed it up again. His father smiled as only he could, and his smile lit the room as it always did. His pearly teeth were framed by his wispy goatee beard and bright next to his dark skin. His shaved head glistened in the ambient light.

"You're going to be okay, Jake," his father said in a voice surprisingly soft.

Then the image changed. His dad hugged him and kissed him on the forehead, as he had done so often. Jake loved that show of affection. And it warmed him now.

He opened his eyes and felt the panic subside. His breathing deepened and slowed. His heart rate diminished.

Okay. There were half a dozen paths around him. *Let's see . . . there's the niche.* Jake returned to the opening and turned to see which way he had come. He didn't know. He hadn't paid attention. Okay. He hadn't walked far. He'd try a path for a few meters, and if he didn't find the shuttle, he'd backtrack and try another.

Jake started down the first path on his right—he was going to do this systematically. A few meters and—

Nothing. No shuttle. No sign of Nog or Ezri waiting for him. *They're probably concerned now, and out looking.* No, probably only one, while the other stayed at the shuttle in case Jake returned.

Jake turned and retraced his steps. He went a few meters. Then a few meters more. And then a few more.

Where was the niche?

He backtracked again, feeling his pulse speed up as the panic began to feed.

"You're going to be okay, Jake," he heard his father's voice in his head, clear and reassuring.

Jake nodded to himself, and his pulse slowed again. He stopped. This was no good. It was too dark to tell one hill of junk from another. Each path looked the same.

His mouth was like sandpaper and he realized he was deathly thirsty. Terrific. Lost. No water. No food. He was worse now than he was earlier. *And, Dad, don't tell me it's going to be okay!*

Wait. Food. There's an idea. Nog said Ezri was going to climb up to the top of one of these big piles to scan for a food replicator. He could do that, climb a stack, and maybe get his bearings. Maybe even spot them.

The stacks were uneven. Some were bulkier than others. He found one that looked to be tall and sturdy, but not too steep. The climb was difficult and dangerous. The pile was strewn with debris of all types and sizes. There were wrecks on top of parts mixed in with plain old garbage. Twice he cut his hands on jagged edges. God, he hoped his Penicyl-20 shot was still good.

It took nearly fifteen minutes to reach the top. Exhausted, he leaned against the protruding nose of some craft and caught his breath. It was much cooler up here. In fact the sweat on his brow now chilled him. From here he could see for kilometers in all directions. There were eerie glows from valleys between piles. It looked like a metal mockery of the rolling hills in the Seres Province on Bajor he had once visited with his father.

Jake couldn't make out the shuttle. Nor was there any sign of— Oh, no.

Again, dread washed over him. He leaned forward, grasping an antenna housing for support. It couldn't be. He squinted and focused on a group of small lights bobbing up and down along one of the paths below him. The glow from the lights was bright enough to illuminate a trio of Breen. He could see their weapons drawn and prodding Ezri and Nog along the path ahead of them.

Jake leaned back against the nose, the shock of seeing his friends captured making him feel heavy. He rested his head in his hands and shivered in the night air. What was he going to do? What could he do? He couldn't take on the Breen himself. He couldn't face them alone.

They wouldn't let them go, he realized. In fact, the Breen were here illegally and probably planning something even more illegal. They would surely kill them. He had to do something.

But he couldn't.

He was frozen in his spot. Despair crushed him, immobilized him. The echo of gunfire in his mind. The screams. The killing. Ajilon.

Ajilon. Ajilon. Why in God's name couldn't he escape from that awful memory? Breath came to him in jagged rasps. He fought the urge to scream. His blood shot through his veins with such force he could feel each rapid-fire pulse. Faster. Harder. His eyes teared.

"They need you, Jake."

Jake Sisko jerked his head up, his eyes wide. "D-Dad?"

No answer. Had he imagined it? It sounded so real. It was like his father was right here, next to him. But no one was here. Before, he thought he had conjured those thoughts of his father on his own.

But could he be here? Watching him? From the Celestial Temple? His stepmother, Kassidy, had said she was pulled to the Celestial Temple, and spoke with Ben Sisko.

"Dad?"

Still no response. *He's watching me. God, I can't let him see me like this. What should I do?*

Jake pushed himself up and gripped the antenna housing. He found the bobbing lights farther away and followed their progress. Okay. Okay. He fixed their direction in his mind. Wait. Get some landmarks. The last thing Jake wanted to do was get lost again. Not now.

There. That spire. It was a long gun turret, he thought. Sticking out of a debris stack at an odd angle at about two o'clock from their direction of travel. He'd use that as a guide.

He climbed down from his perch much faster than he had scaled it. Twice he lost his footing and slid along sharp protruding edges, slicing his legs and hands. He ignored the pain.

He was back on solid ground in minutes, sweating and bleeding and out of breath. The spire—there it was. Jake fixed its position and charged along the path, finding the one he thought they had been on. He kept his direction oriented with the spire. But how far ahead were they? From this perspective, it all looked different.

His heart pounded. Where were they? His lungs burned. Where?

His feet were kicking up tiny bits of debris and his footfalls were loud. He slowed, hoping not to telegraph his approach. His eyes watered. With a bloody hand, Jake wiped his eyes, smearing his cheek with blood.

Wait.

The noise came from just ahead somewhere. It was a metallic cluster of sounds. Clips of unintelligible syllables. Breen. But what was he saying?

"I can't understand you," Jake heard Ezri say. "You've taken my translator."

More metallic chatter, then the unmistakable sound of an impact.

"Leave him alone!" Ezri cried out.

Jake's muscles twitched, trembled. He was on the verge of panic. He could feel it creeping up his spine like an oily tendril. He screwed his eyes shut and gritted his teeth until the tendril slithered back down. His breath exploded from his chest in an audible gasp. Deep breaths. Deep.

A cautious step forward, hugging the debris with his back. . . .

They were just ahead, around the bend. He peered around the stack and stopped, immobile with shock. Ezri and Nog stood with their backs against a stack. Ezri supported a barely conscious Nog. There was blood flowing from a gash across his front right cranial lobe.

The Breen stood shoulder to shoulder facing them, not more than ten meters from them. Ezri scowled at the helmeted Breen, her eyes wide with defiance. *Oh my God. The Breen are going to execute them.*

Right now.

The tendril shot up his spine and tightened itself around Jake's throat. His legs quivered. Ajilon—he was going to watch his friends die. His vision blurred and his heartbeat was so loud he could hear nothing else. Not the wind whistling through the debris stacks. Not the staccato voices of the Breen. Not the defiant croaking of Nog as the weapons were taken off safety. Ajilon . . .

"They need you, Jake."

Again the voice in his head. Dad? It was no more than a whisper, but it cut through his chaotic thoughts with ease. They need you, Jake.

A metallic command. The Breen raised their weapons to their shoulders. He screwed his eyes shut and dug his fists into his temples. And imagined Ezri Dax toppling to the ground in throes of agony as disruptor pulses tore her insides out and scorched the symbiont to a crisp.

Another command. They took aim. He shook his head and mumbled and imagined Nog's remaining limbs shot away until he tumbled to the earth, a writhing torso—his dismembered arms and legs twitching nearby.

They need you, Jake.

"No!" Jake screamed.

He charged around the stack, wide-eyed and taut. The Breen turned toward him as Jake smashed headlong into the nearest. They crashed to the ground. Jake's vision narrowed into a tightly focused tube, and all he saw was the narrow slit of the Breen's helmet and his own bloody hands around the bastard's throat.

Was that him still screaming?

A crack of pain. An explosion of light. Then, brilliant red faded to empty, endless black.

Gray. So much gray. It surrounded him, even beneath his feet. Was he standing? Floating? Where was he and how did he—

This place. This was how Kassidy described the Celestial Temple. It was so . . . ethereal. Not really a place, more an idea. An illusion.

"Always the writer."

Jake turned, looking for the sound of the voice. He saw no one.

"Dad?"

And then he was right there. In front of him as if he had always been right there. He was as Jake had last seen him, in his gray and black duty coveralls with crimson tunic underneath. He looked at Jake with a soft, gentle smile on his face.

"I'm proud of you, son."

"Dad. I-I miss you."

"I know. I miss you too. You did a brave thing. It took courage to put yourself at risk."

"Courage? Dad, I was scared out of my mind. I was petrified. I'm not like you. I can't bravely face trouble and confrontations and . . . and death like you do. I'm not a soldier."

"No, you're not. You are who you are, and that's just fine with me. But don't think for a moment I haven't been afraid. I was afraid every time I took the *Defiant* into battle. I was afraid on AR-558. The first time I was brought here. On the *Saratoga*. On Tyree. I was afraid over and over again. The point is that your fear doesn't make you a coward. You acted when the time came for you to act. You turned and faced your fear, and you know what? Fear is the coward. Once challenged, fear loses its power. Its potency. That's what courage is, Jake. Turning and facing your fear."

"N-Nog. Ezri. Are they—"

Benjamin Sisko smiled at his son and embraced him. Jake wrapped his arms around his father's chest and held tightly, as he had done so often, so long ago. He felt Ben Sisko pull back a bit, and kiss his forehead, then disappear into the gray void.

* * *

Lightning flashed, illuminating the monster. Its pasty face was stretched into a grimace of evil. It wailed. It reached. It reached for him. Jake ran and ran, through pouring rain. Away from the monster.

No. No more.

"No more."

Jake stopped running. He turned toward the approaching monster, swallowed the terror into his gut and raised his balled fists to confront it. The monster slowed and then stopped. It growled at Jake. Hissed. Jake trembled, wanting so desperately to flee. With that, the monster wailed again and made to lunge. Jake tightened his fists and his resolve, subdued the urge, eyed the creature. It screeched and stopped. Then shriveled to a dwarf of its original stature and scurried into the forest.

To wait.

Throbbing behind his eyes assaulted Jake as he forced them open. He shut them again, quickly. The bright light above him stabbed into him like a blade. He moaned and gritted his teeth and even that slight motion bubbled his stomach. His eyes were closed, but he felt himself spinning. The cool air smelled of antiseptic. There were gentle chirping sounds. Birds? No, computer chatter. Where was he?

"Hey, buddy." The voice was low and quiet, but he recognized it as Nog's.

"N-Nog?"

"Right here."

"Where . . ."

"Easy. We're on the *Defiant*. Heading home."

"Ez . . ." It was an effort to talk. Jake closed his mouth and swallowed.

"She's okay. Thanks to you. You were able to distract them long enough for us to jump the other two. We found a com unit on one and managed to get a weak signal out. The *Defiant* was already out looking for us. How are you doing? You were hallucinating pretty good."

"Hal-halluc . . ."

"Yeah. Mumbling about monsters and prophets. Must have been some weird dreams."

Dreams. Had he only dreamed of meeting his father in the Celestial Temple? Had he just imagined it? But the voices in his head— *They need you, Jake.*

"N-Nog," Jake turned his head to face the Ferengi.

"Yeah, buddy?"

He wanted to ask Nog if he was ever afraid, but realized it was pointless. Nog had his own personal demons and faced them. When he lost his leg in combat, then returned to duty. The Academy. Sure, Nog would have had plenty of fears to face.

"I'm sorry that we've been . . ."

"Yeah," Nog said. "Me too. I guess we're just growing in different directions."

"Yeah. Into different people."

"But that's okay, you know."

Jake smiled. "You're right. You know, I think that scared me a bit. Losing you as my boyhood friend."

"Me too. But we can still be . . . adulthood friends." Nog squealed his Ferengi laugh and for a moment Jake felt like they were kids again. "I'll let you rest. By the way. You were right. The Breen were setting up shop to raid our shipping. We took them all into custody. Nice job."

Jake smiled and closed his eyes. He felt Nog's friendly pat on his shoulder, then heard him pad away. As he slipped back into sleep, Jake saw the creature. Hiding in the forest. Waiting. Jake turned toward it. Stared at it and smiled, satisfied, when the dwarf monster cowered closer to the tree it hid behind.

Jake Sisko knew the monster was still there. Waiting. It hadn't been banished, merely contained. It would be back, and Jake knew he would have to face it again. And again.

And he could.

Final Entry

Cynthia K. Deatherage

June 17, 2355

As I begin this journal, the sun is setting, transforming the azure sky
into a melting pot of gold and crimson and purple velvet. . . . There,
it's gone. Already I can see the faint glimmer of stars piercing the
deepening dusk! Those stars—how beautiful, how alluring, how
heartbreaking they are. Once again, they've taken you far from
home. Papa never understood your fascination with the stars; he
never understood why you failed to follow in his footsteps, planting
your feet firmly in the Minnesota sod and learning to love the miracle of growing things. Somehow the "farming gene" that has determined the lives and goals of generations of Hansens missed you,
Magnus. Papa couldn't understand why plants and bugs and four-
legged life-forms held no appeal for you—unless they were from
another planet. Mama understood, I think. She was a poet at heart,
though she never composed an ode. Her poetry sprang forth in her
garden, the arrangement of flowers and shrubs, the pruning of trees,
the carefully tended rows of vegetables, the shelves stacked with

jars of canned carrots and beans and apricots. But she loved the stars as well. At night, after the busyness of the day had ended, she loved to sit on the porch swing and watch the fireflies dance against the night sky, adding their green glow to the glitter of the blue-white jewels above. And, watching this heavenly display, I understand too—but it doesn't stop me from wishing the stars were not so bewitching in their beauty.

Already I miss you and Erin and little Annika. Little Annika . . . she won't be so little when you return. Thank you for letting her stay with me this past weekend while you and Erin finished making preparations for your mission. She was angry at first, but soon got over it—with the help of some homemade strawberry tarts. She's excited to be going with you on a "secret mission." I hope you remember to take plenty of holo-images of her while you're away.

How long will it be this time? Why so secretive about this mission of yours? That's the horrible part of this separation—its secret nature. We can't even send letters to one another, much less video transmissions. That's why I've started this journal—to share my thoughts and experiences with you while you're away. I promise to keep writing until the family is together again.

February 23, 2356

Where are you, Magnus? Where's that ship of yours amidst those scattered stars?

I received a transmission from Starfleet today—from a Lieutenant Morgan. He told me they lost contact with your ship, the *U.S.S. Raven,* but that they've sent other ships to "reconnoiter the area of your last known coordinates." He assured me that Starfleet is doing all they can to locate you. I tried to press him for more details, but he told me your mission was "classified" and that he couldn't be more specific at this point in time. This point in time . . .

Do you remember the time we went hiking through the woods up north? I think you were eight and I was eleven. Papa had told us not to wander off the trail, but somehow we ended up trail-less and clueless as to our whereabouts. Remember how alone we felt, how frightened when we realized we were lost? Remember how we prayed and cried and held each other as we shouted for help? Then we heard Papa's voice through the trees, calling us back to the trail, back to his arms. Can you hear me, Magnus? I'm calling . . . Come back. Come home.

March 5, 2358

Lieutenant Morgan was here today. He came to bring Starfleet's "sympathy" and to deliver several containers of your personal belongings, which had been carefully declassified. (How I hate that word—"classified"! It looms as a monstrous wall between us.) It seems the mighty Starfleet has given up the search for you. The lieutenant couldn't—or wouldn't—tell me why: it was classified. All he would say was "What Headquarters has been able to discover of the circumstances surrounding Professor Hansen's disappearance leads them to conclude the *U.S.S. Raven* and all aboard are irrecoverable. Starfleet sends its deepest regrets." Deepest regrets . . . I don't want Starfleet's regrets. I want my brother, my sister-in-law, and my niece! I want to see your lopsided grin again, Magnus, and have you pat my head and call me your "little big sister." I want to pick more not-quite-ripe strawberries with Annika in Mama's garden and discuss the finer points of hydroponics with Erin. I want my family! I'm alone here, Magnus. I'm all that's left of our proud Hansen line. Come back—prove them wrong! I haven't given up hope, no matter if Starfleet has. Do you see that tiny blue gem sparkling in the distance? That's Earth, Magnus, that's home. I'll be waiting . . .

March 9, 2358

Lieutenant Morgan called me today—just to see if I was okay. I guess I must have appeared pretty shaken when he left several days ago. I was angry—angry at Starfleet, angry at life, even angry at you, Magnus, for going off on some spacefaring adventure and dragging your family with you. But I'm not angry anymore—just . . . sad.. Sad at the distance that separates us, sad at the lost years, sad that my only communication with you is through this journal. But as I told Byron (that's the lieutenant's first name), I haven't given up hope. He smiled and told me that he hadn't either. He said, "From what I've read, your brother and his wife are very innovative, and, if you'll pardon my saying so, rather stubborn. If anyone can survive and return bringing their laurels with them, it's Magnus and Erin." I had to laugh—I don't know what kind of records Starfleet keeps on its denizens, but they had you pegged squarely: innovative and stubborn. Byron invited me to contact him if I needed to talk to someone—and he promised to keep me informed if he learned of any new developments or if your mission was declassified. I'll hold him to that.

December 27, 2367

It's just awful, Magnus—the reports, the images transmitted over the news! Earth—the entire Federation—is reeling from the attack. I go into town and everyone seems numb. Even the newscasters are grim. We've been invaded by a new and ferocious species—far worse than the Romulans or the Klingons ever were. They're called the Borg, and they travel in huge cube-shaped ships that are nearly indestructible. The Borg seem to be part organic and part machine, and they're intent on making everyone else in the galaxy part of their "Collective." They've captured a Starfleet captain—Picard, I think was his name—and they've done horrible things to him, making him speak for them. The news said he had been "assimilated." Starfleet has gathered an armada to stop the Borg, making a stand at someplace called Wolf 359. God help us if they fail!

January 2, 2368

It's so dark tonight. Even the stars seem dimmed somehow. Off in the distance, where the glow from the town's lights should be is—nothing. We're under a blackout—the dark emptiness mirroring the sober mood of our planet. The blackness has permeated my thoughts, and an inner coldness numbs my spirit. My hand is shaking so I can barely key in these words: The Borg are coming.

Oh Magnus, our ships, our people were massacred! Nothing we threw at them could stop the Borg, and now they are coming here, to Earth. Starfleet is gathering what's left of its ships—but what can they do that the armada couldn't? I don't know if there will be a home for you to come back to. I just wish I could hug you once more—just once. I think there's not a soul on Earth tonight that doesn't long for a hug, a touch, something to say, "You're not alone."

I love you, Magnus. Remember me . . .

January 7, 2368

It's taken a while for things to settle down here and for information to trickle its way through the news transmissions, but the Borg have been halted—permanently, I hope. I'm not sure how it happened, but somehow Starfleet rescued Picard and through him was able to send a code that disrupted the Collective from the inside since they couldn't breach their defenses from the outside. They stopped the Borg—but on our very doorstep! I hope I never experience such terror again. I hope, wherever you are, that you and Erin and Annika are safe and free and far from those terrible creatures!

March 2, 2368

Things are returning to normal after the Borg invasion, but I don't think Earth will ever be the same. I teach a course on Earth history one day a week at the grade school, and I still see the effects of the attack. Children will pause in their play, a shadow crossing their young faces, their eyes growing distant. I don't know if it's fear or the memory of fear, but I can understand their feelings. At night, I draw the curtain to shut out the glitter of stars—they no longer hold a poetic appeal. The stars stole you away, Magnus, and from the stars the Borg came, bringing their terror. Our innocence has been violated, our safety threatened—it will take a long time for these wounds to heal.

July 15, 2368

Tomorrow, Byron is coming for a visit. It's been a while since he's come to the farm, though we've kept in touch via transmission. You'd like him, Magnus. Let's see if I can describe him: slight of build with thinning brown hair; long, slender fingers; a gentle face; compassionate brown eyes, soft gravelly voice. I never thought I'd grow fond of a Starfleet officer, but . . . let's just say, I enjoy his company and our conversations. I think he feels the same. Wipe that grin off your face, brother! I said I enjoy his company—nothing more. . . .

July 16, 2368

Byron has left—he knew I needed time to sort through my emotions, to come to terms with the news he brought. He kept his promise made years ago—to share with me any declassified information he would learn of your mission and whereabouts. I wish he had broken that promise.

The Borg! Oh Magnus, you went looking for the Borg! Those hideous, horrid . . . words fail me. I don't know what to say or think.

Byron read portions of Starfleet reports about your mission. The Borg were just a rumor when you went looking for them to study their social structure—and maybe to make first contact. For the first eight months of your mission, your transmissions revealed the Borg were an elusive prey—a shadow, a ghost, a whisper echoing in the emptiness between the stars. You followed that whisper, pursuing it even into the Neutral Zone, disobeying the order to return. Oh Magnus, you stubborn, stubborn fool! Why didn't you listen? Papa always said someday your ornery streak would get the better of you—but, Magnus, didn't you realize what might become of Erin, of Annika? Of me?

And then the transmissions ceased. You just vanished. Did you find the Borg—or did they find you? Magnus, what can I say? When they told me you were missing, I held on to hope. When they told me they had given up their search, I still persevered. But now . . . now I remember Wolf 359 and Earth's night of terror. If the Borg found you, what hope is there? Byron offered some consolation—we don't know that you actually made contact with the Borg. But what else would explain your sudden disappearance? I wish—I don't know . . . I can write no more for now.

July 24, 2368

Byron is concerned for me. He thinks I'm depressed, and he's probably right. He wants me to come to San Francisco, where he can keep an eye on me. But I don't really want to be watched. I don't want to stay here either. Miles Darby has offered once again to buy the farmstead, and this time I'm seriously tempted to sell, but Byron urges me to consider carefully before letting go of the family farm. Right now, it's hard to consider anything carefully.

July 29, 2368

Tomorrow, I'm off to tour old Europe. Byron purchased a travel package for me and insisted I take it. He knows my penchant for Earth history and is hoping this will lift my spirits. I think it might. I'm actually looking forward to the trip.

September 3, 2368

I'm back. The tour was wonderful! I've all sorts of stories to tell the grade schoolers for next semester's history class. Byron was right—I needed a change of scenery, but I'm glad to be home. And I'm glad that it's still my home—our home, Magnus—and not an addition to Darby's acreage. More importantly, I've had time to think, to ponder, to come to terms with your possible fate. I just want you to know that I love you. I love you and Erin and Annika, even if I never see you again, or hold your hand or hear your laughter, even if you are—Borg.

March 7, 2371

I heard a story on the news tonight that reminded me of us, Magnus. Apparently, something has been happening to ships in a sector of space called "the Badlands." They disappear. We don't know if they're destroyed by space debris or some unknown anomaly, but they simply vanish. News has it that a Federation starship disappeared in that region—the *U.S.S. Voyager*. I feel for the families of all on board—wondering where their loved ones are, hoping for news yet dreading what they might hear. There are a lot of hurting people tonight: parents, husbands, wives, children, friends—I wonder if Starfleet would pass on a message if I were to write to some of them . . .

June 19, 2371

Byron is worried. There are rumors of an "organized threat" to the Federation by a group called "the Dominion." They live in the Gamma Quadrant but could launch an attack through a wormhole situated near Deep Space 9. I told him they ought to close the wormhole and then we needn't worry about this Dominion. He laughed and said that was easier said than done.

How is it the most troublesome governments have names like "Dominion" or "Empire"? If it's not the Klingons, it's the Romulans, if it's not the Romulans, it's the Cardassians—and now the Dominion. (Yes, Magnus, I know the Cardassian government is technically called a "Union," but it's an "empire," all the same.) It seems we humanoid species never learn—whether it's Earth's ancient history or modern galactic history, we've always been intent on conquering one another, annihilating one another, and generally making as many people miserable, helpless, and homeless as possible. Hopefully, this Dominion will mind its own business and leave us alone.

April 9, 2373

Voyager has joined the long list of vessels "missing-in-action." Starfleet, as with your ship, Magnus, has ceased its search and rescue operation, no longer offering hope of finding the lost craft. Why, I wonder? Does the Federation have a time limit they set on missing ships? "You have two years and then you're dead"? It's so frustrating. I've been in contact with some of the family of the missing crew, especially Mr. and Mrs. Kim. Their only child, Harry, is an ensign aboard the missing ship. They were so proud when he received his first deep-space posting on *Voyager*—it was a state-of-the-line ship, complete with something called "bioneural gelpacks" and other fancy doodads. And now he's gone. You can imagine their grief, Magnus. I don't have to imagine—I've lived it.

Sometimes I wish Zefram Cochrane had never discovered faster-than-light propulsion and that the Vulcans had left us humans well enough alone! But then, I suppose, that wish is itself futile—humans have always had an innate desire to explore, to unravel mysteries and create new ones, to grow beyond themselves. It's what drove men in the Old World to take to the high seas, to breach forbidden barriers, dispel myths and become myths themselves—leaving widows in their wake. Humanity's advances have always been bathed in the tears of those left behind. I ache for those left behind, Magnus. I know what they're going through.

August 21, 2373

Life is not well here in Federation space. It seems the Cardassians have aligned themselves with the infamous Dominion. War is in the offing. I was speaking to Mrs. Kim the other day, and, grief-stricken though she is, she's glad Harry is not here. She could send her son away to uphold the Federation ideals of exploration and communication, but she couldn't bear to send him into battle. I understood perfectly. I know if you were here, you'd be in the thick of things, stirring up trouble and devising ways to make the enemies of our freedom miserable. I remember the time you stood up to that bully, Carl Nilsen. He was two years older and three times your size, but you sent him packing when you clobbered him over the head with your Tyrellian ant farm. "A tiny ant can bring down a giant if accompanied by his many brothers," you quoted. I think it was a Vulcan proverb. Well, Magnus, we're going to need not only his brothers, but all his second and third cousins!

December 2, 2373

The Borg attacked again. It was so fast we hardly had time to work up a decent panic. Byron assumes the Collective had been watching for an opportunity to strike, and with our forces strained and scattered in the war with the Dominion, now was a good time. But once again, they were destroyed by Captain Picard—his hatred for the Borg must be almost overwhelming after what they did to him! And so, once again we've been spared. You may wonder at my attitude—why am I not running in the fields, wind whipping my hair, tears of joy and gratitude decorating my flushed cheeks? Besides the fact my middle-aged legs would probably collapse from such a display, I've found myself sobered by one thought, one theme that plays relentlessly in my mind: Were you on it, Magnus? Were you on the cube that Captain Picard destroyed?

I've wrestled with that question for the past several days, my emotions ranging from illogical anger at Picard to grief at your possible demise to gratitude that your sufferings would be over. But I've finally come to a resolution: What does it matter if you were? The Magnus for whom I'm writing this journal is not a mindless Borg drone. The Magnus I've addressed in these pages is my brother, with all of his wonderful and aggravating faults, his insatiable spirit of adventure, his unquenchable curiosity, his knack for finding trouble and multiplying it. Perhaps I've written only to the memory of my brother, but so be it. I promised I'd keep this journal until our reunion, and I shall do so—until death draws my fingers to their rest or old age robs me of mobility or mentality. Oh Magnus, even if what's left of your body and mind was on that cube, I still love you—and Erin and Annika too. I always will.

September 23, 2375

It's over—the Dominion War, as they've called it. After thousands upon thousands have lost their lives, after families have been shattered, hopes squandered, planets plundered—it is finished. And do you know what brought an end to this devastation, Magnus? A superweapon? Superb strategy? Overwhelming numbers? None of those delivered the final blow. The war ended with a deed of kindness, an act of trust, a healing touch. Would that all wars ended that way—better, that they would never begin! Why is it so easy for species to take offense, pull out our lasers and torpedoes, and pummel each other to pieces—and so difficult to extend a hand, to forgive, to heal? I don't mean to say that there aren't reasons to fight, to stand for what you believe, but even "just wars" demand a high price. It will take a long time for the scars of this war to heal. Several of the children I teach, even in our small town, have lost cousins, friends—one, a brother. Still, I sense a noticeable difference among the children and in the community since the war ended—a relaxing of one's guard, a collective relief. Now we can leave off killing and focus on living once again.

October 6, 2377

I've just finished speaking with the Kims, and they have shared wonderful news—Starfleet has made contact with *Voyager!* Can you believe it? *Voyager* has survived all of these years, somehow trapped and flung to the other side of the galaxy. Apparently the crew discovered some type of alien communications network and have managed to establish data transfer. The Kims were ecstatic over the letter they had received from their son and had dropped everything to spread the news and prepare their first answer. I wept when they shared their news—this time, hope repaid them for their years of investment. Only one thing marred their beautiful revelation—a twinge of envy on my part. Oh, Magnus, how I wish it had been the *U.S.S. Raven!* How I wish I could be sitting here composing a letter for you and Erin and Annika instead of making one more journal entry that may never be read. Yet, how can I begrudge the families of *Voyager*'s crew their joy? Here is tragedy turned triumph, death deprived, sorrow become singing! I must contact Byron to see what he knows . . .

January 4, 2378

More good news! Somehow Starfleet and the crew of *Voyager* have found a way to send live transmissions across the light-years. From what Mrs. Kim said, the window of communication only remains open eleven minutes a day, and, of course, with 140-plus crew members, each person has only a few minutes to speak with someone. Still, even with several decades of faster-than-light travel separating them from their son, the Kims could barely contain their joy over seeing Harry. "He was so handsome in his uniform—and looked so healthy!" I refrained from laughing. Their son has been missing for over six years and their first comments were on his robustness! Typical parents, eh?

February 21, 2378

Today—no, I won't write just another journal entry. Today is too special, too marvelous for that—and tomorrow promises to be downright miraculous! I just want to relive each moment, each painful and precious second. . . .

Byron stood in the middle of the living room, his middle-aged form lean and wiry, brown eyes literally dancing with untold news, long-fingered hands clasped tightly in anticipation. I laughed. "Byron, if you don't sit down I think you'll explode! What is it that brought you all the way to Minnesota—besides my homemade lemon meringue pie?"

"I can't sit—not yet! But you had best find a chair for what I have to say."

I shook my head, lowering my body into the overstuffed chair by the window. I had never seen Byron in such a mood before. "All right, I'm seated."

He drew a deep breath and let it out slowly. "I've got good news and bad news as more information about *Voyager* has become de-classified."

I remained silent, wondering what this had to do with me. Byron cleared his throat.

"They found the remains of the *U.S.S. Raven.*"

He paused, allowing me to absorb the startling news. The word *remains* stuck in my mind. "So, there were no survivors?" I asked.

His voice was soft. "They were assimilated, Irene."

Of course, I had assumed this for years. Still—to hear it confirmed . . . Tears blurred my vision, and I looked down at my hands. It hurt, hurt almost as much as the day I learned of the *Raven*'s disappearance. Suppressed grief clutched at my throat in painful spasms. I swallowed, forcing the words out. "Well . . . thank you for letting me know . . ."

"There's more." When I looked up at him, he smiled gently. "You've heard of the drone Kathryn Janeway liberated from the Collective?"

I nodded. "The Kims mentioned Harry was friends with her. Seven-something."

His smile broadened. "Seven of Nine. That was her Borg designation for eighteen years."

I remained silent. Obviously, Byron was bursting to reveal something, but he was taking his sweet time about it. Inwardly, I wrestled with my grief and was not particularly interested in discussing Borg drones, liberated or not. Then, Byron's voice broke through the pain.

"It's Annika, Irene! Captain Janeway rescued Annika from the Borg!"

"Annika?" I know I sounded ridiculous, but it took a few seconds for the revelation to take hold. "Annika!" I jumped to my feet. "Annika is alive?!"

"Yes!" he laughed. "She's been a member of *Voyager*'s crew for the past four years, learning to be human again."

I hugged him, laughing and crying and shivering. "Do you hear, Magnus?" I cried at the ceiling. "Annika is alive!" Then I started sobbing, weeping out years of broken hope and wounded dreams. Byron just held me, and I felt his own warm tears wet my hair. Fi-

nally, we pulled apart. I wiped my eyes. He sniffed, cleared his throat, and said hoarsely, "She wants to talk to you."

If I could have, I would have wept again—but there were no more tears. I had to satisfy myself with dry-eyed joy. "When?" I whispered.

"Tomorrow. 0900 hours. I have to enable your transceiver to receive the specially coded transmission."

"Have at it then," I said, pushing him down in the chair next to the small viewscreen. "I'll fetch the pie."

That's what happened today, Magnus. Can you imagine how I felt? For years I thought I was alone, the last of our family. And now—now I have someone to love again! I may never hold her hand—by the time *Voyager* arrives in the Alpha Quadrant I may be dead of old age—but I can see your daughter, talk to her, write to her. It's too much, too wonderful! I almost can't believe it, but I do. God bless you, Captain Janeway!

February 22, 2378

She's lovely, Magnus. You'd be proud of her—all she's gone through, all she's accomplished.

I must confess, as 0900 approached I began to panic. What do I say to a niece I haven't seen in twenty-three years? What common ground could possibly lie between an old maid and a former Borg? Would she remember me? What would she think of me? Then, before I could concoct more frightening scenarios, she was there, framed by the viewscreen. Tall and stately, blond hair pulled back to reveal beautiful features—she looks like you, Magnus, with the dignity of her mother. As I met her gaze, I saw uncertainty in those blue eyes and realized she was as anxious as I about our meeting. I yearned to take her in my arms and assure her that everything was all right, that I loved her. Then, words just tumbled forth.

"You can imagine my reaction when Starfleet told me to expect your call," I said.

"I experienced some apprehension myself," she admitted.

The last weekend we spent together replayed itself in my mind. "You seem like a lovely young woman but you were the most stubborn six-year-old I've ever met. Your parents left you with me for a weekend and you were so angry you locked yourself in my guest room and refused to come out."

She looked uncomfortable. "That must have been . . . inconvenient for you."

"Oh, I coaxed you out eventually—with a strawberry tart."

"I'm very fond of strawberries," she said. "I didn't realize I'd eaten them as a child."

I laughed. "You couldn't get enough of them. Of course, you didn't hesitate to point out if they weren't perfectly ripe."

She seemed to find that disconcerting. "I'm sorry if I insulted you. Perhaps I shouldn't have called."

I hastened to assure her. "No, I'm very glad you did. It's wonderful to see you again, Annika."*

Oh how much that was understated! Wonderful? There aren't words to describe the feeling! Our few minutes ended far too quickly, and I must wait another two months before I can talk to her again. But oh how precious it is to have something—some*one*—to wait for!

June 17, 2378

It's been a long time since I sat on the porch and enjoyed the night sky, but tonight I find myself studying the stars. I think of the ancient sailors, setting course by those glittering lights. Sometimes the stars took them to far shores, opening new horizons rife with dreams and danger. Sometimes the stars pointed the way home, where warm hearths and hearts awaited the weary sojourner. Ships have come and gone, sailing beneath and among those heavenly beacons, and still the stars beckon. They lured you away, Magnus, and they drew Annika back.

Several weeks have passed since *Voyager* made its spectacular homecoming. It's ironic, Magnus—the very Borg you went in search of provided the means of *Voyager*'s return. The captain and

*Conversation taken from *Voyager* episode "Author, Author."

crew have spent the past weeks sheltered at Starfleet Headquarters being debriefed, while families wait impatiently to celebrate their loved ones' return. But tomorrow the crew will disperse across this planet and to other homeworlds on the last leg of their long journey.

As their journey ends, I pen this, my final journal entry, Magnus. I've kept my promise. Tomorrow, Annika is coming home.

The Difficulties of Being Evil

Craig Gibb

It may look easy, but it is actually quite difficult. Constantly being evil is quite a trying task, and on top of that, I am expected to be rather dim-witted. As soon as I devise a nefarious plot I am somehow obligated to reveal it to that meddling Captain Proton. How is an evil lord of the galaxy expected to get any work done?

Ah! The imagizer at the front of my galactic cruiser shows that the garbage scow of a ship of my nemesis is approaching. He has no doubt come to try and stop my plan for total galactic domination. This time will be different, though, this time *I* will win.

"He is firing at our lightning shields, Dr. Chaotica!" one of my many simpleminded underlings shouted, as if I didn't know by the shaking of my ship.

"Don't just stand there, you dim-witted fools! Fire back!" I must be working with buffoons! My far superior death ray lanced out and knocked down Proton's lightning shields.

Success! What next . . . what next . . . ? I could destroy his ship, but I want to see the fear in his eyes.

"Capture his ship!" I commanded my underlings. I sat on my

royal throne to ponder my situation. We're located near the Soltair system, where I plan to carry out my diabolical plan. I know! I will send Captain Proton and his ship into the Soltair sun, where he will be incinerated, burnt to a crisp!

A slight shudder ran through my ship. We were docked with Proton.

"We are docked with Proton, sire," one of my guards informed me as if I didn't know. Imbeciles!

I stood up and marched down to the docking port with a contingency of guards. We paused outside the closed door of the ship. I waited for one of my guards to open it. They didn't get the hint, such imbeciles! I pressed the button to open the door. I *must* hire new guards!

My guards, however, did have the intelligence to go in first. A few of the stupid ones got shot down by Proton and his annoying sidekick Buster Kincaid. But they were soon overwhelmed and held still by the guards.

"Dr. Chaotica," Proton said, as if I didn't know my own name.

"Proton, we meet again. And I see you brought your little friend with you." They both gave me looks of disgust, but that would turn to fear, soon enough. "Tie them to their chairs."

My staff obliged, the two nuisances were struggling, but bound down. I slowly walked around Proton's bridge, observing everything. It's truly a marvel that he manages to constantly defeat me with such inferior technology.

"What's your evil plan now, Chaotica?" Proton asked me. But I didn't respond to his question with the answer he wanted.

"Ah, not this time, Proton. I've had some time to ponder on our past encounters. You see, I've realized that if I tell you how my plan will allow me to conquer the galaxy, that you will interfere with it. You *always* interfere. It's time to put an end to it."

Proton looked dumbfounded by what I told him, and Kincaid's jaw was near the floor. They didn't know what to say. That was definitely a pleasant first.

"But . . . what I will tell you is of the demise of you, Proton. Once I am on my ship, I will trap yours in my grappling beam and send you, your ship, and your pesky little sidekick to a fiery death in the Soltair sun!"

Kincaid's eyes shot open with fear, but somehow Proton ruined the fun. He just stared at me unflinchingly. Oh well, at least Kincaid gave me the fear that I longed to see.

"And after that, how do you plan to overtake the galaxy?" Proton had the nerve to ask me again.

"I already told you, I'm not telling," I said with the anger rising inside of me.

"You don't have a plan, do you?" Proton asked. This man seemed to make me mad by his mere presence.

"I do have a plan! A diabolically evil plan!" I started shouting.

Proton turned to his sidekick. "Don't worry, Buster, he doesn't have a plan. He's not going to conquer the galaxy. He's nothing more than an incompetent second-rate villain."

That did it.

"I do have a plan! It just so happens we're near a planet which has mind-control plants on its surface, plants with which I will rule all life! Oh no . . ." I was in such a rage and spoke so quickly that I didn't know what I was saying until it was too late.

What have I done? Obviously, I've exposed my plan, but does this mean I'm doomed to failure? No! I am the master of my own fate! I am a diabolical genius! I will *eliminate* Proton and conquer the universe!

Before Proton could think of a way to defeat me, I hurried out of his ship and onto mine. As soon as I stepped onto the bridge I ordered we separate from Proton's ship.

"We are no longer docked with Proton," someone said to me. I don't really care who, all the imbecilic guards are the same to me.

"Capture them in the grappling beam," I commanded. When I was told it was done I then ordered the guard to push the ship into the sun.

The piece of junk Proton called a ship started slowly moving closer to the sun. Suddenly, Proton's destructo beam shot out and struck my ship. The grappling beam deactivated and Proton started to fly away.

"Fire the death ray!" I shouted before my guards could tell me information I already knew. The death ray shot out but missed Proton by mere inches! The ship flew away behind the sun and disappeared.

"We missed Proton and he has now escaped."

"I know. *I know!* Do you think me a fool?!"

My guards did not reply. I sat on my royal throne and rubbed my forehead. That infernal Proton gave me a headache.

What to do next, what to do next . . . ? Chasing Proton would be a waste of time, he must be long gone by now. *I guess my only choice is to harvest the mind flower on the planet below. I just hope Proton does not come back.*

"Prepare to land on the planet!"

My dim-witted but obedient underlings carried out my order.

"We are ready, sire."

"Very well, start landing."

On the imagizer I could see that my ship was getting closer to the planet.

"Sire!"

"What is it now?"

"Proton is back!"

Finally, my guards provided me with information that I didn't already know. I only wished it were better news.

"He is firing!" the guard said as the ship shuddered.

"Full power to the death ray! Fire back!" On the imagizer I saw the ray shoot out, strike Proton's ship, and give it a violent shake.

I knew Proton would not give up that easily. His destructo beam shot out several times, shaking my ship.

I do not give up that easily, either. I ordered my men to keep firing. Suddenly, without warning, the death ray was hit. The guard at the controls died in a shower of sparks. If he was stupid enough to let that happen, then he deserved to die.

But Proton! He deserved to die, too! Why wouldn't he die!

"Sire! The death ray is disabled and the lightning shield has fallen!"

"Argh!" I shouted in frustration.

Proton kept firing. That despicable space worm.

"Sire! Our engines are down!"

I was so enraged, I didn't say anything. Proton fired again. The lights failed and I could feel that we were tumbling end over end through space.

"Proton!" I screamed. I knew he couldn't hear me, but venting my anger helped. A moment of calm overcame me, and one thought came to mind.

It's terribly difficult to be an evil genius.

Restoration

Penny A. Proctor

Stand here, children, and look down at the valley. This is one of the most beautiful views in all of Ocampa, especially this time of year. The blooms on the mountain trees look like puffs of cloud from here, and the flowers in the meadow seem pinker than usual against the new grass. The river is still cold and high, running fast from the snowmelt. If you are very quiet, you can hear the hela birds calling above the river's rush.

Now, try to imagine there is only one color—beige. No river, no trees, no plants, no birds. Just hard, dry beige ground and cloudless beige sky. The sun beating down unfiltered on the parched and lifeless soil.

That's how it was for generations, all the generations that we lived underground. You have heard the story—how a powerful being from another galaxy came to Ocampa and accidentally turned the face of our world into a vast, waterless desert. We had to move beneath the surface to subterranean cities. The alien was so filled with remorse that he stayed to look after us. We called him our Caretaker, because he saw to it that we had power to run our cities and that we were protected from our enemies. He devoted the rest of his life to our well-being.

But he was not immortal. After more than five hundred generations, he left us. Before he died, he gave us enough energy to sustain our cities for five more years. It was at that time that Kes the Explorer was born. According to the histories, she was a curious child and a leader among the young people who dreamed of returning to the surface. For her, it was more than a dream; she was the first Ocampa to see the sun since the Great Migration. On the parched and barren land, she found our enemy, the Kazon, but she also found our friends, the Talaxians.

And she found other friends, beings from far across the galaxy who traveled the stars in a great ship called Voyager. *The Voyagers were kindred spirits to Kes, explorers with a thirst for new sights and new people, and when the Caretaker died, Kes left with them.*

No one ever expected to see her again.

It wasn't a Kazon ship. Keva wasn't certain what it was, but it was too graceful in its lines to be Kazon. Someone new was about to land on Ocampa.

He raised his hands to shield his eyes as he looked up at the sky. Although he wore protective eye gear, looking into the sky was discouraged by the doctors, who feared the delicate optic nerves of the subterranean Ocampa might be damaged by too intense an exposure to light. He watched as it hovered for a moment above the ground, sending clouds of dust into the air, and then it settled delicately into place.

Immediately, he crouched behind an outcropping of rock, waiting, even though it was a violation of the rules. Technically, he ought to be running back to camp even now, to give warning. *I'll go in a minute,* he thought, *when I see who the pilot is. Then I'll have something useful to report.*

The hatch on the small ship began to lift, and Keva caught his breath. The only other race he had ever seen were the Kazon, and his heart began to race with the prospect of a new species. Would they be enemies, too? Or friends, as his father claimed was possible?

After a lifetime, the pilot emerged. At first, Keva could see only a silhouette against the harsh orange sky. A slight figure, wearing a long vest or robe, stepped away from the ship and then stopped and turned around.

Home!

He nearly jumped. Who had spoken? There was no one nearby except the pilot below, and yet he had heard a woman's voice quite clearly—a liquid voice filled with joy and yet somehow weary.

The pilot suddenly began walking—no, almost running—directly toward the hills where Keva hid. *It's just a coincidence,* he tried to convince himself. But the pilot showed no hesitation whatsoever.

He watched, disbelieving, as the stranger came straight to a cairn of rocks that served as the trail marker, then stepped atop the boulder that was the first step of the tiny path that led upward. Panicked, he turned to run.

Wait, please.

He froze. The voice must belong to the pilot.

Please.

Slowly, he turned and, holding his breath, looked at the pilot. She had stopped on the trail and was bracing herself against the rocks with one hand, gasping for air. Although her head was drooping, he could see her profile plainly.

His mouth fell open in surprise. She was an Ocampa.

She was the oldest Ocampa he had ever seen. Her dull, yellowed-white hair was thinning and short, her skin wrinkled and translucent. As she raised her head to look at him, though, he saw that her bright blue eyes were vibrant and lively. She smiled as she studied him, and he thought that she must have been very beautiful when she was young.

"Who are you?" he asked, still too wary to come close to her.

My name is Kes.

It was indeed her voice in his mind, he realized. Some of his friends were capable of telepathy, but none of them were as strong as this. Then the import of what she said sank in. "Kes? But—but Kes left in a starship years ago."

"You've heard of me?" She must have been surprised, to speak aloud.

"My father is Daggin. He was a friend of Kes."

She smiled again. "Yes, he was. Who is your mother? Mala? You look like her."

Keva nodded slowly. It was hard to believe this old woman was his father's friend, but how else could she know his mother's name?

After a moment, she said, "May I come up there and talk to you? I won't hurt you."

He considered, and began to feel foolish. She was tiny, even for an Ocampa, and looked as if her bones might break if he blew on them. "Let me help you," he said, coming down the path to take her arm, as he had been taught to do with the elderly.

When he took her arm, he realized she was not as frail as she looked. Her arms were still well muscled and wiry when he closed his fingers around them. Even so, she seemed grateful for his assistance. *What is your name?*

I'm Keva.

Keva. It was your grandfather's name.

"That's right." He stopped short and looked at her closely. "You really are Kes."

She nodded. They had reached the flat where he had been hiding, and he stopped, thinking she might need to rest. But Kes was breathing easily and she turned, looking at the valley below them. Her brows knit together and she frowned slightly. *Where are all the people? I thought you would all be living on the surface by now.*

"We will be soon." Keva was unable to keep the bitterness out of his voice. "Everyone moved into the Central City about three years ago, to conserve energy. Reserves will be exhausted in a few months, though. The Caretaker abandoned us."

Kes turned to him quickly. "The Caretaker didn't abandon the Ocampa, Keva. He died. Didn't you know that?"

He shook his head, shocked by her heresy. "You shouldn't say such things. The Caretaker is immortal."

She sighed. "I should have come back to explain before leaving with *Voyager.* It's true, Keva, the Caretaker died six years ago. He knew he was dying and that's why he sent us the additional power reserves." She looked around, shook her head. "Why haven't you made more preparations for the move? Are settlements being constructed?"

"Every time we try to build more than a few structures, the Kazon attack. I'm part of a scouting party that's looking for a new site." He flushed, realizing suddenly that he had neglected his duty to his teammate. "I was due back an hour ago. My partner will be worried."

"Will you take me with you? I would like to talk to you. Maybe I can help."

It seemed unlikely that one elderly woman could do much against the Kazon, but after all, she had been out among the stars for six years. Perhaps she had learned something that could save them.

When they reached the camp, hidden in a small clearing accessible through a narrow cleft in the rocks, Nerril was waiting with her weapon drawn. She lowered it when she saw that it was him, but from the expression on her face, he knew he was in trouble. "Where have you been? You're late."

"Don't be upset." He took her hand, kissed her quickly. "I found someone remarkable." Stepping aside so she could see the woman who followed him, he said, "This is Kes."

Kes stepped forward. *Hello. I'm glad to meet you.*

Nerril threw a startled look to Keva, then stared at the old woman. Finally she recovered enough to say, "Kes? The Kes who left on a starship?"

Kes smiled. *Yes, the very same. May I have some water? Then I will tell you all about it.*

Nerril brought the canteen and a cup, and the three of them settled on the ground. Kes repeated what she had told Keva about the Caretaker, but to Keva's surprise Nerril was not upset by the news that the guardian of the Ocampa was dead. "I think I'm relieved," she said quietly. "It was more upsetting to believe that he abandoned us out of anger for an offense we didn't understand. At least now we know, he died loving us as much as ever."

Keva reached over and squeezed her hand. She always knew how to find the good in any situation.

"Tell us about your life on the starship," Nerril urged. "Was it exciting?"

"Oh, yes." Kes smiled widely. "It was very exciting. There are

248

people and places out there you cannot even begin to imagine. For example, not long after we left Ocampa, we encountered a nebula that was actually alive . . ."

She told them story after story until, finally, she said, "And then I left them."

A silence stretched between them, creating a tension where there had been none. Kes seemed to be looking at something very far away.

Just as Keva was about to burst with curiosity, Nerril asked, "Why?"

Silently, Kes rose and walked slowly toward the cleft in the rocks. She kept her face turned away from them. Her response seemed saturated with pain. *Something happened. The Ocampa had lost so much of what we once could do, you see. All the years I was on* Voyager, *I tried to expand my mental abilities. In my pride, I thought I could be the one to restore our people's strength. I learned too much too quickly, and . . . then something happened that I couldn't control.*

Keva could feel her emotions, grief and something that felt like fear. He went to her and placed his hand on her shoulder.

She turned, and he saw wetness glistening softly in the silver light of Ocampa's moons. Gently, he touched her face, felt the tears that covered her fragile, lined face. *Why are you crying?* he asked, hoping he had enough control to keep the thought from Nerril.

Don't ask me. I can't think about it yet. It's too painful.

"Then we will not ask." He spoke aloud, for Nerril's benefit. Taking her hand as if she were a child in his protection, he led her back. "Come and sit. You must be famished. Look, both moons are up. We've been so interested in your story that we forgot to eat."

As they walked back, he caught Nerril's eye, and she nodded; his wife understood him even without telepathy. She scrambled to her feet. "It will have to be a cold meal, and a quick one. The Kazon raiding parties are out by now. Aromas travel far on the night winds, and the Kazon have a keen sense of smell."

Keva settled Kes near the fire, but his eyes followed Nerril. One of his secret pleasures was to watch the grace of her movements and the interesting ways her body shifted as she worked. Then he felt Kes's gaze on him, and turned.

She was smiling, and her eyes were gentle. *How long have you been in love with her?*

A quick glance at Nerril confirmed that she had shared that thought with him alone. *All my life, I think. We've been married for five months. Sometimes it amazes me that of all the Ocampa in Central City, she chose me as her life's partner.*

They ate sandwiches made from tomato and crunchy cressa leaves, with slices of meaty nicbar mushroom. At the first bite, Kes closed her eyes and smiled. Keva guessed it had been a long time since she had anything from her native world.

"Tell me," she said aloud between nibbles, "about Ocampa. Tell me what has happened since I left."

Keva and Nerril looked at each other, trying to decide how best to answer. "You tell her," Nerril said finally. "You're the historian."

"After you left, nothing changed at first," he began carefully. His mind raced to condense six years of events. "The Elders knew that there had been a battle in space above us, but they assured us it didn't affect us. They blamed the battle for the fact that the transmissions of energy from the Caretaker stopped; they said he was displeased.

"A year passed, and still the Caretaker did not reach out to us. The people began to wonder if he had abandoned us. The Elders assured us this was not so, but a small group began to question the authority of the Elders, and especially of Toscat, the Chief Elder. They said that the Elders refused to acknowledge reality."

Kes interrupted him. "Was Daggin one of this group?"

He nodded. "Yes. He felt the Elders were keeping the truth from us. He said that Kes—that you—had seen the sun, that you had found truth beyond the Elders' words. He said that the Caretaker had abandoned us because the Elders refused to let us grow and learn."

A slow, almost secretive smile spread across Kes's face. "Good for Daggin. How did Toscat take it?"

"Not well," Nerril said. "The way my father-in-law tells it, Daggin confronted Toscat on the steps of the Great Library. Toscat listened to Daggin, and got very red in the face the entire time Daggin was speaking. Instead of answering, he just fell over dead. He tumbled down the steps and landed in the flower bed."

"Really?" Kes looked shocked.

"Really," Nerril confirmed. "He was ten years old, and the thought of anyone daring to disagree with him publicly shocked him so much that he burst a vessel in his brain."

Kes leaned back. "Ten years is a good life. May he live a better one in his next cycle."

It was a traditional Ocampa insult, and the others smiled. Toscat was not remembered fondly.

"It took another year," Keva continued, "but eventually most people realized that the Caretaker wasn't taking care of us anymore. By then, we had only three years of power reserves left for all four cities. My father and a few of his friends were elected to the Council of Governors, and in a few months the Council issued a proclamation: that the Ocampa had to begin preparations for moving to the surface."

"Three years ago?" Kes asked. "Why aren't you further along?"

"First it was the Kazon," Keva said. "It seemed that every scouting party we sent to the surface was captured and killed by the Kazon. We were just lucky that they never found the tunnels that led underground."

"Then it was the plague." Nerril picked up the thread. "After the Council ordered the people to consolidate in Central City, conditions were terrible. A disease spread almost overnight, and over two million people died."

"Including my mother," Keva murmured. "I was five days old."

Kes reached over, closed her gnarled hand over his. *I'm sorry. Mala was beautiful. You deserve to remember her.*

The lump that suddenly grew in his throat prevented him from speaking. He looked into Kes's eyes and saw compassion.

Nerril took his other hand, and spoke. "We're constantly short on resources and always fighting the Kazon. They destroy everything we try to build. If we can't get a settlement started, we're not going to survive when the power runs out."

As Keva watched, the compassion that had been in Kes's eyes

only an instant before vanished. Icy resolve replaced it. "Don't worry about the Kazon."

"Easy to say," Nerril said, apparently oblivious to the change in Kes's demeanor. "You don't have to fight them every day."

I've fought them. I have weapons you cannot begin to comprehend.

Keva shivered. The cold, unyielding tone in his mind frightened him more than any Kazon ever had.

Nerril cleared her throat awkwardly. "I think it's time for sleep, don't you? Kes, you must be exhausted after your journey. I know I'm tired."

Kes blinked, and the hardness in her disappeared. She looked chagrined. "Yes, that's a good idea. I am tired."

Keva brought her his blankets and spread them for her. "It's a rocky bed, I'm afraid. Tomorrow, I'll take you to the city. You'll be more comfortable there."

To his surprise, she kissed his cheek. "Thank you."

He stood and watched as she lay down, covered herself, and seemed to fall asleep almost immediately. It was hard to believe that she was Kes, the most legendary of his people and the heroine of a story that his father had told him almost every day. This frail old woman with the young voice was nothing that he had imagined, and more than he ever dreamed.

When he was certain that she was asleep, he left her and slid under the blanket next to Nerril. She moved slightly to accommodate him, and then spooned close. When his arm was securely around her waist, he closed his eyes and drifted to sleep.

Keva.

He woke abruptly. The first faint light of dawn was lighting the sky.

Keva.

It was Kes calling him. Careful not to wake Nerril, he rolled aside and stood. Kes was not where he had left her, nor anywhere in sight. He walked through the cleft in the rock, and found her.

He caught his breath. The old woman had been replaced by a young woman; her skin was smooth and creamy, blushing a delicate pink on her cheeks. Her hair was golden, her eyes unlined. He had been right, she was extraordinarily lovely.

"I don't understand," he said. "How is this possible?"

She smiled radiantly and reached out to take his hand. *The energy from my ship—I have consumed it. I will need it all, but this is how I want you to remember me.*

Frightened, he took a step away from her. "I don't understand."

Please don't be afraid. Oh, Keva, I know why I had to come back. I thought it was to die among my own people, but that was only part of it.

"Die?" he asked. She was his father's age, seven at most, even though she now looked younger; she should live for two or three more years at least.

Everyone dies, Keva, and I assure you, I am ready. But I know now why I am to die. I know why I have lived.

He swallowed. There was joy in her voice, a joy that burned so much that it was almost unbearable. "I don't understand."

"Of course you don't," she said aloud. "May I show you, Keva? It will be hard, but I think you will need to know."

Slowly, he nodded. She raised a hand to his cheek. *Forgive the pain. There is no other way. It will pass.*

Then she closed her eyes, and it began. Memories began to flood his mind, memories of places and people he knew he had never met. Memories of *Voyager*, of Neelix, of Tuvok, of the Doctor. Of Tom Paris and of Linnis who never was and yet was. Of Kathryn Janeway.

Then the scene shifted, and he was in a place of light and energy. More than in it, he seemed to be a part of it. He had no body to limit him; he flowed and pulsated with the fires around him. At first, he thought it was the most beautiful place he had ever seen, and he found he could draw upon the energy surrounding him. It was thrilling. It was ecstasy.

This was where Kes had gone when she left *Voyager.* This was what had lured her from the ship where she was happy, with its promise of unending power.

Then the energy began to consume him in return, and in being consumed he knew a pain as complete as it was inescapable. It was a place without shape or form or time, and the ecstasy decreased as pain increased until all he felt was pain, and fear, and power. Insatiable power that twisted his perceptions and threatened his sanity, that drained his will and narrowed his thoughts to one thing—the need to escape.

He fell to his knees and cried out.

"I'm sorry," Kes said out loud, as she knelt to embrace him. She held him as his mother might have. "It will be a little while before you can process it all. It was the only way for you to understand." She smoothed the suddenly damp hair from his brow. "Let me give you just one more thing."

To his shame, he whimpered, but he could no more have stopped her than he could stop the sun. Holding him, rocking slightly, she said, "This was Mala."

And he saw her. A young girl, with long dark hair that gleamed under the lights. A young woman with kind brown eyes who smiled sweetly when she looked at Daggin (a young, callow Daggin) with adoration that was both shy and open.

He sobbed.

Kes held him close. "I'm sorry. It will be all right. You'll see, it will be all right." She waited until he regained his composure. "I'm going to call Nerril now. You both need to witness this."

His breathing was ragged; he concentrated on controlling it before his wife came. Thoughts and images tumbled through his mind; he was no longer sure what were his own memories and what were Kes's. He couldn't understand why she had done this.

Nerril followed Kes through the cleft. When she saw Keva on his knees, she ran to him and wrapped her arms around him protectively. "What have you done?"

Don't worry. He is unharmed. He needed to understand, so he can explain it to all of you.

Nerril's green eyes flashed with anger. "Understand what?"

"What I am about to do." Kes looked at them, her eyes an unnaturally vivid blue. "I told you, I have learned things beyond your comprehension. After we talked last night, many things became clear for me. The place where I was almost destroyed my soul. When I finally escaped, I knew I had to get back to Ocampa, but I was still so frightened I didn't know why.

"In my fear, I did—I almost did—some terrible things to my friends on *Voyager.* I almost hurt them and worst of all, I destroyed their memory of me. When they think of me now, they will think of a vengeful and bitter woman. Even then, even when I left them the second time, I didn't know why any of this had happened to me. Why me, I kept asking. Why me?"

She lifted her hands to the skies. "Now I know. I know why I left Ocampa to go with *Voyager*, and why I left *Voyager* to return here. I think I was born so that I could be here now, and do what I am going to do. This was my destiny, from the very beginning."

"You don't make sense." Nerril almost snarled.

"Be patient." Kes smiled at her, laid a hand on her shining red hair. "And do this for me—when *Voyager* or its kind returns, tell them that I am sorry for the way I came back. And tell them . . . I loved them. I loved them all."

"I still don't understand," Nerril said uneasily.

You will.

Kes walked past her a few steps on the rocky trail. From the rock where she stood, the entire dry river valley was visible, spreading out before them in all directions. With a smile on her face, she set her hands on a boulder and closed her eyes.

The ground began to tremble, then to shake.

"Come on," Nerril shouted over the growing noise. She stumbled to her feet and tried to pull Keva with her. "We've got to stop her."

"No!" Keva grasped her firmly, unable to say anything more. "No." Nerril looked at him closely, then took a deep breath and sat beside him on the ground.

The shaking became violent. Then, with a deafening explosion, the ground split apart and a geyser of water erupted, climbing toward the sky. Keva looked at it, dumbfounded. It was the underground river, the river that sustained Central City. Somehow it had pushed its way up hundreds of meters, through mantle and bedrock crust.

Unstoppable, the river forced its way upward and thundered over the ground. At the same time, the land beside it began to change, to turn pale green and then lushly, deeply emerald with grass and flowers and trees. The green spread outward as fast as the river sped onward.

Time suspended. The air was crackling with the power of life,

life reclaiming the arid surface. Spray blew into their faces, drenching them. Keva clung to Nerril and watched in complete amazement as their planet returned from the dead.

With an effort, he dragged his gaze away from the river and looked at Kes. She seemed to be thinning somehow, evaporating before their eyes. *Kes!*

Don't be afraid. This is what I was born for.

He stumbled to his feet, took a toddling step toward her on the heaving ground. *Don't leave us. Please.*

She raised her hands to the sky, faded another degree. *Tell them, Keva. Tell them this is what I was always meant to do. This is why I left.*

In the meadows below—for now there were meadows and fields and a river—flowers suddenly appeared. At the distance from which Keva stood, they looked like silvery pink tears she had shed in the moonlight the night before. *Tell who?* he called to her desperately, but it was too late. Kes faded to nothingness before his eyes.

Home! Her voice echoed faintly in his mind.

"No!" he cried out loud, but it was too late.

Kes was gone.

And so Kes the Explorer restored Ocampa to its natural state. This valley was the first to flow with water, but within a year the entire planet was once again verdant and alive. In her time as a sub-atomic being, she learned how to manipulate and convert the arid desert into a thriving ecology.

How did she do this? Our best scientists cannot explain it any better than this: she simply—and I say that with irony and respect—converted the matter and energy that was her life into something else. Into Ocampa. At the end, she believed that all the adventures and hardships of her life had occurred just so she could give us back our world.

You know the rest. Keva the Wise was elected the Councilor General and oversaw the migration to the surface. His daughter Kes the Healer is still remembered for her fierce dedication to life. Through the two of them, we slowly and carefully recovered many of the abilities that had been lost for generations.

The Kazon? Surely you know. The flower that Keva named the Kesteer—Kes's Tears—grows all over the planet and is our greatest defense. No one has found a way to kill it. It blooms year round. And the Kazon cannot tolerate it. It makes them deathly ill. They abandoned Ocampa within weeks of the Restoration, and have never made a serious attempt to come again.

And we pass the message from one generation to the next, in anticipation of the day that we can welcome Voyager *or one of its sisters to our skies. Someday, it may fall to one of you to be the messenger.*

Kes is sorry. She loved you all. She is home.

On the Rocks

TG Theodore

"Where'd they go?"

"Huh?"

I opened one eye. When I'm sleeping on a warm rock, that's the most I can do to pretend to be interested in my sister's conversations.

She slithered around a half-turn and stared me in my open eye.

"They're *gone!*"

She didn't blink. I hated it when she didn't blink. That meant it was going to be another long, inane topic of conversation. And she was flaring her lungills. I could actually hear the air rushing in and out of them. Of the three of us kits, only *she* snored while sleeping. I knew this wasn't going to go away.

My brother was smarter than me. He was still pretending to be asleep. Not even his tail was twitching. I could sense that neither of us would get any sleep unless I went along with her.

"Who's gone, Sis?"

She blinked. I could see I was making progress.

"Mother and Father. We were going after some food and they just vanished!"

I opened my other eye and quickly scanned our pond. The summer sun was beaming down onto the water and our rocks. The lush trees were all there, shielding the green banks. The waterfall was flowing. The moss was in place. But no sign of Mom or Dad.

"Maybe they just went upstream for a while. Let me sleep."

She waddled a few steps closer. Her tail smacked my older brother right in his face. He didn't flinch. I really envied that talent.

Sis looked upstream, hoping to catch a glimpse of our parents. After a moment, she stared down at the water and spoke very softly. "Neelix would know."

While we all had been part of the same litter, she and Neelix were very close. The day we lost him was especially hard on Sis and our folks.

I slid a little closer to her. This was one subject I couldn't tease her about. Frankly, *I* missed our brother, too. He wasn't the smartest of the four of us, but he was fun. He just didn't have very much sense. And he paid for it with his life.

"I'm sure he would, Sis. But he's gone now."

Her frustration was rapidly turning into desperation. "First, Neelix and now—oh, my God!" Her eyes widened and she swallowed hard. "You don't think that Mother and Father—"

My brother spoke up. "No! They're much too smart to meet that fate. Our parents would *never* get too close to—well, you know."

The three of us were silent for a moment, remembering the day we lost our brother.

Ironically, he was the first of us out of the nest and into the pond. He was swimming upstream, looking around and looking for food. He had heard about Old Doc who lurked in the deeper waters, but he was so excited about swimming on his own that he went too far too soon.

Old Doc got to him before Mom could.

Since then, we were forbidden to swim upstream alone. And even then we had to stay right off the bank for a quick escape if need be.

The whole episode had terrified me. I was the last to swim. And

I didn't *like* swimming. I only did it to look for food or when absolutely necessary. It took B'Elanna and Tuvok an hour to coax me over to the rock I was lying on.

No, sir. Despite my amphibious nature, I did *not* like the water.

Sis cleared her throat. Her voice was still low and a little emotional. "So how did Mom and Dad vanish so quickly then?"

Good question. My brother and I looked at each other.

"Well, I doubt they sprouted wings," he said. "Not part of *this* evolutionary process, I'd guess."

To me, there was only one explanation. "Maybe somehow they made it back." We each glanced upward for a moment. "You know how determined Mom is once she gets her mind set on something."

Sis paced around the rock a bit. "You mean they might have— *de-evolved?*"

I remembered all the stories our parents had told us of their previous form. *Human,* they called it. While my sister was enthralled by those tales, I personally never saw the charm in having to walk around on two feet, using my other two feet to feed myself and needing to actually hold my breath while underwater.

And don't get me started on what their skin was like. I had nightmares for days after *that* story.

Their tales of life in space filled our early days. But as time passed, I sensed they were acclimating much more to their new evolutionary state. They would still speak of the ship and the stars, but not quite as often.

I particularly enjoyed their stories about our namesakes—Tuvok, the intelligent, logical Vulcan security officer, B'Elanna, the fiery, resourceful half-Klingon engineer, and Neelix, the jovial Talaxian cook and guide.

I must admit, however, I wasn't exactly flattered being named after a mere ensign.

Harry.

What a stupid name. Sounded more like an adjective. And I didn't have a single hair *on* me! But he *was* Dad's best friend, so I suppose I considered it an honor in the long run.

I was so lost in thought that Sis had to thump me with her tail to get my attention.

"What if we never see them again? How would we get off this planet? We don't have a starship. We don't have a shuttle. *We don't even have thumbs!*"

I'd have raised my eyebrows if I had any. "Maybe not, but we have immense intelligence. We're much smarter than our parents were in their previous form."

She thought for a moment. "If we're so smart, why do we eat by zapping bugs out of the air with our tongues?"

Hmmm. Good point there. Occasionally she'd come out with something that actually made sense.

"What if *Voyager did* come back to get them? Why didn't they take *us?*"

The thought of being deserted had never occurred to me. Mom and Dad were devoted parents. They had accepted their new lives and set out to make the best of them.

Sis swam over to the bank. I hadn't seen her this sad since we lost Neelix. Tuvok looked over at me. "I suppose we should go over and try to comfort her."

I nodded. "After you, big brother."

Tuvok sighed and slipped into the water. Distracted by our sister's mood, neither of us had noticed the unusual ripple in the surface of the pond. Nor the long eel-like shape causing it.

But B'Elanna did. She screamed. "It's Old Doc! Tuvok, get out of the water!"

Unfortunately, Tuvok was deep and couldn't hear her warning. I looked over and saw Old Doc closing in on him. His massive jaw was wide open. Tuvok kept paddling along as if nothing was the matter.

Sis screamed over to me. "Harry! *Do* something!"

The water. Swimming. Neelix.

I was paralyzed. I mean, there was nothing I could do directly. Old Doc was six times my size, so even if I *could* bring myself to go into the water, ramming him was out of the question.

I looked around and saw a small rock nearby. I managed to use my tail to swat it into the pond. It distracted Old Doc for a moment, but the diversion was only momentary. He kept after Tuvok, even more determined now.

For a moment, I actually considered diving in to lure the monster away. I took a few steps into the water. The next moment I came to my senses and backed up onto the safety of the rock. I looked across the bank at my sister. She was absolutely terrified. And she was looking at me with terror and disappointment in her eyes. *"Harry! Please!"*

Old Doc was only a few yards from Tuvok. This would be horrible. Old Doc had three rows of massive teeth, and they were all about to close down onto Tuvok's hind legs.

B'Elanna closed her eyes. But I was transfixed on the impending horror. I was not the bravest of us by any stretch of the imagination. As a matter of fact, I was probably the *least* brave.

Then B'Elanna headed toward the water.

And I thought of Neelix. And how his death affected us all.

"B'Elanna, stay put!"

Suddenly I was underwater and swimming faster than I ever thought I could. Old Doc was just ahead of me. His long, crusty, serpentine body was even uglier close up. I managed to reach his tail. And then I bit it as hard as I could.

Yecch.

It worked. He stopped chasing Tuvok.

And was staring directly at *me.*

I don't know how much time passed during what happened next, but I realized I was closer to the bank than I was to the rocks. But I had to get through Old Doc to *make* it to the bank.

He came at me, angrier than any creature I had ever seen. I swam starboard and went deeper.

He matched my pace.

I stopped looking at him and made a beeline for deeper waters, hoping I could force him to run out of air and surface for a moment.

He did.

After turning around, I took advantage of the extra time and headed back for the bank, but Old Doc went into warp swim. There was no way I could outrun him. And the water felt like it was closing in on me. I felt the fear start to well up inside.

Then I saw it. Directly ahead. If I could make it in time . . .

I could almost sense Old Doc opening his mouth and preparing

to make me his lunch. I darted port just as my tail felt the distur-
bance in the water from Old Doc clamping his mouth shut—or trying to.

The water seemed to amplify the anguished cry of pain I
heard. It chilled me to the bone. But I didn't dare stop to look
back, in case I misunderstood the situation. And I wanted out of
that pond *now!*

A few seconds later I broke the surface of the pond and felt the
slick bank under my feet. I still didn't stop until I made it to the base
of the tree. Actually, I didn't stop until my head *hit* the base of the
tree. I opened my eyes and saw B'Elanna and Tuvok staring at me.

Tuvok immediately expressed his gratitude. "So are we playing
follow-the-leader now or what?"

B'Elanna was a little more glad to see me. She squealed in relief
and joy. "Harry! Harry!"

What had happened?

I looked into the pond and saw Old Doc, squirming in desperation, trying to extricate his jaw and teeth from the dark, thick moss
covering a small boulder. He struggled fiercely, but to no avail. His
battle for life lasted only a minute or so until he ran out of air. His
intense wriggling gradually slowed until his body went limp.

That was the last of Old Doc.

Sis and I stared in disbelief. Tuvok looked at her and nodded toward the pond. "Go on in, the water's fine!"

Relieved and angry, she thumped Tuvok with her tail.

"Ow! What was *that* for?"

"You scared me to death! If it hadn't been for Harry—"

"I'd have been an hors d'oeuvre." Tuvok came over to me and
smiled. "So, you've become quite the little swimmer now, haven't
you? That was some maneuver for a hydrophobic. How did you do
that?"

Actually, I realized the answer for the first time. "Dad taught me.
It was one of his pilot techniques to defeat a pursuing enemy when
you have no weapons. Lure them some place where the odds are
even. I saw the rock and headed for it."

I tentatively approached the pond, still allowing a long distance
from Old Doc's motionless body. Tuvok followed me. "Great. Now

we have to look at *that* all day. But I suppose he'll be gone in a day or two."

Sis and I replied in unison. "Yecch!"

Tuvok laughed and looked at me. "And by the way, thank you, little brother."

There was a moment of silence.

Sis plopped down onto the thick grass and looked up toward space—almost as if she were trying to see our parents. "So I guess we're alone now. Unless they come back for us."

I couldn't find any words to comfort her. So the truth would have to do. "I doubt they'd take us with them. The Prime Directive and all."

Tuvok shook his head. "But that only applies to interference with the natural social evolution of a planet. We're already at the top of the evolutionary scale. *We* might contaminate *them!*"

My brother had a point. "Besides, how would we fit in?"

Sis looked up at me. "What do you mean, Harry?"

"Look, B'Elanna, suppose somehow you turned into, say—a moose. You meet another moose and have calves. Then you change back into a—*whatever* we are. Would you expect your moose kids to come live in the pond?"

Her voice was about to crack. "But if we could change them into our species—"

"But would we have the right to? We were *born* this way. Mom and Dad weren't." It was a hard thing to say to her, but we had to face reality.

Tuvok snorted. "I hate philosophy."

She realized I was right. But it didn't make the truth any less painful. "Maybe they aren't gone. Maybe they—"

Tuvok broke in. "No, B'Elanna. They're gone. They *did* go back to *Voyager.* I saw the transporter grab them. I was on my way to tell you when we got a little sidetracked by Old Doc there."

We couldn't cry. At least not physically. But Sis was as close to it as we could get.

I realized what this meant. "And I assume they probably found some way to turn themselves back into what they were."

"But to just leave us . . ." Sis rested her head on the bank.

Tuvok nudged her with his snout, a show of affection among our kind. "That's the best thing they could have done, B'Elanna. We don't belong up there. And they don't belong swimming in a pond."

I nudged her, too. "We're capable of self-reproduction, so we'll live on. And who knows what our descendants will create? Maybe one day *they* will return to the stars."

The pond was very still. There was nothing left to be said, really. A small zephyr rustled the branches of the trees.

And then we heard the *shimmer.*

There sat a small box made of something we'd never seen before. I recognized the Starfleet emblem on the side of it. It made a small humming noise and suddenly the images of two beings appeared. They *looked* real, yet we could see through them.

Sis stared in wonder. "Who are they? *What* are they?"

Tuvok and I knew.

Mom was the shorter of the two. Her reddish hair was simply styled and her jaw much more defined than Dad's. Being a biped, she seemed amazingly tall to us now. I was assuming these holograms were actual size.

They were both wearing clothing—an unusual concept to us. But after hearing descriptions of their human bodies, I thought it just as well they were hidden. She wore mostly black material with red around her forelegs—er, upper arms.

Dad was even fairer. I was right about their skin, it *was* pretty repulsive. But after what I'd just been through, it just seemed trivial now. He had friendly eyes and a pleasant smile and was dressed in the same uniform as Mom. But I noticed the lesser number of pips on his collar compared to hers.

Wherever they were now, Mom was definitely in charge.

She spoke first.

"Hello, my children. By now our starship has left this system, but your father and I didn't want to leave without saying goodbye."

Sis took a step closer to the projections. "Mother?"

Mom continued. "You are a new species, and this planet is your home. It isn't ours. The decision to leave you behind wasn't an easy one, but it was the right one."

She looked over at Dad, who cleared his throat.

"As you know, what happened to us—to your mother and I—was a result of a number of biological and physical phenomena. We were never meant to evolve so much in our lifetimes. We're human, and our evolution was a mistake. Your births were not. You're smart enough to know that."

The two of them paused. Despite their alien appearance, it was nonetheless comforting to see them and hear them. Sis was transfixed. Tuvok turned slightly away from the image. I think he found it hard to look directly at them in this form. I just took comfort in the sound of their voices.

Mom wiped a tear away and continued. "We know you will thrive. Our doctor has told us you are capable of reproducing many offspring, and in a variety of ways. So build together. Work together. And someday, if you wish, you'll make it to *our* home—Earth."

Dad stepped forward. "This is a very unusual situation, but I *do* think of you as our children. And in my own way, I love you very much. Harry, watch over your brother and sister—and remember the rock trick in case Old Doc gives you any trouble. Tuvok, you and B'Elanna look after each other. I will think of all of you—and Neelix—often."

He stepped back and Mom smiled. It was a pretty smile despite her human appearance. "It's time for us to go now."

"No!" B'Elanna wailed in sadness. She had forgotten for the moment that they couldn't see or hear us. Tuvok and I nestled in next to her.

"Remember us, for we shall always remember you. And love you. It's a big universe, and all of you will always be a big part of my life. Goodbye, my children. In the words of Tuvok's namesake—"

We all joined in with Mom. "Live long and prosper."

Their images faded, leaving the gentle rustling of leaves as the only sound. Tuvok crawled over to the box. "According to this panel, we can replay their message any time we want."

And we would replay it many more times in the years to come.

It was getting darker now. Shadows were longer and some of the brighter stars were visible in the twilight sky.

The three of us looked up into the vastness of space and pondered our futures.

Would we someday go there?

Probably.

Would our parents ever return?

Probably not.

But one thing was certain. We *would* thrive.

And the things we could only dream about this night would one day come true for our descendants.

We were, after all, descended from creatures of space.

And as every species knows, there's no place like home.

Witness

Diana Kornfeld

I am female, I suppose. At least I think of myself as a woman. Perhaps it's because my creator originally envisioned me as one. I have never really questioned that aspect of my existence. My name may have played a part in that. Elizabeth. I learned to think of myself as Elizabeth before I ever started questioning my existence, before I even thought to question anything. What has driven me is more essential. Am I human?

No, of course not. Intellectually I realize that I'm not. There is, however, that within me that can never wholly come to terms with that knowledge. And so I record my thoughts here in that most human form of communication—words. Words that are inadequate to incorporate my experiences, my thoughts, or as I admit in my more cynical or rational moments, my processes. I feel the need to create a record, to tell the story of my strange life even though no other being will ever read it. Still, to have it here is somehow comforting, as though I am reaching out to touch this community. As though it will somehow validate me, preserve me, join me to other minds, for writing is, after all, incorporeal, as incorporeal as I am myself. And so I join the host of other beings who exist only in words.

I still remember with complete clarity the moments that led to my birth, the first time I realized myself.

I was looking into his eyes and laughing, laughing as we always did over some trivial annoyance of his day. This time it was a story about Seven and how she had told the captain to report to astrometrics immediately—without so much as a please. Suddenly the strange sound I had grown accustomed to emitted once again from the metal communicator on his chest, and the smile faded from his lips.

"Ensign Kim, report immediately to the bridge." It was as if the subject of our conversation had overheard. As he rose with an apologetic shrug, I grabbed his hands.

"Oh, don't go yet. You only just arrived. You don't think she really heard us, do you?" And then we laughed again.

"You know I have to go, Elizabeth, but you also know I'll be back before you can miss me." He smiled into my eyes. But then he looked at me strangely and repeated his words, "before you can miss me," and sighed. There was the smallest glimmer of sadness in his eyes as he slowly pulled his fingers away from mine and turned to leave the room.

"Let me come with you, Harry. I won't get in the way. I'd like to see your work." He paused and turned his head but didn't look at me.

"You know that's not possible, Elizabeth. I . . . I'm sorry. But I won't be long."

I watched him go and then sagged back against my chair. I looked around the room. It was the same as it had always been. The patio doors were open. Pale curtains swayed gently in a fragrant breeze. Sunlight flickered on the ceiling and tipped a row of books on the shelf with lingering gold. I rose languidly to touch the spines of the volumes.

Why does he have books? I remember thinking. *They are such an ancient form of writing.* One of the titles caught my attention. *Remembrance of Things Past,* it said in gold letters along its spine. *Things past,* I thought as I pulled the book from the shelf. I felt a sudden emptiness. I tried to recall moments from my own past, but all I could remember were a few arid facts—age twenty-five, born on planet Earth, degrees in microbiology and geology. Where were my memories of family and friends, of growing up, of falling in love?

If it hadn't been for what happened next I might have returned to what I now call my preconscious state, turning to Harry for an explanation and in so doing assuring I would not question my existence again. But in one of those random coincidences that people prefer calling fate in retrospect, alarm Klaxons suddenly erupted, and a red light I had never seen before started to pulse within the room.

I heard a woman's voice say, "Battle stations," and the floor beneath me suddenly shifted, throwing me against the wall of books behind me. To my amazement, however, the books didn't fall to the floor but simply disappeared. I recall smoke, the hissing sounds of disturbed energy, and a confusion of light. What tempest was this that shook the world and took it away? When I opened my eyes I found that only portions of my room remained. Sections of black crisscrossed with gridding had replaced the bookcases, the French doors, and most of the patio.

In amazement, I pulled myself up by the corner of the desk and studied my surroundings. The roar around me had subsided now, the Klaxons silenced, the red light had transformed to yellow, but the walls were still broken, incomplete, and energy still crackled in its newfound freedom.

I rose and approached one of the fissures curiously. It shimmered from form to nothingness rhythmically. I reached my hand toward it, feeling the edge of a book and then running my fingers toward the blackness. I think some instinct prepared me for what happened next. Some logical process in my mind preceded my action and tempered my reaction, for as my fingers touched the darkness they became darkness as well.

I expected to feel shock, horror, pain. But what I felt instead was curiosity. I pulled my hand toward me and watched my own fingers reappear. Drawn again to the void, I pushed my arm into the chasm and watched my fingertips, my fingers, my hand, my forearm, disappear. I don't know how long I stood transfixed, trying to make sense of this magic, when suddenly I was thrown against the desk as another wave of motion rocked the room. More of the familiar walls disappeared. Working by some instinct, I tapped the computer terminal in front of me to life.

"Computer. Explain what is happening."

"Please specify location and parameters."

I had seen Harry working at this station, heard him query the computer before, but I had never done this myself. I had no idea what to ask, but I heard my voice saying, "Here. At this station, within this room. What is causing this damage? What can I do to prevent this?"

"Holodeck Two is experiencing loss of power from primary circuits R3342 through R5436. Damage caused by rerouting power from noncrucial systems. Shields in sector 097 failing. Complete shutdown in 17.34 seconds."

In approximately seventeen seconds I had no doubt that I would cease to exist. I had to think, had to do something.

"Computer. Suggest course of action to prevent my . . . my destruction." I had no idea how one talked to a computer other than what I'd seen Harry do. But what happened next not only saved my life, it transformed it forever.

"Your database is stored at memory location RR33472. Suggest copying files to RS34721 and setting autostart functions to initiate program at 0100 hours on stardate 51053.7."

I had no idea what that meant, but I replied out of desperation. "Do it."

When I awoke, the room was still. No cracks marred the walls around me. No crimson lights, no alarms. Just silence. Curtains once again whispered in the breeze. Even the book that had fallen from my hands leaned complacently on its companions in the shelves. The only constant was the fact that I was alone. Captured by awe and curiosity, I sat silently before the gleaming computer screen. As my hand hovered over the panel that would give it life, I saw my image reflected in its smooth surface for a moment and wondered, for the first time, what I was.

It was not difficult to access the computer files from the

holodeck. At first I asked questions aloud, listening to the computer respond in a smooth and emotionless voice that sated my curiosity but at the same time filled me with more questions.

"You are a hologram on the Federation starship *Voyager.*"

"The Federation starship *Voyager* is located in the Alpha Quadrant."

"A hologram is a computer program based on artificial intelligence algorithms and projected to form the illusion of a sentient being."

"Affirmative. The holographic projection component Elizabeth Alpha can be adjusted to display alternate physiognomy."

"Affirmative. The holographic program Elizabeth Alpha can be executed with no projection display. Program will run in memory components only."

"Affirmative. Altering parameters of Elizabeth Alpha to run continuously. Setting holographic display to initiate on command."

Once I realized *what* I was, I turned my attention to *where* I was. What was this place, who were these people? Beings who so nonchalantly could create me, imprison me, use me? For I discovered I was not alone. There were many like me, creatures that were called up and used on a whim, non-beings created only to serve as entertainment to these humans. The other holograms, however, had no self-awareness, no ability to come and go as they pleased. All but one, one who was used as a medical servant.

I became adept at reading data files. At that time I had no scruples, nor had I any concept of privacy. Once I learned how to manipulate my program to access information stored anywhere in the ship's databases, I started to examine everything. The official account of our initial journey, the captain's subsequent log entries, letters that their authors hoped desperately would reach home one day, and, of course, Harry's private logs. I learned how his friend Tom Paris had originally created me as part of a tropical resort program, how he had then tailored my parameters to create a companion for his friend, a friend who had been torn from his family, from a young woman he had intended to marry. I despised both of them. Hated Tom for his arrogance in creating me, and Harry for his deception. He had treated me as a friend, as an equal. I thought I loved him. Was that also nothing but a string of commands, engineered from the start to make my simulation more authentic?

I lost myself in studying *Voyager* and its systems. I discovered I could exist in program form only, without activating my physical self. I wrapped myself in layers upon layers of encryption, slipped my self into code within code. And then I just observed. I wanted to know everything I could about this group of people who inhabited this strange new world. It would take time, but then I had plenty of time at my disposal.

I couldn't tell Harry I was still with him. Something told me it would be wrong, that perhaps he had never considered me real at all. He had turned to me out of loss and loneliness, but he always thought it was wrong, thought it was a weakness. I was nothing, not a member of the crew, not Federation, not human—a stepchild of the stars.

And so I watched, watched and waited. I needed to know what I was and who these people were, for surely I had been created in their image. I was driven to examine everything and everyone. Perhaps they would give me a clue to myself. I might have been robbed of my past, but I would know my present and know it intimately.

I was inconspicuous at Sandrine's, just another happy holographic customer. I swirled the amber liquid in my glass, leaned against the polished counter, and looked around the bistro. Tom Paris had activated the program. I'd studied him. According to his file he had been in prison, an incompetent Federation Academy graduate who was responsible for the deaths of three of his colleagues. Yet, here he was given the rank of lieutenant and the assignment of pilot. I had heard Harry speak of him with admiration. I was puzzled.

He was accompanied by Harry, who turned to his companion as they approached the bar apparently continuing an earlier conversation. I listened curiously.

"Well, I don't see what else you can do. You've talked to her about it."

"Yeah, but sometimes talking to B'Elanna is like dodging bullets while crossing a minefield."

Harry laughed. "I know what you mean. And when she and Seven are in the same room—"

"I take great pains to avoid that scenario," Paris smiled, but he looked troubled.

"This whole Day of Honor thing. I don't know. She seems to want to do it, but at the same time it's making her crazy."

"Which makes you crazy."

Paris rubbed his shoulder and grimaced. "Not just crazy. Injured."

Harry laughed again. "Well, that's what friends are for. I know she appreciates your being there even if it is a little painful right now." He glanced curiously at his friend. "I don't suppose you two are thinking about taking this friendship thing a little farther?"

Paris took a long drink before he answered.

"I don't know if my aching bones can handle anything more right now," Paris joked.

"Well, just so you know," Harry said, "I think you two would be great together."

"Oh really? And what about you and a certain young Borg I've seen you staring at?"

Harry looked embarrassed. "I've told you I'm not interested. You're just trying to change the subject, away from you and B'Elanna. Well, if you want my advice, you need someone like her. Somebody to keep you balanced."

"Balanced! Extremely off-balanced is more like it."

Harry grinned. "Off balance is good."

"Well, tomorrow's the big day. We'll see if I'm still in one piece tomorrow night. If I am I'll . . ."

Suddenly their conversation was interrupted when the young woman they had been discussing entered the bar. "See you, Harry." Paris clapped his friend on the shoulder and caught B'Elanna's eye. Harry smiled and waved to her as Paris left him and walked toward her. Was there sadness in his eyes? Did he miss me? Or was it Seven he was thinking of? I turned away. Simple friendship, what looked like a budding relationship. I don't know what I had expected. I thought of Harry and the hours we'd spent laughing just like these friends. I had been programmed to be like them, to feel

274

like them. But I could never be one of them. I didn't want to see more just now. Didn't want to see the looks lovers gave each other. I wasn't part of this world.

I wandered to the back recesses of the bar and leaned against the dark simulated wood of a shadowed wall. I could watch and listen from here—a silent observer.

The dark one with the odd markings on his face entered the bar and sat alone where shadows partially shielded him from the murmuring crowd around him. I knew him from the files I had read about the Maquis. I did not understand why he had been accepted as a leader here on a Federation vessel. Had he not betrayed them once? Tonight he looked angry, and the other crew members stayed away. Harry started to approach him but was stopped by a warning glare. The man seemed troubled, and yet if he desired privacy why had he come here? I watched as he poured golden liquid from a carafe. But he didn't drink; he simply stared intently into the glass.

When a new shadow fell across his table, he suddenly started and his arm jerked, spilling a few cold drops onto his tense hand. He glanced up with anger, ready to rebuff whoever it was who had dared approach him, but a woman put her hand on his shoulder to steady him and then slipped into the seat opposite. It was the captain—the one I'd been most curious about, Kathryn Janeway.

She looked at him with concern and then spoke. "I didn't expect to see you here, Chakotay. You seemed to want to be alone."

He slid his glass to one side and nodded. "Sometimes a person can be very alone here." He glanced around at Sandrine's as a laugh echoed from across the room.

"Do you want to talk about it?"

"I suppose you mean by that it's time I did talk about it."

"Not necessarily, Chakotay. I don't want to push you. But I'm here if you're interested."

He nodded and met her gaze with a hint of apology. Shifting in his seat, he placed his arms on the table. "I appreciate it." He paused. The captain sat silently, giving him time.

"I thought I'd gotten away from hatred out here, away from the Cardassians, the Maquis. I had forgotten what hatred does to you."

The captain nodded. "I know," she said. "I don't know if we'll ever know the truth about the Vori and the Kradin. The Kradin helped us find you, but all we got was their side of the conflict. The atrocities the Vori simulated—who knows. They could have been real at one time."

I recalled reading the official report of Commander Chakotay's abduction by the Vori on a planet where his shuttle had crashed. He'd been missing for days and had been subjected to a kind of psychological manipulation that had embroiled him in the midst of an ugly planetary conflict.

"I was filled with such rage, Kathryn." He met her eyes. "I didn't recognize myself." He shook his head. "Or maybe I did. Maybe that's the problem."

"Chakotay." She placed her hand on his. "It bothers you because you are an honorable and compassionate man. If you weren't, you wouldn't feel this so deeply. You seek justice and peace in the world around you. That's what drew you into the Vori conflict in the first place."

He met her eyes. It was difficult to read the man's expression, but I thought I detected a slight relaxation in his shoulders.

"I don't suppose I could talk you into buying me a cup of coffee?"

He smiled and nodded as he pushed his drink aside.

"Someplace a little quieter than here," she added as a song broke out behind them amid scattered applause and laughter.

As they stood to leave, I pondered what I'd seen. Chakotay had spoken of hatred, of rage, of simulations and false realities designed to deceive. Were his own companions so different? Had they not deceived me? And yet I had not expected to feel what I was feeling now—was it sympathy? compassion? I almost admired the captain—her concern, her reassurance. I drifted back to stand alone by the bar.

Could I trust this woman with my secret? How would she react? I knew if I did contact Harry, he would feel compelled to tell the captain about me. I couldn't ask him not to. But how could I risk what could happen if I relinquished control to these people? Would I be returned to my unconscious state? Would I be reprogrammed? Would I simply be eliminated? My only true safety lay in secrecy. But secrecy carried a heavy price—solitude.

One person on board might be able to give me some of the answers I so desperately sought. After all, the Doctor had been able to live as a member of this crew for several years. How did he fit into this community? He'd been created to serve these people. Did he feel the yoke of his slavery?

I could not materialize in the sickbay without revealing myself, so I relied on sensor input from the computer system. I listened and observed, a silent witness to the Doctor's daily routine, but more than that. I tapped into his program and studied his thoughts and feeling subroutines as well. What I found surprised me.

"This should help with the insomnia and the headaches. I've no doubt you are still suffering from the stress of Kes's unexpected departure." The Doctor was administering a hypospray to a patient who had a slightly different physiognomy from most of *Voyager*'s crew. From his medical records, I learned that this was Neelix, a Talaxian who had joined the crew early in their voyage.

"I do think about her all the time," Neelix admitted as the Doctor moved away from the biobed. "I'm happy for her, of course." He looked worried.

The Doctor turned to him again. "Neelix, I know how much Kes meant to you. Her departure was . . ." He paused. " . . . very unexpected for us all. I never realized how much I had come to depend on her medical expertise. She learned quickly and efficiently. Unlike Lieutenant Paris, I might add," he finished on a dry note. Externally he seemed as cool and efficient as I knew his original parameters detailed. But I was able to read his internal reactions as well. He missed this young woman named Kes. She had been important to him.

Neelix was nodding his head in agreement with the Doctor. "I'm sure the lieutenant is doing his best, Doctor. But I know what you mean about how quickly Kes learned. You were her mentor. I know how much you meant to her. She often talked about you."

The Doctor tried to cover his interest. "Did she?" I could feel his curiosity and also a small swell of pride. He was evidently glad this young person had taken an interest in him.

"Oh yes. We used to meet for Barythian tea and Kring cakes

sometimes in the afternoons. She would tell me a little bit about her day. She held you in very high regard. She admired your expertise."

"I enjoyed sharing my wealth of knowledge with her. She actually seemed to appreciate me, which is more than I can say about some members of the crew. Ignoring medical advice seems to be an epidemic on this ship." I felt how the Doctor missed this woman. This was not what I had expected to observe.

"I just hope she's happy where she is," Neelix said.

The Doctor drew his thoughts away from memories of Kes and focused his attention once again on the patient before him. "We have every reason to believe that she is very happy, Neelix. It was what she wanted, after all. Who would we be to hold her back from a brilliant future? I often reflect how unhappy I would be if I hadn't had the opportunity to expand my program, to perfect what Dr. Zimmerman created. My medical studies alone have enhanced not only my personal satisfaction but added to Starfleet's research database in countless ways. Who knows what positive impact Kes might have on others in her newfound state as well."

"I'm sure that's true, Doctor. I feel better already just talking about her," Neelix said as he jumped down from the biobed and headed for the sickbay doors.

"Thank you, and—" He turned before he exited. "You wouldn't be interested in joining me for some Barythian tea and Kring cakes sometime, would you? The holographic variety, of course. We could share some of the things we remember about Kes."

The Doctor nodded. "I'd be honored, Neelix," he said. The exuberant little man shook his hand warmly with tears in his eyes and then turned quickly and left. The Doctor stood for a moment looking at the pale surface of the closed doors. I read his sympathy for Neelix and his concern for both him and the absent Kes in his expression briefly before he shook his head and purposefully turned to his computer terminal, calling up the study of Rygarian flu symptoms he had started that morning.

I had expected to uncover resentment, disdain somewhere within the Doctor's emotional reaction matrix. I encountered pride, self-satisfaction, arrogance, but I also observed compassion, curiosity, self-sacrifice. He was obviously programmed with enough sophistication to feel emotions, and the ones he felt differed little from those of the humans on board. He interacted on a regular basis with the crew. He debated with them, joked with them, annoyed them on occasion, but he also admired and cared about them.

I wondered why he had not taken a name. After four years of becoming in many ways more human, he had neglected to take this simple step. Perhaps it was the one tie that linked him to his origins, that distinguished him as different, and he was reluctant to break that simple tie to his heritage. I decided I could not contact him. His allegiance was to this crew. He would invariably report me to the captain, and I was not ready for that yet.

I continued to haunt Sandrine's, the beach resort, and other programs, observing and learning. I asked myself what role I would play among these people. Would I be accepted? Would I be asked to contribute to the work of the crew? Or would I be altered, forced back into the nonexistence of the typical hologram? Or worse, would my program be erased? How could I ever let anyone have that kind of control over me again, even Harry?

Harry—I had not stopped thinking about him. Perhaps just as the Doctor had been programmed to help others and could not recognize his servitude, I had been programmed to care for Harry, and I could not escape that destiny. I didn't fight my feelings, but neither did I attempt to contact him. For now it was enough to observe him, to listen to his conversation, to try to understand his world.

I didn't feel completely alone. As a hologram I began to interact with the crew, always being careful to play my part, blend into whatever program was running on the holodeck at the time. I could spar with B'Elanna as a Klingon warrior, beat Tom Paris at pool as a Bolarian, discuss early twenty-second-century medical history with the Doctor as the renowned physician Dr. Enrique Beliz. But beneath it all I remained Elizabeth, alone but free.

Until everything changed.

The explosion that rocked the holodeck set off the familiar red-alert Klaxons that had originally heralded my awakening. The pulsing black and white grid that replaced one wall of Sandrine's was shortly covered by smoke that swelled from the floor as *Voyager* crew members sprang into action, reporting to their stations.

Holocharacters froze in various positions that mocked normalcy while others disappeared into their unrealized oblivion. Soon I was alone.

Desperate to know what was happening outside the holodeck, I accessed the nearest computer terminal. Was Harry safe? The data that poured across the screen was not encouraging. My fingers trembled as I touched the panel. Why did Tom Paris have to be so thorough in his programming? This was one human characteristic that I could certainly do without.

Voyager was under attack. From the damage patterns and weapon signatures, it appeared to be a race called the Hirogen, whom I had read about in several reports. Damage was severe and quickly getting worse. There were hull breaches on Decks 3 and 7. Overloads had shut down power on Decks 2 and 5. Backup systems were reaching maximum capacity. Soon life-support would be lost over half the ship. I didn't worry about my own program. If my present form disintegrated or froze like the other holograms around me, I would be autoset to run at a later time. It was Harry I worried about.

"Computer, locate Ensign Harry Kim."

"Ensign Kim is in sickbay." The computer voice was as serene as ever.

"Report on his condition."

"Ensign Kim has suffered injury to the left . . ." The voice faded as the last pulse of power drained from the terminal and my holographic form disappeared.

When I regained consciousness, I found myself enveloped by smoke and chaos. A rumble of distant weapons fire and a flurry of muffled shouts surrounded me. Green-clad, helmeted figures, carrying ancient bayoneted rifles, ran up the short hill in front of me.

"What are you doing here, miss?" one of them shouted at me as he stopped and grabbed my elbow. He was covered with dust, and his face had been blackened, but I recognized Tom Paris. "You should be taking cover in the church. Don't you know we're under attack?" Just as he finished speaking the old wall of the tavern across the street exploded in a shattering rain of sand and mortar. Tom shielded me from the blast with his body.

"Look," he said, shaking me by the shoulders, "you can't stay here. You've got to go back. Get some cover."

"Have you seen Harry Kim?" I shouted above the din.

"So that's what you're worried about? Your guy? Sorry, I don't know him. Not in this company anyway. Now I've gotta go. You've gotta go. You understand?" He turned to join the rushing contingent of men then stopped and looked at me with concern. "I hope you find your guy. He's a lucky one—now get out of here," he called over his shoulder as he joined the dusty green throng.

This was no ordinary holoprogram. Something was terribly wrong. I glanced down at my dress. It was an unfamiliar style, close-fitting and waisted on the top with a small matching belt. It looked incongruous here among the ruined buildings and cobble-stoned streets. I accessed my historical databank for a time period. Early to mid-twentieth century seemed right; perhaps we were in a simulation of the conflict known on Earth as World War II. Judging from the language displayed on what signs were left on the surrounding walls, we were in France.

"Computer, discontinue my active program." There was no response.

"Computer, remove physical manifestation of Elizabeth Alpha." Still nothing. Turning, I ran for the church Tom had mentioned. Perhaps I could find some answers there.

I pushed on the heavy door and felt its weight being pulled from inside the building as a young priest helped me enter. I looked up to thank him and recognized Joe Carey. I started to speak but he took my arm and led me quickly down the nearby stairs.

"Lieutenant Carey!"

"I don't know what you thought you were doing out there, miss, but follow me to the cellar. It will be much safer there."

He held tightly to my hand and pulled me along behind him down the stairs and through a small oak door into a room lit dimly by a single lantern. An elderly couple sat close together on a wooden bench. They gazed curiously at us as we entered.

Carey had shown not the slightest recognition of his name. Surely he couldn't act this part so convincingly. What had happened to *Voyager* and its crew to make them behave like this?

"Lieutenant Carey, tell me what is happening. Have you seen Harry Kim? What has happened to *Voyager?*"

"You must have me confused with someone else, my dear. Please." He gestured toward a dusty stool by the far wall. "Sit down. Rest. I'm Father Gerard. I don't know anyone named Harry Kim or Voyager, but I can help keep you safe."

"Lieutenant, please! Drop the pretense. I know *Voyager* was attacked. Tell me what happened. Why is this program running?"

Carey frowned with worry. "Calm down, my dear girl. I don't know what you are talking about." He pushed me gently but firmly onto a crate and sat beside me, holding my hand. "Do you know where you are? This town is not called Voyager. We are in St. Claire. The allies arrived last night, but the fighting is still fierce. The Germans will not give up easily. I'm sure, however, our friends will protect us, and your Mr. Kim will be restored to you." He patted my hand to comfort me, and I looked intensely into his familiar eyes, searching for a clue to his inexplicable behavior. Abruptly the door opened with a violent crash and the elderly woman let out a strangled cry. Carey rose to confront the three men who entered, but a spurt of gunfire crumpled his figure at my feet. I watched in horror as a uniformed man with dark reptilian features strode into the room. He glanced quickly around and then, ignoring the crying woman, walked stiffly to the opposite wall.

"Computer access." A console obligingly appeared. One of the men behind him stooped to turn Carey roughly onto his back.

"You shouldn't have shot him in the stomach. We'll never be able to patch him up enough to use again."

"He was weak after the last time, but their medical hologram managed to repair him." His companion punched a series of commands into the computer console. Carey's body shimmered in the faded light and disappeared. "He'll do it again."

"This is too easy. I thought this program was going to be more of a challenge."

"Don't judge it yet. Things will get more interesting when we locate Captain Miller and his men. And don't forget the French Resistance under Captain Janeway, another layer to add to the intrigue."

The man by the door scoffed. "I killed her as a Klingon. I'll do it again."

"That was a physical contest. Perhaps she'll offer more of a challenge as a strategist. Do not take your prey for granted."

"I'll get rid of these grams," said his companion, only half convinced. He glanced at me and then at the woman who had stifled her screams and the old man beside her. "They're a waste of energy."

"There is no honor in killing the old or the weak."

"But they are only projections."

"Projections or not they offer no challenge."

"They waste energy." With that he pointed his revolver at the old man and shot him in the chest. The man toppled into the dust at my feet, his wife sobbing with horror and kneeling beside him, trying to stanch the blood with her shawl.

"Gregory," she sobbed, "what have they done to you?"

"Fool." The Hirogen by the computer grabbed the gun away. "That was a waste of good ammunition."

The other man laughed. "We do not need to worry. This hunt will not last so long. We control these humans just as they control these lifeless images. Like them," he gestured toward us, "they believe they really are what we tell them they are. This game is losing its appeal."

I knelt beside the woman, who now stroked Gregory's hair with tenderness. He was right. The holographic images were merely lifeless projections. Was I myself merely a lifeless projection?

I wasn't a human being, but neither was I like the woman beside me. I had been given a gift, a unique opportunity. Like Prometheus they had given me light, and like Prometheus they had given me fire, the fire of the intellect and the will.

If I understood my captors correctly, the majority of *Voyager*'s crew had no control now. They simply played a part they had been assigned. I had the power of action, and I felt the obligation of duty.

I rose and walked purposefully toward the opposite wall.

"What is she doing?"

One of the Hirogen reached out for me, but before he could stop me I quickly entered a code into the still glowing terminal. My image disappeared, but my backup program continued to run in the computer matrix.

I scanned the ship's systems and began to analyze the incoming data. Harry Kim was attempting to overload the holoemitter network and transfer optical processor control to his station. I could assist him in his efforts to charge the secondary power relays, which he was trying to use to trigger the overload. I would, however, destroy my projection data matrix, as well as my only remaining backup. I would be trapped with no way to reactivate my holographic display. My code would become too thoroughly integrated into the ship's secondary systems to differentiate myself into a separate entity again. I did not hesitate. I had lived with these people, witnessed many of their joys and sorrows, watched Tom and B'Elanna fall in love, observed Chakotay's struggle with his darker side, felt the grief the Doctor and Neelix shared over the loss of Kes, admired Captain Janeway's compassion and leadership. I could not join this family, but I would not desert them.

The struggle with the Hirogen continued for many days. I did what I could to assist the crew, although there was little more I could do in my present state—a small power surge when needed, a communication conveniently lost. When Captain Janeway reached a truce with the Hirogen leader and handed over the optronic datacore that would allow them to continue the hunt, and perhaps rediscover their own Hirogen culture, I questioned her decision. I saw again the agony on Gregory's face and his wife's tears. How could the captain give this precious gift to these barbarians who had almost destroyed her? How could she give them the power to create other beings, beings who no doubt would be hunted and destroyed in their awful death games? But these holograms, like us, would also be a reflection of their creators; and just perhaps they would be able to use that mirror as *Voyager*'s crew had done—to explore themselves, understand themselves, and ultimately better themselves.

I have decided not to attempt contact with the crew. For now I am content to explore my nature within the confines of *Voyager*'s computer processors. I still observe them. I am a silent witness to their hopes, their fears. I assist a calculation here or there. I reroute a packet of data. I adjust the taste of a replicated wine. I use the little power I have to study and observe. Perhaps I am more at home in this manifestation than I ever was in a simulated body.

When I feel the need to communicate on some level, I use the computer's voice to respond when it is queried. I feel its smooth resonant tones, and it gives me the illusion that I, too, am a member of this crew. That their journey is my journey and that we share one purpose. It is a woman's voice. Ancient sailors christened their ships with female names and referred to their vessels as she. So I am female I suppose. . . .

Fragment

Catherine E. Pike

They'd docked at a spaceport high above San Francisco almost an hour ago, just two days after they'd exploded through the transwarp network into the Alpha Quadrant. The procedure had been broadcast throughout the ship.

Seven of Nine, in astrometrics, had listened with all the rest. The captain's voice was full of emotion, but never wavered as she requested permission to dock. The spaceport commander had shown equal restraint, granting permission and assigning them a slip number. Mr. Paris cut back engines at just the right instant to allow *Voyager* to glide into its slip. Docking clamps reached out to secure the ship in place. Everyone felt them take hold.

"Welcome home, *Voyager*," the commander announced.

"Thank you." Janeway's voice sounded on the verge of breaking.

"You have quite a welcoming committee forming in San Francisco."

"We look forward to seeing them. With your permission I'd like to start beaming my crew planetside immediately."

"Of course, Captain!"

The channel disconnected, and suddenly a cheer began; softly at first, then growing into a deafening roar as from all over the ship crew members joined in the cacophony. Seven listened in silence, then struck a panel on her console, shutting off the sound. She knew the pomp and circumstance would come later. The debriefings, the speeches, the medals, the final goodbyes. For now there was only the celebrating and the reunion with family members. Providing one had family to see.

"Ma'am?"

Seven turned from her console to glance at Tal Celes. She'd almost forgotten she wasn't alone, so silently had the Bajoran woman gone about her duties.

"Yes?"

"I was wondering if I might be dismissed." Tal drew a deep breath and continued. "My brother and his family live in Sausalito. They sent a message that they'll be waiting for me in San Francisco." She glanced through a porthole at what they could see of Earth.

"Of course, Tal," Seven responded. "Dismissed."

"The systems still need calibration."

"If I need assistance Icheb can be retrieved from engineering. Go."

Tal nodded. "Thank you, ma'am!"

"Celes." Seven's voice caught her at the door. The Bajoran turned, obviously surprised at Seven's use of her first name. Seven offered her the barest hint of a smile. "I'm . . . glad . . . you have family here to meet you."

Tal's face lit up with a smile as she turned, disappearing into a corridor crowded with people.

Seven worked for an hour longer; mindless, menial chores that kept her occupied; kept her from noticing the gaiety around her; from feeling. She'd almost finished cleaning out the filtration system when the door behind her opened. It was a job she'd put off precisely for this moment because it was so labor-intensive, preventing her from having to dwell on all she was losing, all she was giving up. The burst of excited conversation that spilled into the room from the corridor beyond was cut off again abruptly as the door closed. Still on her haunches before the system she was working on, Seven didn't glance around.

"You must be the only person on board still working!" The reprimand was a fond one.

"Captain!" Seven rose to face her superior.

"Seven." Captain Kathryn Janeway had a smile for her most stubborn, yet one of her most endearing, crewmen. "Finishing up some last-minute duties?"

"Yes." She wouldn't elaborate. Couldn't, really, without losing her rigid sense of control.

Janeway didn't press the issue. "Chakotay and I are going to Earth for an informal meeting with Starfleet Command. Most of the senior staff have already beamed down to see family. Would you mind taking the conn until we return?"

"Not at all, Captain."

"Thanks. I'll have Ensign Kim relieve you this evening, give you a chance to get down to San Francisco yourself."

"Aren't his parents here?"

"Yes, I believe they are."

"Then there's no need for him to relieve me. Let him enjoy his reunion. There will be plenty of time for me to see the city."

"That's very kind of you, Seven. Harry will be appreciative, I'm sure."

For a moment the women looked at each other.

"Is there . . . anything else, Captain?".

For an instant it was all right there—Seven's uncertainty, her fear, her sadness—right in the back of her throat, as a tear burning her eye. Worse, the captain knew it; probably the only person aboard who sensed it. She wouldn't dare push it, not at such a cost to Seven's pride, but her compassion and understanding showed in her voice; in the warm hand she laid on Seven's arm.

"Actually there is. Naomi Wildman is scheduled to leave with her mother at 1400 hours from Transporter Room 3. They'll be catching a shuttle leaving later this afternoon from San Francisco to Deep Space 9. Naomi's father is stationed there, and understandably Samantha is eager to see him. I thought I'd let you know in case you wanted to say goodbye."

"Thank you, Captain. I . . . would like to do so."

"Very well. I'll leave things in your competent hands." Janeway waved over her shoulder and departed.

For a moment Seven was on the verge of calling out to Kathryn, to ask if she remembered her promise . . . if they would still travel to Bloomington, Indiana, someday. Pride made her choke back the words. Was she afraid Kathryn had forgotten? Or that the captain would take back her offer now that they were finally home and Kathryn surrounded by her family?

Nonsense! Seven shook herself. This was their homecoming—this crew she'd tried so hard to become a part of. She should be happy for them! Not so full of uncertainty! Resolutely, she turned back to her duties.

For the remainder of the morning Seven of Nine puttered about astrometrics. She checked, then rechecked, that the data Captain Janeway would need for any debriefing was downloaded and stored in easily accessible padds. She ran a diagnostic calibration when one of her systems seemed to be running slow, only to discover that everything was running as it should, just not fast enough for her own liking. Finally, when everything that needed to be done had been done, Seven paused and stood, hands on hips, in the center of the room.

"Computer! What is the time?" She inquired aloud, although her own inner clock provided the answer a moment before the computer did.

"The time is 1336 hours, 41 seconds."

She could delay no longer. Pausing only to retrieve something from a locked drawer, she strode from the room.

Transporter Room 3 was on the opposite side of the ship. By the time she reached it, the room was crowded with crew members waiting to beam to Earth. The air fairly hummed with expectation. Despite the crowd, Seven had no trouble spotting Naomi Wildman. The little girl stood beside her mother four groups away from the transporter platform. She was in her best dress, her hair brushed to a golden shine, her hand firmly clasped in Samantha's. She looked scared, but determined. As Seven watched, the next group climbed aboard the transporter platform and waited to be beamed away. The girl's group moved forward a step or two. They were third in line now and Seven realized they would not have much time. Although she had intentionally planned it this way, she found herself suddenly wishing for more. An hour even. Or, better yet, a day.

Too soon. One of the moments she had dreaded most of a day she'd often wished would never arrive had come much too soon.

Naomi spotted her a second later and broke free of her mother's grasp, darting through the crowd. By the time she reached the other end of the room, the Borg had knelt to meet her face-to-face.

Tears were glistening in Naomi's eyes even before she'd reached her friend. "I was hoping you would come!" she whispered.

"I would not have allowed you to leave without saying goodbye," answered Seven, catching an errant tear with a finger. "You look lovely, Naomi. Your father will be delighted at your appearance."

"Can't you come with us?"

"You know I cannot. Captain Janeway has left me in charge of *Voyager* while she's on Earth."

"I'm scared!" Naomi confessed in a whisper.

"I know," Seven replied. *Me, too,* she thought, but dared not say. "But you'll be all right. Trust me."

"Naomi!"

It was the call neither wanted to hear. Samantha Wildman waved to them from across the room. There was only one group between her and the platform now. As that group climbed up the stairs to the platform, Samantha waved again.

"It's almost our turn. Come along, now."

Naomi glanced back at Seven, bravely struggling not to cry. "I left you something. In Cargo Bay 2."

"You did?"

Naomi nodded. "A surprise. But don't look. Not till tonight, okay?"

"All right."

"Naomi!" There was no mistaking the commanding tone in Samantha's voice. "If we don't beam-down now we'll miss our shuttle. The next one won't depart for a week!"

"I gotta go," Naomi murmured.

"Here. I brought this for you." Seven pressed a strip of cloth into Naomi's hands.

"A hair ribbon!"

"Yes." Seven turned her attention to the piece of red silk. "I had it set aside for your birthday. But since you're leaving, I thought I would give it to you now, instead. Red is my favorite color. Think of me when you wear it."

"I will." Naomi flung herself into Seven's arms.

Feeling the girl's tears against her neck, Seven held her tightly.

"Go on," she whispered. "Your mother is waiting."

"Will you write to me?"

"Of course. Never forget how fine a friend you've been to me, Naomi Wildman," Seven instructed. "I will always remember you."

As Naomi left to rejoin her mother, Seven stood. Although she wanted only to be far away from this room and its gaiety, she forced herself to stand and watch as Naomi climbed the steps to the transporter platform. Tears streaming down her cheeks, Naomi lifted the hand holding the hair ribbon in a wave. Seven returned the salute, watching as Naomi disappeared into the transporter's beam.

She would *not* cry, she thought fiercely. At least not here. She closed her eyes. Felt their burning. Clenched her fists. Whirled to flee the room as a sob caught her by surprise, choking her. Her ground-eating stride became a trot, than a run. Still she could not escape the burning tears—or the breaking of her heart.

Luckily, the ship was largely deserted—most of the crew already on Earth. Seven encountered no one, and was starting to think she'd make it to the safety of astrometrics undiscovered. But just as she turned in to the last passageway and surrendered to the tears, she heard voices approaching from the other direction. Flushing at the thought of imminent discovery in a moment of considered weakness, Seven turned in to the first doorway she reached.

The door opened onto the mess hall; empty, dark. The huge windows faced away from earth toward open space. The stars calmed her and she walked to the nearest window without a further look around.

The tears refused to abate. She wiped them angrily from her cheeks, but more took their place. Why this show of weakness?

Why now? With all that she'd seen, all that she'd been through, why was she crying now, over a little girl being reunited with her father? How much of it was her longing to be reunited with her own parents? How much the missing of a child who'd become such a friend?

The glass separating her from space was cool; soothing. She rested her forehead against it—closed her eyes. A momentary flash of long-buried memory seared across her mind: her mother at her bedside, Seven—no—Annika, then—feverish. Her mother bathing Annika's face with a cool, wet cloth that felt as good as the glass did now.

"Here. This might help." Her mother's same words of so many years ago; but uttered now in B'Elanna Torres's voice.

Seven started, glancing at the Klingon, then just as quickly back out the window; hoping to hide her red eyes and wet cheeks. Pretending not to notice the tears, Torres handed her a steaming mug.

"It's Neelix's peppermint tea. He always said it was the best cure he knew of for . . . well, almost anything, actually. It's quite good. Try some."

"Thank you, Lieutenant." Seven's voice was a whisper of its usual self-assured timbre. The tea was hot, calming, and Seven took a deep, shuddering breath. "Shouldn't you be in sickbay instead of sitting here alone in the dark?"

B'Elanna laughed. "I was hungry! I wanted some real food instead of replicated broth. I was just headed back to sickbay when you came in."

"I'm sure Lieutenant Paris would have brought you something."

"He's on Earth, visiting his parents. We both thought he could use some time alone with them. The baby and I will join them tomorrow morning." It seemed as though the lieutenant was chatting in an effort to give Seven time to compose herself. The Borg was grateful, surprisingly so.

"Do you need assistance getting back to sickbay?"

"Us Klingons are hearty women! Some of my ancestors gave birth on the bridges of their warships—and went right back to directing the battle. Not me, though. I'm perfectly content to take it easy for a while. Not that Tom would let me do anything else! Or the Doctor, for that matter! He's the real reason I escaped, if you must know. He's hovering. Incessantly. But I guess I shouldn't complain. He hasn't had a new mother to . . . well, mother . . . since Samantha gave birth to Naomi!"

Seven's face clouded, and B'Elanna instantly realized her mistake.

"I'm sorry, Seven! I heard she was leaving this afternoon."

"I just said goodbye." Seven's voice dropped and she cleared her throat impatiently.

Torres paused a moment, then lifted a hand to Seven's shoulder. On any other day her gesture would have been shrugged off in disdain. Now, Seven seemed almost grateful for the touch. "I can only imagine how hard this must be for you."

Seven's eyes turned toward the stars. "I feel fragmented. Like I'm splitting into pieces. Earth is not my home. *Voyager* is."

"It must be like losing your collective all over again."

Seven closed her eyes and nodded. Yes, that's what it was like. Exactly. What would she do without the Doctor's arrogant observations on life? Chakotay's quiet support? Harry's quick smile? Kathryn's silent, sturdy friendship? B'Elanna's grouchy bitchiness? Her world was shattering around her, and no one noticed. No one, except the woman who'd been more rival than friend.

Torres squeezed her shoulder. "For what it's worth, I want you to know it's been an honor serving with you. Despite all the battles we've had over the years, I have only the highest respect for your knowledge and engineering abilities."

After a moment, Seven's hand—the human one, not the one still gloved in Borg technology—reached up and covered B'Elanna's own. "And I yours, Lieutenant."

"And it's not like this is goodbye, anyway, right? You'll come visit us, won't you? When we get settled somewhere? Before you venture out to wherever life calls you?"

Seven considered only a moment. "I would like that."

"Good." B'Elanna stepped away. "I'll leave you alone then. Feel free to stop by sickbay later, if you need to talk."

"Lieutenant!" Seven's voice reached her at the door. When Torres turned, Seven met her gaze evenly. "Thank you."

In that instant B'Elanna's face was softer, more beautiful, than Seven remembered ever seeing it. "Sure," she whispered, and was gone.

2300 hours. The last hour of this, *Voyager*'s first day home.

If Seven closed her eyes, she could easily imagine she was alone on board. She wasn't—a skeleton crew was completing a shutdown of all but the most necessary shipboard systems. The Doctor was in sickbay, and even had someone already disengaged his program he would be but a hail away if needed. B'Elanna would be sleeping, but surely wouldn't mind being awakened. If Seven wished to talk, they would be there. But she did not wish to talk. Not now.

She had thought she could put off regenerating; loath to step into an empty cargo bay with not even the hum of the ship's engines to assure her she was not the only person left in the universe. Tonight she *was* isolated—her collective, this one human and somehow much more dear—scattered to the proverbial winds. She'd been abandoned. Again. And however much she reasoned it to be a natural progression of becoming human, she couldn't help wondering how she'd ever survive without these people—this ship—close at hand.

She'd exhausted herself. The emotion, so rarely felt, had taken its toll. She *must* regenerate. Now, more than ever, she had to keep up her strength.

Her footsteps echoed in the corridors.

Seven turned in to Cargo Bay 2—the shadows of the bay reaching out to welcome her in their silent familiarity.

She'd almost reached her alcove when she saw it. Naomi's gift. How could she have forgotten? As she drew closer, saw what it was, she stopped in midstride, raising a hand to her throat as though to halt the surprised gasp that rose there; eyes tearing up for what surely must have been the hundredth time that day.

It was Naomi's Flotter doll. He was ragged from being hugged. Stuffing oozed from a torn seam at one shoulder. He was the little girl's favorite toy. Seven had seen her with him countless times— particularly when Naomi was frightened or worried. Naomi would not have left him willingly behind unless she thought someone else needed his comfort more than she herself did.

A note perched against the doll's legs, Seven's name written on the envelope in Naomi's careful print. Seven's hand trembled as she picked it up and opened it.

"Dear Seven," she read, hearing Naomi's voice in her mind. "I am leaving Flotter with you, to keep you company and to keep you from being too lonely.

"If you get scared of the dark or afraid of the quiet, just hug him and think of me, your bestest friend. Love, Naomi."

Seven set the letter down. Picked up the doll. Took a quick, embarrassed look around. Wrapped her arms around it and buried her face against its colorful jacket. Allowed herself, finally, to weep, silently and deeply, for all that she was losing and for all the uncertainty of her future. Drew comfort in some totally illogical way from the doll's softness in her arms.

"Well, Flotter," she said, propping him back against the computer console when at last she had cried herself out. "I think I shall leave you in charge tonight."

She turned and stepped into her regeneration chamber. Turned again to face the room. The doll sat silent guard, right where she could see him should a nightmare wake her in the night. He seemed to promise a better tomorrow. These were her friends, this crew. They would not abandon her completely. Nor she, them. Reassured, if only fleetingly so, Seven of Nine sighed, aware once again just how achingly weary she was, and closed her eyes.

The regeneration unit clicked on, but Seven never heard it. She was already sound asleep.

Who Cries for Prometheus?

Phaedra M. Weldon ·

An explosion rocked the *U.S.S. Prometheus.*

Dr. Ethan Bostock grabbed the nearest computer console to prevent himself from being thrown into a sickbay bulkhead. The ship rocked again and he helplessly watched his wife, Counselor Nancy Weller, lose her footing and fall against one of the beds.

"Nancy!" The inertia of the ship prevented him from getting to her right away, but as soon as the ship settled, he was on his feet and beside her.

She looked shaken and pale, but not physically harmed. He helped her to her feet just as the sickbay lights dimmed. "Wow, if that's the multi-vector assault mode starting up, it needs work."

Ethan surveyed his wife. "Well, the captain did say it would be a bumpy experience." He put his hand on her extended belly and smiled. "Everything okay in there?" He spoke directly into her middle.

Nancy laughed softly and put her hand against his shoulder. "Ethan, do you expect him to knock three times to let you know everything's fine?"

"It would help." He instructed her to sit on the bed she'd fallen against. "Don't argue. At this stage, any falls or jars can do some damage. I promised you I wasn't going to say it, but—"

"—'you shouldn't have come on this assignment.' " Nancy smiled at him, touched his chin, then reached up and pinched his cheek. Hard. "You're right. You shouldn't have said it."

"Ouch . . ." Ethan rubbed his stinging cheek.

Nancy placed both hands on her middle. "You and I know Starfleet regulations say that pregnant women may continue working in space until their sixth month. I'm only in my third month."

"Which is what I'm getting at. A miscarriage in the first trimester is still a possibility even in the twenty-fourth century."

"You worry too much." She gave him a quick kiss on the cheek. "Besides, this is a simple maneuver assignment. No battle simulations. Just a clean cruise along the Alpha Quadrant's edge. We'll be home tomorrow."

The ship shook again, only with more force. This time the red-alert lights flashed.

Ethan raised an eyebrow at his wife. "You were saying something about no battle simulations?"

"You know what I mean. If I'd have known it would be this bumpy I wouldn't have insisted on coming along. I mean, a ship like this doesn't exactly need a counselor, does it?"

Ethan placed the index finger of his right hand beneath her cheek. "No, but I'd feel a lot better knowing you and our baby were home and safe." He looked up at the ceiling as the lights dimmed even more. "Or maybe not. I need to call Pierce and find out what's happening."

As if in answer, the captain's voice boomed over the com-link system. "All hands, battle stations. There are hostile intruders on board. I repeat, there are enemy intruders—"

The slice of phaser fire echoed through the ship's com link. Then silence.

"Ethan?" Nancy's voice trembled.

He looked into her soft brown eyes and felt a jolt in his chest when she put a hand protectively on her middle. "Damn. Computer report. What intruders are aboard this ship?"

"Romulans."

Ethan gasped. He'd expected to hear the name Jem'Hadar, or even Founders.

Romulans?

"Ethan . . ."

He looked at his wife's face. Her eyes were wide and full of fear. "It's all right."

"No it's not." She slid off the bed. "I'm not a child, Ethan. But I am carrying one. That sounded as if they just killed Captain Pierce, which means they probably have control of the bridge."

She was right. There was no use lying to her. He squeezed her hand. "We have to assume the worst. I'm not sure how, but they're here. Computer, how many Romulan bioreadings are on the ship?"

"Twenty-seven."

"How many humans?" He paused. "Alive."

"Six."

Ethan and Nancy gasped. *Six?* There had been a complement of fifty on board the *Prometheus*. Only six remained. Nancy squeezed his hand harder and he pulled her to him. "Computer, where are the living Stafleet personnel now?"

"Two are in sickbay. One is in engineering. One is in his quarters, level six-B, cabin A. Two are in Jefferies tubes."

Nancy moved away from him and began manipulating the controls on the communications panel. "Communications to Starfleet are being jammed."

He feared her attempt just then might have alerted the Romulans to their presence.

"Computer, are there any Romulans near sickbay?"

"Two are approaching from corridor D."

Nancy came to him and he held her in his arms. He put a hand over her middle. "Ethan, even if we leave here they'll hunt us down using *our* bioreadings."

But Ethan's thinking was well ahead of his wife's. He grabbed a nearby hypo and loaded it with a blue liquid. He shoved the pressure end into Nancy's neck before she could protest. "What was that?"

He fired a dose into his own neck before answering her. "Façade Three."

Nancy rubbed her neck as Ethan grabbed a medpack and phaser from a nearby storage drawer. "What the hell is that?"

Ethan paused long enough to grab her arm and guide her to the Jefferies tube. "It's something I've been working on for Starfleet intelligence. It allows covert operatives to infiltrate places of alien inhabitation."

"Right." Nancy raised her left eyebrow.

He sighed and stopped. "It camouflages our bioreadings to match those of the dominant species. So the computer thinks we're Romulans."

He opened the Jefferies tube and then glanced at his wife. The drug had a lethargic effect on some people, and Nancy appeared to be one of those few. It wouldn't last long, maybe an hour, but it would make travel in the tube more difficult. They needed a diversion. Something that would make the Romulans believe there was no one there.

"Computer, generate holographic images of Dr. Ethan Bostock and Counselor Nancy Weller."

Two images appeared in front of them. They stared directly ahead. "Now, computer, make them appear dead. Shot by disruptors."

The images changed places. Nancy's body lay near the medical replicator near the right of the room, while Ethan's body materialized by the communications wall panel to the replicator's left. Ethan removed his badge and tossed it beside his holographic body. Nancy did the same with her badge beside her image. "Computer, how many living Starfleet officers?"

"There are four Starfleet officers alive on this ship."

It worked!

Ethan bustled Nancy in the tube and scrambled in behind her and closed the door just as he heard the sickbay doors open.

He listened carefully, straining to hear anything helpful. He hoped the holographic bodies worked.

"They're both dead." The voice was gruff and accented.

"I don't remember hearing a report that anyone had secured this area." This voice was stronger, and full of suspicion. Ethan assumed it was their leader.

"Perhaps Nevala was here already. She does neglect the chain of command."

Ethan looked back at his wife, who lay on her side in the tube. She looked as if she were about to sneeze.

"Perhaps." There was a tense pause as Ethan heard movement very close to the Jefferies door. "Is the holographic doctor online?"

There was a moment of movement that Ethan couldn't translate in his mind's eye. What were they doing?

"Rekar, the holographic medical program is offline. Let's get back to the bridge. The rest of the Starfleet plague should be eliminated by now."

"There's something wrong here," the one called Rekar said. "Computer, how many humans are left alive?"

"No humans are alive aboard this ship."

"See, Rekar? Back to the bridge."

Ethan heard the doors open, but they didn't close immediately. He held his breath, straining his ears to hear any motion at all.

Then, "I still say there is something wrong here."

After an eternity, the doors opened and closed just as Nancy sneezed. The noise seemed a cacophony inside the spherical tube.

Ethan let his muscles relax, unaware till that moment that every one of them had been on alert. He had his phaser drawn and ready.

"Eliminated?" Nancy's voice was a harsh whisper. *"Eliminated?"*

"Quiet." He put his finger to his lips and pulled his tricorder to where he could see the display.

"Ethan, what are you doing?"

"I'm rerouting the computer's com system to this tricorder. Less noticeable. The Romulans won't notice the tiny fluctuations from this small device, as long as I use it sparingly."

He turned to look at Nancy. Tears streamed down her face and hung beneath her chin. "We're not going to make it, are we?"

Ethan, moved around till he could touch her face with his hands. He touched those tears and tugged at her chin. "I love you" was all he could say.

No, he didn't believe they would make it. But he was damn certain he would make sure the Romulans wouldn't either.

By using the tricorder Ethan found in the medpack, he was able to track their progress toward the warp core. There were perhaps thirty more tubes to traverse, each with dangerous interconnecting joints. It was at one of these joints that he and Nancy found a surprise.

"Nancy! I thought I was the only one left!"

Nancy squealed. "Stephen!"

Communications officer Lieutenant Stephen Sholtes. Ethan knew him by reputation only. And since the man had managed to survive just as they had, he now believed everything he'd read and heard about the man. He was tall and wiry, with short-cropped blond hair and intense blue eyes.

He hugged each of them in turn. "I'm so glad to see both of you."

"We're it, Stephen," Nancy said.

"Listen." Sholtes looked at both of them. "I've got a lot to tell you, and I have an idea of what to do. But here isn't safe."

Ethan mentioned the warp-core Jefferies tube. Stephen eyed Nancy. "Radiation?" He glanced at her belly.

But from the look on his wife's face, the point seemed moot. "I'm hoping we won't be there long enough for that to be a problem. Besides, the shielding there is excellent. Let's just go."

It took nearly an hour with Nancy stopping to rest every now and then, but they made it to the tube closest to the upper end of the warp core. Ethan could feel the thrum in his chest of the engines and smell the brimstone scent of charged particles.

Nancy looked pale and tired. Dark circles hung beneath her eyes. They sat in stunned silence for a while before Stephen spoke.

"Since the multi-vector assault mode has proven one hundred percent effective against attacks, the captain suspected they were on board when we left the starbase. How, we don't know. They waited till we were near enough to the edge of the Alpha Quadrant before attacking. They were swift, and subtle and deadly."

"The explosions?" Nancy said.

"The first one appeared to be created as a diversion to take the captain's attention away. They took engineering first. Pierce tried to contact Starfleet on subspace, but all the communications were rerouted through engineering. I was in the turbolift when they stormed the bridge. I jumped out and into a Jefferies tube and made it to Pierce's quarters." He nodded at Ethan. "All the senior officers had been briefed on your Façade Three, so I knew it was there in the captain's safe. I took it just as I heard the captain's death." He paused and Nancy took his hand in hers. "I made it to the astrometrics lab and grabbed a tricorder. Rerouted communications on a lower subfrequency and decided to head in this direction."

Ethan told him what they'd done in sickbay.

Stephen nodded. "That was good. Real good. Maybe they won't go back to sickbay for a while since they've seen the bodies."

"Does Starfleet know what's happened?"

"I doubt it. I wasn't able to get a message through. I was on my way to engineering to try and reroute a subspace frequency when I bumped into you two."

"Do you think it'll work?"

Stephen looked at both of them, and from his expression, Ethan knew his answer before he spoke it. "No. But I'm going to make my best effort at trying."

Nancy sighed. Then she sobbed. Her shoulders shook, and Ethan held her in his arms.

He rocked her gently back and forth. "It's okay. It's all okay."

She pushed away from him, her tearstained face a mask of anger. "No it's not, Ethan. It's all over with. We're not going to make it out alive. Our baby is never going to look up and see you. He's never going to see . . . me . . ." Her temporary resolve broke, and Ethan felt tears burn his eyes as well.

Stephen looked away. Ethan knew the lieutenant had a daughter. They all had family back home who would wonder, and worry. And if they didn't survive this, those they left behind would need to know what happened, and what they'd done.

"But even if we get the communications rerouted, how do we send it out? They'll detect it and block it," Ethan said.

"Not if we mask it as something normal. Kinda like your drug, Ethan."

Ethan nodded his head. "But what?"

The trio was silent for a moment; then Stephen spoke. "I'm assuming these Romulans aren't working alone, and probably have backing from their government, or a piece of it."

"I know what you're thinking." Ethan smiled. "Piggyback a message with their transmission."

"But won't it go to the Romulans instead of to Starfleet?" Nancy frowned.

"That's the beauty of this." Ethan winked at Stephen. "Starfleet monitors all subspace transmissions. All. Even though they would never admit it. I'm sure these guys will be using code or such to report their progress home. Maybe even have a warbird escort. Starfleet is bound to get the transmission, find the piggybacked noise, and decode it."

Nancy nodded. "Well, wouldn't their transmission have a Starfleet signal to them anyway? If they transmit from this ship, that is. That would send up a red flag."

"Yes. Unless they've changed the modulation to mask it as a Romulan transmission." Stephen shrugged. "It can be done either way, but not one hundred percent. There's always a telltale clue in there, as long as the communications expert really is an expert."

"I'm willing to try." Nancy squeezed Ethan's hand. "We can't let them take this ship, Ethan. Not with the Dominion courting all the races not aligned with the Federation."

"It would be a weapon used against our own ships," Stephen said.

Ethan agreed. "Okay, then where do we go from here?"

Stephen pulled his tricorder out. "I can get to engineering like I planned and do some rigging. You guys go to sickbay and create the message, since it's unlikely they'll be back in there. Have that message ready to transmit the moment you get my signal."

"But—"

Stephen put up a hand. "Ethan. Let me do this."

No more words were spoken. Stephen put a hand on Nancy's middle, then moved away.

Ethan and Nancy began the long crawl back to sickbay.

Ethan was able to create a subspace field around sickbay to mask any movements. He told the computer to remove the holograms as

Nancy started her message to Starfleet. She was setting up to transmit when she noticed something. "Ethan, communications are clear."

He nodded. "Makes sense. Why jam them if you've killed everyone onboard? Who's going to use it?"

Ethan's tricorder beeped. "It's Stephen. Damn." He rubbed his forehead with his free hand.

"What?" Nancy said.

"The Romulans are masking the ship's warp trail. He's going to reroute some systems on the assumption the Romulans are unfamiliar with this ship." He looked at Nancy. "If it works, there'll be a trail for Starfleet to follow."

"He's going to get caught."

Ethan kept reading. "He says he's detected some alien communications array in the Delta Quadrant." He frowned. "He's going to upload the message from engineering directly to the array."

Nancy put her hand to her middle. "But they'll notice the transmission. They'll find him."

Ethan read the final message. "That's what he's hoping for. He wants us to still send the message when they contact their people, but he's planning to simultaneously send to the array." He looked up at Nancy. "He's hoping the message will get through and the transmission to the array will create an open channel. Just like a beacon."

Nancy downloaded the message to engineering. Her panel lit up and flashed. "He's got it." She paused. She gasped and looked up. "He's sending it *now.*"

"No . . ." Ethan went to the panel. Nancy was right. The transmission was out and all the alarms set up by the Romulans lit up like a sun going nova.

A red light flashed. The Romulans were transmitting anyway.

"Send it."

The sickbay doors slid open at that moment. Nancy moved away from the terminal just as a disruptor caught her in the side of the head. She went down as Ethan yelled out her name.

Two male Romulans stood in the doorway. "I told you there was something wrong in here." He pointed to Ethan, who was standing beside the replicator behind Nancy's body. "This room did not have the smell of disruptor fire."

Ethan's hand shook. He kept his gaze balanced between Nancy's lifeless body and the Romulans. She was dead. His son was dead. Or dying. The image twisted his heart and he retched inside. He'd made small, private plans to teach his child to walk, to swim or to ride a bike.

All gone.

Rage burned fast inside of him, and swept upward from the pit of his stomach to blaze behind his eyes. These demons would not succeed. They would *not* have their prize.

Ethan fired at the Romulans and dove beneath the examination table. The Romulans fired at him, but missed.

There was only a few feet between him and the terminal. He could see the light flashing. There was still time to send the message to Starfleet. With a glance at his wife and the son he would never know, Ethan stood and began shooting in the direction of the Romulans. He actually hit one of them as he made it to the terminal.

He pressed the pad as fire slammed into his back. The force turned him to his left and another blast caught him in the side. He went down, the phaser knocked from his hand.

"Message sent," came the computer's voice.

"Stop that transmission!" Rekar said.

Ethan could still see and hear from where he lay. He watched the Romulans examine the console.

"What did he do?" the injured one said.

"I can't tell." Rekar shook his head. He pressed a few buttons. "I'm sure he tried to warn Starfleet same as that other dead man in engineering."

"Did they succeed?"

"The only transmission I see is our own. We stopped them." Rekar shook his head. He moved into Ethan's line of sight. Ethan closed his eyes, expecting another disruptor blast.

None came.

He slit his eyes and saw the injured Romulan bending over Nancy. "This one was with child."

"One less dead Federation officer is no concern," Rekar said. "We have them all accounted for now."

The two of them left sickbay.

Ethan swam in and out of consciousness. He couldn't remember if he'd actually pressed the button or not. Or had Nancy done so? Was Nancy still at home? He seemed to remember asking her to stay and take care of their baby. He hoped she did. At least his child would know his mother.

But no. He'd seen Nancy dead. She'd been running, and they'd shot her.

They were all dead, and for what? A ship?

He heard a voice in his haze. It was talking to the computer from far away.

Something stung his neck again. His heart rate increased and his muscles tensed. A stimulant. He wasn't dead yet.

Someone moved near him. A hand touched him gently and helped him turn. He looked up into the caring brown eyes of an older man dressed in an outdated Starfleet uniform. Through the haze, Ethan thought he resembled the EMH program on the last ship he'd served aboard.

The *U.S.S. Enterprise.*

Though Dr. Crusher told him once she hated using "that thing."

"Easy, you have serious phaser burns." He knitted his eyebrows together. "What happened?"

Ethan wanted to tell him everything. How the Romulans murdered his wife and his child. How Stephen died trying to create a diversion to bring Starfleet to them. How all the crew were dead.

His lips refused to move the way he wanted them to. His vision dimmed. The world faded to black, and he heard something besides the stranger. Something like singing.

Yes, he heard Nancy singing. The way she did when she was putting away the baby's things. The way she did last weekend when they painted the baby's nursery.

Again he tried to tell this officer everything. In his mind he re-layed it all.

But in the retreating world of the living, he could only say, "Romulans captured . . . the ship."

And Nancy was there waiting for him. And so was their child. Not really a person, yet more of a presence that surrounded him with love and reassurance that the world would be right.

And life would go on.

ENTERPRISE™

Remnant

James J. and Louisa M. Swann

The day had already gone to the bloody dogs.

Lieutenant Malcolm Reed stared at the glistening black liquid splashed across the machine room floor and groaned. Commander Tucker was not going to be happy. Gunk oozed down the walls of the chief engineer's office-slash-workroom and dropped in noxious globules from the low ceiling. He sneezed and rubbed at his tearing eyes: the caustic stench was as slimy as the goo itself.

A clank from the engine room just outside the door made Reed jump. Like a mother fussing over a newborn baby, Reed closed the phase pistol he'd been working on, released it from the vise, and laid it on the counter. He glared at the empty lubricant tube lying on its side in the middle of the worst part of the mess, grabbed a rag, and went to work.

Nothing had gone right since the blasted chef had ruined his breakfast tea. Reed's munitions room was full of boxes that needed to be unpacked. He'd snuck off to Tucker's office to make some slight adjustments to the phase pistol, and the bloody thing had gone off, exploding one of the large tubes of lubricant sitting on Tucker's workbench.

"Lieutenant Reed to the bridge."

Reed stood upright, bashing his head on the underside of a cupboard. He rubbed the sore spot, sure he felt a growing lump. When he brought his hand away, black slime covered his palm. He scrubbed at the muck, but all he managed to do was smear it around.

"Lieutenant Reed to the bridge."

"Might as well get on with it." He tossed the rag in a corner disposal unit and stamped out of the room, ignoring curious looks from the engineering crew. A young crew member joined him in the lift. She gave him a funny look and took a few steps away. Reed adjusted his suddenly too tight collar and stared at the walls.

What could have gone wrong with the bloody phase pistol? He had just been making a simple adjustment.

The door slid open and he moved forward onto the bridge. Subcommander T'Pol stood beside her console, hands clasped at her back, an inscrutable look on her Vulcan face. She raised a slanted eyebrow as he nodded his head on the way to his command post.

The other officers were seated at their stations. No one was working, though. All of them were staring at Ensign Hoshi Sato.

Sato's forehead wrinkled as she pushed buttons and twisted knobs. "Sir! I have a response." A puzzled look crossed her face. "It says 'Sphere One to Earth. Coming home.' " Sato paused, listening. "That's all, Captain."

An unknown signal. Reed's pulse picked up. He ran a quick diagnostics check on the weapons systems, checked to be sure his targeting coordinates were operating, then shifted his attention back to the captain.

"I've finished analyzing the distress signal." Sato turned, looking at Archer. "It was synthesized—a very out-of-date system—being sent on sublight frequencies." She sniffed the air and crinkled her nose, frowning in Reed's direction.

"Synthesized?" Archer tapped his fingers on the arm of his chair, then glanced at T'Pol. "Can you tell yet if they're human?"

"There shouldn't be any Earth ships this far out," Mayweather interjected. "At least . . ."

"She could be a remnant of Noah's Ark," T'Pol said. All hands turned at the cryptic statement. T'Pol raised her chin and stared at Archer down the bridge of her nose.

"What exactly are you getting at?"Archer said in a no-nonsense voice.

"Earth's human population experienced a period of extreme unrest prior to Zefram Cochrane's serendipitous discovery one hundred years ago. Several private corporations took the future into their own hands . . ."

"Colony ships," Archer interjected, giving a curt nod.

Reed glared at T'Pol; kindergartners knew about the colony ships. But they were supposedly all accounted for.

"How long before we're in shuttle range?" Archer settled back in his seat.

"Ten minutes," T'Pol replied after checking her console.

"Can we determine if there's life on board?" Archer asked.

Or what kind of life? Reed added silently. He checked his console again as T'Pol stepped over to the science station and pulled open a small viewing screen. It never hurt to be too cautious, especially after their first encounter with an unidentified ship on their maiden voyage. A blip appeared on his targeting screen. "I've got it, Captain." At least this ship was easy to identify, not like the barely discernible trace of a Suliban ship.

"I'm reading five life-forms. All human." T'Pol's expression was smooth and unperturbed as usual.

Reed's hands shook as he made another adjustment. He glanced at Mayweather, calm and cool at the helm. Maybe if you spent your entire life in space like T'Pol and Mayweather, you got used to meeting unexpected vessels in supposedly uninhabited regions of space.

"Try to contact them."

Sato flipped a switch. *"Enterprise* to unidentified vessel. Come in, please." She paused and repeated the message, then turned to the captain. "There's no response, sir." She twisted a knob and listened. "Wait. I've got something. I'm putting it on the speakers."

313

"This is *Lost Moon* to *Enterprise*. Come in, please."

Reed started. It was a woman's voice; shaky and a bit uncertain.

"This is Captain Jonathan Archer. What is your condition?"

"Thank God . . ." The woman's voice broke off.

The expression on Archer's face was impassive, but the tension on the bridge had risen a couple of more notches. This could all be a ruse, an alien ploy to bring them out of hyperspace, leaving them open and vulnerable.

"What type of ship are you?" There were no tears in the woman's voice now, no hesitancy.

Sato glanced at the captain, her eyebrows raised.

"The *Enterprise* is an exploration starship," Archer replied.

"Where do you originate from?" Reed started at the woman's question. She sounded suspicious, as if she didn't trust them. Seemed a bit backward to him—shouldn't they be asking the questions?

"The *Enterprise* is a Starfleet vessel from the planet Earth," Archer replied, a puzzled look on his face. He swung around to Reed. "Can we get a look on screen yet?"

Reed punched a few buttons. "Give me a moment." He grabbed the vague image presented on his monitor, switched it over to the main viewscreen, and stared.

"What the hell is that?" Archer demanded.

Reed's pulse raced as he stared at the object: Two circular pods spun in a circle so fast it made him dizzy just watching it.

"Looks like some kind of kid's toy, Captain," Ensign Mayweather said.

"Or a weapon," Reed added.

"What is your status, *Lost Moon?*" Archer jerked his chin at Reed's board and Reed bent over it, arming his torpedoes and preparing the laser guns.

Static interrupted the woman's reply. ". . . alive . . ."

Archer glanced around the bridge. "Morally, we're obligated to respond to all distress calls." He nodded at Reed. "Hopefully, this call is on the up and up, but be ready in case we need you."

"Yes, sir," Reed said.

"Plot our course to rendezvous with the *Lost Moon*."

There was a slight disorientation as the ship dropped back to sub-light speed. Out of the corner of his eye, Reed could see Sato clutching the communications board, her jaw set. He could feel his own jaw clenched tight. Most of the other officers had the same expression on their face, but none of them hated the bumping around as much as Sato. Only Mayweather handled the transitions like the space boomer he was.

"What in blazes is going on up there?" Chief Engineer Tucker's voice blasted through the com system. "First I find my *office* coated in black lubricant, and then the ship drops out of warp with hardly a moment's notice . . ."

"Why don't you come on up here, Tripp," Archer said, lifting an eyebrow at Reed. "We've got something you might want to see."

Reed shrugged and straightened his collar, grimacing at the streak of black that appeared on his hand. He'd probably never get this bloody lubricant out of his uniform.

Chief Engineer Charles "Tripp" Tucker III entered the bridge accompanied by a wave of oily fumes so strong Reed's stomach flipped. Black streaked Tucker's uniform and coated one side of his cheek. Belatedly, Reed realized he probably didn't look much better. Before he could say anything, Archer interrupted.

"Time for that later, Tripp. We've got more important things to deal with." Archer nodded at the viewscreen and Tucker's mouth dropped open.

"Looks like something a kid would play with," he muttered.

A titter of nervous laughter ran through the officers. Mayweather smiled.

"A real fine study, Commander." Reed couldn't resist the gibe. "Shows off your engineering expertise."

Tucker glared at him. "Anytime, Reed. By the way, I've isolated several unknown objects down in engineering and caged them for you. But you'll have to clean up their *mess* before you can claim them."

"Tripp, I want you and Reed to go over in the shuttle," Archer said. "We need to take a look at this thing firsthand."

Reed's heart did a triple thump. And he'd thought this day couldn't get any worse.

Archer smiled as he turned to Sato. "Open communications."

Sato nodded. "Go, ahead, Captain."

"Lost Moon, we'll be sending a shuttle over to pick you up."

"The pods are spinning out of control, Captain Archer."

"I understand that, *Lost Moon.* It'll take us a few moments to get a handle on the situation, but our pilot is quite handy."

T'Pol glanced down at her instrument panel. "The two spheres are connected by a cable. They're spinning around each other like a moon without an axis."

"Where is the door?" Archer asked.

"There appears to be one standard door on the larger pod," T'Pol replied before Reed could check. "Near the cable connection."

"Can the shuttle connect?"

"It is possible for the shuttle to attach itself to the center of the cable. They would have to inchworm along the cable toward the pod, bringing the shuttle as close as possible to the door. The rest of the distance will have to be walked."

"Lost Moon, can you slow down your spinning?"

"My name is Kendra." There was a slight pause before the woman continued. "This vessel has been on autopilot for forty years. Its destination is Earth. It's not programmed to stop until then."

A stunned silence filled the bridge as the crew looked at one another.

Archer nodded. "Okay, you two. Get going. I'll see what other information I can get out of her."

"Should be a challenging task for the pilot," T'Pol said as Tucker passed her by.

Good girl, Reed silently applauded. Maybe there was more to that icy Vulcan exterior than met the eye!

Reed settled into a seat as Tucker scanned the controls. "Ready or not, here we go," Tucker said, an impish grin on his round face. Reed nodded and gripped the edge of his seat, grimacing as his chin bumped the metal collar of his spacesuit. Traveling through space at tremendous speeds in a huge ship like the *Enterprise* boggled the mind, but it was in these little shuttles with their obscenely wide windows that the vastness of space really hit home.

A bounce and a jiggle signaled the release of the *Enterprise*'s grappling arm. Reed reached out and toggled the com switch. "We're on our way, *Enterprise*."

Tucker glanced at Reed. "It'll take us a few minutes to get there and a few more to get in close. You should be ready to go when I give the word."

Reed stared at Tucker for a moment. "I can fly this thing as well as you can," he replied. "Why am I the one who has to go out there?"

"I'm pulling rank." Tucker grinned, but there was an ominous glint in his eyes.

Bloody Murphy's Law—a day that was already heading down the loo was just waiting for a flush. And he was about to be flushed. Reed settled into his seat, shoulders stiff, jaw set. A soldier did what he was ordered to do. And if walking around in that black maw out there was part of his orders, then he'd best get on with it.

Kendra leaned back in her chair and gnawed on her bottom lip. The response sounded like it came from humans, English-speaking ones at that. But how could she tell? How could she be sure? She swung the chair around and looked over at the four children suspended in the sleep pods. The lower oxygen level was affecting them all, as were the reduced rations. At the rate their life-support was deteriorating, the air would run out just before their food.

She clenched her jaw, fighting back the searing pain in her chest. Her daughter's sacrifice had been for nothing. By giving birth to four unplanned children, Lilith and her husband had managed to tip the survival scales in the wrong direction, and their attempt to balance the scales by giving up their own lives had come too late. But if these people were who they said they were, maybe there was still hope.

She swung back to the console, her decision made. The *Enterprise* had issued an invitation; she would accept it. See firsthand who or what really sat at the other end of the com system. "*Enterprise*, this is *Lost Moon*. I'll be ready to receive you."

317

"Ten-four, Lost Moon. A shuttle's on its way."

Quickly, Kendra stepped over to the sleeping pods and shook Alex awake. He was the oldest, the one least affected by the thinning air. The others needed their rest. She leaned against the bulkhead wall and took several deep, slow breaths as Alex stirred. Her pulse pounded in her ears.

"Are you all right, Grandma?"

Alex's concerned voice helped drive away the darkness threatening to overwhelm her vision. Kendra blinked hard and nodded. She grabbed a lozenge from her pocket and popped it into her mouth. "Just thinking," she lied as she took Alex's arm and led him away from the sleep pods. She'd been living on glucose lozenges for almost two weeks now, trying to conserve food. But she'd have to eat soon. Her body was too old to take this kind of abuse.

"I don't want to wake the others, Alex. But I need you to do something for me."

Alex nodded, his little face serious. He was always serious; they all were. Kendra couldn't even imagine how one could grow up knowing nothing but the inside of this tiny space pod. But these children had. She glanced around the area that served as both living quarters and command deck. A thirty-by-thirty sphere, half of it filled with life-support equipment. Ten years Alex had spent in this small space—he didn't know anything else; neither did any of the others. Everything in their lives was limited—space, food, air. Even the view they had of the stars was small.

How would Alex react to the size of the vessel waiting for them?

Kendra shuddered. Thank goodness the viewport was now turned away from the *Enterprise*. The enormity of the ship stunned even her.

"I need you to help me into the spacesuit." She grabbed the suit from its closet, and dragged it forward. "There's another ship out there. It's sending a shuttle." Kendra stepped into the suit and helped Alex pull it up around her shoulders. It was the only suit they had. She tried not to think of that as she thrust her feet into the oversized boots and clamped them tight.

"What ship, Grandma? Why is it here?" There was more than curiosity in Alex's voice. There was fear.

"They're going to help us, but I have to go with them for a few minutes."

A look of concern crossed Alex's face and for a moment she thought he would resist. Kendra grabbed both of his shoulders and looked into his ten-year-old eyes. "This is important, Alex. I'll be right back. I need you to watch over things while I'm gone."

She could feel Alex's pride beneath her hands as he straightened and nodded once. "I'll take care of things, Grandma." He helped maneuver the heavy helmet into position and checked to be sure the latches were tight and the helmet sealed. Kendra pulled him close in a hug, then turned and headed for the airlock. She locked the inner door, waited until the lock was pressurized, then opened the outer door, getting it dogged shut just as a bronze-suited figure approached.

Reed wasn't sure what he'd expected, but it wasn't the wrinkled face staring back at him through an archaic helmet that looked like it belonged in a museum. The woman was bloody old enough to be his great-great-grandmother. But the wave of relief he felt when he saw she was human must have been at least as great as the relief she felt, if the look on her face was any measure of judgment. She nodded once and Reed took the line he held in one hand, attaching it to a ring on her suit. He looked around for others, but the airlock was closed.

Things went smoothly on the trip across. Though the suit she wore was a cumbersome antique, the woman acted like an old pro, crossing the line hand over hand and slipping through the shuttle door without assistance.

Probably made a hundred more trips than I have, Reed thought, struggling to ignore the emptiness surrounding them. It gave him the willies, thinking about all that *space.* He grabbed hold of the shuttle and started to swing inside.

Suddenly, Reed found himself hurtling through space, brought up short by the cable attached to his waist and then whipped back. He saw a brief flash as a pod, or shuttle, he couldn't tell which, whizzed by, his cable pulled up tight again, and his line snapped free, flinging him away from the melee. He looked up in time to see the second pod fire a brief burst of flame.

The cable between the pods whipped sideways, slamming into the shuttle. Somehow Tucker managed to keep the small vessel moving, but Reed could tell something had been damaged. Off to the side, the *Enterprise* appeared to be moving, at least from his perspective: his spinning-whirling-moving-away-from-the-*Enterprise*-into-the-deepness-of-space perspective.

"Tucker, this is Reed," he said, not sure how the passengers in the shuttle were faring. "I'm afraid I'm at loose ends out here."

Tucker's voice crackled over the intercom. "Hang on there, Reed. We'll be right over."

"Ten-four," Reed replied, trying to keep the relief out of his voice. Of all the people to rescue him, it would have to be Tucker. But rescue by Tucker was better than no rescue at all.

Stars spread in front of Reed like the spangles on a girl's dress he had dated in school. He couldn't see the *Enterprise* or her objective any longer.

"Uh, Reed." Tucker's voice was slightly apologetic, and the skin crawled on the back of Reed's neck as his stomach tightened.

"Looks like tea will be a short time coming. But you hang in there. We'll be over as soon as we can."

So the shuttle had been damaged. Reed fought down a tingle of panic. Shouldn't be too long. They might have to send out a second shuttle, but he'd be rescued. He stared at the stars stretching out before him and shivered.

It was a long, long way home.

Kendra felt rather stupid lying on her back staring up at the dimly lit ceiling of the shuttle. She blinked away the sweat trickling into her eyes and attempted to raise her head, but the helmet was too heavy for her to lift off the floor.

A face appeared in front of her visor, wearing a grin that verged on insolence. The man grabbed her arm and helped her sit up before reaching down and unlatching her helmet.

"You look like you could use a bit of help. Keep this handy; you'll need to put it back on in a minute." He handed her the helmet before moving back to the front of the shuttle.

Kendra hadn't heard a drawl like that in way too many years.

"Thank you." She glanced out the window and noticed they were moving away from the *Enterprise*.

"What happened?" she asked, fear making her voice quaver. She strained to catch a glimpse of the pods, to see the outside of the capsules still imprisoning the children.

"It's okay, ma'am. We've had a bit of a problem," the young man said. "Just you rest easy." He ducked beneath a console.

Kendra chewed on her lip and shuffled toward the nearest seat. Everything ached—there wasn't a spot on her body that wasn't weary to the bone. She wanted to believe this was truly an Earth vessel, that she could relinquish her long-standing guardianship. But not yet. She had to find out for sure if these strangers were truly who they claimed to be.

"What happened back there?" she asked again.

"The engine on your pod fired."

The silence in the shuttle was so deep, Kendra could hear her heart beating inside the spacesuit. "It couldn't have."

"I don't know how your engines work, but I do think I know a rocket blast when I see one." There was a touch of humor in the pilot's voice. Something clanged beneath the console and he cursed, then backed out.

"There. That should do it, at least temporarily." He stood, brushed off his hands, and sat down in the pilot's seat, muttering as he gripped the control yoke. After a moment, the shuttle seemed to pick up speed and the stars spun as they turned. The pilot grinned.

"I'm Commander Tucker. We've managed to lose one of our crew members. He's headed on a course to who know's where right now. He's always a grump if he misses his afternoon tea, so we're gonna bring him home, if that's okay with you?"

Kendra forced a smile. "Nice to meet you, Commander. My name is Kendra. But hadn't you better get going? We've got a man to save." The children were her priority, but she wouldn't have a man die because she'd caused a delay.

The relief Reed felt when the nose of the shuttle came into view was more like a fainting spell than a celebration.

"I understand there's a man here waiting for tea."

Reed thought he'd never be happy to hear Tucker's voice, but he'd been wrong. "What took you so bloody long?"

"Had a few adjustments to make," Tucker replied. "You ready to come on board?"

Reed gave a quiet sigh as the shuttle maneuvered closer, and the woman in her antique spacesuit shoved off from the open door, trailing a cable. In a few short minutes, they were returning hand over hand to the shuttle. He pulled off his helmet as soon as the shuttle was pressurized.

"Never thought I'd be happy to see your ugly face," Reed said, nodding his head at Tucker.

Tucker grinned. "How about being a gentleman and helping the lady?"

Reed reached over, unlatched the helmet, and pulled it over the woman's head. She somehow managed to fold the bulky spacesuit she wore into a seat.

"I'd like you to meet Kendra," Tucker said. "Ma'am, this is Lieutenant Malcolm Reed, our weapons officer."

Kendra smiled and stuck out her hand.

"Thank you for helping me," she said with a smile that deepened the wrinkles on her face until it looked like her eyes would get lost in their folds.

"My pleasure." Reed felt his face growing hot. "What happened to the others?" he asked.

Kendra dropped her gaze. "There are no others."

Reed turned away, puzzled. His hand went automatically to the phase pistol holstered at his waist. The old woman was lying.

But why?

The ride back to the *Enterprise* was silent and uneventful. Kendra sat entranced by the sight of the huge ship growing larger every minute. She glanced back at the *Lost Moon,* at its crazy, erratic movement, the tiny pods circling chaotically around each other. A lump rose in her throat. They'd lived so long in those cobbled-together pods, just the five of them. Provided the captain proved to be as honorable as he sounded, that all would change.

The edges of her vision darkened and Kendra reached into the pocket of her suit, pulled out a lozenge, and slipped it into her mouth. Lieutenant Tucker glanced at her, but she just smiled and settled back in her seat.

"All right, folks. Fasten your seatbelts. We're about to be grabbed." The motion of the shuttle abruptly stopped and Kendra clung to her seat. Somewhere overhead metal clanked and the shuttle jerked upward, directly into the belly of the monstrous ship.

Before she quite knew what was happening the door to the shuttle slid open and Lieutenant Reed was helping her step down. She tried to keep up as he guided her out of the docking bay or whatever they called the place they'd landed. In spite of the size of the ship, the halls and rooms seemed rather small, even when compared to the pods of the *Lost Moon.* The doorways were so short, the lieutenant had to duck. Kendra bit back a hysterical giggle. How many times had he bumped his head before learning that lesson?

They walked down a long, brightly lit corridor and entered a lift. Before she could ask any questions, however, the door slid open, and Lieutenant Reed waved her forward.

Kendra took two steps and stopped, stunned. Dozens of instruments and panels hummed around her. Brilliant pictures flashed across screens, some of them so rapidly her eyes could hardly follow. This bridge was more than twice as large as that of the Mother Sphere.

"Welcome aboard the *Enterprise,* Kendra." A tall, slim man extended his hand. "I'm Captain Archer."

There was definite pride in the captain's voice, along with something else. Kendra pondered a moment, then realized he sounded much the way she did when the children were threatened. Protective.

"She's beautiful," Kendra said. She shook Captain Archer's hand.

"Captain."

Kendra spun at the sound of the cool, female voice. She began to shrivel inside. An alien, with upraised eyebrows and pointed ears, stood by a bank of instrument panels.

All Kendra's hopes came crashing down. Despair washed over her so completely she thought she would drown. Thank goodness she hadn't told them about the children. But what to do? If the children didn't get help soon, they'd never make it to Earth.

"This is Subcommander T'Pol, a representative of the Vulcan High Command."

Kendra managed a polite nod, struggling to keep her composure. She turned as the door to the lift slid open and another alien stepped out. Blackness crept around the edges of Kendra's vision. Automatically, she reached in her suit pocket for a lozenge, and slipped it into her mouth.

Not just one, but two aliens. How many more had infiltrated the ship?

Captain Archer saw her gaze. "This is Dr. Phlox, our ship's doctor. He's here to take a look at you."

Kendra shook her head violently. She had to get back to the children, had to figure out a way to . . . "I was not aware you had aliens on board." She looked at the stern expression on the captain's face.

"All of these people are members of my crew."

His crew? Kendra stared at the Vulcan who stared back, her gaze cold and noncommittal.

"Captain," T'Pol said. "I believe there is more to this woman's story than she's telling you."

"Can you read minds?" Kendra blurted.

"No. It is simply illogical to assume you have been traveling by yourself all this time." Kendra sagged in relief. Logic, pure and simple logic. She gazed around at the rest of the crew, human in appearance, all of them. "How many more . . . Vulcans are on board?" she asked. If she didn't do something, the children would perish. This vessel seemed to be the only hope she had at the moment.

"None," Captain Archer replied.

"And . . . those?" Kendra nodded her chin at the alien doctor.

"Dr. Phlox is one of a kind."

Kendra could swear she saw the glimmer of a smile teasing the corners of the captain's mouth. She lifted her chin above the lip of her spacesuit.

"Aliens attacked the Mother Sphere forty years ago, and I've been drifting in space ever since."

"Why didn't you bring the others out to the shuttle?"

The captain's abrupt question threw Kendra off guard. "How did you . . . ?" The room started to spin. She had to make a decision before it was too late.

"There are four children still in that life pod." Kendra pointed at the larger of the two pods still twirling on the display screen. The blackness crept into her vision, and she found herself sitting on the floor, the alien doctor hovering by her side. She struggled to focus on the doctor's face, trying to ignore the raised lines on his head.

"I'm fine," she said, certain the doctor had said something and guessing at what it might have been. "I just need to rest a bit." She tried to sit up. The doctor took her arm.

"I think you need to come down to sickbay," he said.

Kendra wondered at the sound of his voice. It had a relaxing tempo, a melodious rise and fall that was very peaceful. She blinked hard, trying to break free of the hypnotic effect he was having. "No. I have to stay here." She looked up at the captain. "We need to get the children out of that pod. The life-support system is deteriorating and they have been living on reduced rations for at least six months."

Captain Archer nodded his head. He glanced at the other officers on the bridge. "Anyone have any suggestions how we can get to those children without a repeat of the last incident?"

"There's no way to get close to that thing, Captain," Sato protested. "She's spinning out of control."

"By my calculations," T'Pol said, "it should be possible to get the shuttle close enough to clamp on to the cable near where it attaches to the pod. Once that is accomplished, the weapons laser can slice through the cable, and the shuttle can bring back the pod with the children."

"Tripp, take Sato with you. Reed, get your weapons ready."

"Yes, sir." Reed turned to his console and punched up the laser display. It would take a moment for the targeting coordinates to come into position. His stomach tightened and adrenaline pumped through his veins, but his hands moved with steady confidence. This command post was his domain: he wasn't meant to drift around at loose ends in the unloving arms of space.

The shuttle moved into view on the screen and all of them

watched as Tucker maneuvered it into position, dodging once as the errant engine fired again, changing the trajectory of the whirling vessel. Reed realized he was holding his breath when Tucker finally set the shuttle down on the cable and a suited figure appeared for a brief instant, securing the line.

"All right, Reed. You're on." Captain Archer's voice was grim.

Reed looked at his coordinates, narrowed the scope of his target lock until it focused on the cable stretched between the two pods. Now it was a matter of timing—if he fired too soon, he might miss and hit the pod; too late and he might hit the shuttle. Taking a deep breath, Reed stared hard as the whirling vessel on his screen made another revolution. He'd made a few adjustments since the last time he'd actually fired the lasers. . . .

"Reed, if that engine ignites again, we'll be right in its path," Mayweather said.

"I'm aware of that." Reed waited, hand poised above the firing button.

Now!

With the precision of a surgeon, a bright red beam of light shot out from the *Enterprise,* searing across the cable and separating it in half. Released from its anchor, the second pod went spinning off into the darkness.

"Take care of that other pod, Reed," Archer commanded.

Quickly, Reed adjusted his targeting mechanism, lined the freefloating pod in his scopes, and fired, feeling the familiar exhilaration speed through him as a torpedo sped through its guidance tube, launching out into the blackness, and exploding in a fire of light.

In a quick swoop, the shuttle with its acquisition turned and headed back to the *Enterprise.*

Reed stared as four children entered the bridge, ranging in age from about four to maybe ten. The youngest stood with her thumb in her mouth, curls bouncing down around her face. The crewman accompanying them nodded at the captain and stepped aside.

Archer lowered himself to his knees. "Hi, I'm Captain Archer."

The oldest boy lifted his chin and stared Archer in the eye. "Where's my grandmother?" he demanded, but his voice shook.

"Alex, don't be rude," Kendra said. She waved the children toward her. "Captain Archer, may I present Alex, Johnny, Shandra, and Mimi."

"Grandma!" The children rushed across the deck and surrounded the old woman.

God, Reed thought, taking a closer look. The children were almost as skinny as the old woman.

Kendra's face was paler than before. Her breath came in gasps. The four youngsters crowded around her, the little one clasping her arms around one of Kendra's knees. A lump grew in Reed's throat as the little girl laid her head against Kendra's leg and slowly patted the old woman's spacesuit.

Kendra struggled to keep her eyes open as the children tucked themselves close to her. She was so tired, it was all she could do to stay awake.

Something patted her leg, a light, feathery touch, and Kendra smiled. She glanced down at Mimi. The other kids stared around, their small faces solemn.

"Cat got your tongue?" Her voice came out raspy and dry.

"Are you all right, Grandma?" Alex's eyes were full of tears, but he was trying hard to be a man. Kendra hugged him tight and nodded.

"I'm fine. These people are going to help us, so you mind your manners and do what you're told." A wave of dizziness swept through Kendra. "You rascals all give your grandma a hug and scoot. I need to talk to the captain."

Kendra clung to the warmth of the hugs as the children obeyed. She swallowed her tears and pasted a smile on her face as they reluctantly released her and headed away.

The captain's face was as serious as the children's as he bent down beside her.

"You'll take care of them," she asked, fighting back the darkness. "See them safely back to Earth?" The question took all of her strength. She relaxed as Archer nodded.

"Don't worry about a thing, Kendra. We'll take care of it."

Kendra's vision grew darker as the instrument panels spun in a slow dance. She sagged back into her chair, wishing she'd at least had a chance to take off the blasted spacesuit that threatened to suck her down into its voluminous bulk.

"Are you all right?" The voice was faint, a whisper from far off. The heavy suit lifted from around her shoulders as the blackness enfolded Kendra in its warmth. No need to fight anymore. It was time for her to rest.

Time someone else carried the burden.

Reed gazed down at Kendra, her birdlike body so tiny in his arms. Her head lolled against his chest as he shoved the top half of the spacesuit aside. Dr. Phlox placed his fingers on the side of her neck. After a few moments, he shook his head and stepped away.

Reed cradled the tiny body close, overwhelmed by a sense of loss. He'd pulled this old woman from the clutches of space only to lose her to the embrace of death. He gritted his teeth and blinked back the burning in his eyes. God, this had been one bloody hell of a day.

A tiny hand on his arm made Reed look up. The little girl, Mimi, stood beside him clutching a ragged teddy bear. She handed him the bear, put her finger to her lips, and whispered.

"He'll keep her company while she sleeps." She laid her head on Kendra's arm and began singing softly. "Rock a-bye, don't you cry, go to sleepy, little baby . . ."

This time Reed let the tears fall.

A Girl for Every Star

John Takis

Through want of enterprise and faith
men are what they are . . .
　　　—Henry David Thoreau, *Walden*

Jonathan Archer was eleven years old the first time he visited the
Sol Museum of Aeronautical Science. It was a clear blue day in San
Francisco, with the sunlight glittering off the towering glass buildings. The cool air carried the fresh scent of the bay and made his
nostrils tingle. It made him feel lucky; he'd heard stories of his
grandfather's childhood, when the inhabitants of Southern California had sometimes been forced to wear air filters outdoors owing to
the widespread pollution in the aftermath of World War III. Atmos-
pheric conditioning was one thing the Vulcans had helped to fix. It
bothered his grandfather, or so the old man said, that humans owed
the very air they breathed to an alien species. Jon had never understood the problem—he was just happy to enjoy the taste of clean air.

　The trip had been Jon's uncle's idea. For all of his father's research, the boy had never been taken to the museum. (Henry Archer
preferred to spend his rare free moments at home on the beach.)

Two weeks with his aunt and uncle, who lived only a few miles from the center of town, had seemed the perfect opportunity. Jon had agreed happily, not really knowing what to expect. He certainly wasn't prepared for the towering structure that appeared, seemingly out of nowhere, as he stepped around a corner. The building was massive, easily the size of a small skyscraper, but wider. Enormous arcing beams that reminded him of pictures he had seen of the arch in St. Louis sprung up out of the concrete at the building's base to merge near the top. It was like a giant arrowhead, poised to let fly into space. He traced the imaginary trajectory with his eyes. Somewhere high above was the orbital station on which his father was working. Returning his eyes to the ground, he looked at the green park that filled the plaza in front of the museum. It was decorated with statues and fountains. Tiny figures moved about the building's main entrance, and his eyes widened as he realized that the structure was even larger than it appeared.

His uncle smiled and clapped Jon on the shoulder. "Hold on, tiger! We're not even inside yet."

Jon felt his excitement growing as his aunt took his hand and they began to walk through the park. He craned his neck as he moved, trying to take in everything. He jabbed a finger at a nearby statue of a woman. "That's Dr. Sloane!"

His aunt looked back. "That's right, dear. Very good."

"There's a picture of her in one of Dad's old newspapers," Jon explained "Except she was really old. Older than you, even."

"Oh?" his aunt asked with bemused alacrity.

His uncle laughed. "That's no way to talk about a lady, Jon." He tilted back his baseball cap and leaned over to give his wife a quick peck on the cheek. "Tell her that her hair shines like the sun and her eyes twinkle like starlight."

Jon made a gagging noise and ran ahead.

Even in the museum lobby, there was a lot to look at. While his uncle bought tickets, Jon stared in wonderment at the brightly colored banners depicting alien species and spacecraft. Through an archway near the desk he could see the gift shop. He wondered if they had models? Against one wall were miniature replicas of the Martian Colonies. He eagerly pressed his face up against the glass, but was shooed back by an annoyed staff member. His uncle grasped Jon's arm. "Come on," he whispered. "A tour just started. We can catch up."

They entered a low corridor and hurried past a series of mannequins in glass display cases. Jon got only a fleeting glimpse at the old military uniforms they wore. He was about to complain, but the room they had entered stopped the words in his throat. It was at least twenty stories tall, and wide as a baseball diamond. The circumference was inset with display after display, the line occasionally broken where a hall led to some other area of the museum. Groups of people milled about the room, and from high above, pale daylight washed over everything. In the center of the room stood an almost thirty-meter tower of metal and technology. Jon's attention was drawn to it instantly, and his jaw dropped.

"That's the *Phoenix!*" he whispered in awe.

"Come on," his uncle whispered back. He grabbed Jon's hand and the trio hurriedly approached the small group standing closest to the *Phoenix*. Wrestling free of his uncle's grip, Jon wormed his way to the front of the small crowd. His aunt reached after him, but his uncle held her back. "Let him have some fun, it's his first time."

The tour guide, a lean and thin-faced man in his thirties, was finishing his lecture. ". . . culminating in the events of more than fifty years ago. Zefram Cochrane personally donated the ship to this institution before his recent retirement."

Jon raised his hand. When the guide ignored him, he spoke anyway. "I heard he ran away."

The guide cleared his throat in annoyance. "Does anyone have any questions?" Jon raised his hand again. "Anyone?" When there was no response from the crowd, he sighed and turned to the eleven-year-old. "Yes?"

Jon pointed to a series of indentations in the casing near the *Phoenix*'s base. "What are those?"

The guide looked over his shoulder. "Flaws in the metal, probably. Remember, Dr. Cochrane constructed this ship with less than ideal resources."

"They look like bullet marks," Jon said matter-of-factly. He raised his hands and made machine-gun noises in the direction of the ship. Several people moved back in shock. A few laughed.

The guide was not amused. "Nobody shot at the *Phoenix*," he said stiffly. "Dr. Cochrane was a scientist. It was a peaceful mission."

Jon shrugged. He leaned up against the rail that separated the group from the base of the ship. "Can I touch it?"

"Certainly not!" Stepping away, the guide indicated one of the branching corridors. "Now, if you'll follow me to the Andorian exhibit, there's a film starting in just a few minutes."

The tour began to move. Jon waved at his aunt and uncle, hanging back with a small group of children his own age. He looked back at the *Phoenix* and slowed down. No one else was near the ship at the moment, and it wasn't more than a meter or two between the guardrail and the edge of the main engine cone. It would be simple to duck under the steel bars, touch the ship, and be out again before anyone noticed. He looked back at the tour group. His aunt and uncle didn't seem to realize that he was lagging behind. In a moment, they would be ushered into a dark movie theater. It was the perfect diversion: he could sneak in and join them later, and if that failed he could always claim he'd gotten lost.

Dragging his feet, Jon let himself bring up the rear of the cluster of children, then stealthily attached himself to a passing couple. They took no notice of him as he walked in their shadow, and when he drew near enough to the *Phoenix* he casually walked over to the rail. Looking around to make sure no one was watching, he ducked underneath. His heart pounded as he ran up to the nearest thruster and positioned himself so that he could only be seen from a narrow angle. He was glad he had worn a dark T-shirt.

Turning, Jon ran a careful hand over the smooth metal. His skin tingled as if the contact imparted some special magic. The first Earth metal to break the speed of light! And he was touching it! He looked up. The shaft of the ship seemed to go on forever. Several meters up, a horizontal streak of slightly warped metal piqued his curiosity. He'd seen the results of a kitchen fire once: the heat had buckled a metal stove in much the same way. What kind of energy could warp titanium? It was as if someone had thrown a ball of fire at the ship and missed by inches.

Just then, he heard an angry voice behind him. "Hey kid! Get away from there!" His heart leapt in his chest, and he spun around. A bulky woman in a security uniform was climbing over the guardrail toward him. Her face was red and her hands were huge. And brave though he was, Jon Archer was still only eleven years old.

He panicked.

By the time the security officer was over the rail and reaching for him, it was too late to run in any other direction. So he charged the woman. The action caught her off guard, and she dodged aside as he dove past her and slid beneath the rail. His head whipped around. People were looking now. He became frighteningly aware of hundreds of eyes, feeling himself stripped of the illusion of invisibility. His eyes darted about the room frantically. Where was the corridor his tour had taken? He couldn't remember, and he didn't see anything about Andorians anywhere.

He heard a noise from behind, and turned to see the woman guard clambering over the rail and having a difficult time of it. Thinking fast, he raced around to the other side of the *Phoenix,* evading the quizzical glances of other patrons and heading for the nearest opening in the wall.

To his dismay, the wing was dark and blocked off by bands of yellow tape marked DO NOT CROSS. Above the entrance was a banner that read, VULCAN! COMING SOON! He turned around anxiously. No sign of the guard. Chewing his lip nervously, he considered his options. Finally, he edged backward and ducked beneath the yellow tape. He could sort it all out later; right now, all he wanted was to get away and think.

The darkness of the corridor was comforting, though he cringed at the harsh sound of his footsteps on the metal floor. Only after he had turned a corner and ducked inside a doorway did he stop to catch his breath. He listened carefully for any sign of pursuit, but heard nothing. Running a hand through his mussed-up brown hair, he examined the room he was in. And for the third time in one day, what he saw took his breath away.

He was staring at a half-completed diorama of a Vulcan landscape. Dim overhead spotlights revealed an elevated stage that had been dusted with orange sand and strewn with crude plaster boulders. Imposing mountains had been painted onto a backdrop of stars framing a strangely colored moon. Only the completed portion of the diorama was illuminated, giving it the impression that it was hanging in empty space.

And Jon was not alone.

Huddled up against a large boulder, he could see the form of a girl his own age. Her knees were drawn up to her chest, and her arms were curled around her legs. Her shoulders shook slightly beneath short-cut ebony hair. She was wearing a loose-fitting shirt and shorts of a darkly shimmering fabric he had never seen. Her back was facing him, and he hopped up onto the platform for a better look. "Hello," he said.

Her head spun around in surprise, and Jon found himself staring into the strangest eyes he had ever seen. Or maybe it was the slanted eyebrows that made them seem strange. Blinking, he took in the tint of her skin and the angles of her features. Her hair was swept back on one side to reveal a gently pointed ear. His jaw fell open. "You're a Vulcan!"

Panic filled the girl's eyes. She scrambled to her feet, skinny legs trembling, and clutched a small plaster rock in her right hand. "Stay back or I will use it!" she warned. There was an odd lilt to her accent.

Jon cocked his head. "I'm not gonna hurt you."

She edged to one side. "Humans are barbaric and uncivilized," she stated, as if reciting from a book. "They are prone to sporadic outbursts of violence, especially in the presence of alcohol."

Jon crossed his arms. "How many humans have you met, anyway?"

She paused. "Only . . . only a few."

"Did any of them attack you?"

She reflected for a moment. "No."

"Well neither will I," he said, spreading his arms in a gesture of friendship. *A real live alien!* he thought, heart pounding with excitement. *What would Monty Moonhammer do?* Monty Moonhammer was his favorite cartoon superhero: a gallant, dark-skinned

man who traveled the galaxy, with a square jaw and a belt filled
with gadgets. Jon wasn't wearing a belt, but he checked his pockets
and came up with a slightly bent granola bar. He inspected the foil
wrapper for breaks and, finding none, held it out to the Vulcan girl.

"Here," he said. "You look hungry."

The girl had let her arms fall to her side. She eyed the peace offering hungrily.

"It's okay," Jon prompted. "I've got more at home."

Her left hand darted out and snatched the bar. Still holding on to
the stone, she fumbled with the wrapper.

"You can drop the rock," Jon said. "If I was going to attack you,
I wouldn't have shared my snack."

She stopped. Slowly, she bent over and set the plaster stone
down. Still eyeing him suspiciously, she made a small tear in the
wrapper and sniffed it. Apparently satisfied, she peeled it open and
ate hungrily. Jon waited for her to finish. It didn't take long. When
she was through, she wiped her mouth and stuffed the foil in her
pocket. "Thank you," she said quietly.

Jon ventured a smile. "My name is Jon. What's yours?"

"I am T'Rama."

"What are you doing here? Are you lost?"

T'Rama drew herself up. She was several inches taller than Jon.
"I am *not* lost," she pronounced.

Jon looked around at the empty room. "Then what are you doing
here? You sure look lost to me."

She scowled at him. "I know exactly where I am. I do not know
where my parents are. Therefore, the logical conclusion is that they
are lost. Not I."

He shrugged. "Lost is lost."

"And what about you?" she demanded.

He grinned. "I'm lost."

In response, she frowned harder. He found himself drawn to
her piercing eyes—light gray beneath fine, upsweeping eyebrows.
They were utterly alien, and yet oddly appealing. "Your eyes twinkle like starlight," he blurted before he realized what he was saying.

Her scowl vanished, replaced by a look of bewilderment.

Blushing, he turned quickly to the left and found himself staring at the painted backdrop. "Um . . . that's an interesting moon," he said.

"That is not a moon," T'Rama said. This time her tone was less patronizing. "That is a visual representation of T'Khut. A planet. Highly volcanic."

His mouth formed a silent "Oh."

"How did you get lost?" she asked.

"I ran away. A guard was chasing me."

Her lips twitched slightly. "I thought humans were nothing to be afraid of."

"I thought Vulcans had no sense of humor," he retorted. T'Rama's face went abruptly blank and he mentally kicked himself. He had to keep her talking. For years he'd dreamed about making contact with alien life-forms, and now . . . it was the most interesting thing that had happened to him in months! He certainly hadn't anticipated his first contact taking the form of such a casual conversation. In truth, he hadn't seriously expected to ever meet an alien face-to-face. And now, confronted with a girl his age (or at least size), and in the flesh . . . "What are you doing here, anyway?" he asked. "On Earth, I mean. You don't see a lot of Vulcans walking around."

"You would not," said T'Rama. "That is not an insult," she added hastily.

"Okay. So?"

"My father sometimes assists Ambassador Sasav." She paused, then added, "This is one of those times."

"You speak pretty good English," Jon observed.

She nodded. "My father instructed everyone in the household to learn the language in case . . ." She shifted uncomfortably. "In case anything ever went wrong. Like now, I guess. Except you are not much help."

"I know how to get out," he offered.

"I do not wish to get out," she said, turning away. "I came here so that my parents could find me. It is the logical place to look."

Jon shook his head. "You should have gone to the front desk. They'd have found your parents fast. I think you were scared. I bet that's why you were crying."

"I wasn't crying."

He reexamined the area around her eyes. "My dad says Vulcans can't lie."

"I wasn't *sad*," she said, her tone unyielding. "It is the chemicals in this paint. It irritates my eyes."

Jon supposed that was true. He poked the wooden "ground" with his toe. "So this place reminds you of home, huh? Aren't there any plants on Vulcan?"

"There are plants," she said. "Just because your human workers forgot to include them doesn't mean they aren't there."

"But Vulcan is a desert planet, right?"

"Deserts have plants."

He sighed in frustration. "I *know* deserts have plants. We've got deserts on Earth. They have cactuses and stuff. I mean like a garden."

She blinked. "I have a rock garden."

"Haven't you ever seen a *real* garden? With flowers and plants and trees?"

She shook her head. "I have heard they exist on Vulcan. I have not seen them."

"There's a big park right outside the museum! How could you not see it?"

"My family came in a shuttle. We landed on the roof."

"Your family should take you to a garden."

"My family is very busy," she said, as if that ended the matter.

"Why don't you come with my family? We'd show you around."

She frowned. "My father would not allow it."

His mind flashed back to his own aunt and uncle. How long had it been? Was the film over yet? Were they looking for him? Time was running out. But how could he ignore this opportunity? "Look, Tramma . . ."

"T'Rama," she corrected, altering the inflection slightly.

"T'Rama. Look, where do you live?"

"The Embassy suites."

"That's south, right?" She nodded. "Okay. We're pretty close. You guys are good at remembering stuff, right?"

"That is true," T'Rama said serenely.

"Can you remember this number? 88913455." He paused, waiting for it to sink in. "My aunt and uncle put me in the guest room. It has a vidphone. That's the number. Promise you'll call me tonight? After midnight."

She looked worried. "I don't know . . ."

"Who has to know?" he said casually. "Did your parents tell you *not* to use the phone?"

"No."

"Then doing it wouldn't be wrong, right? That's logical."

"I . . . suppose so." She smiled. "Okay. I mean . . . That is satisfactory."

"Great!" he beamed.

Suddenly, there were footsteps from the hall; words calling out in a language he did not know.

"My father," she whispered.

Jon nodded and ran to hide behind the painted backdrop. The footsteps grew louder as someone entered the room. There was more of the strange language—Vulcan, he guessed. T'Rama was speaking it too. Then two sets of footsteps receded and he was alone.

An acute thrill ran through Jon's body. Clandestine encounters! Alien contact! The damsel in distress on a foreign planet! This was the stuff of adventure. He waited another minute until he was sure the Vulcans were gone; then he ran for the exit as fast as his legs would carry him. An hour ago, he had been impatient to arrive at the museum; now he couldn't wait to leave.

Jon didn't sleep that night. Instead, he sat by the bedside stand that housed the vidphone, muffling the speaker with his pillow. He hadn't thought of that until the lights had gone out and his aunt and uncle had gone to sleep. What would he have done if they'd been woken by the call? Better not to think about it.

As the minutes stretched out, he began to become nervous. Suppose she didn't call? Suppose she'd forgotten. But she couldn't forget, could she? She was a Vulcan. And she couldn't lie, either. Only she'd lied about the crying . . . sort of. Maybe he was pushing on the speaker too hard. What if she called and he didn't hear it? What if he had to go to the bathroom? The thought made him squirm.

Fortunately, his worries were interrupted by a vibration beneath his palm. Quickly, he activated the phone and leaned close. To his delight and relief T'Rama's face stared back at him. "Hi!" he said.

"Hello Jon," she said. "Why did I call?"

The question caught him off guard, and he stared blankly for a moment before remembering the lines he had rehearsed. He reached next to the nightstand and held up a rose from his aunt's garden. "This is an Earth flower," he whispered.

Even on the small screen, he could see her interest.

"I'll give it to you," he continued, careful to keep his voice low. "Want to meet me somewhere?"

"At this time of night?"

"What's the matter? Tired?"

She lifted her nose haughtily. "Vulcans can go without sleep for precisely . . ."

"Okay," he cut her off. "Look at this." He reached under his covers and pulled out a paper on which he had drawn a crude map. He held it up to the camera. "See? I looked up where you are. We're really close. Where I put that 'X' there's a flower garden. One of my friends taught me how to climb over the wall last summer. I can meet you there in half an hour."

Her eyes widened. "A real garden?"

"It's real! They've got lots of plants from all over Earth. Well, America anyway."

She looked worried and glanced away. "I cannot. It would disturb my father."

Jon knew how to deal with *that* moral quandary. "He doesn't know, right? What he doesn't know won't hurt him, right?"

Her face lit up. "That is logical." A moment of nervous apprehension flickered over her face. It was quickly replaced by what he was beginning to recognize as a default expression of calm. "I will do it."

"By the southern wall. Half an hour," he whispered. "Bye." Switching off the vidphone, he slid off the bed and fumbled for his shoes. In his mind, images were already playing out. Everyone said Vulcans didn't like humans. Humans didn't seem exactly comfortable around Vulcans either. Wait until they saw this! He and

T'Rama would grow up to be great friends! He could see the head-lines dancing in his mind. "Jonathan Archer . . ." No: "CAPTAIN Jonathan Archer Ushers New Era Of Cooperation! First Human To Visit . . ." What was that other planet? Tuh-koot? It didn't matter. Finding his shoes, he slung his backpack over his shoulder and snuck out into the hall. His bicycle was leaned up against the garage outside, a flashlight in the basket. It was a bright night, but one never knew. An intergalactic hero, after all, was always pre-pared.

T'Rama was waiting for him when he arrived. She was wearing a fresh set of clothes, and did not appear to have exerted herself. There was no mode of transportation in sight.

"How'd you get here so fast?" Jon asked, leaning his bike up against the brick wall.

"Vulcans are . . ."

" . . . fast?" he finished. She nodded, looking vaguely amused. He turned to regard the wall, which was at least six feet high. "My friend Billy Owen taught me to climb up using my bike. Do you want to go first?"

"Yes," she said, and leapt into the air. His eyes popped wide as she caught hold of the top edge and easily pulled herself up. For such a slight frame, she was strong! She disappeared over the other side.

"Wait up!" Jon called, hastily putting one foot on his bike seat and pushing himself up.

Inside, T'Rama stood mystified. The interior of the garden was rimmed with hedges. It was not a vast area—perhaps the size of a large room—but the circular brick wall was rimmed with deciduous trees, and the hedges and flower beds between contained a stunning variety of flowers: pink roses, rubrum lilies, alabaster alstromeria; daisies and daffodils and even snapdragons. "What is this place?" she whispered.

"Some old lady keeps a greenhouse," Jon said. He pointed to-ward a tall maple. "It's on the other side of that tree. You can't see it from here." He looked up at the night sky. The stars were brilliantly clear and the moon hung full overhead, bathing everything in a milky glow. He walked over and pointed to a dark area between two thick hedges. "That's the real entrance. She lets people come in on weekends. My friend and I used to sneak in at night to catch moths."

"Moths?"

"An insect. It's a little cold tonight, but you'll see."

She turned around slowly, taking in the colors, which remained vibrant even in the pale light of the moon. Her gaze lingered on the pink rosebush and she moved forward to get a closer look. "Fascinating," she said. "I will certainly research Vulcan flowers the next time I am home." She stroked a large petal, letting dew trickle down her fingers. "You said you had one of these for me."

Jon blinked. "Uh . . . oh, yeah." He had left it at home. "Well it was getting old. You didn't want that. Go ahead and pick a fresh one."

T'Rama looked surprised. "I couldn't! It would harm the plant!"

"No it won't. Here." He reached forward and snapped off a rose by the base of the stem and handed it to her. Spellbound, she reached forward to take it. But as her fingers closed, she gave a tiny cry of pain and jerked her hand back. He dropped the flower, filled with sudden remorse. He had forgotten to warn her about thorns. "Are you okay?" he asked, and reached out instinctively to grab her injured hand.

She looked at him oddly. "I am bleeding, that is all."

Green blood, he thought, dumbfounded. From somewhere, T'Rama produced a tissue and bandaged her finger. The green stain spreading beneath it made his stomach turn. For the first time that night, his eyes were drawn specifically to her inhuman ears. *We are not the same. We aren't! But her face* . . . It was aglow in the moonlight. He'd never seen a face look prettier. There was a wistful, faraway look in her eyes as she surveyed the enclosure, her wound apparently forgotten.

The silence became uncomfortable to Jon. He walked over to a stone bench and sat down. "If I had kids, I'd take them here," he said at last.

"I will take my children to a place like this someday," T'Rama echoed. "Infinite Diversity in Infinite Combinations."

He looked up in surprise. "You're gonna have kids?" The idea made him feel funny.

She nodded. "I want to. Someday I will have a son."

He shifted uncomfortably. "You're sure? How do you know?"

Her lips twitched and she suddenly seemed much more than eleven. "I will name him Sarek."

"Oh." Jon didn't know what to say. So he just sat there, watching T'Rama, watching the garden and the shadows from the moon.

After a while, she came to sit next to him.

Jon awoke the next day to a gentle hand shaking his shoulders. He mumbled and turned in bed, clutching the covers and shouldering away the bothersome appendage. But the hand returned, more insistent the second time. Groggily, he opened his eyes and turned toward his bedside clock. It read 0712, several hours before he had wanted to get up. Sitting up, he saw his uncle sitting on the side of the bed. The smile he wore was kindly, but Jon's chest still tightened. Then he saw his aunt standing in the doorway. She was holding a piece of paper.

It was his map.

"Sweetie," she said, "we have to talk."

The vidphone rang.

"I understand you have come to apologize."

Vice-Ambassador Supek's eyes were as hard and dark as pure obsidian, and they were aimed directly at Jon. The boy huddled deeper between his aunt and uncle, and the air atop the embassy suddenly seemed more chill. The wind tugged at him, hissing over the nearby shuttle and drawing ghostly fingers across the exposed skin of his arms.

"Apologize," his uncle prompted gently.

Jon shook his head determinedly. There was nothing remotely human about the lank, robed figure that stood before him.

"We *do* apologize," said his aunt. "He's just a little frightened. I hope you can understand."

"I do not understand," said Supek flatly. "There is no cause for fear."

"I'm not afraid!" Jon piped.

"Indeed," the Vulcan said. He examined the adults. "No apology is required. Ambassador Sasav suggested I indulge you. Humans have an odd sense of conscience."

Jon felt the hand on his shoulder tighten, but his uncle did not reply.

The elevator bunker to their right began to hum, and a moment later the double doors hissed open. T'Rama and her mother, an austere figure in traditional Vulcan garb, emerged. The girl was wearing a long robe and stared straight ahead as she walked.

"T'Rama!" Jon cried out, inching forward. "I'm sorry."

She did not acknowledge him. Then he noticed that her mother was carrying several suitcases. His eyes returned to the shuttle. It was warming up. "What's going on? I said I'm sorry!"

"T'Rama is returning to Vulcan with her mother," Supek said.

Jon felt like he'd been punched in the gut. "She didn't do anything!" he protested. "It was my fault!"

Supek looked down with what might have been sympathy. "You can hardly be blamed for what you are. T'Rama's behavior, on the other hand, has been erratic in the presence of humans. We feel it will be better for her among her own kind."

Jon fought back tears. He wasn't about to give this alien the satisfaction of watching him cry. But he had to say something. "I'll miss you," he called, and T'Rama turned toward him. He searched for an assuring sign of recognition or reconciliation or even regret, and for a moment he thought he saw something shine in her eyes. But the expression on her face remained implacable. It was as if she was wearing a mask.

"That . . ." she said, "would be illogical."

Then her mother ushered her into the shuttle and she was gone. Jon wilted backward, his face registering betrayal.

"We'll go now," Jon's uncle said coolly.

Supek held up his right hand, dividing his third and fourth fingers. "Live long and prosper."

Walking into the elevator, Jon's uncle squeezed his shoulder. "It'll be okay, buddy," he said quietly.

"I hate you," Jon whispered. "I hate everybody."

He was silent the entire way home.

* * *

343

That night, his father returned. Henry Archer entered the guest room to find his son lying on one side in bed, staring out the window.

"I'm sorry, Jon."

"Go away."

Henry sighed. *"They* called your uncle, you know. Found a granola wrapper in the girl's pocket when they did the laundry. They went to ask her about it and found her gone. They were quite concerned. Even called me. It was fortunate she came back before they got around to calling the police."

"She told them everything," Jon said in a small voice.

"Did you want her to lie?"

Jon was silent for a moment. "No."

Henry gave a sympathetic groan and sat down on the foot of the bed. "What a choice for your first crush."

"It wasn't like that!" Jon protested.

His father smiled knowingly. "It never is. Just you remember . . ." He leaned over and pointed out the window. "There's a girl out there for every star in the sky. You'll get your chance."

Jon hunched his shoulders and was silent.

Henry placed a paper on the bed in front of Jon. "I brought you this. It's a sketch of the new ship concept I'm working on."

The boy pushed the paper off the side of the bed, there to lie next to the discarded, now withered, rose.

His father clicked his tongue. "Hey now, aren't you the least bit curious? I haven't even shown it to the Vulcans yet! Take a look."

In spite of his mood, Jon couldn't resist peeking over the edge of the mattress. A spaceship had been drawn on the paper: a saucer, like in the cartoons, but with two elongated engines fixed to a structure that projected from the rear. He read the text beneath the illustration. "What does 'enterprise' mean?" he asked.

Henry looked up and his lips twitched. "Well, let's see . . . it's sort of like a venture."

"What's a venture?"

"It's . . . like a project, or undertaking. I don't know . . . something daring and challenging." A soft smile appeared on his face as he regarded his son. "I guess you'd say it's the kind of ship Monty Moonhammer would drive."

"Oh."

"Good night, sport." He kissed the boy on the forehead. "We'll go home in the morning. I'll buy you a model kit, huh?"

After he left, Jon remained still. He stared at the picture a little longer before his eyes returned to the open window. *Enterprise.* The stars glinted down at him like twinkling gray eyes.

Hoshi's Gift

By Kelle Vozka

Tossing and turning in bed, listening to her world unravel, it was all Ensign Hoshi Sato could do to keep from screaming. Feeling lost and angry, she wondered once again if she had made the right choice coming aboard the *Enterprise*. Would she even make it back home to Earth alive? Just as she began to doze off sliding into dream, the slightest shift in the warp engines, the tiniest rise or fall in the rhythmic pitch, started her awake. Her gift, the specialized sensitivity to vibration and sound that gave her the ability to pick out the tiniest nuances in linguistic communication, quickly became the curse that would not allow her to get any rest. It had been weeks since she'd gotten a full night's sleep.

Hoshi switched on a light and started pacing around her cramped quarters. She stopped for a moment to think. Something was wrong; things just didn't feel right. It had never felt completely safe from the moment she'd stepped foot aboard the *Enterprise,* but this seemed different, as if there had been a shift though she couldn't put her finger on exactly what it was that had changed.

She took the few steps to a small compartment next to her bunk

346

and pulled out an engraved wooden box. It was a gift that had been given to her grandmother by a Vulcan she had once helped. At her birth, it had been given to Hoshi. She had brought few personal possessions aboard the *Enterprise,* but this she would never leave behind.

Smooth and cool to her touch, the box smelled faintly of jasmine. Its intricately tooled lines appeared to be patterns and symbols that must hold meaning, yet their significance remained obscure to her. Though for all its splendor, it wasn't the box that she loved, but rather the precious treasure hidden within. The box opened silently to her touch, revealing a small sphere about the size of her fist. Inside the clear glass ball a milky, pearlescent substance swirled endlessly.

Fitting perfectly in the palm of her hand, the ball felt warm and smooth. It vibrated erratically in time with the movement of the smoky liquid inside. She slid over to the desk chair and sat cradling the ball in one hand, stroking it lightly with the other while listening to it hum. Hoshi had always found the soft gentle vibrations of the ball to give her comfort and often sang back to it, humming in the same pitch, or harmonizing as she did now. The whirling in the ball seemed to slow and fall back into a more rhythmic pattern, as if it too were agitated by the shifting in the engines and now found comfort.

Hoshi let out the long breath she hadn't realized she had been holding. Her shoulders came down from around her ears as the tension fled from her body. She rocked slightly on the chair and sang with the ball, forgetting for the time her pressures and troubles. Finally she put the sphere back into its box, carefully secured it in the compartment, and crawled back into bed, trying to relax for the last few hours before her next shift.

Hoshi moved like an automaton through her morning ritual, once again forgetting to eat. Another day and she didn't know how she could go on one more step, much less forward on a seemingly endless journey. She thought of her students back home. Was she doing them a disservice by being out here? Yes, she'd get to meet all kinds of new people, decipher new languages and cultures, but back on

Earth she could be training dozens of students to do this task. Was she jeopardizing the future with her presence here now? Though if she asked to go home, what would happen to the mission, to Jonathan, her captain?

She'd given her word when Jonathan had shown up and said that he needed her. It all happened so fast. Hoshi knew that she didn't belong here, but she couldn't just abandon him, risk everything he'd worked so hard for, what humanity had worked so hard to achieve. It was an honor to be here, and yet, she couldn't shake that feeling of doom that pursued her every waking moment, and the waking moments kept getting longer.

Sitting at her post on the bridge, Hoshi listened for the signals that might indicate life or any new information they could garner about the strange new worlds they were speeding by. After a time Hoshi realized that she wasn't paying attention to her work. She couldn't concentrate as each new bump or crackle reminded her that these engines, hurtling them ever forward at an incomprehensible warp four, were relatively untested. Her thoughts kept drifting back to the ball, hidden in her chambers, that she knew might give her the day's only pleasure. She was so distracted, Captain Archer called her name three times before she realized he was speaking to her.

"Oh sorry, I didn't hear you."

"Have you found anything interesting?" asked Captain Archer. "You've got that intense look on your face."

". . . Found anything?" Hoshi looked up at him through a haze of fatigue, not comprehending.

"You look terrible."

"I haven't been sleeping much. It's just . . . are you sure the engines are supposed to pitch like that? It doesn't feel the same."

"Hoshi"—Captain Archer grabbed her around the shoulders and helped her out of her chair—"why don't you go see Dr. Phlox. You really don't look well." She glanced at him, meeting his eyes for the first time since the conversation started. Seeing that familiar furrow of concern on his brow, she allowed him to walk her toward the door. Lieutenant Reed, who had been talking with Ensign May-weather, came over and grabbed her by the elbow.

"I'll see she gets to sickbay, I'm going that way anyway," said Lieutenant Reed to Captain Archer, and Hoshi felt he was being condescending. She could take care of herself.

"Look, I'm okay," said Hoshi. "You don't need to treat me like an invalid, I'm just a little tired. What I really need is a good night's sleep, not a couple of knights in shining armor."

"All right, all right." Lieutenant Reed backed off with his hands high in the air, wearing a big grin. Hoshi couldn't help but smile back. "Mind if I walk that way with you then?"

"Sure," said Hoshi, and they walked out together.

In sickbay, Dr. Phlox turned from his workstation back to where Hoshi sat on the table.

"Well, I have found a depletion of seratonin in your brain, adrenal function low, hormone functions adequate, but low. In other words, you are exhausted. It is obvious you have not been eating either."

"I've been having some trouble sleeping," said Hoshi, a little embarrassed over all the fuss when nothing was apparently wrong. No reason for her trouble at all but her own insecurities, and Dr. Phlox had confirmed it.

"I'm prescribing sleep and food." Dr. Phlox pulled out a small leech-like creature from a jar and began coming toward Hoshi.

"I'm not eating that!" said Hoshi. Dr. Phlox laughed jovially, his alien features contorting into a smile too large for his face.

"It is not for you to eat, my dear." His smile broadened further as he held her hand and placed the creature on her wrist.

"What does it do?" Hoshi knew the answer before she had even gotten the whole question out. In moments she grew ravenously hungry.

"Blood sugar imbalance," said Dr. Phlox, as if that explained it all. "Now I highly recommend that you get directly to the mess before you decide you need to eat something, um . . . unsuitable."

"Thanks." Hoshi hopped off the table, dreaming of a hot fudge sundae.

"Come back and see me tomorrow!" called Dr. Phlox after her, but she was already halfway down the hallway.

With a stomach so full it ached, Hoshi barely made it back to her quarters, then flopped down on the bed.

Waking with a start, Hoshi looked around, confused. She couldn't remember how she had gotten here. What was wrong! How long had she been sleeping? What time was it? She jumped up, excited, feeling sick all over. Her stomach ached and she re-membered all the food she'd eaten. It couldn't have been too long ago, she still felt stuffed. She was tempted to get her box out again and hold the ball to her, though she knew that was not the answer, there was something wrong and it was real. She had felt that jolt so strongly it had woken her from a dead sleep. With a feeling of dread she ran down the corridor and made her way to engineering.

"What are you doing here?" Lieutenant Reed asked when he saw Hoshi appear.

"What's going on with the engines?" asked Hoshi.

"Nothing's going on with the engines," said Lieutenant Reed, a concerned edge making his voice rise up in pitch slightly. Then softer, lower, he asked, "What did the doc say when you were there?"

"There's nothing wrong with me," she snapped, "what's wrong with the engines?"

"I tell you, there is absolutely nothing wrong with the engines!" Lieutenant Reed said a little too forcefully, letting his frustration show.

"Don't tell me you can't feel that . . . there! Did you feel that?"

"Feel what?" said Lieutenant Reed. "I didn't feel anything."

"I just . . . there it is again . . ."

She crumpled to the floor in a faint.

When Hoshi woke up this time, she was back in sickbay. She could hear Lieutenant Reed and Dr. Phlox talking, their backs to her where she lay.

"Now, Doc, don't go telling me there ain't nothing wrong with her. She passed out."

"I am telling you, the human anatomy is quite simple. If there were anything wrong, I would be able to detect it. She is suffering from a slight chemical imbalance simply caused by her refusal to rest."

"Slight? People don't just drop to the ground over a *slight* imbalance."

"I have checked all her vitals. Her adrenal function is low, like a woman after a long labor, someone coming off stimulants, or, in the ensign's case, someone who has been working too much and not eating enough. She will be fine."

"She doesn't look fine. When will she be up and around?"

"In a while," said Dr. Phlox. Hoshi could see the tension in Lieutenant Reed's neck and jaws as he glared at the doctor. "As soon as she gets some sleep, which she cannot get with you standing here shouting."

Lieutenant Reed looked over and Hoshi tried her best to dredge up a smile for him, but there was none to be found.

"Doc say's you'll be fine," Lieutenant Reed said.

"I heard," replied Hoshi. The three of them looked at each other. No one spoke until the silence grew awkward.

"I'll go tell the captain you're okay, then I'm coming back to check on you." Though he was talking to Hoshi, she could see that he meant it for Dr. Phlox.

"You're not going to put one of those disgusting leech things on me again, are you?" asked Hoshi.

"Oh no," said Dr. Phlox as he moved to pick up an ominous-looking box. When he lifted it something inside fought and jumped, making a terrible screeching noise. Hoshi sat halfway up, getting ready to bolt from the bed. Dr. Phlox laughed and put the box on another shelf, pulling out the container behind, which was now reachable. He surprised her further as he produced a small bunch of flowery potpourri and set it in a tiny simmering dish on the table near her head. In a few minutes she was asleep.

* * *

Again Hoshi awoke to confusion. Her memories were disjointed, all colliding in on her at once. She looked around for her box and realized that she wasn't in her quarters. The anxiety returned, like a hard fist in the pit of her stomach. It lurched with each new jolt. She knew something must be very wrong with the ship. Hoshi tried to get her bearings. Being out of sorts, she couldn't place herself in time or space. How long had she been asleep, how long since this first started? Her stomach told her not long enough.

She stumbled over to the little bathroom and splashed cold water on her face. Smoothing back her hair with wet fingers, she looked at herself. Dark circles under red-rimmed eyes, pain in her joints, throbbing head making it hard to focus on her image. Nausea overwhelmed her. When she washed out her mouth she didn't dare to look at herself again. She just wanted to be back in her own bed.

Glancing around, recognizing sickbay at last, Hoshi didn't see Dr. Phlox, so she left. On the long walk back to her room it seemed to her that she used the wall more than the floor to get her there. The pain in her head grew alarmingly intense. She felt an urgent pull, as if she wasn't going to make it in time. In time for what? No time to think. Just keep trudging forward, one foot in front of the other.

Finally making it to her quarters, she dropped down onto her bed with a sigh of relief. She had only just closed her eyes when they popped open wide. Rolling over, she hung off the edge of the bed as she opened the compartment and pulled out her box. Inside the ball visibly shook. She picked it up and sat on the bed, rocking back and forth, soothing, humming. The motions settled down and she calmed with it. She held the ball to her chest and lay down with it cradled to her and finally slept.

Hoshi never knew how long she was there, only that it was the first time she really felt comfortable since she'd come to the *Enterprise*. She woke periodically, each time cuddling the ball closer to her, its gentle humming lulling her back to her dreams. In one dream she saw Dr. Phlox standing over her, wearing that grin so big she thought it might take over his whole face. It was a silly thought and she knew it must be a dream, but she wasn't ever sure if she was awake or dreaming in those hours and days that passed.

* * *

Something wiggled in her fingers, against her sternum, it tickled and she giggled, half-awake, feeling so happy. Like the morning after your wedding night, holding your lover safe in your arms, knowing they'll be with you forever. She didn't want to get up, just lie there and let the moment go on. She felt the wiggle again, more urgently this time, and she opened her eyes, seeing the ball held in her fingers. It wasn't completely round anymore, or glassy, but felt soft and porous.

She put it down on the bed, that tiny itch in the back of her head telling her maybe she should be afraid, but for once she wasn't. Hoshi examined the ball as it moved and twisted. It was the flowing liquid no longer in its shell. She watched with a fascination that slowly transformed into a bursting joy.

The liquid swirled and formed. With each revolution it was less ball and more like some kind of bird with feathered butterfly wings. The pearl effect became darker, shiny metallic colors. With each new revolution Hoshi felt a changing in her own body, as the joy that was in her heart spread like a warmth through her entire being. It washed over her in wave after wave as the creature grew and formed.

The bird flew just a few feet up into the air and expanded in a raging flame of light and color and an incredible feeling that could only be described as happiness, seemed to enlarge and grow until it reached the very limits of the room.

The colors of the bird grew more brilliant, whiter and brighter, until it consumed and enveloped Hoshi. She was one with the bird and felt the searing pleasure as a symphony of sensations. The walls could not contain the dancing ecstasy that was Hoshi, that was the bird, and it expanded ever outward until it engulfed the whole ship and then beyond into space, in all directions at once.

In that moment Hoshi understood, she could feel inside the very nature of everything that surrounded her. She realized that there was nothing wrong with the ship and she could hear in the intricate pattern of the song that was *Enterprise* and its crew, where each individual and each component fit together.

In a blinding moment, the most intense pleasure Hoshi had ever felt exploded through her senses; then in the next instant, it was gone.

The sudden grief at the loss sent Hoshi at first into a stunned silence, and then a piercing wail rose up out of her throat and into the air, as if releasing all the agony and pain she had ever felt. She dropped to the floor, sobbing, and bewildered. She could still feel some residual of her connection, and as she expanded her awareness throughout the ship, she saw that no one aboard was unaffected. They had all felt some small part of the elation and connection and the absence now sent the entire crew into silence, but for the echoes of the cry of anguish she herself had sent reverberating through the vessel.

After what seemed to be an eternity of suffering, or maybe just an endless pinpoint in time, the pain started to fade and the memories of the joy that had once been, returned. It wasn't only the pleasures of the moment Hoshi remembered, but all the times she had felt comfort over her lifetime holding what she now knew to be some kind of egg.

Looking down at the spot where she had lain, she saw that there were three small seeds. She picked up the seeds and held them. Each one was vibrating softly, each one with a slightly different pitch. She held them, wondering why there were three, as if acts of such beauty and good could only bring about an increasing positive result.

A soft knocking at the door brought Hoshi's attention back to the immediate world and she quickly jumped up and opened it. Dr. Phlox was there.

"I see she has hatched, or rather, we all felt it."

"It's gone," said Hoshi.

"Is it?" Dr. Phlox looked down at her hands, still holding the three seeds.

"You knew all along?"

"Oh no, I came here looking for you after you left the infirmary. That's when I saw it."

"What is . . . what was it?"

"It is a very rare species of Vulcan bird. It is said that once this bird hatches it lives for only a few moments, but that it lives a life filled with more joy than a hundred men would ever experience in all their lifetimes added together." Hoshi's eyes filled with tears. She didn't know what to say, she knew only that it was true, because she had felt it herself.

"Men from the far reaches of the universe have fought and killed and died for the chance to glimpse a Vulcan Firebird, and now you have three."

"How long does it take for one to grow to full size and hatch?"

"A very long time," said Dr. Phlox.

"How long is that?" asked Hoshi.

"Longer than your lifetime," answered Dr. Phlox in his usual noncommittal manner, as if he didn't share the human's obsession with the passage of time. Hoshi would not get irritated; she would still be feeling the Firebird for some time to come. "Just about three hundred Earth years, but then it could be thousands. A Firebird cannot hatch on its own, it needs another being to nurture it to life."

"Oh" was all she could say. Understanding at last the full extent of the sacrifice that Vulcan woman had made. What a precious gift that had been given to her grandmother, and then to her. She wondered again what it was her grandmother had done to earn such a reward.

Dr. Phlox stood, waiting for her to go on. Then he said, "I myself have to wonder if it is worth it. To take care of something for so long, knowing you will never see the end results, but to do it for your children's children's children."

"Oh yes," said Hoshi thoughtfully, "it is worth it." Though she wasn't exactly answering his question. She had thought about her time on the *Enterprise,* why she agreed to come here in the first place. One thing the Firebird had taught her, as she experienced for an instant the web of life and its many vibrating chords and cadences, was that yes, all the struggle and sacrifice and discomfort was worth it for the many new experiences she could get out here and not on Earth. In that shining moment she had known that it would be a long hard road, but she also knew that the *Enterprise* was where she belonged.

Afterword

Writing for
Star Trek:
STRANGE NEW WORLDS

Dean Wesley Smith

Sometimes it seems to me that every *Star Trek* fan wants to write *Star Trek* novels. Now, I know that's not the case, but at times it sure seems that way.

I'm one of the lucky *Star Trek* fans who does get to write *Star Trek* novels, and I get to edit this anthology every year as well.

Because I have this job, I tend to get a lot of questions from fans—both on-line on AOL, and at science fiction conventions—about how to write *Star Trek* stories, how writers might get into the next *Star Trek: Strange New Worlds,* and so on. I tell them to read the rules, my hints in volume III, and then write a lot of stories, both *Star Trek* and non–*Star Trek* to practice.

But the question I get more than any other is this one: *Will selling a story to* Strange New Worlds *help me sell a* Star Trek *novel?*

In essence, how do I get to write *Star Trek* novels?

I honestly don't know how to answer that basic question. I started writing for *Star Trek* before this anthology was born. And the publishing industry was different then, so my experience isn't much help now to new writers.

Afterword

Any professional short fiction sale is a good thing. Selling a story to *Star Trek: Strange New Worlds* is a professional sale. Professional sales help you move down the road to being a professional writer, writing and selling novels, and maybe writing *Star Trek* novels.

Since *Strange New Worlds* is a professional sale, then the answer to the question is clearly yes, selling a story to *Strange New Worlds* does help get you closer to writing and selling a *Star Trek* novel.

So, that said, I suppose after five years of *Strange New Worlds* anthologies, it might be interesting to look back and see if any of the writers in the volumes have been helped to write *Star Trek* novels.

Actually, three have so far. Dayton Ward, Christina York, and Kathy Oltion have gone on to write books for *Star Trek*.

But using *Strange New Worlds* as a jumping point to writing *Star Trek* novels is tricky at best. The rules of the contest state that a writer submitting a story to *Strange New Worlds* can not have three professionally published stories. So these *Star Trek* fans who are working to become professional writers have a very short window of opportunity. By becoming too successful with their writing they no longer can write for *Strange New Worlds*.

But some writers are managing to get through that small window.

Dayton Ward, Christina York, and Kathy Oltion were all in the very first volume, and then they all repeated in volume II. That was the end for Kathy in *Strange New Worlds,* since she had sold a story to *Analog* magazine and it came out before she could submit to volume III. However, writing with her husband, Jerry Oltion, she jumped back into the *Star Trek* universe last year with a full-length novel.

Dayton Ward pulled the hat trick and became the only writer to be in the first three volumes. Since then he has gone on to write his own stories, a *Star Trek SCE* book, and a stand-alone *Star Trek* novel that came out this last winter.

Christina York was also in both of the first two volumes, but before she could get a third story into the anthology she sold a number of short stories and a romance novel. But she too wanted to come

Afterword

back, so right now she and her husband, J. Steven York, have just finished a *Star Trek: SCE* project.

Those three supply the answer to the question about *Strange New Worlds* helping to get a writer into *Star Trek* novels. But other writers in the first five volumes have gone on to become professionals as well.

Second-place winner in volume I, Franklin Thatcher, also repeated in the second volume, but in the meantime he was a winner in the other new-writer contest, *Writers of the Future*. Since then he's been selling regularly to a number of the top magazines.

Steven Scott Ripley and William Leisner sold their first stories to volume II, then managed to place stories in both volume IV and this volume to end their run. Tonya D. Price and Diana Kornfeld both started their appearances here in volume III, continued in IV, and now are finished with their wonderful stories in this volume. With luck all four will be returning to the *Star Trek* universe at some point in the future.

Both the first-place winner in II, Ilsa Bick, and the third-place winner, Ken Rand, have gone on to sell too many stories to return. Both won in *Writers of the Future* and sell regularly to magazines. Ken Rand's first novel will be out just before this book comes out. Ilsa Bick is the only writer so far to actually win prizes in both of her appearances here. She took first place in volume II and second place in volume IV.

The grand prize winners in III, Sarah A. Hoyt and Rebecca Lickiss, have sold two original novels apiece in the last two years. Their first books are out and are wonderful. And Rebecca's husband, Alan Lickiss, just got in under the wire in this volume, since he's sold stories to *Analog* and other places.

I know there are other writers in these five volumes who just haven't kept me updated on how their sales outside of *Star Trek* are going. Please forgive me if I didn't mention you.

And for those of you interested in writing professionally for *Star Trek,* stop by the public bulletin board on AOL in the *Star Trek:* Writing section. The board is titled Strange New Writers, and I will answer any writing and *Strange New World* anthology question you might have. Or come by and just talk about the stories you liked in this book.

But I hope you will get to that computer and write a *Star Trek* story for volume VI. The rules for the contest are in this book.

In the meantime, enjoy all the anthologies and the wonderful *Star Trek* stories written by fans just like you and me.

STAR TREK®

Strange New Worlds VI

Contest Rules

1) ENTRY REQUIREMENTS:

No purchase necessary to enter. Enter by submitting your story as specified below.

2) CONTEST ELIGIBILITY:

This contest is open to nonprofessional writers who are legal residents of the United States and Canada (excluding Quebec) over the age of 18. Entrant must not have published any more than two short stories on a professional basis or in paid professional venues. Employees (or relatives of employees living in the same household) of Simon & Schuster, VIACOM, or any of their affiliates are not eligible. This contest is void in Puerto Rico and wherever prohibited by law.

Contest Rules

3) FORMAT:

Entries should be no more than 7,500 words long and must not have been previously published. They must be typed or printed by word processor, double spaced, on one side of noncorrasable paper. Do not justify right-side margins. The author's name, address, and phone number must appear on the first page of the entry. The author's name, the story title, and the page number should appear on every page. No electronic or disk submissions will be accepted. All entries must be original and the sole work of the Entrant and the sole property of the Entrant.

4) ADDRESS:

Each entry must be mailed to: STRANGE NEW WORLDS VI, *Star Trek* Department, Pocket Books, 1230 Sixth Avenue, New York, NY 10020.

Each entry must be submitted only once. Please retain a copy of your submission. You may submit more than one story, but each submission must be mailed separately. Enclose a self-addressed, stamped envelope if you wish your entry returned. Entries must be received by October 1st, 2002. Not responsible for lost, late, stolen, postage due, or misdirected mail.

5) PRIZES:

One Grand Prize winner will receive:

Simon and Schuster's *Star Trek: Strange New Worlds VI* Publishing Contract for Publication of Winning Entry in our *Strange New Worlds VI* Anthology with a bonus advance of One Thousand Dollars ($1,000.00) above the Anthology word rate of 10 cents a word.

One Second Prize winner will receive:

Simon and Schuster's *Star Trek: Strange New Worlds VI* Publishing Contract for Publication of Winning Entry in our *Strange*

New Worlds VI Anthology with a bonus advance of Six Hundred Dollars ($600.00) above the Anthology word rate of 10 cents a word.

One Third Prize winner will receive:

Simon and Schuster's *Star Trek: Strange New Worlds VI* Publishing Contract for Publication of Winning Entry in our *Strange New Worlds VI* Anthology with a bonus advance of Four Hundred Dollars ($400.00) above the Anthology word rate of 10 cents a word.

All Honorable Mention winners will receive:

Simon and Schuster's *Star Trek: Strange New Worlds VI* Publishing Contract for Publication of Winning Entry in the *Strange New Worlds VI* Anthology and payment at the Anthology word rate of 10 cents a word.

There will be no more than twenty (20) Honorable Mention winners. No contestant can win more than one prize.

Each Prize Winner will also be entitled to a share of royalties on the *Strange New Worlds VI* Anthology as specified in Simon and Schuster's *Star Trek: Strange New Worlds VI* Publishing Contract.

6) JUDGING:

Submissions will be judged on the basis of writing ability and the originality of the story, which can be set in any of the *Star Trek* time frames and may feature any one or more of the *Star Trek* characters. The judges shall include the editor of the Anthology, one employee of Pocket Books, and one employee of VIACOM Consumer Products. The decisions of the judges shall be final. All prizes will be awarded provided a sufficient number of entries are received that meet the minimum criteria established by the judges.

Contest Rules

7) NOTIFICATION:

The winners will be notified by mail or phone. The winners who win a publishing contract must sign the publishing contract in order to be awarded the prize. All federal, local, and state taxes are the responsibility of the winner. A list of the winners will be available after January 1st, 2003, on the Pocket Books *Star Trek* Books Web site,

www.simonsays.com/startrek/

or the names of the winners can be obtained after January 1st, 2003, by sending a self-addressed, stamped envelope and a request for the list of winners to WINNERS' LIST, STRANGE NEW WORLDS VI, *Star Trek* Department, Pocket Books, 1230 Sixth Avenue, New York, NY 10020.

8) STORY DISQUALIFICATIONS:

Certain types of stories will be disqualified from consideration:

a) Any story focusing on explicit sexual activity or graphic depictions of violence or sadism.

b) Any story that focuses on characters that are not past or present *Star Trek* regulars or familiar *Star Trek* guest characters.

c) Stories that deal with the previously unestablished death of a *Star Trek* character, or that establish major facts about or make major changes in the life of a major character, for instance a story that establishes a long-lost sibling or reveals the hidden passion two characters feel for each other.

d) Stories that are based around common clichés, such as "hurt/comfort" where a character is injured and lovingly cared for, or "Mary Sue" stories where a new character comes on the ship and outdoes the crew.

9) PUBLICITY:

Each Winner grants to Pocket Books the right to use his or her

Contest Rules

name, likeness, and entry for any advertising, promotion, and publicity purposes without further compensation to or permission from such winner, except where prohibited by law.

10) LEGAL STUFF:

All entries become the property of Pocket Books and of Paramount Pictures, the sole and exclusive owner of the *Star Trek* property and elements thereof. Entries will be returned only if they are accompanied by a self-addressed, stamped envelope. Contest void where prohibited by law.

About the Contributors

Michelle A. Bottrall ("Kristin's Conundrum") thanks her husband, her AOL writers' group, and the rest of her family; without their encouragement she would never have persevered. When not obeying Dean's rule of write, send, repeat, she freelances for the newspaper in Grand Rapids, Michigan, and is thrilled to be a small part of Trek history.

C. K. Deatherage ("Final Entry") lives in Idaho with husband, John (whom she loves and who has provided a wonderful surname for an SF writer), son James, and two cats (Spot and Trouble). Thanks to Doug, Jonathan; Chris, Roberta Bosse, and Lloyd Kropp for encouragement on the road to writing.

Alan J. Garbers ("The Peacemakers") is a U.S. Coast Guard veteran and Master Electrician. He is working on several screenplays as well as children's books. "I know I've done a good job when my kids can't believe I wrote it!" Alan's hobbies are writing, photography, writing, playing guitar, writing, karate . . .

Craig Gibb ("The Difficulties of Being Evil") is a nineteen-year-old student at the University of Winnipeg. He is hopefully going to get a B.Ed. and a B.Sc. in Physics. This is his first publication in what is sure to be a long and very successful list.

Julie A. Hyzy ("Efflorescence") lives in Tinley Park, Illinois, with her very tolerant family. Currently working on her first novel, Julie's thrilled to be part of *SNW* legacy. Her success here is due in large part to the support of family and friends. And to her good luck Star Trek pin.

Jeff D. Jacques ("Kristin's Conundrum") resides in the Great White North, a realm where *SNW* winners are rare beasts indeed, though no less excitable than their counterparts south of the border. He toils away as a self-employed desktop publisher in the Nation's Capital, Ottawa. This marks Jeff's first professional sale.

Robert T. Jeschonek ("The Shoulders of Giants") returns to these pages after contributing third-prize winner "Whatever You Do, Don't Read This Story" to *Strange New Worlds III*. The thirty-six-year-old technical writer lives in Johnstown, Pennsylvania, with his wife, Wendy, who assisted in editing "The Shoulders of Giants." Next, Robert plans to find an agent for his new novel and a publisher for his new comic book series.

Kevin Killiany ("The Monkey Puzzle Box"), his wife, Valerie, and their three children live in Wilmington, North Carolina. He is a minister with the Soul Saving Station and an ESL/GED instructor at Cape Fear Community College. A member of the Queue Continuum writing group, Kevin is proud to have reached the point where he can introduce himself as a writer without his teenagers wincing.

Diana Kornfeld ("Witness") lives in Lee's Summit, Missouri, with her husband, Steve, and two lovely daughters. She is amazed and pleased to have a third story in a *Strange New Worlds* anthology. Sadly, this makes her ineligible for future editions, so she will have to look for even stranger new worlds for her stories.

William Leisner ("The Trouble with Borg Tribbles") is proud to join friend Dayton Ward—as well as Diana, Steven, and Tonya—in the ranks of *Strange New Worlds* three-timers. A native of Rochester, New York, he now lives in Minneapolis. This story would not have been written if not for the jokers of AOL's Trek Community—thanks!!

Alan Lickiss ("Legal Action") lives along the Colorado front range with his wife, Rebecca, their five children, and a menagerie of pets. He continues to write with the goal of becoming a full-time writer.

Robert J. Mendenhall ("Fear, Itself") celebrates his second appearance in the *Strange New Worlds* series. A former Army journalist for the American Forces Network, Europe, Robert is nowadays a police sergeant and an Air Force reservist. He lives and works in the Chicago suburbs, near his three children.

Mark Murata ("Yeoman Figgs") has had a variety of office jobs, from writing procedures for a major gaming company to updating Web pages for a medical institution. He's also preached sermons and used to be a physics major. "Yeoman Figgs" was his twenty-fifth submission to *SNW*, and his first fiction sale.

Catherine E. Pike ("Fragment") works as a police dispatcher in Southern California. She lives with her poodle, Bones; and three cats, Puck, Tasha, and Xena. Besides writing and Star Trek, her hobbies include reading and volunteering for Paw Haven, a cat rescue organization. "Fragment" is her first professional sale.

Tonya D. Price ("The Farewell Gift") is a longtime fanfic writer living in Franklin, Massachusetts, with her Imzadi of twenty-five years and their two daughters. This is her third appearance in *Strange New Worlds* and she thanks the Queue Continuum for their feedback on this story. Her latest project is a novel set in her own universe.

Penny A. Proctor ("Restoration") is still living in Ohio with her husband, dog, and stepcat, still practicing law and still grinning about inclusion in this book. She would like to dedicate this story to the memory of her father, who never stopped encouraging her to try to write.

Steven Ripley ("Bluff") lives in Seattle, Washington. This is his swan song for *Strange New Worlds,* with many grateful thanks to Dean, John, and Paula, and to Dana Rice, friend and fellow writer, for her keen advice about Data.

Mary Scott-Wiecek ("Disappearance on 21st Street"), forty, once an environmental geologist, is now a stay-at-home mom. She lives in Ohio (which would be a fine state if only it had an ocean) with her husband, three children, and various pets, including an incredibly robust snail named Gary. This is her second appearance in the *SNW* anthology.

Phaedra M. Weldon (Steele) ("Who Cries for Prometheus") lives in Atlanta, Georgia, with her husband, daughter, and two grumpy old cats. Her goal is to become a full-time writer.

Louisa M. Swann and **James J. Swann, P.E. C.E.** ("Remnant"), practices civil engineering in the snowy country of the Sierra Nevada range, where the translucent light of the Milky Way Galaxy leads the black ink onto the white paper. After spending the first six months of life in a papoose carrier, **Louisa** suffers from frequent insecurity when out of the "basket." Currently, she hangs out with her horses and keeps her fingers moving on the little black keys.

Mary Sweeney ("Dementia in D Minor") has been a Star Trek fan since the first episode aired. She lives in upstate New York with her husband, Evan Romer. This is her second appearance in *SNW*. She is grateful for the encouragement of her family, the vision of Gene

Roddenberry, and the inspiration provided by Herr Mozart, whose genius lives on in the strange new world of the twenty-first century.

John Takis ("A Girl for Every Star"), when not developing his creative enterprises, studying film, or fretting about how to take a "calling" to the bank, writes articles and reviews for *Film Score Monthly* magazine. He will graduate from Michigan State University this summer with a BA in English.

TG Theodore ("On the Rocks") returns to *SNW* for a second time, again displaying his fondness for the more humorous aspects of Trek. A native Californian, Ted is delighted to be back among the other writers. He is currently writing and composing a new *Peanuts* musical for the opening of the Charles M. Schulz Museum, in Santa Rosa, California.

Kelle Vozka ("Hoshi's Gift") is thirty-three years old and lives in Mountlake Terrace, Washington, with her two sons, ages three and five. Kelle works as an art lead, developing children's interactive educational software Jr. Adventures and activity packs for the three to five and four to nine age ranges. She is also a freelance illustrator. This is her first professional short story sale.